Summer Vibes Anthology

Cover Art by Melissa Russell
Copyediting by Elizabeth Flynn

ISBN: 978-0-9908429-9-6

Table of Contents

FOREWARD

Summer means warmer weather, longer days, and hotter nights. This anthology was inspired by the desire to bring the warmth and joy of summer to our readers during a time when social distancing may be disrupting many of our traditions. While we may not be able to gather with our friends and family, or travel to sunny beaches, or wander down to our favorite restaurant, we can still open a book and get lost in the beauty of a summer romance.

All of the authors, editors, cover designers, and contributors to this anthology have donated their time and efforts so proceeds can go directly to Washington Women In Need (WWIN), an organization that focuses on empowering women to reach their dreams. During our current crisis, WWIN is extending their programs to provide additional financial assistance to women affected by COVID-19 while still funding scholarships, offering mentorship opportunities, facilitating career coaching, and expanding their online systems of support to meet new demands.

In our most challenging times, we see the power of hope, the beauty of connection, and the strength of our relationships. Love has never been more important than now, so pour yourself something cool and delicious, find a slice of sunshine, and let the *Summer Vibes Romance Anthology* sweep you away to happily ever after.

During this project, a fellow artist reached out via social media. This gentleman's name is Nick Morgan (@SteelandStrings on Instagram). After Danica Winters told Nick about her story, he generously agreed to write a special song for Danica, and the project as a whole. He is a tremendously talented country music singer/song writer and we're proud to have worked with him on this project. Head over to YouTube and check out Nick Morgan's song: *Short and Precious Time!*

Short and Precious Time

by

Danica Winters

Chapter One

After living in quarantine for so long, Harmony had learned a few things about herself: boredom was awesome so long as there were drinks on hand, her cats loved salmon paté more than tuna, and she needed a boyfriend. Preferably a boyfriend with a big, muscular chest, a six-pack and a billion dollars in the bank. As of right now, the only men who kept hitting her up on Tinder were balding, rocking the dad bod, and looking for sugar mamas.

So much for having her fairy tale kind of love.

So yeah, online dating... While it had worked for a number of her friends, if this was the future of relationship building, she was going to be single forever.

Not that she hadn't had a little fun laughing and texting with a few potentially interesting men, but as soon as she seemed to catch the feels and move toward maybe actually meeting up for more than a sidewalk coffee, things always seemed to hit the skids. It felt as if no man in modern America wanted to be exclusive—or did it have nothing to do with exclusivity and more to do with her? Did something change when she started *actually liking* a guy? Did they sniff it in the air like it was some kind of pheromone release and know that they would actually have to make a commitment and therefore they ran?

Maybe it was just that men were devolving thanks to the internet and isolation. It certainly felt as if they were going back to being cave dwellers. In fact, the last guy she had talked to on the phone had even attempted to make full conversations out of grumbles and grunts. At one point, she could have sworn she heard him grumble something to the effect of "Me like boobies."

On second thought, maybe she didn't need a boyfriend or real adult relationship. Her cats were really great, though they did tend to run down the hallway at night and keep her awake then meet her in the morning with some kind of coughed-up hairball.

Looking to the common denominator...maybe *she* was the one at fault here as even her cats didn't want to treat her with any sort of respect. Then again, they were cats. She was lucky they even allowed her in their furry lives.

She just needed to get out more.

She looked up from the computer screen as she signed off from her last Zoom meeting, another day working as a claims adjuster in the books. Perhaps her real problem was that she was solidly average. Or maybe that was just in her head. She was different than most women, but didn't all women say that?

Or was that just what all the men she talked to online told her women said?

Gah. I give up. Single. Single for life.

Yes, she definitely didn't need a man. What she needed was to not question herself. Instead, it would have been nice if thinking she was different actually meant she was *different*. She didn't want to question it and she didn't want to feel the pressure to prove it or to force herself to fit some idealistic mold in which a man wanted her to conform.

She needed to be unapologetically herself and unafraid to speak her truth.

As she stood up from her desk, Mr. Darcy, her gray cat, wrapped himself around her legs, wanting food.

"Yes, buddy, I got you." She walked down the hall to the kitchen and picked up his bowl. The sound called the rest of the herd.

See...all the dudes love me, she thought, laughing to herself.

After feeding her pack of little lions, she walked by the window. A finger of sunshine poked through from a crack in her curtains, beckoning her outside.

If she went outside, she would have to put on real pants and get out of her soft polka-dotted pajama bottoms. She loved these bottoms. As she walked, though, she looked back at the finger of sun and the warmth it promised. Maybe changing into real clothes and getting outside wouldn't be terrible. Just ten minutes. She could pop out and walk around the park and then come back. She wouldn't even have to wear a mask if she was quick and the park was not too busy.

She sighed, but as soon as the sound escaped her lips, she was embarrassed with herself. Was she really upset that she was *going outside*? Yeah, she needed to get out of the house.

Life had become so strange, such a juxtaposition to the normal coming and going at this time last year. But months ago, she had realized the worst thing she could do was think about life as she had known it; eventually, it might go back to something close to what it once was, but to wish for the past only held back the future. The only thing to do was to make the best of any situation, be grateful, and forget to focus on the rest.

She slipped into a pair of shorts and grabbed her fanny pack, putting her phone and mask inside. Mr. Darcy walked up to her and sat down, looking at his chest harness.

"You want to go with me, buddy?" she asked.

Mr. Darcy meowed up at her.

A walk would do them good. Mr. Darcy let her slip the harness over his head and clicked it into place. He strutted out ahead of her, used to the leash—obviously knowing it was more to keep her in line than it was for him.

The Montana sun was bright and the world outside her doors smelled of dust, freshly cut hay, and pine. She loved that smell, the unmistakable scent of home. Taking in a deep breath, she started her walk toward the park. Her neighbor's rose bushes were in full bloom, their red heads so heavy that they had started to droop in the evening sun. Walking by, she lifted their faces ever so gently, hoping that she could remind them to keep their heads up even when the world around them was too heavy to bear.

From the park wafted the scent of greasy food trucks and it made her mouth water. All day she'd eaten a protein bar in between what must have been eight hundred cups of coffee. She could go for Chinese food or maybe a burger...or ice cream. And that right there was why her pants had seemed to have shrunk.

Take it easy on yourself, she thought, rubbing her hand over her cheek and sniffing the rosebud on her fingers. Like the rose, it was easy to let her head fall down and then be left only able to see the ground.

Chin up.

As she and Mr. Darcy walked through the gates at the entrance of the park, she was met with country music. It wasn't like the new wave of country that sounded more like pop; instead, it was funkier, something closer to Chris Stapleton mixed with a little bluegrass flavor. As she was drawn to the sound, she found her footsteps moving in beat with the music.

If she had to guess, even the rhythm of her heart was in sync.

The park was full of sugar maples, ponderosa pines, and potentilla bushes. The bushes were covered with dainty yellow flowers and they brushed against her skin as she walked by them, tickling her.

How long had it been since she'd been touched by someone? As she made her way on the gravel footpath that sat at the outside edges of the park, she thought about her last relationship. Together too quickly, hurt feelings too soon, and it ended even faster.

The music stopped and as it did, she came to a standstill. For a long moment, there was only the voices of kids running and screaming in play and the sound of a fountain in the distance.

Come back. Keep singing and playing guitar.

She had been enjoying the music, but like everything else in her life recently, it wasn't until it was really gone that she had wished she had grasped the experience with both hands and held on with all of her might.

Halfway around the mile-long path, Mr. Darcy was still prancing but occasionally stopping to sniff the wayward piece of grass. Thankfully, the music started again; this time the sound was so much closer, crisper, and it mixed with the swirling scents of food and the outdoors. With the sensations came the feelings of real, true life. Throwing her head back, she opened her hands—making sure to keep the leash on her wrist—and took it all in. This—this moment of bliss was shared with all those around her, and yet entirely private.

The man crooned of love and loss, and though she heard all of his words, some came louder than others and she found herself floating through the thrummed chords of the guitar as the man sang the chorus, "Falling in love would be easy, if it wasn't so hard to do."

He had her there.

If only it wasn't so damned hard.

Around the next bend, she came to the small amphitheater. It was set down into the ground, amplifying the sound of the musicians so all in the park could hear and yet when a person was near, it was not too loud. This little place, this concrete oasis in her normally masked world, was so full of life and energy that she couldn't help but stop and sit down at the edge of the ring. Mr. Darcy wrapped around her legs and then jumped up into her lap, happy for the reprieve in their swaggering around the park.

On stage—wait, was it even called a stage? Well, on the concrete slab that acted as the stage, there stood a man. He was all alone, performing though she was the only one sitting there, listening.

Though she was sure she should have felt pity for the man, standing alone, instead she felt honored. Not an hour before, she had been wilting away in her house, and now she was getting a private serenade. Life had a beautiful way of reminding a person what was really important and how fleeting the world could be, but in this moment, her soul was rejuvenated and her heart felt lighter. Nothing mattered but sitting here, listening to the timbre of the man's voice as his song vibrated against her skin, and just letting the moment happen.

He had broad, muscular shoulders and as he moved forward toward the microphone, his blue eyes closed. She loved the sound of his song, but she could have stared at those eyes forever. As if on cue, he looked over at her and gave her a sexy half-smile as he sang the next line of his song. Though she heard the words, all she could think about was the way he was looking at her right now, as if they were the only two people in the world. She swam in the deep blue sea of his eyes and her body ached with longing for a man whom she didn't know and would probably only share this one look.

He held out his hand like he was asking her to dance. It was sweet, soft, and all-encompassing. She started to sway in time with his side-to-side steps. It could have been her imagination getting away with her, but they were dancing together and yet a world and a life apart.

She crossed her arms over her chest as if embracing him and she beamed. He met her gaze and grinned, running his fingers through his hair. The simple action made her long to do the same to his hair. Did he have soft hair or was it coarse? Thick or fine? His dark hair looked like it was a little thick, and as she watched a curl drop down his forehead, she could almost feel its softness in her fingers.

She forced herself to look away as he lamented about lonely nights. This was pathetic. She was pathetic. What woman took a single look at a man and wanted to dance alone and *touch his hair*?

Before the song ended, she forced herself to walk away, around the bend in the path and just out of sight from the stage. Whatever that moment was, the daydream had to be better than whatever the reality would entail. As his song came to an end, a sadness filled her.

Why did she have to be so weak and not stay and talk to him? Why couldn't she be the kind of girl who had the strength to just walk up to him and tell him how much she enjoyed his music? That wouldn't have been weird, admiring his work and his talent. And yet, here she stood just on the other side of the bushes from him, wanting his songs to fill her soul.

Single. She was staying single. She walked toward home. The last thing she needed was to fall for the troubadour who had broken through her world of silence.

Chapter Two

The next day she found herself yearning for another midday walk. Sure, her thoughts had been fluttering around the handsome musician all night and most of the morning, but thanks to work her mind had finally broken free of the crushing-hard cycle.

In fact, she had barely thought of the guy.

As she grabbed her pack and made her way to the door outside, she nearly patted herself on the back. Yep, she wasn't the kind of girl who blithely fell for some strange dude because of nothing more than the way his singing made her feel.

Wait, if she fell for him would she be considered a groupie? Or was a groupie only for a full band? If it was just a guitarist alone on a stage, would she be called something else? Maybe a solo-ey? Souly? Permanently single? Daydreamer extraordinaire?

Wow... Yeah, she needed to stop swirling this drain.

Mr. Darcy plodded over next to her, his footfalls sounding like soft drumbeats on the hardwood floor. He sat, meowing up at her and then looking at his chest harness.

"Buddy, you don't need to go. Why don't you stay here with your friends?" she asked, motioning to the other two cats who didn't seem to care she was leaving their domain.

Mr. Darcy wrapped himself around her legs and then plopped back down, glancing back up at the harness.

"No one could ever accuse you of not knowing your own mind," she said, laughing. "Maybe if I was half as assertive as you, I wouldn't be as confused as I am. You certainly have no problem telling others what you want and then doing your best to make them bend to your whim."

Mr. Darcy meowed proudly, stood up and stretched, readying himself for their jaunt like he was some kind of Olympic sprinter instead of a nine-to-five couch potato. He walked to the door, scratched it, and then looked back over his shoulder in what she recognized as his best attempt to get her to hurry up.

"You know you are a cat, right?" she asked, grabbing the harness and clicking it into place on the cat.

Mr. Darcy gave her a side eye that told her she would need to check her shoes for dead mice in the morning.

"Come now, I didn't mean it like a jab." She paused, realizing she was having a full-fledged conversation with a cat. "All I was saying," she continued, opening the door, "is that it is somewhat odd that you are a cat who likes to be taken on leashed walks."

He kicked up his tail as he ignored her and strolled out the door, ahead of her. If he didn't care that they looked like the odd couple, then she didn't either.

But what about my troubadour? Did he care? Did he think I was crazy for walking my cat?

She chuckled at herself. What did it really matter what he thought? She wasn't going to see him again. The odds were solidly stacked against them ever even seeing each other and if they were to see each other on the street sometime he would never recognize her. She was, undoubtedly, just another woman who had sat and watched him play his music—one of a million faces he had seen in his travels.

Thinking about all of his adventures in bar towns and amphitheaters, she realized he probably had more than his fair share of women. A man like him didn't have to go home alone at night. One sweet chord, the whisper of a song in a woman's ear, and *poof!* Panties would drop and inhibitions would disappear.

What a difference from her own life. In hers, one of the men she had met on Tinder had not wished for her panties to drop, he had rather that he wear them. That had been a quick couple of clicks and a block.

Maybe the singer was just like that guy, a dude who had some weird fetish tendencies. Or worse, he would be just another dude who wasted an hour of her life.

She had recently read a book that stated all people were hard-wired to win and succeed at whatever it was that their subconscious was gearing them toward. Was she permanently destined to be alone? Was that what she really, truly wanted?

Really, in being somewhat weak in her decision to not approach the thick, well-muscled singer, she had been winning. She'd saved herself any possible embarrassment caused by being rejected, and if things had gone in a direction that landed her a date, she had saved herself from wasting time. Yes, it had all worked out splendidly.

Sighing, she followed behind Mr. Darcy, making the first corner on the trail as her thoughts turned to winning. What did it really mean to *win*? She thought of her sister who was one of the most successful women she knew. She ran her own company, made millions of dollars and could travel the world—when there wasn't a quarantine—at the drop of a hat, and had the perfect husband. Or, rather, she'd *had* the perfect husband and everything else that made up the epitome of a perfect life.

Harmony would have called everything her sister had done *winning*. And yet, even when everything had seemed perfect in her sister's life, it hadn't been enough. He sister hadn't felt as though she had won; instead, she had felt like something was still missing.

Did anyone ever feel good enough, smart enough, humble enough? Just *enough*?

Winning didn't mean enough, it didn't mean happiness; it didn't even mean success. All it meant, at the base level, was that a person had accomplished the goals that they had set out to accomplish—even if those things were negative. By winning in not speaking to the singer, what if she had shot herself in the foot? What if in her accomplishment of being passive and self-defeating, she had actually missed a wonderful opportunity?

Was she unlovable because at a subconscious level she chose to be unlovable?

No more.

She was lovable. She deserved to be loved.

If she saw the singer today, she was going to march right up to him and tell him how hot she thought he was... Okay, maybe not the hot part, but she would at least *talk* to him.

Subconscious, get with it.

This was her day. Her time. Quarantine and social distancing be damned. She could yell at him from six feet if she had to, but damn it, she was going to do this.

She walked around the corner, and in the distance, she could make out the sounds of the guitar. It was a different song than she remembered from yesterday, but the melody was reminiscent of his sound. It had to be him, beckoning her forward with his siren's song.

Winning would be a positive.

She smiled as she looked down at Mr. Darcy. He had his fuzzy face stuffed into a bush and promptly stopped, making it impossible for her to keep going.

"Pst pst. Come on, let's go, buddy." She gently pulled at the leash.

Didn't he know that she was on a mission? She had love to be had. What if, in these few missed seconds where she waited for Mr. Darcy to putter about, that she missed her mystery man?

She loved Mr. Darcy—and his namesake, for that matter—but if he messed up her groove, he would be eating nothing but dry food for a week.

And then he'd probably pee on her bath mat, but...*whatever.*

She gave another gentle tug on the leash, but instead of stepping back toward her, Mr. Darcy disappeared into the bush, pulling her after him.

Gahhh. "Come on, Mr. Darcy. Really. Mommy doesn't have time for this," she said, annoyed. "If you don't come out right now, I'm going to come in there and lift you. Your walk will be over." There was the rustle of leaves, but he didn't emerge.

"You're not going to like this," she continued. "You know how you hate it when I carry you on our walks."

Another rustle of leaves, deeper into the bush this time.

"Fine." She grumbled as she dropped to her knees and moved toward the bush.

Pushing back the outer limbs, she followed the angle of the leash into what looked like some kind of pinion bush. The needles were rubbing against her, giving off a strong odor like that of turpentine and something earthy, oily. She knew that smell.

"Oh my God. Get out of the bush," she squealed, rummaging as quickly toward Mr. Darcy as humanely possible. "Get out. Get out. Get out." She repeated her mantra until she spotted the white tip of Mr. Darcy's tail.

She grabbed hold of his belly and started to lift the cat and pull them free of the grip of the bush. As she moved, a little black and white head popped out from the left side of the bush, followed by a striped black and white body.

Harmony turned to run, but before she could take a step the tail was up and... *Psst....*

Full hit.

The skunk's oil slipped down the back of her legs as the pungent, putrid odor hit her nostrils. In all of her life there had never been anything as strong or as disgusting that she had ever smelled. It was as if the skunk had opened up Harmony's mouth and released its stench right onto her tongue.

She gagged, retching. Mr. Darcy tried to bunny-kick her boobs and propel himself out of her arms, clearly as shocked and disgusted by the turn of events as she was. Instead of letting him go, she pulled him tighter, letting his nails dig into the soft skin of her belly.

The skunk scurried away from them in the direction in which they came, probably going toward some other unsuspecting woman with daydreams filling her head.

Mr. Darcy clawed harder, the pain of his attempted escape making the stink seem that much more pungent while also keeping her moving. Pain was good. Pain meant she was still alive.

Not really paying attention or looking around, she started to jog toward home, taking the quickest route that she could think of.

They had to get this off.

Retch.

The music grew louder as they jogged toward the amphitheater. A breeze kicked up, blowing the powerful stench back at her instead of away as she jogged.

Retch.

By now, everyone in the entire park had to be smelling what had happened to her, *them.* Kick. Mr. Darcy yowled, sneezing and rubbing his face furiously as she tried to hold him.

"Don't worry," she said, trying to keep moving even though all she wanted to do was stop, drop, and roll like her body was on fire.

Water. They needed to find water. Maybe a shower. There was one by the kids' swimming area. But they hadn't turned it on this year because of everything. And even if they had, somehow it seemed wrong to make the whole entire place some kind of biohazard thanks to the stench that was steadily seeping into her pores.

Yes, they had to get home. She had a hose there. They could douse off.

The music grew louder and she heard the soft crooning of *his* voice.

He couldn't see her like this if she wanted even the slightest chance of ever having him in her life. And yet, it was longer if she went back the way she came, not to mention the skunk having gone that direction.

She'd just have to move fast. Maybe there would be more people today and he wouldn't even notice a wayward woman slipping past him and around the stage.

Yes. That would be it. It would be fine.

She jogged as Mr. Darcy kicked maniacally at her stomach. "Stop."

The cat looked at her with the devil in his eyes and he swiped at her face. In a knee-jerk reaction, she let go of the cat and he took off. His leash trailed behind him as he approached light speed in the direction of the amphitheater.

Shit...

She ran in the direction of the damned cat, but as she turned the corner and the amphitheater came into view, she stopped.

If she hadn't smelled so bad, she was sure she could have tracked him by the cat's scent, but as it was, she was trying hard just not to cry from her own stench.

Why? Why, when she had finally decided to do something for herself and be brave, did the world have to come crashing down?

Tears pelted down her face.

Even her cat was gone.

"Mr. Darcy, here kitty, kitty. *Psp. Psp. Psp.*" Her voice cracked and she repeated the call again and again.

Mr. Darcy didn't reappear. And she couldn't blame him for running away.

The music stopped, and she looked up from her frantic search for her cat. Standing on stage, looking directly at her, was the blue-eyed singer from yesterday. As she stared at him, his brows furrowed and he covered his nose and mouth like he had just caught the smell of her.

Dead embarrassed, she ran.

This wasn't supposed to be how it went when she saw him again. Not even close.

Chapter Three

Did the universe hate her?

Tears streamed down Harmony's face as she ran as quickly as she could back home. Opening up the back gate, afraid to go inside, she made her way around to the back faucet. Turning on the water, she sprayed herself down. The initial spray was warm, the water heated by the sun, but the icy pricks soon followed. As the cold water hit her skin, she sucked in a breath and held it. Goose bumps rose on her skin. She worked fast. Rubbing the skin of her face, hard. She stripped off her clothes and threw them toward the garage door. She could burn those later. Or, at the very least, bag them up and put them in the dumpster.

She glanced around, making sure none of her neighbors were outside before unclasping her bra and slipping out of her underwear. No one wanted to see her naked, taking a freezing-cold hose bath, and lamenting the reality of her life. But if they did, she was sure they would start to feel better about themselves.

Maybe that was what she was, some reminder to all of those around her that their lives could be worse. Yes, she was the universe's greatest clown.

So much for winning. She was the biggest loser.

Scrubbing the last bits of her legs, the smell was still strong, but at least she had gotten off what she could before going inside. Turning off the hose, she looked up, and sitting in the back window, joyfully watching, were her other cats. The ginger cat, Leonidas, was positively smiling—no doubt, laughing at her predicament.

What a jerk.

Knowing Leonidas, if he could figure out how to lock the back door, he would.

Going inside, she made a bee line toward the cupboard where she kept a few bottles of tomato juice for summer beers. Grabbing them, she hustled to her bathtub and poured the cold tomato juice in her hair. It streamed down her face and as she caught a glimpse of herself in the mirror, the scene reminded her of something out of the movie *Carrie*.

Thank goodness she lived alone.

She scrubbed until her skin was nearly the same color as the tomato juice and then she sat there, marinating. Out of nowhere, maybe it was self-pity or just an acceptance over everything that had happened in the last forty-eight hours, but she started to laugh. And not just little giggle laughs one reserved for polite company—no, it was the snorting, side-gripping laughs of the exhausted.

She laughed so hard that her eyes welled up once again. Who in the world had this kind of thing happen to them? And she was going to have to write a "Missing cat" sign for the park. She could barely even imagine what it would read, something to the effect of:

LOST
Cat who likes to go on walks,
smells like skunk,
named after a romance hero,

thinks he's the boss,
and kicked the crap out of his owner.
Reward if located, but
only if you keep him.

Then again, she did want him back. Her other cats weren't into snuggling.

She looked down at her stomach and, for the first time, really looked at the deep gouges and scrapes from his back claws. They were red and angry, needing care and, as she touched them, she finally noted how badly the acid from the tomato juice was stinging. Her laughing stopped, but the exhaustion and pain remained in its wake.

After a quick shower to get the tomato juice off and applying a few Band-Aids, she made her way to the kitchen. The air was still thick with skunk, but it was better than before. At least now she could breathe without too much cringing. At least she wouldn't have anyone over for a while, thanks to the pandemic, and no one would be any the wiser about the predicament in which she had found herself.

Though she would have to tell her mother when she called. She would at least feel her pain and get a kick out of it. She would definitely have to leave out the part of the good-looking man. That was one element of the story her mother would never let go. In fact, her mother would make it her mission to set her up on a date, possibly going to the extreme of finding the man and setting him up on the date herself.

Her mother was the desperate-to-see-her-daughter-married type. She'd always teased her and told her that her husband would be named Cole—the name of her favorite literary character. However, Harmony was in no hurry. Especially not now.

About an hour later and after getting as cleaned up as Harmony could, she grabbed a fresh pair of shoes and made her way to the door. She had to find Mr. Darcy before she started making signs and posting about her lost cat on social media. Maybe he would even find his way home. She'd heard of cats traveling thousands of miles in order to find their way to the families. He was smart enough, but that was if nothing had happened to him and he wanted to come back to her. Maybe he would just get hungry.

She had been a good owner and they had a bond—at least in her mind—but she doubted that she would come in even a close second to a cute Siamese. Kittens were out of the question for her boy, but that didn't mean he wouldn't give it a good college try until he wore himself out. Then maybe he would drag himself home.

Maybe.

As she grabbed her mask and her cell phone, which had exactly zero alerts, she moved toward the door. But before she could touch the door handle, there was a knock.

Was she getting a package? She frowned as she thought about her recent drunken online purchases. Yes, there was supposed to be a kitschy cat-shaped cheese grater on the way, but that hadn't even been marked as shipped yet.

Opening the door, sitting patiently to be let in, was an unleashed Mr. Darcy and a box of canned tomato juice. Mr. Darcy appeared to have been cleaned, his wet fur in little spikes on his head, and he had the squinted eyes of one pissed-off feline. He stood up and walked inside, giving her a flick of the tail and his nose in the air as he walked by her.

"Welcome home! Glad you wished to grace me with your presence, Mr. Darcy," she said, matching his icy disposition.

There was laughter from out on the sidewalk, drawing her attention. Standing there, pink roses in hand, was her troubadour.

As she stepped out on her front porch, he held up his hands, motioning for her to stop. "Hi," he said, his smile even brighter than she remembered.

"Hi," she said, her voice soft as she suddenly felt so shy that she almost couldn't look at him.

She stopped herself from looking away—this was her time to be brave. He had come to her rescue and literally saved her cat, almost like something out of one of her favorite romances. If her life was something out of the Victorian novels she loved so much, no doubt he would have been here to offer her his hand in marriage.

That thought nearly made every bit of her courage slip from her. While he definitely wasn't here for that kind of nonsense—though her mother would have loved it—what was he here for?

"I hope your cat is okay," he said, turning his hands so she could see the angry red slashes on the backs. "When I saw you walking him, I thought he would be the docile kind. I was *wrong*. But hey," he said with a laugh, "at least now I know how he slipped from your grasp. This dude's a beast."

"Yeah, don't let his sweet little face fool you," she said, looking back at Mr. Darcy, who was now sitting on her favorite chair and licking himself.

"I'm just glad I found his house." He smiled, rubbing the back of his neck awkwardly.

"That's true. How did you find my place?"

He shot her that big smile and he held onto his neck and looked up at her. "Well, I hate to tell you this, but it was easy to follow the smell."

Her face went instantly ablaze. Of course. How could she *not* have known that?

Running her hands over her mouth, she wished she could hole up and disappear from out in front of her dream man. "I am a walking shit show." She didn't mean to say it aloud, but there was just no other way to put it.

"No, you're not. I could tell yesterday that you are definitely a bit shy."

A *bit* was an understatement. "To be honest, I haven't really talked to many people lately. I think I've gotten more awkward over the last few months."

"I know the feeling," he said, glancing down at his feet. "It's why I have taken to playing music in the park. At least I get out."

"I wish I had found you sooner. Your music is amazing." She stumbled over her words as they came out jerky and fumbling. "I...err...you have a great voice. Really. I know I don't sound like I mean it, but that's me. I'm...well...like you said—"

"I think you're perfect. Albeit, you and your cat could use a little tomato bathing for a few days." He laughed, but it didn't do anything to diminish her embarrassment. "If it makes you feel better, thanks to your cat, I don't smell any better. And neither does my car," he said, pointing in the direction of a Subaru parked on the opposite side of the street.

"Oh my God, I'm so sorry. You shouldn't have..." She walked out of her house, closing the door behind her. "I'll pay to get your car cleaned, and get you some new clothes."

He laughed and shook his head. "No, really. It's been a long time...err... actually, I've never been skunked. If anything, it was a great opportunity to test out several methods of getting rid of the stink. The hardest part of all of it was catching him. It wasn't until your cat went up a tree that I was finally able to get close to him."

She cringed as she thought of the look her jerk of a cat must have given their hero. "Are you sure there isn't something I can do to repay you?" As soon as she said the words, she wished she hadn't. She sounded so stupid. "I mean, I was going to offer a reward if someone found him. Does five hundred sound good?"

His eyebrows rose and then pinched into a frown. "I didn't bring him home out of hopes of getting some kind of reward." He dropped his hand from his neck and started to play with the edge of his gray T-shirt. "Actually, I was hoping you would stop by today. Maybe even dance with me again. I wasn't expecting to see a rodeo." He laughed, but stopped as he looked at her and must have noticed how embarrassed she was feeling. "It was *adorable*."

"Ack," she said, making a disgusted face. "If that was adorable, I can't imagine what kind of thing you are used to." She paused. "Wait...you *wanted to dance with me* again?"

He nodded. "And I had something to give to you," he said, extending the roses. "But I don't want it to be weird. I mean, we don't even know each other's names. And I promise I'm not a creeper or anything... I just... Well, there was something yesterday. You know?"

She did know, but she had no idea what to say. This kind of thing didn't happen to her. Ever. Not even in her dreams. No. "I don't know what to say."

His cheeks turned red and she noted a thin sheen of sweat on his forehead.

"I mean," she continued, making her way over to him, "thank you for the flowers. That is, if they are for me."

"Uh yeah," he said, handing them to her. "There's a card in there too."

Goodness, they were both so awkward. And yet, she loved it. She loved that in a way, this sexy and smiling man was all too much like her, skunked and all.

She took them, their fingers brushing as they broke all the social distancing rules. There was something even more sensual than normal in the way their fingers grazed, as if in that simple touch they were playing some kind of game with the forbidden.

Maybe this was a bit like her own Victorian romance.

"My name is Harmony," she said, her voice barely above a whisper.

"That's a cool name. Perfect, actually. I've always been looking for harmony in my life." He smiled. "I'm Cole Tilney."

"No shit? Cole?" she said, the words erupting from her ever so eloquently. "Like Jane Austen's *Northanger Abbey*, Tilney?"

He cocked his head to the side. "One and the same, but not commonly brought into day-to-day conversation."

She opened and closed her mouth. "I, uh, I'm a big Austen fan."

"I could see that," he said. "I like that about you. It's one of the reasons I knew I had to meet you. I'm just sorry it couldn't be a tad bit more romantic. Maybe something Austen-esque."

The. Man. Was. Talking. *Austen*. With. Her.

Put a ring on it, now.

"That kind of thing, while my style, would completely overwhelm me. If you had come at me all perfect, I don't know if I would have been able to have the courage to have even said hello."

"Then it's a good thing I came with my C-game." He smiled. "I would have hated not to have gotten the chance to talk to you."

He was killing her with this. If this was his C-game, she would have literally died if he had brought his A-level game. As it was, she was solidly playing out of her league with this handsome, talented man.

"Open your card," he said, suddenly looking shy. "I'll hold the flowers for a second." He held them for her as she took out the card at their center and opened it up.

A sheet of paper slipped out and fell onto the ground. Picking it up, she read the note at the top.

Hi,

I know we've never met and we may never meet, but I knew the moment we saw one another that we needed each other.

I need to see you each morning and each night. Even though I don't even know your name, there is something in you that draws me.

This kind of thing isn't like me, and for me regular words aren't enough. So, I wrote you this song:

I never believed in love at first sight, Until you
showed up in my atmosphere,
That summer night.
I never believed I'd ever feel at home,

'Til I knew the warmth of your embrace,
To a country song.
CHORUS**
So baby let your walls down,
You already knocked down mine,
Life is more than tragedy,
Just let your soul shine,
Be free and who you want to be,
Press your heart here close to mine,
Because we're only here on earth,
For a short and precious time.
**

And I know it scares you,
Opening yourself up to someone
For the first time.
But baby you can breathe,
Because I want all of you,
Girl I'll walk that line.
CHORUS:
So baby let your walls down,
You already knocked down mine,
Life is more than tragedy,
Just let your soul shine,
Be free and who you want to be,
Press your heart here close to mine,
Because we're only here on earth,
For a short and precious time.
BRIDGE
Just let go, hold on to me,

Be the one you're meant to be,
And know that when you call,
I'll be waiting here for you
CHORUS:
So baby let your walls down,
You already knocked down mine,
Life is more than tragedy,
Just let your soul shine,
Be free and who you want to be,
Press your heart here close to mine,
Because we're only here on earth,
For a short and precious time.

Here is hoping for forever,
Cole Tilney

Harmony stared at the lyrics of the song for a long moment, unsure how she should react. Her hands were shaking so violently that the words of the song were no longer even legible. This man, this stranger, knew her.

For this short and precious time, this life, she would be free to be herself. They would let their walls down, together.

Without a single word, she took him by the hand and they slipped into her house. There would be no social distancing, no meaningless chitchats, wasted time, or bad coffee.

Until now, just like him, she had thought love at first sight was merely some myth. He had just proven her wrong. And in a single moment, she felt her life change.

She had found true, once in a lifetime love in a man whom she had only just met.

As the door closed behind him, she took the lead and pushed him back against the door and took his lips. As his lips danced with hers it struck her, she was finally living the different, amazing, and passionate life she had always wanted.

This man, Cole, had helped and would continue to help make her soul shine.

Here was to dancing together forever.

Danica Winters is a Publishers Weekly, Walmart, and Amazon bestselling author who has won multiple awards for writing books that grip readers with their ability to drive emotion through suspense and occasionally a touch of magic. Her books have won numerous awards, but she says that her greatest joy is hearing that the worlds she creates have helped to provide escapes for those who need it most.

She is also the co-owner of Self-Publishing Services, LLC. SPS is a successful and lucrative company owned and run by Montana women. SPS is partnered with Apple Books, Barnes and Noble, and Draft 2 Digital.

In addition to her writing and publishing, she spends a great deal of her time mentoring up-and-coming authors in every genre from children's fiction to science fiction. Books are her passion and her life.

When she's not working, she can be found in the wilds of Montana with her husband and two children (all love books). Her daughter often helps her handle her fan mail.

Website | Blog | Amazon | Apple | Barnes & Noble | Goodreads | Twitter | Facebook | Instagram

Other recent books by Danica Winters include:

Protective Operation *(Stealth-Book 4)*, Harlequin Intrigue

Her Assassin for Hire *(Stealth-Book 3)*, Harlequin Intrigue

In His Sights *(Stealth-Book 2)*, Harlequin Intrigue

Hidden Truth *(Stealth-Book 1)*, Harlequin Intrigue

A Summer Sail

by

Eliana West

Chapter One

"Nurse Christmas, do you have a pet reindeer?" the little girl asked, looking up at Noelle with a combination of awe and curiosity. Her large, light brown eyes were exaggerated without hair to frame her tiny head, and a mask covering her mouth. She studied Noelle's movements warily as she adjusted her catheter port.

Noelle gently patted the little girl's arm once the clear liquid that provided the child's body with lifesaving medication began its journey into her body.

"No, sweetheart, the reindeer need to stay at the North Pole with Santa. It's too warm for them in Seattle during the summer."

Her little wise woman nodded solemnly in agreement with her explanation.

The little girl's mother came back into the room with a grateful smile and motioned for Noelle to speak to her out of earshot.

"I'll be back to check on you tomorrow, okay, Zoe?"

"Thank you, Nurse Christmas."

Her first patient on her first day at Seattle Children's Hospital had called her "Nurse Christmas" when she introduced herself as Noelle and the name stuck. The irony was, Christmas was her least favorite holiday. She avoided the bleak childhood memories learned at a young age. A present in a nicely wrapped package didn't always contain a thoughtful gift.

The current season was the one she loved. Summer in Seattle was enchanting. It began in fits and starts with a sunny day here and there. And then, all of a sudden, bright blue sky met emerald green mountains with glacier-fed waters, luring more than one person to move to the Pacific Northwest on a whim. Summer in Seattle made up for being called Nurse Christmas all year round.

Noelle met Zoe's mother at the door. She grabbed Noelle's arm, her eyes shining with excitement.

"Dr. Sankaar just gave me the news. The new immunotherapy looks like it's working," she said in a hushed whisper.

"That's wonderful news. I'm so happy for you."

Zoe's mother gave Noelle a hug. "Everyone here has been amazing, but you have been so kind to Zoe. I know you try to spend extra time with her and I'll never be able to thank you enough."

Every nurse at Children's Hospital gave their charges the same amount of care and attention, but they all had patients who touched them in a special way. Zoe had captured a piece of Noelle's heart from the moment she met the sweet, precocious six-year-old.

Zoe asked the first time she came into her room, "Nurse Christmas, our skin is the same color. Is your mommy white and your daddy Black like mine?"

Noelle always marveled at how the biracial kids knew she was one of them.

The little girl and her mother had traveled across the state to seek treatment while her father stayed behind to run the family farm. He could only come for visits every couple of weeks. Sadly, such cases weren't unusual. The parking lot at the hospital was peppered with license plates not only from Washington, but from Oregon, Idaho, and Wyoming. Sometimes the cars arrived with travel trailers attached so families had somewhere to live if their child was admitted for an extended period of time.

Noelle said her good-byes to Zoe and her mother, and then bumped right into the one person she tried to avoid every week.

Hugh Donavan smiled at her. "Just the person I was looking for."

Noelle sighed. "The answer is still no."

"But I haven't asked the question yet."

Noelle rested her hand on her hip and raised an eyebrow. "Are you going to ask me something different this week?"

"No, not exactly. Let's see." He scratched his head, looking at her thoughtfully. "I've asked you out to dinner, lunch, breakfast, coffee, tea..." He listed all the ways he had asked her out since Noelle started working at the hospital six months ago.

The star midfielder for the Seattle Emeralds MLS team smiled at her, his hazel eyes hopeful as always. The hospital would occasionally host a professional athlete or celebrity who would come to visit the kids, but Hugh came every week. Noelle's heart softened for just a moment. She admired his commitment to the young patients at the hospital, but then she reminded herself about her ex-husband, and any sympathy she felt vanished.

"The answer is still no, Hugh. I appreciate you asking," she said politely; she would never be intentionally unkind, "but you should find another girl. I'm sure there are plenty out there who would've said yes to you by now."

Hugh frowned and shook his head. "But none of them are you."

Her heart skipped a beat. She was taller than most women at five-eight, but she still had to lift her head to look him in the eye, but she didn't dare. She was still trying to decide if he was just another pretty package who would lead to disappointment.

She wasn't going to pretend Hugh Donavan wasn't a handsome man. More than one nurse had swooned over the ad campaign he did for an athletic company a few months ago. Noelle was embarrassed to admit she did sneak a peek at the picture of Hugh wearing nothing but a pair of form-fitting athletic shorts in his team colors, looking intently at the camera while holding a soccer ball.

He didn't have the bulky muscles of her football player ex-husband; his arms and legs were sinewy, each muscle well defined. He wore his hair long enough to flop over his forehead and his beard close -cropped. The picture didn't capture the auburn color of his hair or the way his eyes reminded Noelle of her favorite lake. The same eyes that were looking at her now, with a determination that made her heart beat a little faster.

A little voice called out of the room. "Nurse Christmas, if you don't like tea, maybe you can go out for ice cream."

Noelle's head jerked toward the room where the door was slightly ajar. Zoe's mom poked her head out and lowered her mask to mouth, "Sorry," her eyes sparkling with amusement.

She heard Hugh chuckling softly next to her and closed her eyes, wishing the floor would open up and swallow her.

"I like vanilla because you can add whatever you want and make it something different every time," he said.

Damn it, he even liked the same flavor of ice cream for the same reason. It was getting harder and harder to come up with excuses to dislike Hugh Donavan. When she opened her eyes, he was smiling at her with a hopeful look.

"So, ice cream?" he raised his eyebrows.

Little Zoe's voice rang in her ears. "We'll see," she said.

You'd think she'd agreed to marry him the way he beamed at her. "What time do you get off?"

Noelle shook her head. "Not today, I'll... I'll let you know when I'm ready."

"And I'll be here when you are."

When she returned to the nurses' station, Thanh, her best friend and co-worker, was waiting for her with his arms crossed and his lips pressed into a thin line.

"What?" Noelle asked.

"It's time," he said.

"Time for what?" Thanh's husband, Milo, walked up, handing his husband his lunch tote.

Noelle admired the way the two of them cared for one another. With Milo working as an ER doc and Thanh's schedule as a nurse, there were some days their lunch handoff was the only time they would see each other.

Thanh sniffed. "Black-eyed pea salad?" he asked, with a hopeful expression.

Milo grinned and kissed his husband on the cheek. "With your mother's lemongrass chicken."

Thanh groaned in appreciation. "You are the best husband ever."

"I know," Milo said with a wink. "Now, what is it time for?" His gaze went between Noelle and Thanh.

"It's time for Noelle to give Hugh Donavan a break and go out on a date."

Milo's eyes widened. "Oh, *that* time."

"You're going to take his side, aren't you?" Noelle grumbled.

"I am," Milo said with a nod, "and not just because I'm his husband, but because I'm also your friend. I want you to be happy. Athletes, actors, and celebrities, some show up because they need good press, but Hugh does because he wants to be here. I've gotten to know him, Thanh and I have met up with him for drinks a few times, and I've never gotten a bad vibe from him, ever. I've watched him treat the people around him with respect and kindness, not just the kids but the staff as well. I don't know your ex, but I know Hugh and I like him."

"I know he's nice. I've seen the way he is with the kids and how he treats everyone here. I overheard him checking in on Debbie a few weeks ago after she lost a patient and the way he spoke to her was beautiful," Noelle sighed, "but I'm just...not ready," she finished, quietly.

Milo put his arm around her shoulder. "You're just scared, and there's nothing wrong with that."

Thanh came over and took Noelle's hands in his. "When I was a little boy, I took swimming lessons and on the last day of class we all got to jump off the high dive. Most of the kids climbed up, looked over the edge, and climbed back down without jumping. When it was my turn, I climbed up and looked over the edge. The water seemed so far away, and I was scared. I started to walk back to the ladder and climb down, and then I stopped. I took a deep breath, turned around, started running and I jumped," he finished, giving her hands a squeeze. "It's time for you to jump."

Noelle sniffed, blinking back her tears before they could fall. "Thank you," she whispered.

That night, Noelle bobbed in her kayak in the waters of Lake Washington while she watched the evening commuters slowly made their way across the 520 bridge, happy she wasn't among them. She'd always wanted to be a nurse; the idea of any kind of job where she had to work in a cubicle never appealed to her. After a brief disastrous turn as a trophy wife, she achieved her goal and completed the nursing program she'd started in college.

Noelle had done everything she needed to do to make herself happy, and yet something was missing. She'd made wonderful friends in Seattle, especially her coworker Thanh and his husband, Milo, who took her under their wing on day one.

As she looked out over the expanse of blue sky reflected in the water, she thought about how nice it would be to have someone to share it with. The ink was dry from her divorce, but her heart was still frozen. She rested the paddle across her lap and let her fingers trail in the cool water while her mind drifted to her conversation with Hugh that afternoon.

He was slowly but surely worming his way into her heart. Noelle craned her neck to watch an eagle make slow circles in the sky, searching for its evening meal. Another benefit to summer in the Pacific Northwest were the long days; at this time of year, it would be after nine p.m. before the sun set. A summer night on the water was the perfect way to end her day.

The eagle flexed his wings and glided through the warm air. It was time for Noelle to follow his lead and stretch her wings. The next time she saw Hugh, she'd say yes to ice cream.

Chapter Two

The automatic doors opened with a quiet hiss, and a blast of air conditioning welcomed Hugh when he walked back into the hospital for his weekly visit.

"Morning, Mr. Donavan. How's the leg feeling?"

The young man at the check-in desk handed Hugh the ID badge that all visitors were required to wear.

"It's much better, Gabe. I think I'll get the all-clear to start rehab next week."

Gabe's eyes lit up. "Maybe you'll be back on the field by the playoffs."

Hugh noted the eagerness in his voice. He was doubtful he would play at all this season, and the idea didn't bother him as much as he thought it would. He'd been playing hard both at his sport and life. It was time to take a break, but he didn't want to disappoint a fan, so he smiled and said, "I'll do my best, but the decision is up to the training staff and the coach."

"I'll keep my fingers crossed." Gabe held up both of his hands.

"Thanks." Hugh waved and made his way to the bank of elevators. He took one several floors down and then walked through the familiar maze of hallways painted with a colorful forest mural to the pediatric oncology wing of the hospital.

He shifted the bag of signed soccer balls, scarves, and Seattle Emerald's blankets he brought with him to give out to the kids he would visit this week. Normally, he wasn't able to come every week during the season, but this year he wasn't traveling with the team, giving him more time to spend with the kids and the one person he couldn't stop thinking about. Injuries were a part of life for a professional athlete, and Hugh had had his fair share. This one was different, the most severe so far, and a reminder that he was getting older and his career wasn't going to last forever. He needed to start making plans for his future, and that included settling down with the right partner.

Hugh tried to tamp down his excitement. He'd been trying to get Noelle Williams to talk to him beyond the patients he would visit since the first time he saw her. He didn't believe in love at first sight—until he met the beautiful, reserved pediatric nurse. He had it pretty easy when it came to dating, or he could, if he were attracted to the kind of women who threw themselves at him. Through high school and college, Hugh had learned pretty quickly that certain people were always attracted to talent, popularity, and fame. He also figured out that most of those people weren't always genuine. Noelle was the only person he'd encountered since he became a professional player who seemed to disapprove of him being an athlete.

She was sitting at the nurses' station when he arrived to pick up the list of patients he would visit that day. Her dark blue scrub bottoms were paired with a top covered in colorful mermaids on a turquoise background that complemented her light brown skin. She glanced up, her amber eyes flickering toward him, and then bowed her head so her hair hid her face.

"Morning, Hugh," her coworker Thanh greeted him with a wave.

Hugh's gaze darted to where Noelle sat staring at her tablet, avoiding eye contact, though a faint blush spread over her cheeks. He exchanged a look with Thanh, who shrugged.

He cleared his throat. "Good morning, Noelle."

She reached for a piece of paper and handed it to him. "Here's today's list. Make sure you review it carefully."

Hugh set the bag on the floor and rested his elbows on the counter. "Could you take a few minutes to look at it with me?"

Noelle sighed and spun around in her chair. "I have patients I need to check on," she said as she jumped up, pulling her wavy, dark brown hair into a ponytail while she walked away.

Thanh folded his arms and sat back. "If it's any help, she's interested. She's just...scared."

"What's she afraid of?" he muttered, watching her disappear down the hallway.

"She doesn't talk about it much, but her marriage didn't end well, and she's still a little gun-shy. Be patient. She'll come around when she's ready and hey, Milo and I are rooting for you." Thanh grinned at him.

"Thanks, man. I appreciate it."

"By the way, thanks again for the tickets to the last home game. Those seats were awesome. Milo's voice is still hoarse from all the yelling."

Thanh's husband was a big Emeralds fan, and Hugh was happy to pass on tickets for a game when he could. He'd made the same offer to Noelle, but she always turned him down.

"There's gotta be something," he muttered.

Thanh leaned forward, his eyes darting back and forth to make sure they weren't overheard. "She likes water."

Hugh's eyebrows shot up. "I can work with that," he said with a grin.

When he was finished with his visit, Noelle called out to him as he walked past her station.

"Hugh?" Her voice carried a slight tremor as she stood next to the desk, twisting her hands in front of her. "About that ice cream. I can go... I mean, if you still want to," she said, her gaze darting to where Thanh stood by, nodding his encouragement.

Hugh smiled at her. "I'd like that."

Thanh beamed at the two of them and rubbed his hands together. "Great, this is good."

Noelle bowed her head, trying to hide her grin at her friend's antics.

"You're supposed to ask when you can take her." Thanh gestured between Hugh and Noelle.

"Okay, I think I can take it from here," Hugh said with a pointed look at him.

Thanh backed away, holding his hands up. "Just trying to help."

Once Thanh was out of earshot, Noelle gave him a shy smile. "I can meet you after my shift tomorrow, if that works for you."

"That sounds perfect."

Chapter Three

That evening, Hugh sat on the deck of his house overlooking Lake Washington, watching a kayaker paddle past, looking serene in the evening water. He heard the click of the gate in the fence that separated his property from the house next door and his neighbor climbed the stairway up to his deck, dropping into a chair next to him. Hugh reached down and handed him a beer.

Dane Prescott took a long swig and stared out at the water.

"Long day?" Hugh asked.

"You know, when I founded PresTec in college, I never thought I'd end up spending all my time in board meetings and putting out fires instead of coding."

"Better you than me." Hugh saluted him with his beer.

They drank in silence for a while before Dane sighed. "Maya wants me to cut my hours back and spend more time with her and Jamie."

"If I had a great little boy and a beautiful wife, I'd spend every minute I could with them."

Hugh envied his friend. He hoped to have a wife and family someday. His mind drifted to Noelle again, and he shifted in his seat, trying to tamp down the physical effects of his lustful thoughts.

Dane glanced over at him with a raised eyebrow. "How are things going with your nurse?"

"She's not my nurse—at least, not yet."

"You know, my sister has a friend..."

Hugh held up his hand. "Stop. The last time I let you set me up with one of your sister's friends, I had to hear about how she was having a hard time finding someone who would make matching outfits for her and her chihuahua."

"Sorry." Dane snorted a laugh.

His best friend meant well, but his last few attempts at setting Hugh up had been disastrous. He didn't bother to add that once he met Noelle, he compared every other woman to her. Hugh would never forget the first time he saw her at the hospital. He'd been finishing up one of his visits when Thanh introduced him to the new nurse who would be working with him. He was used to people being excited to meet him, so he was thrown off when she gave his hand the briefest shake and avoided eye contact. When she finally met his gaze, those light brown eyes were hesitant, but he caught the slight spark of interest. Her dusky pink lips turned down, and she excused herself, practically running away. It took weeks of patience before she stopped being skittish around him. Each smile had been hard won, but every time that dimple appeared and her eyes lit up, he knew it was worth the effort.

Hugh pinched the bridge of his nose. "Don't forget the one before that who came to the date with a stack of bridal magazines."

"Dude," Dane said, rolling his eyes, "I owe you a case of wine for that one."

"No more blind dates."

Dane cocked his head, studying him. "So it's the nurse, is it?"

"It is."

"I hope it works out for you."

"So do I." Hugh sighed.

Dane downed the rest of his beer and stood. "I've got to get back. I promised Jamie two bedtime stories to make up for the one I missed last night."

"Give him a good-night hug from his uncle Hugh."

Dane nodded and headed back toward the other side of the fence, leaving Hugh alone with his thoughts. He tried to tamp down his excitement for his date the next night. It wasn't even a date, just ice cream, but it was a start. It had taken six months to reach this point, and he wasn't going to take it for granted. Now wasn't the time to be cocky.

Hugh scanned the lake looking for the kayak he spotted earlier, but it was long gone. He went up and rested his elbows on the deck railing, taking in the view of Mt. Rainier that he would never get tired of. It had taken a long time to reach a point in his life where he was ready for the life his friend Dane had with a wife and child to enjoy nights like this with him. He should have been more upset about missing the season than he was, but in a way he was thankful for the injury. It forced him to slow down and take stock of what was important to him—family, friends, and a partner in life who saw him as more than the sport he played. Noelle could be that person, and he hoped this would be the summer he finally got the chance to find out.

Chapter Four

Noelle looked up at the menu board for Annie Elliot's Homemade Ice Cream, feeling silly because with all the choices she knew she would still pick vanilla, and feeling self-conscious because she was with Hugh. *This isn't a date, it's just ice cream,* she reminded herself for the hundredth time since she finally agreed to meet Hugh after her shift the next week when he came to the hospital.

"Do you know what you want?" Hugh stood beside her, looking up at the menu with her.

"I should probably order something more exciting with all of these options, but I'll have the double cream vanilla."

Hugh nodded to the server. "Two double cream vanillas, please."

"Mister Donavan." A little boy tugged on Hugh's shirt. "Can I please get your autograph?" He held out a piece of paper and a pen.

Hugh took the pen from the boy and eyed his Seattle Emerald T-shirt. He turned back to the server and asked, "Excuse me, do you have a permanent marker?"

The server smiled and handed him a black marker. He knelt down and signed the boy's shirt while the boy stared at Hugh, wide-eyed, and his parents stood by beaming at him. Noelle took the cones from the server and paid for the ice cream while Hugh spent a few more minutes asking the little boy what position he played and giving him a few words of encouragement before sending him on his way.

Hugh handed the pen back to the server and pulled out his wallet.

She shook her head and pointed to Noelle. "She took care of it."

Hugh turned to her. "This was supposed to be my treat."

"I don't mind." Noelle shrugged. "You were busy."

"Thanks for understanding."

Noelle did understand, more than he knew, and it made her appreciate the extra effort he took with the little boy even more. Her ex wouldn't have shown the same kindness and patience that Hugh had just done.

They wandered through the outdoor mall with their cones, eventually stopping at a shady seating area.

"So what made you come to Seattle?" Hugh asked between bites.

"There was a movie, *Singles*, set in Seattle. I saw it on TV when I was in junior high and I fell in love with the idea of living here one day."

"You've only been here for six months. Where did you live before you came here?"

Noelle licked the frozen mixture of cream and sugar, appreciating how something so simple could taste so good. "Life happened," she finally said. "I let go of the dream of coming here for a different one and it turned out to be a mistake. Luckily, I figured it out in time. I've been here for over a year, actually. I had to spend a semester finishing my nursing degree, and then I was lucky enough to get a job at Children's."

"I'm really glad you did." Hugh's gaze held hers just long enough for her to feel the heat rise in her cheeks.

"What about you? Were you disappointed when you were traded to Seattle?"

"I was hoping to play for San Diego so I could be close to my parents, but I've loved playing for the Emeralds. I'd like to finish my career and retire here."

"Do you know what you're going to do when you've finished playing?"

Hugh finished off his cone and dusted his hands on his pants. He leaned forward, resting his arms on his thighs. "I'd like to coach if I can." He paused and waved to the little boy who had asked for his autograph when he walked by with his parents. "I like the idea of working with kids and passing on what I've learned."

"I've seen how great you are with the patients at the hospital and the extra time you took with that little boy just now. You would be a wonderful coach."

"See, I'm not such a bad guy after all." Hugh lifted an eyebrow.

"I never said you were."

"But I can see it in your eyes. What can I do to show you that you can trust me?"

Noelle blew out a shaky breath. "I was married, and my ex-husband played professional football."

"I know," Hugh said quietly.

Her head jerked up. "You..." She swallowed. "You know?"

"We didn't meet, but I saw you at an awards show a couple of years ago. You carried yourself so differently, I didn't recognize you when I met you at the hospital."

Noelle stared at him, trying to remember.

Hugh gave her a slight smile. "Your hair was straightened and almost blond. You wore a tight dress with high heels and," his brow furrowed, "you looked really uncomfortable."

Noelle shuddered as a wave of embarrassment washed over her. "That was me."

Hugh reached out and took her hand. "I noticed you then, but I see you now."

The awards show was the last event she went to before finally gathering the courage to ask for a divorce. Her hair and clothes were what her husband had demanded of her. Hugh was right, that wasn't her, and she knew that night she had to leave before she disappeared altogether. She moved to Seattle, finished her nursing degree, and started working at Children's Hospital. Opening her heart again and taking a chance on love were the only things left for her to do.

"You'll have to be patient with me. I have to remind myself that not all athletes are like my ex," she admitted with a small smile.

Hugh turned her hand over and brushed his thumb over her palm. "I'm a very patient man."

She saw the desire in his eyes, and the libido that she thought was long dead flared back to life.

"I should go," she said, pulling her hand out of his and hurriedly rising from her seat.

Hugh stood up slowly, his gaze locked on hers. "It's a shame to waste any of these beautiful summer days. Will you have dinner with me this weekend?"

Noelle remembered the promise she made to herself and said yes.

She said yes! Hugh couldn't stop grinning while he packed a picnic basket with food. He was so excited he barely slept the night before. Every time he closed his eyes, he pictured Noelle's shy smile and the slight flush on her cheeks when she agreed to go out with him. This was his chance, and he wasn't going to blow it.

There was a knock at the door and his neighbor Dane walked in. "Did you want me to buy the house next door just so you could come in and raid my refrigerator?" Hugh asked, watching Dane rummage through his refrigerator out of the corner of this eye.

Dane pulled out a bottle of flavored water and took a swig, grimacing he looked at the label. "What's the point of persuading your friend to buy a house next to you when all he has is healthy stuff to eat?"

Hugh laughed and added a bottle of wine to the basket.

Dane came over and peered at the contents with his eyebrows raised. "Wow, this looks good."

"I hope so." Hugh frowned. "I should have asked what she likes to eat," he muttered.

Hugh pulled out his phone and sent a quick text to Thanh, asking if Noelle had any food allergies and if she liked salmon. He stared at his phone, watching the three dots waiting for Thanh's reply.

His friendship with Thanh and his husband Milo was another unexpected benefit to his visits to the hospital, one he was particularly grateful for right now. He finally got a reply that there wouldn't be any issues with the picnic he planned and sent his thanks.

Dane watched him with amusement. "I haven't seen you this worked up over a date in... I've never seen you like this now, that I think about it. What makes this girl so special?"

"She's kind and thoughtful, and when she lets her guard down, she's funny and..." He shrugged. "She doesn't care if I play soccer. When she looks at me, it's like she's looking for the real me, and not just a guy wearing his underwear in a magazine ad," he added with a wry smile. "When I met her at the hospital the first time, I just knew she was the one for me."

"I remember that feeling. I felt that way the first time I met Maya," Dane said, his voice softening.

"And why aren't you with your wife and son now?"

Dane checked his watch. "They should be home any minute now. Jamie had a doctor's appointment today," he said, starting toward the door, calling out over his shoulder, "I'll be expecting a full update tomorrow."

Hugh shook his head, laughing. Dane was more invested in his dating life as he was. They met in college and his friend was thrilled when Hugh was traded to the Emeralds. When Dane heard that the house next door to him was going on the market, he had pressured Hugh to come see it. He wasn't sure he wanted or needed a big home, but he took one look at the mid-century modern house overlooking the water and realized this was where he wanted to live and raise a family one day.

Hugh looked around the kitchen and wondered if Noelle would like the house as much as he did. One step at a time, he told himself, grabbing the picnic basket and heading to his car.

Chapter Five

"I don't know...do you think it's too casual?" Noelle asked, twisting and turning in the mirror.

Her friend Aviva lounged on Noelle's bed, scrutinizing her outfit.

"Turn again," she said in her heavy Israeli accent, waving her hand at Noelle.

She obliged, and Aviva scrunched up her nose. "Where did he say he was taking you again?"

"He didn't," she said with a frustrated groan as she pulled off the silk dress she just tried on. "He just said it's casual, and to bring a sweater because it might get cold."

Aviva tapped her lips. "Okay. Then you definitely need to wear the ripped skinny jeans with that pink T-shirt that has the fluttery sleeves that show off your arms."

Noelle dug into her closet and wiggled into the jeans Aviva suggested and pulled the pink top over her head. She turned to the mirror. The jeans were capri length and would look good paired with the white sneakers she'd pulled out. The peony pink top was sleeveless, and the arm openings were capped with a short ruffle that showed off her toned arms. The color flattered the deeper golden glow she had from the summer sun.

Aviva grinned at her. "That's perfect," she exclaimed.

They went into the bathroom and, with Noelle's limited makeup supplies, decided on a touch of dark brown eyeliner, mascara, and pink lip gloss. Her hair fell in loose curls around her shoulders, and she finished off her outfit with a pair of small, gold hoop earrings.

Aviva came up behind her and put her hands on her shoulders. "I'm really proud of you. This is a big step you're taking."

Noelle gazed at her friend's reflection in the mirror and reached up to pat her hand. "Thank you so much for coming over to help. I'd be tempted to call the whole thing off if you weren't here."

Aviva turned her around and pulled her into a hug. "It's time for you to have some fun. It's summer, the sun is shining, and the air is filled with the smell of flowers. This is the best time of year to fall in love."

Noelle pulled back. "Let's start with a date, and then we'll see about love. One thing at a time."

Aviva laughed, her dark brown eyes filled with merriment. "You already half-like him, I can tell."

"Okay. I'll admit I half-like him." Noelle's lips twitched.

"Good." Aviva nodded. "Now I have to get going before he gets here."

Within minutes of her friend leaving, Noelle's doorbell rang. She opened it to find Hugh grinning at her.

He was wearing jeans and a faded blue T-shirt that stretched across his broad shoulders and athletic build. Noelle's heart sped up a beat. Hugh cleared his throat, and she realized she had been staring.

He looked down at her with a wry smile. "Are you ready?"

She grabbed a cardigan and her handbag. "I'm ready."

The top had been removed from Hugh's sage-green Bronco and the summer sun made the Puget Sound's waters sparkle as they headed west.

"Are you going to tell me where we're going?" she asked.

Hugh's lips curled up. "You'll see."

Trusting men wasn't easy for Noelle. Hugh managed to break through the defensive wall she had built, but it was still difficult to trust him. She remembered Thanh's story and decided it was time for her to take a leap of faith. Whatever Hugh had in mind for their date, she would enjoy their time together.

He pulled into the parking lot of the Shilshole Bay Marina and parked. Getting out, he came around and opened the door for Noelle, holding his hand out to her. Hugh grabbed a picnic basket out of the back seat with the other hand and led her toward the marina. They walked through the maze of boats until he stopped at a beautiful cobalt blue and white sailboat with gold striping on the side and *Henry's Gift* painted in gold and white lettering on the stern. He lifted the basket onto the deck and climbed aboard, turning to hold his hand out to her. Noelle reached up and felt like she'd stepped onto a marshmallow, from the gentle rocking under her feet. She swayed forward with the boat, and Hugh gently grasped her arms.

"Whoa, steady there," he said in a low, soft voice.

Noelle looked up into his hazel eyes, so close she could see tiny flecks of green and brown and the laugh lines that framed them. They were the eyes of someone who enjoyed life, someone who had laughed a lot. At that moment, Noelle knew he was the kind of man who would love with his whole heart. In her twenty-eight years, she'd never known a man like that before, and it scared her as much as it thrilled her.

Hugh let go and stepped aside with a sweeping motion. "I'd like to introduce you to *Henry's Gift*."

"It's beautiful," Noelle said, reaching out to run her hand over the teak trim. "So who is Henry?"

Hugh's smile dimmed. "Henry was my big brother."

From the change in his voice, Noelle knew Henry was no longer living.

"I had leukemia when I was four years old. Henry was my big brother and his bone marrow saved my life. He followed in our dad's footsteps and joined the navy." Hugh's voice shook with emotion, "Henry died on his last tour."

"Hugh, I'm so sorry." Noelle reached out and stroked his arm.

"He loved sailing as much as I did, and he gave me the gift of life, so..."

"*Henry's Gift*." She nodded. "And that's why you come to the hospital, isn't it?"

Hugh smiled faintly. "I just want to make sure I give back."

Noelle reached up and cupped his cheek.

"You're a good man, Hugh Donavan, and I'm sure your brother is proud of you."

Hugh nodded and took a deep breath. "Thank you for saying that." He took her by the hand and pointed toward a short staircase leading to the cabin. "The galley and head are downstairs. Make yourself at home while I take care of the anchor and ropes."

"Can I do anything to help?" Noelle offered.

"If you don't mind storing the food in the galley, that would be great."

Noelle picked up the basket and headed into the interior of the boat. The cabin was just as elegantly appointed as the outside. It continued the blue theme, with a seating area upholstered in white, with blue accent pillows scattered all around, and teak and mahogany woodwork was featured throughout. She set the basket on the counter and unloaded everything into the small cooler in the galley area.

When she finished, she explored the rest of the cabin. Beyond the seating area, there was a small wet bath and at the very back, a stateroom that consisted of a full-sized bed with built-in cabinets on either side. The engine started, and the boat began to sway. Noelle climbed back up to the deck and made her way over to where Hugh stood at the wheel. He maneuvered the boat slowly out of the marina toward the open waters of Puget Sound. As soon as they were clear of the other boats, Hugh motioned for her to stand at the wheel. He stood behind her, solid and calm, and placed her hands on the wheel.

"Don't worry, I'll make sure you get wherever you want to go," he said.

His deep voice washed over her, making her stomach dip and swell with the waves. The sun hovered over the top of the Olympic Mountains, making the last bits of snow that still clung to the tips glisten pale pink and orange in the late afternoon light.

Hugh pointed to the right. "Let's head up toward Golden Gardens, and then we can circle back to Elliott Bay."

Noelle nodded and turned the wheel, loving the way the boat cut through the water. With the sail tied down, she had a clear view of the water ahead. She looked up at the mast, imagining flying through the water with full sails on a windy day.

As if he could tell what she was thinking, Hugh leaned forward and whispered in her ear. "We'll come back out when there's more wind so you can really see her fly."

They passed the park and continued north. The moment Whidbey Island came into view, Hugh reached around her and cut the engine. "Look," he said in a hushed voice, pointing ahead.

At first, she couldn't see anything, and then. "Oh my God," she said in an awed whisper, watching as the flash of gleaming black and white emerge from the water. A trio of orcas breached the surface and swam up ahead of them

Noelle and Hugh stood in silence as the whales continued on their way, dipping in and out of the waves on their way to hunting grounds farther north.

After the orcas were no longer in sight, Noelle turned to Hugh. "Thank you. I never thought I'd actually have a chance to see them. That was..." She shook her head, searching for the right words. "Magical...incredible."

Hugh smiled at her, reaching up to tuck her hair behind her ear. Her breath caught, his eyes filling with desire and something more. He didn't see her as an object; he wasn't scrutinizing her, looking for flaws. He saw her as she was, and it was enough.

The wake from a passing boat rocked them, breaking the spell. Noelle spun around and gripped the wheel.

Hugh chuckled and started the motor again, resting his hands over hers. He steered the boat around toward Seattle. As they came into Elliott Bay, cruise ships and massive container ships came into view. Two ferries passed each other, one on the way to Bainbridge Island and one on its way back to Seattle. Hugh steered the boat toward a spot near the Space Needle, well out of the way of the larger ships and set the anchor. The city lights were just starting to come on, the last of the sun's rays reflecting gold off the windows on the buildings in the city center, casting downtown Seattle in a golden glow.

"Take a seat, and I'll get dinner ready," Hugh said, gesturing to a u-shaped seating area behind the wheel.

"I feel guilty letting you do all the work. Are you sure I can't do anything to help?" she asked.

"Nope," he said, shaking his head, "you're my guest. Make yourself at home and enjoy the view."

Hugh disappeared into the cabin, and Noelle settled herself against the dark blue cushions to watch the city lights grow brighter. The Ferris wheel lit up, and the lights came on at the baseball stadium, announcing the transition from day to night.

Hugh came back out with a blanket and a bottle of wine with two glasses, setting them down on the seat next to her. "I'll be right back with dinner," he said as he headed back into the galley.

Noelle took a deep breath, taking in the warm summer air. Standing at the wheel with Hugh at her back, watching the whales swimming through the Sound, had been one of the most amazing things she'd ever experienced.

A smile tugged at her lips. Aviva was right, summer was the best time of year to fall in love.

Chapter Six

Hugh quickly prepared the grilled salmon Caesar salads, using the time to pull himself together. Having Noelle on the boat with him was incredible. He could spend the rest of his life watching her eyes light up with each new discovery. The way her face filled with joy when she saw the orcas had his heart bursting. He put the finishing touches on their dinner and carried the plates back up, eager for more of Noelle's smiles.

She poured out two glasses of wine and cleared a spot on the bench for him. Noelle sighed, looking out toward the city lights. "This may be my favorite view of the city."

"I never get tired of it," he replied, his gaze following hers.

"I don't think I could ever live in a landlocked city after living here," she said wistfully.

"Where did you grow up?"

"Indianapolis."

She said the name as if it left a bad taste in her mouth, and the light in her eyes dimmed just a bit. Hugh decided not to push any further, this was an evening for happiness.

"Where did you grow up?" she asked.

"San Diego. My dad was in the navy and we bounced around when I was little, but then we got lucky. He was stationed there from the time I was in junior high through the end of high school."

"Is that where you learned to sail?"

Hugh nodded. "Sailing and soccer were my favorite things, but eventually, soccer took over, and I didn't have time for sailing. When I was transferred to Seattle, this was the first thing I bought," he said, patting the hull. "I couldn't live here and not have a boat. I even lived on her for a few months before I bought a house."

Noelle smiled. "I love to paddle by the houseboats on Lake Union. I've always thought it would be wonderful to live in one."

"Do you have a kayak or a paddleboard?"

"A kayak. I try to go out every chance I can when the weather is warm."

"Where else do you like to go?"

"I keep my kayak at a boatyard on Sandpoint so I can go after work. Most of the time I'm on Lake Washington or Lake Union."

"There's something special about the view of the world when you're right on the water, isn't there?"

"Everything seems calmer." She nodded. "I miss being on the water when the weather turns too cold."

An image of Noelle bundled up with him next to a fire flashed in his mind. Maybe winter wouldn't be so bad after all.

"I don't mind the winter so much, but this is my favorite time of year," he said.

Noelle took a deep breath, smiling as she admired the view. "No matter how gray the winters are, one sunny day here makes up for everything."

Hugh nodded. He shared his favorite spots for sailing and some trips he planned to explore the San Juan Islands in the future, and Noelle told him about some of her adventures kayaking while they ate their dinner, watching other boats both big and small pass by. Hugh put the dishes away, and when he came back up he noticed Noelle shiver and tug at her sleeves while she gazed out over the water. He picked up the blanket he had brought up earlier and wrapped it around her shoulders. She smiled and thanked him, the city lights reflecting in her eyes and the wind gently playing with her curls.

"Noelle, I promised myself I wouldn't put any pressure on you, and I mean to keep my promise, but I'd like to kiss—"

Before he could finish, she reached up and cupped the back of his head and pulled him down until his lips met hers. Her lips were soft and slightly cool from the night air, but the minute she opened her mouth, he was consumed with warmth and heat. Hugh reached under the blanket and pulled her close. She moaned and deepened their kiss. He reveled in the knowledge that she was as hungry for him as he was for her. He explored the curve of her waist and the small of her back with his hands, and now that he finally had her in his arms, he didn't know how he could ever let her go. Reluctantly, he tore his lips away.

She looked up at him with a dazed expression, her lips pink and swollen. She grasped his shoulders to steady herself as the boat swayed.

"I didn't know," she whispered.

Hugh pressed his forehead to hers, running his hands up and down her arms. "That one kiss could be everything? I didn't know either," he said in a breathless murmur. He nuzzled her neck, placing soft kisses behind her ear and along her collar bone, inhaling blackberry and vanilla scents of her shampoo. "You smell like summer," he said with a smile.

Noelle wound her arms around his neck and drew him in for another kiss. When they finally parted, he said, "It's late. I should take you home."

"Can we go sailing again?" she asked, her face luminous and full of hope in the moonlight.

He kissed her forehead. "I can't imagine a better way to spend the summer than sailing away with you."

This is a new story that is not a part of any series... yet (wink).

Eliana West writes multi-cultural romance with diverse characters. When not writing, Eliana can be found exploring the many wineries in Oregon and Washington with her husband in their vintage Volkswagen Westfalia named Bianca.

She is the founder of Writers for Diversity, a community for writers interested in creating diverse characters and worlds.

Eliana's debut *The Way Forward* with Tule Publishing will be out August 25, 2020.

https://tulepublishing.com/books/the-way-forward/

You can find Eliana online at: www.elianawest.com

The Search

by

Nichole Severn

Chapter One

The first forty-eight hours were critical.

Sweat built under Deputy US Marshal Lucy Whitlock's blouse as she walked the scene. August heat battled with whipping winds coming off the water and thickened the air in her throat. Boiler Bay State Scenic Viewpoint just north of Depoe Bay, Oregon, provided panoramic views of the Pacific Ocean. It was a perfect location for kids looking to hook up in the backs of their cars. But no one had seen seventeen-year-old London Zinnes disappear.

"The tracking app on her mother's phone says London Zinnes is still here." Deputy Dermot Hathaway rounded into her peripheral vision, his shadow casting across a dark set of tire treads at her feet. His light green eyes followed the same pattern of burnt rubber toward the southern entrance to the overview. Six-four, thick, light brown hair perfectly angled along his jaw, mountainous shoulders capable of more than blocking the sea-salted gusts attacking from the west. With buzzed sides and longer styled hair on top, her partner fit the tall, dark, and dangerous fantasy in every sense of the word as well as he fit his suit. "Someone sure got out of here in a hurry."

Their victim? The perpetrator? Or someone completely unrelated to the case? Lucy covered her eyes from the blistering sun above and pointed to the length of parked vehicles along the curve of the lot. The collar from her blazer rubbed against the sensitive skin at the back of her neck as she moved, but discomfort had to be the last thing of her mind right now.

The call had come in less than twelve hours ago. If London Zinnes had been abducted as her parents believed, she could be anywhere by now. They needed something more than a gut instinct. They needed evidence of a crime. "Have the Lincoln County sheriff's department run the license plates on all these vehicles. I know they're already interviewing the kids and tourists who were here when we arrived, but I want to make sure we aren't dropping the ball when the FBI hits the scene."

The US Marshals Service Missing Child Program supported the National Center for Missing and Exploited Children to protect underaged youth from victimization. With more than a dozen successful recoveries under hers and Dermot's belts, the FBI had specifically requested she and her partner take point during the investigation until their own agents landed. In Lucy's experience, the quicker the response to the initial call, the better chance of bringing the victim home, but nothing here suggested London Zinnes hadn't simply met up with the friend she'd planned to hang out with for the night and forgotten her curfew.

Lucy stared out over the rough, brown rock leading down into the ocean as a familiar pool of dread solidified at the base of her spine. That didn't explain why the mother's phone said London was still here.

"I can see the wheels spinning in your head." Dermot's voice penetrated through the thick haze building in her head, kept her in the moment. "Talk to me, goose."

"Those tracking apps use GPS data from nearby cell towers to triangulate any given device's position, and you know as well as I do that kids these days are practically born with a phone in their hand. They don't go anywhere without them. We've swept the parking lot, checked the restrooms, and searched all the vehicles. London isn't here." Instinct drew Lucy toward the edge of the parking lot, closer to the rocks. Sheets of saltwater spit into the air. Her hair whipped behind her. Mist coated her skin in an electrifying wake-up call to her senses. Rough grass tickled her ankles as she stepped down from the parking lot and crossed the short distance toward the rocks.

There, a few feet below, she caught sight of the rectangular black device. A wave filled the cracks below the phone and dislodged it from its position for just a moment before setting it back down. Extracting a latex glove from her jacket pocket, Lucy stepped down and crouched to pick up the device. She held it up for Dermot. "But her phone is."

Dermot settled large hands on his hips. "London Zinnes was abducted."

"Do either of you know who London was meeting up with last night?" Deputy Dermot Hathaway had memorized the layout of the Zinnes home the moment he'd stepped through the door, an old habit he couldn't seem to shake, even after his military discharge two years ago. Spectacular panoramic ocean views from Cascade Head to Fishing Rock encircled the remodeled home-in-the-round. Family photos filled with smiling faces watched his every move from the walls as he studied the wraparound deck. The home flooded with natural light from the sixteen individual windows as the mesmerizing sound of surf on sand filled his ears.

The recovery of London Zinnes's phone at the scenic overlook had been enough for the bureau to issue an AMBER alert for the girl, but whoever'd abducted her would've had just as good of a chance taking her from her own home. No security. No neighbors. Complete isolation. "Was she dating someone special that you can think of?"

"If she was, she didn't tell us." Harrison Zinnes, a fit, blond man with a better-than-average build and a collection of high school football trophies behind him, slid one arm around his wife. The defense attorney had made a lot of enemies over the years, gotten a lot of threats for making a living out of defending the worst kind of killers. It was possible one of them had caught up to the man standing between his clients and justice. "London didn't have many friends. She mostly kept to herself and worked on her art."

"Those are hers." Christine Zinnes motioned to the bookcase on the other side of the room near the dining table. Dozens of books stood erect with pages open to depict cut-apart scenes of dragons, knights, hearts, and skulls. "She sold them to a boutique in town. Tourists loved them. The owner had put in another order last week, but..." She cast her tear-filled gaze to the floor and seemed to compose herself. Wiping tears from her cheeks, Christine drew in a shaky inhale. "I'm sorry. I don't understand who'd want to hurt London. She's an artist. She keeps her grades up. She volunteers at the battered women's shelter. She's a child, for crying out loud."

Dermot's stomach flipped as the past threatened to take control. He wasn't at war anymore, but search and rescue, whether on American soil or in a combat zone, consisted of the same rules. This was what he'd been trained for, what he was good at. "We'll do whatever it takes to bring her home alive, Mr. and Mrs. Zinnes. I give you my word."

"We'll need a list of anyone she's been talking to recently." Deputy Lucy Whitlock slid a dark leather notebook and a pen across the coffee table toward the couple. Her case notes. Long, black hair slid over her shoulder as she leaned back in her seat with nothing but grace and control. Her Chinese-American features, with constructed perfectly shaped brows over dark eyes, wide nose, and full pink lips he hadn't stopped thinking about since the moment they'd been partnered two years ago. Confident, resourceful, determined. She was the marshal Harrison and Christine Zinnes needed on this case, the one who'd dedicated her entire career to bringing home the missing. "Anyone she sees regularly, including teachers, church leaders, friends' parents?"

Christine took the notebook and started making a list. "Will you be talking with Gwen Oliver's parents, too?"

The name wasn't familiar. Dermot pressed his elbows into his knees, the edge of the sheaf of paper from his own notebook cutting into his thumb. "Gwen Oliver? Is she one of London's friends?"

"They're best friends, ever since they were toddlers. The girls have been inseparable for years," Harrison said.

"You think Gwen might know who London planned on meeting last night at the overlook." The hairs on the back of Dermot's neck stood on end. It wasn't much, but with CCS still trying to crack the encryption on London's phone, it was a start.

"No, you don't understand." Christine shook her head, the pen still poised above Lucy's notebook. "Gwen Oliver disappeared six days ago."

Chapter Two

Crystal blue water reflected a clear sky and mossy green growth from boulders peppered throughout the stream. Fogarty Creek, approximately twenty minutes north from where the victim had disappeared, hadn't suffered from the lack of visitors and tourists since the sheriff department's warning to avoid the area due to a possible abduction less than a week ago—Gwen Oliver's. Miles of ocean stretched beyond the horizon to the west, but families seemed perfectly happy picnicking along the sand as kids chased each other along the beach and kicked up water in their paths. As though they didn't have a care in the world. Or concern for their lives.

Lucy's heels sank lower in the damp sand as she surveyed the large collection of boulders making up the fisherman's rock ahead, London Zinnes's notebook in hand. "According to London's notes, this was the location she believed Gwen had met up with the guy she'd been seeing, but any chance of finding evidence the girl was abducted here would've been destroyed days ago."

"If Gwen was trying to keep their relationship a secret, even from her best friend, there's a chance they would've gone somewhere private." Dermot pointed to a trailhead nearby, leading deeper into Sitka spruce, western hemlock, shore pine, and alder forest. "There are trails all throughout these woods. Plenty of areas a perp could isolate and get the jump on a seventeen-year-old girl. I'm having the sheriff send over the initial incident report and supplemental reports, but we might be able to find something they missed during their search."

"You think if we find out what happened to Gwen Oliver, we'll find London Zinnes." It was worth a shot. Their victim had already been gone fifteen hours. Every second they were out here could cost London Zinnes her life. They headed for the trailhead, sand clinging to the hems of their slacks.

Once in the trailhead, thick canopy blocked the summer's unrelenting heat but failed to cool the nervous energy skittering down Lucy's spine. She'd never told anyone other than the police the details of what'd happened all those years ago. Not even her parents, for fear they would've combatted her terror with you-should-have-known-better dismissals. They'd learned she'd been abducted, held, but anything more than that, Lucy had kept to herself. The shame had been too much to face, the self-blame.

She knew better now. She'd developed a healthy routine of keeping potential threats at arm's length, but something had convinced her she could trust Dermot, that he'd never use what she'd told him to hurt her.

Another layer of sweat trickled down her collarbone as they hiked along the trail. Lucy took the right side of the path, Dermot the left. They watched for anything out of the ordinary, anything that could tell them if there'd been a struggle. Disturbed foliage, a piece of clothing. Blood. She slowed her pace after as the trail leveled out before taking them over a bridge, nothing but the sound of their combined breathing in her ears. "So are things going to be awkward between us now?"

"What do you mean?" Dermot pulled up short along the path a few steps ahead and offered her a bottle of water. Sweat beaded at his temples and accentuated the ripple of tendons along his neck.

"I tell you I was abducted as a teenager, and you suddenly don't have the need to fill every second with conversation." She accepted the water from him and twisted off the lid. The bottles had been cold when they'd left the Zinnes home. Now they were stuck with room temperature water that did nothing to douse the burn under her skin. She squinted up at him, one eye closed against the sunlight coming through the trees. "Kind of feels personal."

"We've been partners for two years, and you never told me." He replaced the top on his bottle. "I figured you'd said everything you'd wanted to say back in that room. Was I wrong?"

"No, but that doesn't mean anything has to change between us." Had telling him been a mistake? "We can still be—"

"What, Luce? Friends? Partners?" His voice dipped into dangerous territory, and a warmth that had nothing to do with the brutal temperature swirled through her. He took a step down the trail, closing the space between them until only a few inches remained. "I think you've worked with me long enough to know neither of those options are good enough for me. Not anymore."

He crushed his mouth to hers.

Her taste filled him. He reveled in the firmness of her mouth, the edges of her teeth grazing his bottom lip, and the whole world threatened to rip straight out from under him. A soft humming noise escaped her throat as she rose on her toes to match his height and press against him.

She was kissing him back. He'd only intended to kiss her to make a point, to prove that her trust had meant more to him than anyone else's, but now Dermot couldn't seem to let her go. All the cases they'd worked together, all the missing victims they'd recovered, the late nights, the early mornings, the inside jokes—it'd all been leading to this. To Lucy. He didn't give a damn about what anyone else had to say. He'd resign from the marshals service right the hell now if hanging onto her a little longer was his reward.

Heavy footsteps and low voices echoed down to him from across the bridge, and the bubble they'd created around themselves in the past few minutes burst. Lucy pressed a hand over his heart and broke the kiss, staring up at him as though she'd never considered they could be more than partners. Her fingers slid down his chest as she stepped away and swiped at her mouth with the back of her hand. Long black hair lifted off her shoulders as a tendril of wind breezed through the trees and accentuated the flush of pink in her neck and face. He'd done that. He'd broken through her carefully controlled exterior and made her feel, and a satisfaction he'd never experienced before burned beneath his skin.

A group of hikers descended down the trail and maneuvered between them with nods and hellos. She waited until the small group had passed out of earshot, giving him just enough time to pull himself together. "We should keep going. If London is still alive, she doesn't have much time."

"After you." He motioned higher up the trail with the half-full water bottle still in his grip, the warm plastic crackling under the stiffness in his hand. Insects buzzed in his ears as they neared the bridge leading across this section of the creek. Steel girders reverberated as they stepped over the old wood planks leading to the other side of the shallow gulf. A single tree fought to invade the bridge's space off to his right, and Dermot slowed.

A couple of thin branches had been broken here. Could've been an accident, a tourist's backpack catching on the tree or some kid determined to destroy anything he came into contact with, but they were searching for a missing young woman. He couldn't discount anything. Pressing the pad of his thumb into the dry break, he narrowed his attention on a dark stain in the wood at his feet. "Lucy."

She turned back toward him from nearly halfway across the bridge. "Got something?"

"Broken branches, maybe blood." He crouched, following the path of the remnant of a single droplet from the top handrail. The evidence had been smeared and baked by the sun, but Dermot was positive. There'd been a struggle here. Lucy's shadow cast over him as he straightened. "Could be random."

"Or it could be Gwen Oliver." Head down, she searched the rest of the planks, careful of where she stepped. "The blood seems to be confined to this one area. I'll get a crime scene unit to collect a sample. We should be able to compare it to DNA taken from the Oliver home when she was initially reported missing."

Stepping around the evidence, Dermot maneuvered to one side to get a full look at the base of the tree. And froze. "It'll be a match."

Lucy rounded to his other side and inhaled sharply once she caught sight of the body. "London Zinnes's suspicion was valid. Her best friend didn't run away with her boyfriend. She was murdered."

Chapter Three

The medicolegal investigators were examining Gwen Oliver's remains, documenting everything they could, and getting the body ready for transportation back to the county morgue for autopsy. But Lucy didn't feel the relief that usually came with closing an investigation. London Zinnes was still out there, still in danger.

Lincoln County sheriff's deputies had already taken their statements, but she couldn't seem to move from the scene. Gwen Oliver had been lured here, killed, and discarded as nothing more than garbage. Was it only a matter of time before they found London out here, too? Park rangers waited on the sidelines as the homicide investigators kept tourists from disturbing the evidence, but Lucy only had attention for the bruised, battered, swollen face of the victim.

"She fought back." Dermot's voice broke through the soft ringing in her ears, doing its best to keep her from shattering right there in the middle of a crime scene. "The medicolegal investigator said there are defensive wounds along her forearms, fingers, and palms. Her nails are broken, too. There's a good chance she scratched her attacker. They'll know more after the autopsy."

Lucy crossed her arms as though she could hold herself together on her own, but she knew the truth. Every victim she hadn't been able to bring home alive stole another piece of the sixteen-year-old girl who'd survived two weeks in that shed. She'd dedicated her life to saving others. But at what point had she stopped living for herself? "London is still out there. Unless something in Gwen Oliver's life or on her body tells us where, we're back at square one."

"We're going to find her, Luce," he said.

Luce. Her lips tingled with the explosive memory of that kiss they'd shared before crossing the bridge, and the emotional armor she'd used to keep him out—to keep everyone out—cracked. The constant fear of him seeing past the guards she'd put into place had dissipated with every stroke of his mouth against hers, and for the first time she could remember since her abduction, she'd been able to take a full breath. She'd used her work to help victims move on with their lives, but seeing Gwen Oliver's body, knowing London Zinnes was still out there, increased her awareness that she'd done nothing more than survive.

She'd forgotten what it'd been like to live, to embrace life, to cling to it. Until Dermot had kissed her. One kiss. That was all it'd taken to remind herself she wasn't that scared girl anymore. She was a damned US marshal. She was strong, confident, assertive, and protective, and she deserved to be more than a shadow of her former self. She deserved to be happy. "We're done here."

They took the trail back the way they'd come as the sun dipped lower in the western half of the sky. Heat billowed off the parking lot in waves and worked under her blazer. Wrenching the SUV's door wide, she collapsed into the driver's seat and started the ignition. Dermot climbed inside, the cabin immediately filling with a mixture of his aftershave and man. Air conditioning worked overtime as she pulled out of the state park's lot and headed back to Depoe Bay. Miles of coastline blurred past them as they raced down the highway.

"You got someplace to be?" He clung to the handle above his head, the weight of his gaze pressurizing the air in her lungs.

Lucy tapped the brakes and maneuvered the SUV to the side of the road. Speeding cars and semi haulers shook the vehicle as she struggled to make sense of the exposed nerves inside, and she shifted the SUV into park.

She stared out his window as the sun lowered over the horizon. Red, oranges, pinks melted together within a few seconds and cast a soft glow over Dermot's features. She unbuckled her seat belt and swung one leg over the center console to wedge her knees on either side of his hips. Surprise brightened the light in his light green eyes as she peeled her blazer from her shoulders, and she brushed her mouth against his. "I'm exactly where I want to be."

She was asleep in his arms.

Stitched purple flowers stretched from the mess of bedding up toward his chest. The rental they'd found for the night wasn't much. Three bedrooms, two bathrooms. It'd been the best they could do during tourist season and would serve as a safe house until they could come at their investigation into London Zinnes's disappearance from another angle in the morning. The slap of ocean waves against bouldering rock right outside the window kept in rhythm with his heart rate, and Dermot closed his eyes.

Every kiss, every touch, every sensation burned into his brain. *This.* This was what he'd been waiting for. Not just someone who waltzed in and out of his life because of an assignment, but a real partner. Someone he could count on for support, trust. Someone who would come looking for him if he were the one to disappear. Someone he could love.

Lucy.

Hell. He'd fallen for her. He wasn't exactly sure when, but it'd been long before she'd climbed into his lap on the side of the road a few hours ago. Maybe the day he'd met her. Her persistence, her strength, her self-reliance. He needed all of it right then, because no matter how long they ignored what was waiting for them outside these walls, they couldn't push away reality forever. A young woman was dead, another missing, and he'd do whatever it took to make sure they weren't forgotten.

"I can see the wheels spinning in your head." Lucy used his earlier words against him as she feathered her index finger along his jaw. Hiking one leg from beneath the covers, she slid it up and over his thigh until she fit right against him. Right where she belonged. A perfect piece to the puzzle he'd been trying to assemble his entire life. "We won't have the autopsy results until tomorrow afternoon at the earliest. Why are you still awake?"

He caught her hand in his, kissed his way down the backs of her fingers and to the thin, sensitive skin along her wrist. "You know I'd never stop looking for you if something happened, right? I'll always be there for you."

"What are you talking about? Nothing is going to happen to me." Confusion brought her sculpted eyebrows together and deepened the lines at the bridge of her nose. Lucy pressed her hand into his chest and leveled her gaze with his. Understanding deepened the brown depths of her eyes, and his gut clenched. He hadn't given her an answer, but she knew. "Dermot, you and I are partners. What we've built these past two years goes beyond us working cases together. It goes beyond the occasional drink we've had after work as friends." She threaded her hand in his. "Even before you kissed me on that trail, I knew we were more than partners. We're two people who care about each other, and there's nothing—no case— that is going to change that."

He claimed her mouth, threading his hand into the hair at the base of her neck in order to hold onto her a little longer. She cared about him, and he cared about her. She was right. Nothing would change that, and he'd spend the rest of his life guaranteeing that outcome if that was what she required of him.

Three low knocks penetrated through the thick haze of rising desire, and Lucy smiled as she pulled away.

"I told the medical examiner where we were staying in case she had news on Gwen Oliver's autopsy." Sliding from the bed, she grabbed her oversized T-shirt and sweats and dressed quickly. "I guess she couldn't wait. I'll be right back."

The sound of her bare feet sticking to the hardwood floor faded, and Dermot reached for his clothes. They'd taken all the time they could. Didn't matter they were still waiting for autopsy results. It was time to bring London Zinnes home.

A gunshot exploded down the hall, and Dermot pulled his weapon from his shoulder holster at the side of the bed. He raced around the end of the bed and pressed his back against the wall for cover. Craning his neck, he caught sight of the body near the front door, and blood. So much blood. His heart threatened to beat out of his chest as he swung the gun up and closed in on his partner's position. "Lucy!"

He collapsed at her side, panic taking hold, and set his gun down to apply pressure to the wound. No. This wasn't how it was supposed to be. He had to get her out of here.

Clamping a hand over her shoulder, she set her head back against the floor. Pain filled her voice. "Still...here."

"Of course I'm still here. You're out of your damn mind if you think I'm going to leave you here." Dermot pulled his phone from his back pocket and dialed 911. "This is Deputy US Marshal Dermot Hathaway. I need emergency response at my location. Now!" He gave them the address and hung up. "They're coming. Hold on."

She wrapped her bloodied hand around his discarded weapon and thrust it straight into his chest. "He's...still here."

Understanding hit. Movement registered out of the corner of Dermot's eyes, a mere glimpse. Pain exploded through the side of his face, and the world tilted on its axis and went dark.

Chapter Four

Dermot hit the floor, unconscious.

"I really wish you hadn't gone looking for Gwen, Marshal Whitlock." Harrison Zinnes stood over her partner, the gun he'd used to get through the door still in his hand. Crouching, he confiscated Dermot's weapon and studied it in the single slice of moonlight coming through the cutout in front door. "None of this would've happened if you'd let her disappearance slip under the radar like the rest of the investigators."

"You killed her." A groan escaped her control as she increased the pressure on her wound. Blood slipped through her fingers. Pressing her feet into the floor, Lucy struggled to increase the distance between her and the gunman and set her back against the nearest wall. "Then you left her in the middle of that park like a piece of garbage to be cleaned up by someone else."

"I tried to keep her quiet about what she'd found, but she wouldn't listen to me. She wanted to get to know me. She was excited by the possibility she and London were sisters." Harrison Zinnes straightened, towering over her. "She was going to ruin everything. Do you have any idea how much money I would lose in the divorce if my wife found out I'd had the affair? Do you think I would've been able to make partner with something like that on my record?"

"You were Gwen Oliver's biological father." The investigation was coming into focus. "You had an affair with her mother, and Gwen was going to expose you. She wasn't meeting with a mystery boyfriend. She was meeting with you."

"She wouldn't listen to me," he said. "I gave her a choice, and she chose wrong. She wanted a relationship that I couldn't give her. I couldn't let her destroy everything I've worked for. I couldn't let her tear apart my family."

"So you lured her to Fogarty Creek, and you killed her." Lucy had to keep him talking, distracted. She wedged herself higher along the wall. She was unarmed and outweighed by her attacker, but that wouldn't stop her from making sure she and Dermot got out of here alive. "And London? You found her notebook, didn't you? You knew she was looking into her best friend's disappearance, and you couldn't have that."

Zinnes's face relaxed, his dark, engraved gaze distant. Distracted. "She hired a private investigator with the money she made selling her book art in town. That's who she was scheduled to meet with last night. I couldn't let that happen."

Lucy shot to her feet and landed a kick to her attacker's gut. Pain ripped through the wound in her shoulder and stole the air from her lungs. She stumbled to the side as lightning shot across her vision. A fist slammed into the side of her face, and she hit the floor.

"I can't have you and your partner getting in my way, Marshal Whitlock." His footsteps reverberated through the hardwood beneath her a split second before stinging pain exploded across her skull. He hefted her off the floor by her hair. "Not again."

He threw her straight back into the wall, and her head snapped back.

She couldn't breathe, couldn't think. A moan slipped past her lips as the world battled to right itself. The fight drained out of her. She struggled to sit upright. "Where is she? Where is London?"

"Someplace you'll never find her." Harrison Zinnes pressed a foot into her wound, effectively pinning her to the floor, and elicited a desperate scream from her. "Where no one will find her."

"You're going to want to get the hell away from my partner now," a familiar voice said.

Harrison Zinnes turned, gun raised, but Dermot was faster. Her partner locked onto her attacker's wrist and jerked down. The crack of bone filled her ears before Zinnes's scream echoed throughout the house. In one fluid move, Dermot swept the bastard's legs from underneath him and planted their perp facedown. Cuffs reflected the moonlight coming from the rectangular glass in the front door as the man she'd fallen in love with secured the suspect.

Sirens and shouts penetrated the pounding of her heart behind her ears. "Where is she, Harrison? Where is your daughter?"

"I'll lose everything," Zinnes said.

"You've already lost everything that matters. Where is London?" Dermot increased the pressure on her attacker's wrist.

"I never meant to hurt her. I wanted us to stay together as a family, so I kept her close." Dark eyes locked on Lucy, and dread pooled at the base of her spine. "I wanted to keep my family."

Her partner claimed his own weapon and took aim, stance wide. "Tell me you're okay."

"I'd like an ambulance now, please." She set her head back against the wall. "And I don't think a brownie would hurt."

Pain ricocheted around his head as the EMT with the flashlight made another pass in front of his eyes. Dermot turned away, every cell in his body focused on the two sheriff's deputies hauling Harrison Zinnes between them in cuffs. The bastard would spend the rest of his life in prison for what he'd done to Gwen Oliver, but that still left law enforcement without a clue as to where he'd hidden London. He pushed the EMT off. "I'm fine."

"You look like hell." That voice. *Her* voice. It wound through him, heightened his senses and anchored him at the same time. Lucy settled against the bumper of the ambulance, her arm strapped close to her chest. Emergency techs had been able to patch the wound in her shoulder well enough to stop the bleeding. After that, it'd be a matter of cleaning and stitching once she made it to the hospital herself.

A smile broke free from the hard set of his mouth. "You're one to talk."

"The medical examiner called." Red and blue patrol lights highlighted the sharp angles of her face as she stared out over the scene. "You were right. Gwen Oliver fought back before Harrison Zinnes threw her over the side of that bridge. The DNA under her fingernails was a fifty percent match to her own, revealing a parent or sibling relation. I imagine once Zinnes is compelled to provide his DNA at booking, we'll be able to verify if what he said was the truth. The district attorney will have a field day, for sure."

"Has he said anything about what he did with London?" he asked.

"Only that he wanted to keep her close." A haunted mask spilled across her expression, and his gut twisted. The similarities between Harrison Zinnes's motives and Lucy's own abductor were glaring. Neither had wanted to accept the possibility of losing someone close to them, but Lucy was still here. A little worse for wear but alive. He had to believe there was still hope for London Zinnes.

"If she's alive, we've arrested the man who was keeping her that way." The FBI would take Gwen's killer into custody, leaving the marshals service and the Lincoln County sheriff's department to clean up the mess. By the time they managed to get any information out of the perp, it could be too late for London. And that wasn't good enough. "Zinnes said he wanted to keep her close. What if he hadn't just meant metaphorically?"

Lucy pushed off the edge of the ambulance. "He was trying to keep his family together. What better location to do that than his own home?"

"We need to get to the Zinnes home. Now. I'll drive." Dermot called after two deputies as he and Lucy ran toward the SUV. In seconds, they fishtailed out of the neighborhood and headed for the home-in-the-round on the beach. Sirens filtered through the low sound of his own breathing. He shook his head. Unbelievable. "He's had her there this entire time, and we never knew."

"We'll make it." Lucy's confidence bled past his doubt.

Fifteen minutes later, Dermot slammed on the brakes in the Zinnes driveway and shouldered out of the vehicle. Both deputies were out of their patrol car and awaited orders. "Search the house. Every room, every closet. I don't care if you have to break that door down. We need to find her."

Lucy rounded behind the circular home. "Dermot!"

He followed her voice until her outline stood stark against the darkened backdrop of open beach behind her.

"There." She ducked beneath the wraparound deck to what looked like a doorway to a crawlspace beneath the house. Tugging on the handle with her free hand, she stepped back. "There's a new padlock."

"Get behind me." Dermot unholstered his weapon and aimed at the latch from an angle to prevent the shot from piercing through the siding. The bullet destroyed the lock, and he lunged for the three-foot-by-three-foot door. Ripping the padlock free, he discarded the crude metal into the sand and wrenched open the makeshift door.

Silence enveloped him as he crawled inside. He reached back for Lucy, and she handed him a flashlight. "London, can you hear me? I'm a US marshal. I came to get you out of here."

A small moan broke through the darkness, and the hairs on the back of his head stood on end. His eyes adjusted to the dim light from the flashlight, and the beam illuminated a pair of bare feet. The breath rushed out of him. "London." Deep throated sobs intensified as Dermot approached. "It's okay. You're safe. I'm going to get you out of here."

Slowly, he unwound the duct tape around the young woman's wrists, ankles, and mouth and maneuvered her through the opening before climbing out himself. Sheriff's deputies took the girl and led her toward their patrol car as frantic cries filled the night. Christine Zinnes, dressed in her nightgown, reached for her daughter before an ambulance pulled into the driveway.

"You found her." Lucy settled her head against his shoulder as a set of EMTs helped their victim into the back of the ambulance. "London Zinnes is alive."

"We found her." He couldn't have done it alone.

"Partners?" She stared up at him, her smile igniting a rush of fire across his nerve endings.

"Partners." Dermot leaned down, careful of her shoulder, and wrapped his arms around her lower back.

He teased her with a brush of his mouth against hers. "On the job and off. Forever."

Thank you for reading this introduction to Nichole Severn's Marshal Law series, debuting with The Fugitive in December 2020 from Harlequin Intrigue!

Nichole Severn writes mind-twisting suspense and bullet-proof romance with a hell of a lot of guns. She graduated from Utah Valley University with a degree in Psychology and from Nevada State College with a degree in English Literature.

She resides with her very supportive and patient husband, as well as her demon spawn, in Utah. When she's not writing, she's constantly injuring herself running, rock climbing, practicing yoga, and snowboarding.

Nichole's recent releases include Midnight Abduction (Tactical Crime Division) and Caught in the Crossfire (Blackhawk Security).

Keep in touch, and grab yourself a free search and rescue novella from Nichole by joining the Syndicate!

Outlaw Ghost

by

Kat Martin

Chapter One

Sweet Springs, Texas

A harsh wind pulled at the branches outside the window. The howl of a coyote echoed mournfully from the hills overlooking the property at the edge of town. Beneath the old-fashioned quilt on the antique iron bed, Callie Sutton listened to a different sound, this one coming from inside the old Victorian house.

It was an eerie sound, disturbing, a strangely human sound. As if someone walked through the silent rooms then climbed the stairs. As if someone opened the door and came into her room. As if he stood at the foot of her bed.

Since the door was firmly closed and locked, it was impossible, yet the feeling of being watched would not go away.

The tempo of her heart increased and her nerves stretched taut as Callie searched the darkness but found no one there. She told herself it was all in her mind, nothing more than the normal creaks and groans of a house this old. The Victorian home she had inherited from a distant aunt had been empty and in disrepair for more than thirty years.

But the moment she had seen the charming turret in front and wrap-around porch, the lovely built-in bookcases, molded ceilings and ornate woodwork, she had fallen in love with the place.

The renovations she'd had done before she moved in were mostly finished, the kitchen and baths remodeled, the hardwood floors refinished, the fireplace repaired and a fire crackling in the hearth in the evenings.

The work that remained was mostly superficial and of course she had a ton of decorating to do. Callie was looking forward to that. Or at least she had been until the ghostly sounds in the house at night continued to grow more pronounced.

Awake now, Callie stared up at the ceiling, her ears straining for any indication of a threat, but the house had fallen silent. Eventually, her heartbeat returned to normal and her body relaxed.

She yawned, sleepy from a long day at the clinic and putting up wallpaper in the kitchen when she got home after work.

As a veterinarian technician, she had been hired by the county vet, Dr. Reynolds, who was badly in need of help. Callie worked mostly with small animals, while Doc Reynolds specialized in large animals, a necessity in a ranching community like the tiny Texas town of Sweet Springs.

Since the clinic at the end of Main Street was always busy, Callie would be facing another hectic day tomorrow. She needed to get some sleep. She yawned again and her eyes drifted closed as an odd sense of peace stole over her. It had happened before and perhaps that was the reason she wasn't more afraid.

She didn't believe in ghosts. On the other hand, if there were such a thing, this one seemed strangely protective. A smile touched her lips as she drifted deeper into sleep and Callie started to dream.

He was tall, in snug dark pants, a full-sleeved white linen shirt, and tall black boots. He wore a black flat-brimmed hat, and a gun belt hung from his lean hips, the pistol strapped to a muscled thigh. She tried to see his face beneath the brim of the hat but caught just the hint of a hard jaw covered by several days' growth of dark beard.

He stood at the foot of the bed as if he watched over her. He looked like an outlaw, she thought in some corner of her mind, a gunslinger right out of the Wild West. She should have been frightened but she wasn't afraid. Instead she felt safe, protected.

She settled into an even deeper sleep and didn't wake up until morning, the dream no more than a hazy memory.

Callie showered and dressed in jeans and a lightweight sweater just warm enough for the end- of-October weather, then headed downstairs for coffee and toast before she drove to work.

She loved her newly remodeled country kitchen. She'd almost had the servant's stairs removed but they were part of the original structure so she had left them. Turned out they were handy and added a certain charm. She'd found an antique oak table and topped it with pretty yellow placemats that matched the walls, making the big kitchen feel cozy.

Callie glanced at the table, an uneasy feeling creeping through her. At the sight of the single red rose lying on top, her insides tightened. Someone had been inside the house!

Her hands shook as she pulled the phone out of her pocket and dialed 9-1-1. Dear God, was the intruder still somewhere inside? Her gaze shot to the back door, saw that the lock had been pried open, and a chill rolled down her spine.

She thought of the eerie sounds in the house last night and how she had felt safe and protected.

Clearly she wasn't as safe as she thought.

Chapter Two

"Sweet Springs Sheriff's Office," a woman's voice answered. "Millie speaking, what's your emergency?"

"Someone broke into my house last night. They left a rose on my kitchen table while I was asleep upstairs."

"A rose, huh? Old boyfriend, maybe?" Clearly a town the size of Sweet Springs didn't have a lot of crime.

"I don't have any old boyfriends," Callie said. "I just moved here. I-I'm afraid he might still be in the house."

Millie's voice sobered. "What's your address?"

Callie gave her the property address on Pecan Lane. "It's the old Victorian at the edge of town." "Stay on the line. I'm calling Sheriff Trask. He isn't that far away."

Callie's stomach churned for the entire five minutes that passed before she heard the crunch of gravel and the engine of a vehicle pulling up in front. Through the dining room window, she saw a white extended cab pickup, the word SHERIFF in big blue letters on the door.

The sheriff got out, a tall man in dark brown uniform pants and a light beige short-sleeved shirt, a badge pinned to the front. He wore a beige cowboy hat and a pistol holstered on the belt at his waist.

"He's here," Callie said to Millie with relief. The call ended and she hurried to the front door to let him in.

"Callie Sutton?" the sheriff asked, looking down at her from beneath the brim of his hat. He had the bluest eyes Callie had ever seen.

"That's me. Please come in."

"Sheriff Brendan Trask. Let me take a look around then we'll talk." "Thank you. I don't think he's still here, but I don't know for sure."

He nodded and started moving silently through the house. She noticed he unsnapped the flap on his holster, and the chill returned.

Callie was five foot three, the sheriff at least a foot taller. He was swarthy and with his strong jaw and incredible blue eyes, he was handsome. A pair of powerful biceps stretched the sleeves of his uniform shirt. His shoulders were wide, his waist and hips narrow.

If he wasn't married, he was probably the most eligible bachelor in Sweet Springs County.

He returned a few minutes later. "Nobody here. Looks like he came in through the back door." "I guess I should have bought a better lock."

"Rob Solomon over at the hardware store can sell you something reliable. He can put it on for you, too."

"Okay, thanks."

"Millie mentioned the rose. You found it on the kitchen table?"

"Yes. I haven't touched anything." She glanced toward the kitchen. "I suppose it could be kids or someone's idea of a joke. If it is, it isn't funny."

"Breaking and entering is never a joke, Ms. Sutton."

They walked together into the kitchen and he took a second look around, focused his attention on the rose. "You didn't hear anything?"

How to answer. She heard the same noises she'd been hearing every night, the sound of a man's boots on the stairs and someone walking into her bedroom. But she couldn't tell the sheriff there might be a ghost in the house.

It was ridiculous. She didn't even believe in ghosts.

"I didn't hear anything that sounded like a door being forced open or anyone moving around in the kitchen. Just someone upstairs in my room. But she didn't think a ghost could force open a door or carry a rose into the kitchen.

"I want to dust the door for prints. I'll be right back." The sheriff disappeared outside and returned with what she assumed was a fingerprint kit.

He set his hat aside as he dusted the door and the table, and she admired his thick, slightly too long, dark brown hair. He bagged the rose as evidence and asked her a few more questions, then she walked him to the door.

"Be sure and take care of that lock," he said. "I'll call Rob Solomon right away."

He nodded, glanced around the living room. "You did a nice job restoring the place. Looks like it must have more than a hundred years ago, only better."

She smiled at the compliment. "Thank you." Not many people had been over for a visit since she'd moved in, just her best friend, Lanni Bridges, who'd come down from San

Antonia, and one of the girls who worked part time for Dr. Reynolds.

The sheriff pulled open the front door. "Like you said, it's probably just kids, but you don't want to take any chances." Those amazing blue eyes fixed on her face. "I'll give you my cell phone

number. I don't live far away. If you hear something, call me."

She punched his number into her phone. As the sheriff put his hat back on and settled the brim low across his forehead, Callie felt a warm tug in the pit of her stomach.

She blinked in surprise. She hadn't felt the least attraction to a man since she and Adam had split up almost a year ago.

"I'll keep you posted on what I find out," Sheriff Trask said.

Callie watched him walk away and tried not to think he looked nearly as good from the back as the front. She hadn't noticed a wedding ring, but that didn't mean he wasn't married or seriously involved with someone. A man like that had his choice of women.

Not that it really mattered. She was too busy getting settled at the clinic to think about a man. Well, other than the ghost upstairs.

Chapter Three

After a hard day at the animal clinic that included a battle with a wily Siamese cat named Hugo armed with the sharpest claws Callie ever had seen, she prayed for an uneventful evening. Besides working late to help the doctor sew up a car-chasing dog hit by a pickup, she had worried about her intruder all day.

The house was quiet when she got home, no sign of anything out of place. She zapped a frozen lasagna dinner in the newly installed microwave, ate and went straight up to bed. She drifted off more easily than she had expected and settled into a deep slumber.

She wasn't sure when she started to dream, only that the tall outlaw cowboy was back in her room and this time he was in her bed.

He was leaning over her, kissing the side of her neck, his big hands lightly caressing her breasts through her thin white nylon nightgown. She moaned as he trailed kisses along her throat and over her cheek, and soft male lips settled on her mouth.

Warmth spread through her, slid into her core. It's a dream, she told herself as a memory of last night's dream returned. Why not enjoy it?

Parting her lips, she opened to invite her dream lover in and the kiss turned hot and deep. A hard chest pressed against her breasts and big calloused hands roamed over her body.

It had been so long since anyone had touched her that way, so long since she had actually felt this kind of desire.

The dream shifted a little and he was naked, his body hard and muscled over hers. She could feel his heavy arousal nestled between her legs--for a dream, it was incredibly real.

She allowed the fantasy to continue, her body responding to the skillful touches of the outlaw's hands and the saturating pleasure of his mouth moving hotly over hers.

When a noise downstairs penetrated her senses, threatening to disturb the dream, irritation trickled through her. Damn, she didn't want the dream to end. With a sigh of resignation, Callie stirred awake and opened her eyes, expecting to be looking at the ceiling above the bed.

Instead, she stared into the bluest eyes she had ever seen. Callie screamed.

Chapter Four

In an instant, the man was gone, vanished like the ghostly vision he had been.

Her heart was racing, her body still flushed with heat. Callie tried to tell herself the face of the outlaw she had seen was just part of the dream, that she hadn't awoken and seen a blue-eyed man in bed with her who looked almost exactly like the handsome county sheriff.

It was the almost that was the problem. The outlaw had a scar along the bottom of his jaw that the sheriff did not have.

The noise came again, pulling her back from the fantasy, the sound of glass shattering downstairs-- someone breaking the window in the kitchen. Fresh fear assailed her. The ghost was gone but what about the man who had broken into her house last night?

She grabbed her phone off the nightstand and hit the sheriff's contact number. "Trask," he said, his voice crystal clear, as if he'd instantly come awake.

"Sheriff, it's...it's Callie Sutton. He's...he's in the house. He broke out a window. Oh, God...he's...coming up the stairs."

"On my way. Lock yourself in the bathroom, Callie. Stay there till I tell you to come out. I'll keep the line open, but the call may drop. I'll be there as fast as I can."

She heard fabric rustling as Trask pulled on his clothes. Callie grabbed her white terry robe and hurriedly shrugged it on.

As she turned toward the bathroom, she heard sounds outside the bedroom door. A struggle, some kind of fight going on, a foul curse, then the heavy thud of something crashing down the stairs.

Oh, dear God. "Sheriff? Sheriff Trask are you there?"

But as he had warned, the call had dropped and the line was dead. He's on his way, she reminded herself. All I have to do is survive until he gets here.

Her gaze shot to the bedroom door. Rob Solomon had installed a new lock on the kitchen door downstairs, but the lock on the bedroom door was old and hadn't been replaced. She should barricade herself in the bathroom as Sheriff Trask had told her, but the lock was no better in there and she didn't like the idea of being trapped inside.

Callie listened. The only sound was the fierce beating of her heart. Instead of the usual creaks and groans, the house was eerily silent. Too silent, she thought, a shiver running over her skin.

Headlights flashed into the bedroom. She hurried to the window and saw Sheriff Trask's pickup pull up in front of the house. Thank you, God.

Her cell phone rang. She answered with unsteady hands. "Callie, are you all right?"

"I think he's gone. Just in case, I'll come down the back stairs and let you in through the kitchen."

"Be careful," Trask said.

Callie grabbed the flashlight she kept beside the bed, unlocked the bedroom door, and peered into the hall. Seeing nothing, she quietly headed for the servants' stairs leading down to the kitchen.

As she passed the round oak table, she shined a light on top and there it was--another long-stemmed red rose.

Fear quickened her footsteps. She unlocked the newly installed deadbolt, the sheriff strode into the kitchen, and relief poured through her.

"Stay here." His gun was in his hand as he made his way out of the kitchen and began to search the house.

She couldn't help noticing the lack of a scar beneath his hard jaw.

Chapter Five

Brendan moved silently though the house, quietly checking each room. First floor clear. He headed for the staircase, shined his light in that direction and stopped cold in his tracks.

Death had an aura about it. The bald, muscular man sprawled on the stairs with his mouth gaping open, sightless eyes staring up at the ceiling, reeked of it.

Brendan knelt to check for a pulse, but there was really no need. He stepped back and took a moment to study the scene. From the angle of the man's neck and the way the body had landed, it didn't look like the guy could have accidentally fallen down the stairs.

Brendan's gaze shot to the landing at the top. If it wasn't an accident, who had killed him? Was the perp still in the house? Brendan made a room-by-room search, but found no sign of an intruder. He returned to the crime scene and phoned the coroner, a local physician named Elias Halpern, rousing him from sleep.

Brendan looked back at the dead man on the stairs. The guy was big and strong. Had the pretty little brunette in the kitchen somehow managed to overpower him? It didn't seem likely. Even if by some miracle she had killed him, he was trespassing in her house. The lady would have been justified, at least as far as Brendan was concerned. Still, she could be in for a lot of trouble and legal expense.

Brendan thought about her as he returned to the kitchen. He had run a check on her after the first call she'd made. Callie Marie Sutton was twenty seven, just five years younger than he was, originally from San Antonio. With her big brown eyes, long dark brown curls, and dynamite figure, he hadn't been able to get her out of his mind since the first time he had seen her.

He and Deb Younger were no longer dating. If Callie gave any indication she was interested, Brendan planned to ask her out.

He just hoped like hell she wasn't a killer.

Chapter Six

Awaiting the sheriff's return, which seemed to take forever, Callie tightened the sash on her

robe and wished she'd had time to put on some clothes. Finally, Trask walked back into the kitchen, his features grim.

His glance strayed to the table and he noticed the long-stemmed red rose. "It was him," she said, her pulse hammering again.

"Looks like." He fixed her with a stare. "But you don't need to worry about him anymore." "You caught him?"

"Your admirer is lying at the bottom of the staircase. He's dead."

Callie gripped the back of a kitchen chair. "He...he fell down the stairs?" "No, Callie. He was pushed."

The coroner arrived, a local physical who said his name was Elias Halpern. While Dr. Halpern examined the body, Callie sat in the kitchen drinking coffee, doing her best not to think of the dead man in the other room and answer the sheriff's questions.

"So you heard noises on the stairs but you didn't go outside your bedroom to see what was going on?"

"I told you, I was waiting for you to get here." She frowned. "In a roundabout way, that's the third time you've asked me the same question. You don't think I'm the one who pushed that man down the stairs?"

Before Sheriff Trask had time to answer, Dr. Halpern walked in, an older man with thinning gray hair and glasses. "It wasn't Ms. Sutton," he said. "Bruising on the neck indicates a big man's hands, someone strong and extremely fit. The struggle didn't last long, then one good shove and it was over. This little gal ain't big enough nor strong enough to do the job."

Trask looked relieved. "Looks like you're in the clear, Ms. Sutton." "I wasn't really worried since I knew I didn't kill him."

Trask's sexy mouth edged up and she felt a slide of heat. It was crazy considering the circumstances.

His smile faded. "This is a crime scene. Is there somewhere you can stay for a day, maybe two?"

"I just moved here. I don't know many people. The Westerner Motel will have to do."

He nodded. "Pack what you need and I'll follow you over there. Use the back stairs so you don't disturb anything."

"All right. So...who do you think killed him?" "We'll no more in a couple of days."

Callie hoped so. But as she climbed the backstairs to her room, a strange thought occurred.

Was it possible for a ghost to kill?

While the sheriff spent the next few days searching for a killer, Callie went to work searching the past for the man she thought of as her protector.

Chapter Seven

Barb shook her head. "Nope, not that I ever heard. Kids used to make up stuff to try to scare each other, but none of the owners ever said anything like that. At least nothing that was ever passed down."

Callie wasn't sure if that was good news or bad. "Thanks, Barb. You've been a great help." "No problem. Always fun to talk history."

From the library, Callie drove to the Sheriff's office on Main Street at the opposite end of town.

With its false front brick buildings and slant parking in front of the stores, Sweet Springs had an appealing, old-fashioned charm. Or at Callie thought so.

The sheriff's white pickup sat in front of the office when Callie walked in, ringing the bell over the door.

"May I help you?" a large woman behind the counter asked, MILLIE, read the sign on her desk. "I'm looking for Sheriff Trask. I talked to you the other night. Thanks for your help, by the way." "You must be Callie Sutton. I'm glad you're okay. Welcome to Sweet Springs."

Callie looked up as the sheriff walked out of his office. He smiled when he saw her and she felt a little kick. There was something about a man uniform, or so it was said. Plus this man was just flat hot.

"I'm glad you stopped by, Callie," he said. "I was on my way out to get something to eat. You got time to join me?"

"I'm off today. I could use something myself."

The sheriff seemed pleased. She figured he probably just wanted to discuss the case but she couldn't help hoping it was more.

At the Sweet Springs Café, they sat down in a red vinyl booth across from each other and both ordered burgers and fries.

"So how is the case coming along?" Callie asked as the waitress brought their food. "Do you have any leads?"

Trask swallowed the bite of burger he had taken and set the rest back down on his plate. "On the killer? No. No DNA, no fingerprints. Nothing left at the crime scene. The guy did a spectacular job of cleaning up. Must have been a pro."

Or he wasn't really a guy, or at least not the living, breathing kind.

"We IDed the man who broke into your house. His name's Raymond Whitley. He's wanted for serial rape."

The French fry she had just picked up dropped from her suddenly nerveless fingers. "Oh, my God."

"Whitley's signature was a single red rose. He broke into his victim's home and left a rose while she was sleeping. Then he returned on a different night to attack her. He was brutal, liked to inflict pain. Four women that we know of--all ended up in the hospital."

Callie swallowed, no longer hungry.

"His last victim was in a small town outside Shreveport, Louisiana. No reason to think he'd show up here. You're a very lucky woman, Callie."

"Yes...yes, I am." But maybe it wasn't luck. Maybe someone had saved her. Someone who looked a lot like Sheriff Trask. "I was wondering...I've been researching the history of the house.

Barb Dawson told me it once belonged to your family. Would you happen to have any information on the Trask family who lived there?"

The sheriff smiled, a flash of white against his swarthy skin. "I've got a ton of old stuff out at the ranch. I'm not a great cook, but I'm a kick-ass barbeque griller. I could fix you dinner and show you what I've got."

"No wife or kids?"

"Nope. Never found the right woman."

She toyed with another fry. "Barb told me about Brendan and Priscilla. I guess you're waiting for that kind of romance."

The look in those intense blue eyes softened on her face. "Yeah, I guess I am." Callie couldn't tear her gaze away. "I'd love to come out for supper," she said softly. Trask's eyes remained on her face. "How about tonight?"

"What time?"

"Gets dark early. I could pick you up around six. It's not that far to the ranch house."

Chapter Eight

Brendan was right. It wasn't that far. The original ranch house was gone, he told her as they drove along the two lane road. She couldn't see much through the darkness, but she knew the terrain was rugged in places, lots of trees and the river not far away. The house had been built by his parents, Brendan said, who had wanted to be closer to town. He'd moved back in a few years ago, when his dad and mom retired to Florida, a longtime dream.

He pulled up to a two-story brick house with upstairs dormer windows and a long covered porch out front. "Welcome to my humble abode." Brendan went around and helped her down from his truck then walked her to the door.

"I haven't changed much since I moved in," he said as they stepped into the entry. "I'll get around to it eventually."

Callie glanced at the comfortable living room furniture, the antique buffet, and the handmade doilies. "I like it. It has a very warm feeling."

"It's homey, I guess." "Nothing wrong with that."

They went into the kitchen and Brendan poured her a glass of white wine. He grabbed a beer for himself then started making supper.

As eager as she was to see the information Brendan might have on his family, she decided to relax and enjoy herself. She was out with a gorgeous man and she hadn't done anything but work since she had moved to Sweet Springs.

She smiled as she watched him work. Brendan was a serious griller. While Callie made a salad and put a couple of potatoes in to bake, the sheriff used his big stainless barbeque to perfectly cook two medium rare steaks.

It was a delicious meal and Brendan was a good conversationalist, asking questions about her job and telling stories about his work as county sheriff.

From the moment she had met him, she'd felt a deep pull of attraction, not just because of his good looks and hard muscled body, but because he was smart, and she felt that she could trust him.

The attraction seemed to be mutual, reflected in those amazing blue eyes. There was heat there, plenty of it. Like the blue tip of a flame.

When the meal was over, she helped him clear the dishes, then he led her into the living where an overstuffed burgundy sofa and chairs sat in front of a mantled brick fireplace. Photos dominated the wall above an antique mahogany buffet.

"You wanted to know about my family. I've got old letters, photo albums, and all kinds of stuff.

The photos are my favorite."

Callie walked over for a closer look, an odd sensation prickling her skin. "Some of these pictures are really old."

He nodded. "The daguerreotypes date back to the eighteen sixties."

She studied the early tin types. Two in particular caught her eye, a man and a woman in oval mahogany frames facing each other. Her pulse quickened. "It's them, isn't it? Those two photos. Brendan and Priscilla."

He nodded. "Silla, he called her. He would have been in his late thirties, early forties at the time the picture was made." He turned toward her. "There're a lot of photos up there. How did you which ones they were?"

She toyed with a pretty lace doily on the sideboard. "If I tell you, you'll think I'm crazy." She gazed up at him. "I don't want that to happen. I really like you, Brendan."

He smiled. God, she loved the way he smiled, like it was always close, ready to surface at the first opportunity.

"I really like you, too, Callie." One of his big hands settled at her waist and he drew her closer, until they were touching full length. He framed her face between his palms and Callie closed her eyes as he tipped her head back and settled his mouth over hers. Softly at first, then deeper, their lips melding, fitting perfectly together.

A little whimper escaped at the rush of heat that burned through her and her arms slid up around his neck. She could feel the muscles moving beneath his shirt as Brendan deepened the kiss, which went on and on, long, hot, and hungry, thoroughly arousing.

The ghostly Trask had nothing on the living, breathing version standing right in front of her.

When the kiss finally ended, Callie swayed toward him, and Brendan steadied her. He ran a finger along her cheek. "I had a feeling it was going to be like that." Callie looked up at him. "So did I." But then she'd had a sneak preview.

Brendan's gaze returned to the pictures on the wall and Callie's gaze followed. "You thought it was the outlaw Trask because he looks like me?" he asked.

Outlaw. Shock rolled through her. "Your great great grandfather was an outlaw?"

"For a while he was. He was pardoned. Something about helping catch a bunch of smugglers down in Natchez. They wrote a book about him, one of those pulp fiction westerns that made him more of a hero than he probably was. It's called Natchez Flame."

"I'd love to read it sometime."

Brendan studied the photos, including one taken with the couple and their kids years later. "You know, you look a lot like Priscilla."

She'd noticed that, too. "I've done some family genealogy. I don't think we're related, but looking at her picture, I can certainly see the resemblance. It's uncanny how much I look like her." She studied the face of the woman with big dark eyes and thick dark hair. Same chin, same nose, same mouth. "Maybe that explains it."

"Explains what?"

She turned and looked up at him, into those amazing blue eyes. "The reason he came back to the house. Maybe he thinks I'm Silla."

"Wait a minute--"

"I know, I know. But he's been coming into my bedroom at night. At first I thought I was dreaming, but one night...one night he kissed me and I opened my eyes and I saw him. He was dressed like an outlaw or a gunslinger. He looked just like you, Brendan, except for the scar below his jaw."

"Whoa. You think the ghost of my great great grandfather is in your house?" She managed to nod. "He's young, though. Somewhere around your age." "Sorry. I don't believe in ghosts."

"Neither do I. At least I never did. You know what's even crazier? I think he protected me the night Raymond Whitley broke into the house to rape me. I think Brendan killed him."

Chapter Nine

She hadn't seen Brendan for the last three days. She'd said she had seen a ghost. He thought she was crazy. No way would he ever call her again. It bothered her more than it should have, considering how little time they'd spent together.

It was probably that amazing kiss. She couldn't remember a kiss affecting her so strongly, turning her knees to jelly and setting her body on fire. She'd wanted to tear off his clothes and drag him into the bedroom. She'd wanted to make love with him all night long and start again in the morning.

It wasn't like her. She hadn't thought about sex for nearly a year, not since she had ended things with Adam. Now Brendan was gone and there was no way he was coming back. It made her heart hurt a little.

She was working at the clinic when her cell phone rang, just finished stitching up a little white schnauzer that had cuts its paw on a barbed wire fence.

"I'll finish up," Dr. Reynolds said. He was mid-forties, a little too thin and a really nice guy. "Go ahead and take the call."

Callie hurried over and picked up the phone. "This is Callie." "It's Brendan. Have you got a minute?"

Her stomach clenched. For him, she had all the time in the world. "I'm not busy at the moment." She walked into the back room for a little privacy, the phone pressed against her ear. "I can't stop thinking about you, Callie. I really want to see you."

A warm feeling spread through her. She'd begun to accept that she wouldn't be seeing him again. "I'd like that, too."

"Good. That's great. Has the...ahh...ghost been back?"

Her fingers tightened around the phone. She didn't want to talk about ghosts. She didn't to ruin things again. "No, not since...not since the night of the murder."

"I'm glad to hear it," he said firmly. Something in his voice. Impossible as it seemed, it sounded a lot like jealousy.

"I know someone who...ahh...thinks she can help," he said. "Any chance the two of us could come over tonight?"

He wanted to see her. He wanted to help her. He wanted to come over to the house. The warm feelings expanded. "Tonight would work."

"Say eight o'clock?"

"All right. I'll see you then." She ended the call but still held onto the phone. Brendan was coming over. She glanced at the clock. It was almost six. If nothing last-minute came up, she could go home and figure out what to wear. She wanted to look good for him.

She just hoped all this talk about ghosts wasn't going to send him running again.

Chapter Ten

Brendan stood on her doorstep at exactly eight p.m. "Miss Aggie, this is Callie Sutton. Callie, I'd like you to meet Agatha Hennessey. Everyone calls her Miss Aggie."

Callie smiled. "It's nice to meet you, Miss Aggie."

"Miss Aggie's from over in Jasper County." His gaze went to the woman beside him. She was huge. Not tall, but square, built like a box. She must have weighed three hundred pounds. "Miss Aggie is a seer. My mom used to visit her for...ahh...advice."

Callie inwardly smiled. The sheriff must have had an interesting family.

"I appreciate your trying to help, Miss Aggie. Please come in." Callie stepped back to welcome her guests into the house. "Why don't we sit in the parlor? There's coffee and chocolate chip cookies. Not homemade, unfortunately, but the bakery in town is always good."

They all took seats, Brendan next to Callie on the sofa, Miss Aggie in an overstuffed chair. Callie filled her aunt's pretty porcelain cups with coffee and passed them around, and Miss Aggie helped herself to cookies. At least five of them vanished in her direction.

"I told Miss Aggie a little of what's been going on," Brendan said. "She knows the story. Hell, everyone in Sweet Springs County knows the story of Brendan and Priscilla. It's kind of the old West version of Romeo and Juliet except with a happy ending."

"Or mostly happy," Miss Aggie said. "They had a long, happy life, but the end wasn't so good for Brendan. A problem came up at the ranch. While he was gone, Priscilla took a turn for the worst. She died while he was away. As the story goes, he never forgave himself. He died a few months after she did."

Callie set her cup and saucer down on the coffee table. "I know it sounds crazy, but I think he might still be here."

Miss Aggie smiled. "To someone like me, it doesn't sound crazy at all." She finished the last of her cookie and heaved her big bulk up from the chair. "I'm going to take a walk. I'll be back." She didn't say more, just lumbered off down the hall.

Callie's gaze went to Brendan. "I didn't think I'd hear from you again." A faint smile touched his lips. "Because of the ghost?"

"Most guys wouldn't want anything to do with a woman who thinks she lives in a house with a ghost."

"You don't seem like the kind of person who goes around making up stories. Plus there's the dead man on the stairs and no prints, no DNA, nothing. In this day and age, that's not easy to do."

"That's sort of what I was thinking."

"Miss Aggie's been a friend of the family for years. I went to see her to ask her opinion. She said she wanted to see for herself."

Callie hadn't seen the woman go upstairs, but she watched her making her way carefully back down. She looked different somehow, calmer, an oddly vacant expression on her face.

"Have you got any candles?" she asked.

"Of course. In case the power goes off. I'll get them." Callie returned with an assortment of candles. She set two of them on the coffee table and one on the oak sideboard against the wall. Brendan pulled a box of wooden matches out of his jeans and lit them. It gave the living room a soft eerie glow.

"Be patient," Miss Aggie said. "He's here. I could feel him."

Callie's heart began to pound. Brendan flashed her a glance, but made no comment. He reached over and caught her hand, steadying her.

They sat in silence for half an hour, by the antique mantel clock. It was strangely peaceful, until the candle flames started to flicker and Callie felt the sensation of a big hand sliding beneath her hair, settling possessively around the nape of her neck.

It wasn't Brendan, whose hand still held hers. Callie made a little sound in her throat that drew his attention. His expression changed as he watched the dark curls move though no one else was touching her.

"I know you're here, Brendan," Miss Aggie said. "And I know why you came. But the lady in the house isn't Priscilla. She looks like your Silla, but her name is Callie. Your Priscilla has gone on to the other side. She's waiting for you there. She misses you terribly. She's been waiting a very long

time."

The candle on the sideboard flickered and went out.

"It's true," Miss Aggie said. "She was gone when you came home, but you can find her again.

You don't have to live without her. You just have to look for the light. Do you see it, Brendan?" A loud whooshing sound filled the room, stirring the draperies.

"Callie belongs to the Brendan of this time. He'll take care of her. He'll protect her."

In the candlelight, Brendan's features looked hard. He glanced at Miss Aggie, who nodded. "Callie's mine," he said. "She belongs to me. She's mine to protect. I give you my solemn pledge that I will."

Callie's heart was beating. Brendan sounded like he meant every word.

"Go on now," Miss Aggie said. "Move toward the light. Go and find your Priscilla. She's waiting. She loves you. Just the way you love her."

The house began to shake, rattling the windows, jiggling the antique stemware in the glass curio case. A sudden burst of light lit the room, so bright Callie had to close her eyes.

Brendan's hand tightened around hers. "Jesus," he said.

A roaring began, rising to a crescendo. The bright light flashed again and something whooshed past them. A fierce crack sounded, then a long heavy roll, like lightening followed by thunder.

Silence fell. The old house slowly settled. Brendan drew Callie into his arms and she felt a tremor run through his hard body.

"It's over," Miss Aggie said. "He won't be back." She smiled. "He's found her again after all these years."

Callie turned her face into Brendan's chest and started to cry.

Epilogue

It was the biggest social event in Sweet Springs that year. The wedding of Sheriff Brendan Trask to the town's new resident, Callie Sutton. Those that couldn't make it to the ceremony in the little white church showed up for the party out at the ranch. Bets were made how long it would take before the first little Trask was born.

Not long, Callie figured, considered how much practice they got. She grinned.

The ghost of the outlaw Trask had never reappeared. Callie firmly believed he was happy with his beloved Priscilla on the other side.

The search for the man who had killed the Red Rose rapist eventually came to an end. Brendan let the case fade away on its own accord. Though he never mentioned it again, like Callie, he believed the outlaw Brendan had saved Callie that night.

All was well in the little town of Sweet Springs.

Callie believed, at last, all was well on the other side, too.

I hope you enjoyed OUTLAW GHOST. I have no idea where the idea came from to write a ghost story about characters from one of my old books, but suddenly there it was inside my head.

The outlaw, Brendan Trask, and his lady, Priscilla Wills, appear in NATCHEZ FLAME, a tale set in Texas in 1846. If you liked OUTLAW GHOST and you're curious about the first Brendan Trask and his lady, I hope you'll look for NATCHEZ FLAME and that you enjoy the book! Till next time, all best wishes and happy reading, Kat

Currently living outside Missoula, Montana, Kat Martin is the New York Times bestselling author of over sixty-five Historical and Contemporary Romantic Suspense novels. Before she started writing, Kat was a real estate broker. During that time, she met her husband, L. J. Martin, an author of Westerns and high-action Thrillers. Kat is a graduate of the University of California at Santa Barbara where she majored in Anthropology and also studied History. She spends her winters in Arizona.

"I love to travel and especially like visiting the places where my books are set," Kat says. "I love history and enjoy spending time in museums and art galleries. My husband and I often stay in out-of-the-way inns and historical houses. It's fun and it gives a wonderful sense of a by-gone era."

To date, Kat has over seventeen million copies of her books in print. She is published in more than two dozen foreign countries, including Germany, France, Norway, Sweden, China, Korea, Bulgaria, Russia, England, South Africa, Italy, Spain, Argentina, Japan and Greece.

Kat is currently writing her next Romantic thriller.

Social Media Links:

Facebook:
https://www.facebook.com/KatMartinAuthor

Twitter: https://twitter.com/katmartinauthor

Website: http://www.katmartin.com/

Enter contest: https://www.katmartin.com/monthly-contest/

Links to more of Kat's romantic suspense books!

Beyond Control
Beyond Danger
Beyond Reason

Into the Firestorm
Into the Whirlwind
Into the Fury

Against the Tide
Against the Sky
Against the Wild

Against the Mark
Against the Edge
Against the Odds

Against the Sun
Against the Night
Against the Storm

Table for One

by

Katy Lee

Chapter One

I need to get off this boat.

Becca Shane gripped the cruise ship's handrail and looked over to see the gangway being removed below. The *Heart of the Sea* was about to set sail. From the top decks, swarms of travelers waved enthusiastically to those on shore: family, friends, strangers, it didn't matter. They were just happy to be setting out to sea.

There was nothing happy about this trip for her.

The ship's horn blared through the Miami port. Becca jumped and squeezed back more tears of humiliation. The ship pushed back from the dock.

Too late.

Short of jumping, there was no going back now.

She felt something tug on the hem of her strapless sundress. "Excuse me," she heard a young child's voice. "May I see the shore?"

Becca turned to find a small girl, maybe six years old. A scan of the crowd showed her alone. "Would your mommy mind you being so close to the railing?" Becca asked.

The child squinted up in the late afternoon sunlight. Her red ringlets glowed with flecks of gold. "I don't live with my mom."

Becca bit her tongue. "Well, ah, then your parent or grandparent, or the adult with you?" Another glance around. There seemed to be no one in the crowd looking for a wandering child.

"I'm Jenny," the child said. "My dad wouldn't mind. Honest."

Apparently not.

Becca had to bite her tongue again to refrain from speaking her dissatisfaction about the father aloud. He wasn't the first man in the last twenty-four hours to disappoint her.

She loosened the white scarf tied around her neck. The long, netted silk whipped in the wind, its soft threads of the utmost finery. She had spared no expense for her bridal veil.

"I like your flowers," Jenny said, glancing down at the satchel at Becca's feet. Her bridal bouquet of bright pink peonies protruded from the top, threatening to spill out.

Without a thought, Becca bent down and pulled one out from the arrangement. "Here, for you," she said and passed it to Jenny. The child's green eyes widened in delight.

"Jenny! Jenny, where are you?" a frantic voice called from somewhere on the deck.

The child whipped around. "That's my dad." She waved high above her head. "I'm over here! Look, Daddy, I got a flower!"

Becca still didn't see anyone looking. People amassed, laughing and cheering, ecstatic to be heading out to sea for six days on the Eastern Caribbean waters. The island of

Barbados awaited them, and just yesterday, Becca would have been joining them in their reverie.

What a difference one day could make. What a difference being stood up at the altar could make.

"Jenny!" the father called again.

The mingling crowds began to step aside, a parting of tides, revealing Jenny's disgruntled dad. The man appeared disheveled in an expensive suit, the navy tie loose around his neck and his short black hair mussed a bit in the front.

He was also in a wheelchair.

Instant remorse swept over Becca. She shouldn't have let her recent dissatisfaction with her ex-fiancé form incorrect assumptions about another man.

"Why did you take off like that?" The man rolled up to his daughter. Anger mixed with relief covered his lightly bearded face. Specks of gray came through his facial hair and a bit more at his temples. Becca didn't think he was over forty. The stress of parenting could do that, she thought, or at least that was what her own dad used to tell her whenever she caused him to worry.

"I'm sorry, Daddy. I wanted to wave 'bon vogage.' "

"Bon voyage," he corrected her. "You should have told me. And where did you get the flower?"

Jenny looked up at Becca. "From this nice lady. Isn't she pretty? She has a whole bag full. Ma'am, would you give my dad one too?"

Becca glanced down at her satchel and back at Jenny's father. She cleared her throat. "Sure, if he would like—"

"No," the man cut her off. "I'm all set. *We're* all set. I appreciate your kindness, but that's not necessary. Jenny, let's go. The maitre'd is holding our table for dinner."

Jenny obeyed her dad now, climbing up into his lap with her flower placed in her own. She looked up at Becca. "Thank you for my flower. What's your name?"

"Becca." Becca wondered if she should have responded.

The piercing anger in the man's blue eyes said probably not. He turned his wheelchair on a spin and was gone before she could make sense of his disdain. It was as though *he* was the one left at the altar twenty-four hours ago.

"Mr. Joyce, we are thrilled to have you aboard again." The waiter in the dining room led the way to a table with handicap accessibility.

"Miguel, I've told you before, please call me Patrick. I've been on this boat enough times to warrant a first-name basis, don't you think?" Patrick pulled up to a space without a chair and lifted the black napkin for his lap.

"As you wish, Mr. Joyce. Will you be sailing with us the whole voyage this time?"

So much for familiarity with the staff. "No, Jenny and I will be disembarking in Barbados, right after some business here on the ship."

"Very well. I look forward to serving you both while you are aboard." Miguel held a chair out for Jenny and pushed it in once she was situated. He lifted her triangular folded napkin and shook it out for her. "Miss Jennifer, your napkin."

Jenny giggled. She thrust the pink flower at Miguel. "And I need water for my flower."

Patrick eyed his daughter. "Don't forget your manners, Jenny."

"Please and thank you." She beamed a smile.

Patrick relaxed a bit at Miguel's wink. "Of course. I will be right back with a glass of water for your beautiful blossom. Wherever did you get it?"

"From my friend Becca. She has a whole pocketbook of them."

Miguel left, and Patrick picked up the menu. "You have a choice of salmon or beef tenderloin tonight."

"Chicken nuggets." Jenny lifted her chin.

Patrick sighed, trying to hold back his frustration in his daughter's defiance. He had witnessed it more and more lately—like her running off today. "The dining room is formal with an elegant meal. Won't you try something new?"

Jenny frowned. "But I don't want to." She looked away and instantly perked up. "Becca! Over here!"

Patrick glanced in the direction of the wide-open double doors. The woman from the upper deck locked her gaze on him. A reddening blush grew up out of that long, white scarf around her neck. The maitre'd looked that way too. And before anyone knew what was happening, he was leading Becca their way.

"Oh, no, really this isn't necessary," the woman could be heard from behind the maitre'd.

But Franz wasn't hearing her—or ignoring her. "Mr. Joyce, Jenny, you know Ms. Shane? Would you like her to dine with you tonight?"

"Yes!" Jenny announced. "Sit next to me, Becca."

Becca's pale skin blotched all the way up to her forehead, redder than her perfect twist of strawberry-blond hair. "I was trying to say this isn't necessary. Please, a table for one is all I need." She backed away, an apology written on her face to Patrick.

Great. Now I'm the bad guy. A table for one? How could he send her away now? "We would be delighted if you dined with us," Patrick said, waving to the chair across from him. "Please, sit. I would get up, but, well, we all know that's not going to happen."

No one laughed.

"A joke, guys." He forced a smile, but after his rudeness earlier, could he really blame anyone for being uncertain? "Seriously, I really want you to join us. I want to make up for my actions up on deck."

Becca gave a short nod and took the chair. She had a reserved poise about her that he found familiar, even appreciated. An image of her entering the hall of his manor with a collection of his most prominent acquaintances flashed in his mind. However, in his mind's eye she was without the scarf.

The waiter returned with the flower in a fluted champagne glass. "For Miss Jenny," Miguel said and flourished a bow.

Jenny smiled and clapped her hands. "This is Becca. She gave me the flower. She has lots of them."

Becca's lips grew rigid and trembled before she pressed them tight. The flowers didn't bring her joy, Patrick reasoned, and wondered why. She picked up the menu and gave her full attention to it.

"I'm having chicken nuggets," Jenny announced.

"The salmon for me, please," Patrick and Becca spoke at the same time. An awkwardness fell over the table. The waiter took his leave quietly.

"I apologize," Patrick said. "I should have let you go first. I thought you might want more time." Before she could respond, he thought it best to clear the air right away. "And I apologize for my behavior above deck."

She waved her left hand his way. A sparkling diamond flashed between them. A diamond but no wedding ring.

Speculation was what he did best. Observe the details—because that's how good deals were made.

Flowers from a bouquet.

A white scarf that resembled a bridal veil.

A honeymoon with no groom.

"Did you leave him? Or did he leave you?" Patrick got right to the punch. Also, how he did business.

Becca's lips parted on a puff of air. She glanced Jenny's way. The child ate from the breadbasket, oblivious to the lie Becca appeared to be forming in her mind.

He raised his eyebrows her way, daring her to deny his conclusion.

She dropped her ringed hand in her lap, out of sight.

But not out of mind.

He leaned back in his chair. "Don't worry about answering. The fact you're still wearing the ring is answer enough." He chose a piece of bread and lifted the basket to her. She shook her head, and he put it down.

"Do you always go straight to the point?" she asked.

"Time is short. I see no reason to drag out the inevitable."

"And my relationship status is an evitable discussion?"

"Isn't it? As is mine? You must have questions. So ask them." Patrick smirked at the way Becca lost her footing. He had rendered her speechless.

Another business tactic, tried and true.

"That's none of my business," she said and visibly sighed when Miguel placed their dinners before them. She looked at Jenny's plate and said, "They're shaped like dolphins." Her smile brightened her face and eyes, bringing a shine to their blue-green hue. "How fun!"

"They're my favorite. I get them all the time here." Jenny spoke with her mouth full.

"Manners," Patrick reminded his child. "No talking with food in your mouth."

Becca's head tilted in a dainty way, her creamy skin along her jawline beckoned to be caressed, to be kissed. He imagined feather kisses, trailing all the way to those perfect pink lips.

His mouth went dry, and he reached for his water glass.

What made him go there?

"Do you come here a lot?" Becca asked.

"Yup," Jenny said. "We live in—"

"Miami," Patrick found enough of his voice to cut his daughter off from sharing too much about their private lives. In his line of work, it was best to be cautious.

"Oh, so you're able to take a lot of cruises. How nice for the two of you." *So she knew there was no Mrs. Joyce. He probably had Jenny to thank for that.*

Dinner progressed with the smallest of useless talk. He waited for Becca to inquire about the biggest elephant in the room—his missing legs—but by the time dessert was served, she'd yet to ask.

Jenny yawned loudly.

Patrick motioned for her to cover her mouth. To Becca, he said, "If you'll excuse us, I think I will take her back to our suite. I apologize for cutting our dinner short." He rolled back and watched how Becca's eyes widened for a moment. It wasn't anything new. For the short time at the dinner table, his missing legs were forgotten. "Come on, kiddo," he said, inviting his daughter back onto his lap for the ride back to their room. She nestled in sleepily and waved her free hand to Becca. The other held her flower in its glass.

"Enjoy your evening," Becca said and stood to say good-bye.

"That's it?" he asked. "Are you always this passive?"

Her lips pursed. "Some might call it respectful."

"I call it a waste of time." He looked down at where his pant legs were folded under at the knees. "Like I said, life is short. I don't waste a moment."

Put on the spot, he gave her no choice but to ask. She lowered her voice and said, "All right, what happened? Were you called up for duty?"

He shook his head. "Nothing so heroic. I was on a business trip to Mexico and contracted meningitis. By the time I was airlifted to a hospital, my legs were toast. When I woke up, they were gone. My wife left soon after that."

Becca scoffed and pursed her lips. "Figures." She shook her head and sat back down, grabbing her teacup with both hands. "Thank you for sharing. Believe it or not, your story makes me feel a little better." She lifted her teacup to him. "Glad I'm not the only one who chose horribly."

Chapter Two

The bottle of champagne and chocolate-covered strawberries in her cabin told Becca someone didn't get the memo about Brad not boarding. But who would ever think the jilted bride would still attend the honeymoon?

Life is short. Patrick's words returned to her.

"Or more like the trip was paid for." Becca picked up a strawberry and bit into the juicy fruit. She dropped the champagne into the trash bin. She wasn't much of a drinker on a typical day, and definitely not one to drink alone after such a humiliating experience. That was asking for trouble.

The small cabin felt claustrophobic. Brad definitely didn't splurge on anything extravagant. Not even a window with a view of the sea. She might as well be home.

Home.

Becca didn't know where home was anymore. She had let her lease go and moved her belongings into Brad's apartment last week. They had picked out paint colors to tackle the rooms when they returned from the cruise. They would have made a home as husband and wife.

Except Brad changed his mind.

The cabin's walls seemed to press in even more. Becca gripped at her neck, pulling the scarf away from her skin.

Who was she kidding? One look at the material and everyone knew it had been her veil, ripped from the headdress in a moment of defiance.

This whole trip was an act of defiance.

She had one week to figure out what she was going to do when she returned to Seattle. Find a new apartment or go home to live with her parents. How humiliating for a twenty-nine-year-old with her own business.

Becca untied the scarf at her neck and flung the silky fabric behind her. She located her running attire quickly from her luggage and dressed for a night up on the track. Lacing up her sneakers, she raced from the tiny cabin and soon could breathe easier. The night and the sea air refreshed her. She breathed deep, filling her lungs completely when she raced out to the upper decks and hit the rubber track. She lifted her head to the multitude of stars glittering over the expanse of black water and remembered there was a Creator who wasn't fazed by Brad Turner's cold feet. She took solace knowing God had bigger plans for her, even if she wanted to hang her head in shame.

" 'For I know the plans I have for you. Plans to give you a hope and a future,' " she recited His promise from the Book of Jeremiah aloud and began her run.

The first three laps came easy. She pressed harder, faster, reaching for the zone that runners aimed for. It was close. She pushed harder. Lap 10 came and went, then someone passed her.

A man.

He threw her off her goal, then she zeroed in on his feet.

The man wore prosthetic legs that curved at the bottom and offered a spring to every step. It wasn't long before he approached from behind again. But this time he slowed by her side. She glanced to her left to see Patrick Joyce.

Becca tripped. The front of one foot hit the other. She felt her body falling and there was nothing she could do to stop the momentum. She put her hands out to break the fall, but the rubber turf never came up to meet her.

"Whoa. Careful now." Patrick held her around her waist, catching her and righting her back on her feet, surefooted again. "That stuff looks soft, but it still hurts if you hit it. And your face is too pretty to scuff up."

His own face was mere inches away, their noses an inch, if that. Neither of them moved away. Becca didn't think she could...or strangely, wanted to.

"What are you doing here?" she asked, her breathing slow and deep from running.

His eyes darkened. "I should ask you the same thing. This is my time up here. I'm usually alone this late at night. Most people are taking in the shows or singing their hearts out at the piano bar. Not much for entertainment, are you?" His hand slipped down her forearm, lingering at her hand.

She whispered, "No." A shiver ran up her spine. She stepped back, flustered. "I'm sorry for intruding. I can come back in the morning."

"Becca, I was kidding. Actually, I would enjoy the company. Stay. Run with me."

She glanced down at his prosthetics. "Something tells me you have an advantage."

A huge knowing smile grew on his too-perfect face. Every angle seemed chiseled and shaped to accentuate his piercing eyes and bright smile. His physique as well. After ten laps, Becca knew she had to look a mess. He bounced on his prosthetics. "They do allow me to work less than you, true, but I would still choose real legs over them."

Again, Becca cringed at her heartless remark. "I am such an idiot." All she wanted to do was slink away. The exit beckoned.

Patrick grabbed her hand and pulled her attention to his face. "Run with me." She saw no mirth, but she also saw no judgment. At her nod he led the way.

They set off, slow at first. Becca didn't know how fast she should go. It was a steady jog with a tight silence between them.

"Where's Jenny?" she asked on lap 3, breaking the tension.

"Asleep. The ship has babysitting through the night."

"Through the night? That's convenient." She cringed at her choice of words again. As if he planned to stay out all night. "I mean if you needed to stay out late for some reason."

He sent her a side smile. "Are we going to actually run tonight or just stroll along?"

That was all the approval Becca needed. She let loose, holding nothing back. Lap 20 flew by before Patrick pulled ahead. She pushed her body harder than ever before, racing ahead of him. He came back up beside her quickly, huffing and puffing but bypassing her again.

Becca wasn't sure she had much strength left to pull ahead. She wanted to slow down more than anything but refused to quit. She let out a shout. Power surged her forward to complete lap 30 ahead of him.

She lifted her arms in victory and hooted with joy. She turned around to bask in the glory—and saw Patrick sprawled out on the track.

"Patrick!" Becca raced back to where she had unknowingly left him behind. "Are you hurt?" She fell to her knees to meet him at his level. She hovered her hands over him, first his arm, then his prosthetic legs. She didn't know where she could touch. What part of him was safe to touch.

"I'm fine," he assured, but flinched a bit. "They're not the most comfortable things."

"Where are you hurt?" she asked. "Should I call for medical help?"

"Becca." He reached for her shoulder. "I said I'm fine. This isn't the first time I've fallen. And it won't be the last."

"Can I help you up?"

"In a minute. That would be great." Patrick maneuvered to sit up and adjusted one of his prosthetic legs. "I'll admit, this is kind of embarrassing."

"You don't have to be embarrassed," she assured him. "A disability isn't something to ever be embarrassed about."

Patrick laughed. "I wasn't talking about my legs. You are one fast runner. I was eating your dust. I never thought *that* would happen."

Becca joined him with his laughter, relieved at what he had been referring to. "Track star all through school," she said.

"I should have asked first." He moved to start to stand. Becca quickly leaned in to assist with her arm wrapped around his back. He stopped in mid-movement.

"Take as much time as you need. I'm not going anywhere." When he didn't move at all, she glanced up to find him watching her. Their heads were so close. She glanced at his parted lips and felt her own go dry. "Is something wrong?" she whispered.

He nodded. "Everything's wrong."

"I don't understand."

"Me neither." He looked down at her lips. "Who are you?"

She swallowed hard. "Becca Shane from Seattle. I'm an interior designer." She dropped her gaze away. "I was...left at the altar yesterday."

"Fool." Patrick's single-word response came out guttural and raspy.

"I hope you don't mean me." She huffed a short laugh that died quickly when she saw anger flash in his blue eyes.

"He didn't deserve you."

Silence fell on them. Becca appreciated his opinion but wasn't 100 percent sure she hadn't played a part in her own jilting. "Thank you, but I can be a bit overpowering."

Patrick feigned shock. "You don't say," he said in a playfully sarcastic tone.

She lightly punched him in his biceps. The rock-hard arm muscle took her by surprise.

"But seriously," he said. "If I can't apologize for a handicap, you can't apologize for a strength. Understand?"

Becca nodded slowly.

"Good, now help me up."

"*Please.*" She couldn't help herself. After spending dinner with him and his sweet daughter, she'd heard him remind Jenny enough times to use her manners.

"Tell me why I let you eat dinner with us?" He presented his question in all seriousness, but his smirk was back on his lips.

Becca brought him to a standing position. She stepped back when he was stable. The space between them felt cavernous after being so close. "That's easy. You adore your daughter and would do anything for her."

He gave a single nod. "Anything."

"Eat all your fruit," Patrick instructed Jenny the following morning. They sat at their kitchen table in their suite. The full floor-to-ceiling windows and sliding doors gave a panorama view of the sea and the course of blue waters set before them.

"But I'm full," she whined and dropped her cheek into the palm of one hand while the other hand toyed with a bowl of fruit salad.

He peered over his laptop of the figures he was working on for a new cruise ship rehab and studied his daughter's sleepy eyes. "You look tired. I hope you were actually sleeping last night when the sitter was here. Should I make a call and find out?"

Jenny sat straight up. "I'm not tired." She shoved a pineapple chunk into her mouth.

Patrick folded the cover of his laptop. "Good. I would be extremely disappointed in you if you were giving the child-care workers a hard time. They are important people to this cruise line. We need them. Lots of families come aboard, and they need to trust us with their children's safety." He glanced at his watch. "Speaking of which, it's time to drop you off at the playroom."

"Can't I stay with you today? Please, Daddy?" Jenny tilted her head and pouted. "I'll be really quiet during your business deal. I promise."

Patrick backed his wheelchair away from the table. "Not today, sweetie pie, but I promise to come pick you up right after. Although why you would want to be with an old man like me, when you can be a pirate on the high seas and go on a treasure hunt is beyond me."

"Arrrrrrh," Jenny made her best pirate speak, followed up by a fit of giggles.

"Uh-oh, I better be careful around here. You're starting to sound like a real pirate."

"That's because I am." She took another bite of fruit, leaving all the melon untouched. "Can I please be done now?"

"Only because we're going to be late. Hop up, and we'll hightail it out of here."

Jenny climbed up on his lap. Patrick turned his chair toward the hallway. He passed by his bedroom then Jenny's and came to the entrance to their quarters. Down the corridor, he headed to the elevator and took it up a couple flights to the deck with the playroom. The gym was also on the same level.

Jenny saw Becca before he did. His little girl jumped from his lap and wrapped her little arms around Becca's smooth, toned thighs. Her workout wear accentuated every sculpted muscle. A slight sheen glowed her skin.

"Good workout?" Patrick asked as he rolled up.

"It was okay. I had some problems with one of the workers."

"How so?" Her displeasure concerned him.

She waved his question away. "It's nothing. I like to use one of the weight machines. The guy didn't think I should. Directed me to the smaller free weights. I assured him I wasn't taking on more than I could handle. He's just doing his job and keeping people safe. I get it."

"What's his name?" Patrick asked.

"Tom, I think. Why? You gonna beat him up for me?" Her smile struck him right in the chest.

Patrick thought about it for all of two seconds. "Maybe I will."

"Well, be sure to tell me when. I want to be there, front and center." She gave Jenny a pat on her red curls. "Tomorrow we dock in Barbados. I've never been there. I was thinking of taking in one of those excursions, like snorkeling. Have you been there before?"

Jenny replied, "We live—"

Patrick cut her off. "We practically live there, is what she means. Yes, we frequent Barbados quite a bit. But don't sign up for the excursion. If you're looking for something to do, why don't you join us out on a catamaran? There will be plenty of places to jump off and snorkel. The coral reefs are beautiful, and I know of an amazing cove with still, clear water."

Jenny jumped up and down. "Becca, please say yes! It would make me the happiest person ever if you came on the boat with us."

Becca bent down to his daughter and poked her belly. "We'll see."

She then turned those stunning blue-green eyes up on him, so like the cove waters. The vision of her sunbathing on the rocks swelled his heart in his chest, and he thought he also just might be the happiest person ever to see her in his place of refuge—the one place he felt like a whole man.

Suddenly, he wanted her there. "Say you'll come," he said, his voice rasped.

"Only if I buy my own ticket."

"Ticket?" Jenny squinted Becca.

"Fine," Patrick replied. "You can pay me back." *As if.*

"Then it's a date," Becca said and stood. "I'm looking forward to it. Now, if you'll excuse me, I'm going to head back down to my cabin. Or I should say closet." She winked his way. "I might develop claustrophobia on this trip. How do you handle it with your chair?"

"My room's handicap accessible. A little extra wide." He left out that he had the Presidential Suite, and by "wide," he meant quite spacious.

"That's great. I'm so glad the cruise line has accommodations like that. And I am so excited for tomorrow."

Patrick watched Becca head to the elevators. Words escaped him, but he wanted to say something. "Dinner tonight?" he called out. "I mean, you're welcome to join us again."

She hit the elevator button and gave the same response she had given his daughter. "We'll see."

The door closed on her. "Daddy, how come you don't want Becca knowing where we live?"

"It's hard to explain to someone your age, but sometimes ladies pretend to like Daddy, but what they really like is my money. So for now, let's just keep it our secret, all right?"

"Pirates are good at keeping secrets. So no one finds our loot."

He ruffled her curls. "I knew I could count on you."

"Don't you have to go to your meeting?" Jenny asked as she climbed back onto his lap.

"I do, but first I have something else I have to fix—right after I get you boarded on your pirate ship."

He wheeled off, with them both practicing their pirate speak.

Chapter Three

The tip of Becca's nose burned from the extra time she had spent poolside all afternoon. In her bathing suit and coverup, she headed back to her cabin, tucking her summer reading book into her satchel and removing her keycard at the same time. She took the next turn down her hall and noticed a note on her door before she reached it.

A letter from the cruise line's concierge informed her of a possible issue in the room's air conditioning system. She was to report to the concierge desk right away for a room change and was promised an upgrade for the trouble.

Becca smiled and kissed the letter. "Maybe I'll even get a window."

She headed back up to the Promenade deck and approached the desk with staff waiting on other customers. She took her place in line about four people deep. The clock on the wall said she would miss her dinner time at this rate. She needed to shower and dress for the dining room. Tonight was the captain's dinner and formal attire was required. She reasoned it was just as well to miss it. A table for one would be humiliating on such an evening. She didn't need more of Patrick's pity. She also didn't want to give him the wrong impression.

The buffet on the Lido deck would suffice, she reasoned, as someone tapped her on the shoulder. Becca turned to find a man dressed in the cruise's professional suit.

"Becca Shane?" he asked with a slight bow. The flip of his perfectly groomed hair stayed in place.

She gripped the collar of her bathing suit's coverup to close it. "Yes, I apologize for coming up here in my pool clothes, but I received a notice on my door to come right away."

"Of course, miss. Please come with me. I will get this dilemma fixed for you immediately." He waved a hand for her to cross the Promenade to a private sit-down desk.

She left the line to follow, taking the seat he held for her. It all felt so unnecessary. She could have waited her turn and spoken to one of the employees in customer service.

"I want you to know I've been quite pleased so far with the cruise," she assured him. "My air conditioning worked fine last night."

"That's wonderful to hear. Here on *Heart of the Sea* we aim to provide perfection to all our guests. Your room service attendant felt the air was a bit off, and as we head closer to the equator the temperature will spike. To be sure you don't have even one uncomfortable night, we would like to move you to another room." He opened a side drawer and withdrew an envelope. Withdrawing the contents, he held a new room key. "I'll take your previous key and swap you with your new one."

"Oh, but I still have to grab my baggage."

"Your attendant noticed you hadn't unpacked and already moved your bags up to your new room. You will find everything in its place, I assure you." He slipped the keycard over.

This all felt surreal, but if anything was missing, she knew where to find everyone. Nobody would be getting off the boat in a grand escape. Besides, she didn't have much. Her most valuable thing was her engagement ring, and that was still on her finger. She gave it a swirl with her thumb. Why did she keep it on?

Was she holding out hope Brad would change his mind?

"Miss Shane?"

Becca glanced back up to the concierge. "Yes?"

"Your keycard?"

"Oh, right." She rummaged through her satchel and withdrew it again. Passing it over, she scooped up her new keycard, along with the envelope that listed her new room number. She noticed it was much higher. "I'm on a different floor then?"

"Yes, take the elevators up to Deck 12 and head forward."

"Forward?"

"To the bow of the ship. The front."

"I see." She stood. "This is so proactive and generous. Thank you."

He stood and gave a slight bow again. "May the rest of your trip exceed your expectations."

Becca studied the number of her new room and made her way toward the elevator. When the doors opened to her floor, she found it exceptionally quiet. The doors seemed more spread apart than her floor below. She found her room number and unlocked it with her card. Stepping inside, she froze on the threshold.

"Is this a joke?" she whispered and checked the number on the door. It matched the envelope. Her key worked. She looked back out in the hall, first to her left, then to her right.

No one snickered behind cupped hands.

She looked back into the room and at the end of a hall saw her bouquet of peonies in a vase of water on a table.

An actual table.

She stepped inside and let the door shut behind her. In a daze, she looked around, absorbing the large suite with a full kitchen and lounge. Her bedroom was a room all by itself. She reached the kitchen and moved in a circle.

"I can dance in here." She twirled just to prove it to herself.

The interior designer in her appreciated the island colors of teals and peach hues. The couch looked inviting with its plush cushions. A glance at the clock told her it would have to wait. She could still make it to the captain's dinner if she hurried.

With a squeal of delight, she headed to her bedroom and made fast work, so glad she had splurged on a certain green-blue gown that matched her eyes perfectly. Brad loved her eyes.

Or so she had thought.

A glance at the floral arrangement on the way out of the bedroom stopped her. Suddenly they paled in comparison to the beauty of the room. Their bright pink didn't match at all.

Becca grabbed the stems all at once. One lift and they were upside down in the trash bin.

"There. That's better." Her thumb twirled the ring on her finger.

That one she wasn't ready to toss.

With a deep breath, she took one last look at herself in the mirror and smiled at what she saw.

A woman trying to begin again.

"I think I'm ready. I think."

Captain Meryl Sinclair sat at the head of the captain's table. She was a recent addition to the cruise line, and Patrick was quite pleased with the direction she was taking the company. Her navigational skills extended past the bridge of the ship into making the cruise line stand out above the rest.

"When are you going to bring Jenny up to sit at the helm?" Meryl asked him. Her bright smile put everyone at ease. This was not a stodgy old captain. She exuded a fun atmosphere. Her feathery brown, pixie haircut encircled a youthful face. She had many years at sea ahead of her.

"When I can pull her away from her new mateys in the playroom," Patrick replied to her question about his daughter. He appreciated Meryl's welcoming demeanor and all that would mean for this business venture of his. Investing and building ships was only one part of the success. Trusted employees mattered most. Without them, he would be ruined. And judging by the full table of fifteen important people and repeat guests, he had chosen well in this captain. "But even beyond the stellar child-care workers, the ship has a solid crew this tour."

"I am quite pleased with each department," the captain said.

The woman next to him in a flashy gold dress nodded to the empty seat beside him. "Are you expecting your daughter to join us for dinner?"

He referenced the meals before him. "We're still working on appreciating a fine cuisine."

Everyone gave a knowing laugh. "Picky eating is a phase," the woman replied. She patted his hand, lingering a beat too long, he thought. But maybe he'd only imagined it.

Doubt it.

Patrick cleared his throat. "Actually, I was saving the seat for a certain woman aboard."

The woman's demure look faltered for a mere second before she gave a nod of understanding. He hoped she understood anyway.

Patrick scanned the room for at least the tenth time. Maybe Becca was bowing out of the formal dinner. He touched the black bow tie at his neck. He would have gladly met her for a private dinner elsewhere.

Sipping from his water glass, he wondered again what it was about the woman that intrigued him. While the conversations continued without him, Patrick swirled the liquid in his glass. He studied it as though it had the answers he was looking for. One response came to mind.

She helped him when he fell.

That fall drudged up another time he had fallen. It was three years ago, and the night his wife left him. She watched him struggle on the floor and couldn't handle it. She turned her back on him and Jenny and never looked back.

But Becca helped him.

Patrick lifted his gaze from his glass. He knew she was there before he even looked. The feeling wasn't anything he could explain. A sense? A magnet? A supernatural force?

He locked his gaze on her in a sea-green satin gown. Its cut draped loosely off her pale shoulders and over her body. He curled his fingers from the urge to touch her again, from along her slender jaw line, down her neck and over her shoulders.

She walked toward him, the maitre'd leading the way, per the instructions Patrick had given him. At this point, every department aboard ship and on island for tomorrow had received their instructions to be sure Becca Shane was treated as the most important person.

As she drew closer, he realized she was.

Patrick's chest tightened as he forgot to breathe. Every curve on her body moved in a mesmerizing way. His lips parted and he tried to swallow. He tried again.

And then she stood at the table.

The maitre'd pulled out the chair beside Patrick. "Miss Becca Shane," he announced to the table.

Becca's complexion bloomed red instantly. "It's nice to meet you all. I'm a bit stunned by your invitation to your table. Thank you for having me." She touched Patrick's shoulder and said under her breath, "Something tells me you arranged this?"

He reached for her hand and led her the rest of the way around her seat. *Oh, to be the one pushing her in*, he thought as Franz held the honors. Patrick would have leaned down and kissed her shoulder, lingering there to take in the fragrance of her...and the taste of her.

"It's lovely to meet you, Miss Shane," an investment banker elder said from across the table. Patrick realized all the men were standing as Becca took her seat.

All of them except him.

What was he doing? Who was he kidding? Just because Becca showed kindness to him and helped him stand the other night did not mean she had any interest in dating a cripple.

"Please, call me Becca," she told the group. "Only Rebecca if you're mad at me." Her laugh came with ease.

From there the guests asked her questions about her career and her home in Seattle. Dinner was served and cleared, and coffee was being poured. Becca had a natural ability to fit in. There was nothing fake about her.

"I see you're engaged," the woman beside Patrick said, and instantly, he sensed Becca falter in her confidence. He should have known the woman would look for a reason to cut Becca down. He knew from his business dealings people could be vicious when they sensed competition.

"Um..." Becca brought her hand to her lap and covered the ring. "It's complicated."

"What she means is we're not telling anyone yet," Patrick jumped in to explain, saving her from having to admit about her no-show fiancé.

Delighted faces lit up all around them. A few of the ladies clapped and congratulated them. The woman beside Patrick downed her champagne—officially silenced.

The announcement made for an easy segue to excuse themselves from dinner. They had a special evening planned. They were bid good-bye with many blessings, but Becca remained silent all the way back to her suite.

"This is your cabin?" He feigned knowledge of it, trying to lighten the mood. "I'm right next door."

She turned abruptly. Anger flashed. "Something tells me you had something to do with my room change as well. Room changes, table changes...and now apparently *name* changes?"

"Of course not. I was only trying to save you from explaining about that loser you nearly married."

"You don't have to save me from anything. I make my own choices, and when I make mistakes, I make my own amends. I came on my honeymoon alone. Doesn't that show you I can stand on my own two feet?"

Her face blanched. Her eyes grew wide. She covered her mouth in horror at her choice of words. "Oh, Patrick, I am so sorry. I did not mean to sound so insensitive. Please, forgive me."

Patrick paused before responding. The look of panic on her face was priceless. Suddenly, a laugh burst from his lips, and it just kept coming. "Darling, 'standing on your own two feet' is a figure of speech. I'm not offended or hurt."

Slowly, she dropped her hand and trusted herself to laugh with him. Her humanity shined through. He found her so endearing.

Pushing up in his chair, he reached for both her hands. "I need to make you laugh more," he said. "You are stunning."

Her smile fell. Her gaze found his eyes, then lowered to his lips. Did he dare believe she wanted to kiss him as much as he wanted to kiss her? To taste her and fill his senses with everything that was Becca Shane. He would never be so bold to ask it of her. To put her on the spot to kiss him out of pity.

Except...he watched her slowly lower herself to her knees. Her gaze never left his lips as she leaned in. "Kiss me, Patrick. Please." A desperate sound emitted from her plea. "Make me feel wanted."

"That won't be hard to do." He shifted forward, letting go of her hands and reaching one hand behind her soft hair tied up in a twist. His fingers splayed through and loosened the clasp. His other hand finally found the smooth skin of her cheek. His thumb rubbed over her lower lip as he brought her closer to him. "You are wanted. Do you hear me, Becca? I want you."

With that he met her the rest of the way and captured her lips with his own. Pressing in hard, driving in a need he thought long dormant. This woman awoke a fire in him he thought he had extinguished. He wasn't supposed to let another woman in. Ever.

A tiny moan escaped her lips.

He plunged deeper within her mouth. His hand traveled down to her side and slowly grabbed the satiny material of her dress.

Her shoulders trembled.

He moved his other hand down to cover her smooth shoulder. Her firm body felt like silk to touch. At another tremble, it took Patrick a moment to realize she was crying.

Crying.

Pulling away from her felt like a long, spinning tunnel. A vortex that pulled his life's breath from him. But there was no other choice.

A wail escaped her lips and her arms wrapped tightly around his neck. She buried her face into the crook of his neck and wept deeply. Her pain of rejection was still so fresh. Patrick had three years on her in the healing department. His three years to her three days wasn't fair, and he knew it.

"I'm sorry," he said. "I shouldn't have pressed you. It won't happen again."

She shook her head against his neck. Her cries slowed, and he withdrew the cloth from his tux's front pocket. She pulled back and took it to wipe her nose. She couldn't even look at him.

He lifted her chin and met her with a soft smile. "You are an amazing woman. Don't ever forget that."

She smiled through her tears. On a nod and sigh, she pushed back and stood to her feet. She backed toward her door and touched the doorknob with her keycard. The door clicked, and she opened it a crack. "By the way," she whispered. "I love my new room. Thank you."

She disappeared inside and the door clicked back closed.

"You deserve so much more," he said quietly to the closed door and backed up to head to his suite next door.

Chapter Four

Nausea rolled through Becca as the catamaran bounced over another choppy wave. "I should have chosen a land excursion," she mumbled from a bench inside. With eyes shut, she rested her head back, trying not to be sick.

"Here, try putting this on your forehead," Patrick said from somewhere in front of her.

She tried to lift a hand but groaned instead. Any movement brought on another wave of seasickness. Her hands felt like dead weights in her lap.

She felt him place a cool, damp cloth on her head. She sighed. "I am so sorry, Patrick."

She heard a shuffling sound beside her but didn't dare open her eyes.

"You have nothing to be sorry for." He was closer now, right next to her.

"I ruined your day on the water. You don't have to stay here with me. Just pretend you left me at the port."

He chuckled as he brought the damp cloth down the side of her cheek, gently cooling her skin. "If I had left you at the port, I would have been miserable."

"Not as miserable as I am for coming."

"You're wrong."

They hit another wave, and she groaned and closed her eyes again. "Where's Jenny? I hope I'm not ruining her day too."

"Will you stop about ruining our day? Jenny is concerned for you. She's with the crew, and they are keeping her occupied. We only want you to feel better. We're almost at the cove. Once your feet are back on dry land, you'll feel better."

"What if I don't want to get back on this boat? I'll be stuck here forever."

"Would that really be that bad?" He brought the cloth to the back of her neck, and she could feel his warm breath on her cheek.

"No, but seriously, how am I going to get back to the ship? I don't want to get back on this catamaran."

"I can drive you across the island, back to the port, or you could..."

Becca leaned a bit his way. She missed the rest of his sentence. "Could you repeat that? I didn't hear the rest of what you said. Did you say 'stay'?"

"It's nothing. It was a silly idea. I promise, you won't have to take the catamaran back. We're at the cove now. You'll be off as soon as we dock."

"Oh, thank God. On both accounts." Relief swept over her faster than the waves. She slowly opened her eyes, testing the nausea now that they were at shore. Patrick's face was closer than she thought. His lightly stubbled face practically tickled her. She realized he was sitting on the bench beside her.

"Take it slow. We have all day," he assured her. His eyes held a compassion she hadn't seen before. But then she hadn't known him for very long. Still, the whole scene didn't make sense.

"Patrick, where is your chair?"

"It's beside me. I couldn't get close enough to help you, so I hopped onto the bench."

"In those waves?" She sat up straight, and instantly regretted it. She covered her mouth just in case.

"Slow, I said. You're not on terra firma yet. Breathe deep and let it out." He put the cloth back on her forehead, but it was no longer cool.

She settled back but kept her eyes on him. She hoped he saw her anger in them. "You could have been hurt. What if the chair started rolling? You would have fallen, and I couldn't have helped you, that's for sure. Not in my state of seasickness."

"But you would have, if you were able to, right?" His question caught her off guard.

"What kind of person do you think I am?" She was affronted.

He brought the damp cloth down to his lap. His throat convulsed, and now he was the one who felt a bit green. "I think I know who you are, but my track record causes me to question my judgment of character. The last woman ran out on me...leaving me on the floor."

"Oh, Patrick," Becca whispered, struck silent at the thought of someone being so cruel to him. She reached for his cheek. How humiliating that must have been, but even more so, painful that he trusted someone so completely, and she turned her back on him. "Yes, I would have helped you. Of course I would have helped you. You can believe that."

His lips cracked into a slight smile. "Thank you. I knew I was right about you."

"Sir?" one of the crewmen interrupted. "You are all set to disembark."

"Thank you, Juan." Patrick looked over to the men. "We won't be taking the catamaran back, so you all are free to go. I will need the van."

Jenny appeared behind them. "Daddy, can I come over now? I've waited the whole time. I was a good girl, like you asked me to be."

"I know you were, sweetie. Come on over. Becca is starting to feel better, I think." He looked her way for confirmation.

"Yes, absolutely," Becca said and outstretched her arm to the child. "I'm sorry if I scared you." The young girl ran straight into Becca's arms and wrapped her own around her neck. "I'm from a city and never been on a boat like this. I guess I'm not much of an island girl like you."

Patrick frowned. "Don't jump to any conclusions yet. You haven't stepped foot on the island, and I hope after our day at the cove, you will change your mind." He looked to his chair then back at her. "Why don't the two of you head on shore. I'll be along in a few minutes."

Becca pursed her lips. "So you'll be all alone to get back in your chair? I don't think so. You tell me what help you need, and I'll do it."

"I don't need help." His voice lowered to a near whisper. "But if I should happen to fall, I might need help then. If for no other reason to shield my fall from the men. I'm not up for a humbling experience right now."

Becca got to her feet, taking a few seconds to let her legs grow accustomed. She rolled the wheelchair in front of him and locked the wheels, per his instructions. He grabbed hold of the arms of the chair and used his upper body strength to lift the rest of his body up and around to swing back into the seat. Even with his pale blue T-shirt on, there was no mistaking the hard, sculpted physique he had under it. The sight of him took Becca's breath away.

"Are you ready?" He turned his head to ask her. "Becca, are you all right?"

"Yes," she jumped to respond, but had to start to breathe deeply again. *In and out, slow and steady*, she repeated to herself as she followed him off the gangway. Jenny grabbed hold of her hand, having no idea Becca was so affected by her daddy.

Becca didn't even understand it.

Becca was avoiding him. Patrick couldn't pinpoint why for sure, but ever since they had disembarked the catamaran, she'd been uncomfortably quiet. No eye contact was made during the lunch he had ordered ahead of time. They ate in silence under the canopy, except to answer the endless barrage of questions Jenny had for them. At one point, they both reached for the strawberries at the same time and their hands touched. When he tried to entwine his fingers in hers, she pulled away, and the berries remained untouched for the duration of the meal.

Now, Patrick moved his sand wheelchair away from Jenny, who was asleep in her favorite hammock. He scanned the rocks of the cove for where Becca had gone off to, but he couldn't see her anywhere. Last he saw her, she had been walking along them, circling the blue-green water, her skirt whipping in the sea breeze.

He moved closer to the inlet, finding her as she swam underwater. She was finally getting to snorkel like she had wanted to. He should leave her to her exploration, he reasoned, even as he lowered himself into the water and set out toward her with smooth, long strokes. With his eyes open under water, he noticed the moment she saw him in her mask. Her own eyes widened, and she rushed to the surface.

They both broke through at the same time.

"You scared me," she said after she pulled the snorkel from her mouth and ripped the mask from her face.

"You're avoiding me," he responded.

At her lowered gaze on the snorkel and mask, he knew he hadn't imagined it. "Why? What happened? Did I gross you out getting in my chair?"

She snapped her head up. "How dare you? I'm tired of you thinking the worst of me. I am not like your wife."

"Ex. And what do you want me to think, Becca? It's obvious you don't want to be near me."

"Is it now? Well, you would be wrong. Way wrong." She turned to swim back to shore.

Patrick reached her in shallower water. When his hands could touch the sandy bottom, he gripped her forearm, pulling her down to her knees before him. "Then what is it? What did I do wrong? Tell me so I can fix it."

"You didn't do anything wrong. It's me, okay? I'm not being fair to you."

"How so? You've been nothing but kind to me."

She sputtered and said, "If you only knew the thoughts going on in my head. I'm supposed to be helping you, but instead all I can think about is your body."

Patrick jerked back. "My body? You mean my legs, or lack of them."

"No." She touched his chest with her free hand. "Your body, and how beautiful it is. It's not right for me to think such things."

Patrick covered her hand on him and moved closer to her. "That's what this is all about? You're feeling guilty about desiring me?"

She squeezed her eyes shut. "Why do you have to put it like that?"

He bit his tongue. He found her adorable. "Is it not true? Do you not desire me?" He dropped his voice low, and he moved in even closer to her, wrapping an arm around her back and pulling her up against him. Water sloshed between them and around them as he waited for her admission. "Tell me, Becca. Do you feel the same way...as I feel about you?"

Her head tilted.

He nodded. "It's true. I can't get you out of my mind." He huffed. "And if you want to talk about bodies, when you showed up to dinner last night in that satin dress, I very nearly had a heart attack."

She giggled.

"It's not funny. I *am* older than you, you know." He took the mask and snorkel from her hand and let them go in the water. He entwined his fingers into hers and brought her arm up around his neck.

"Not by that much," she said. "Ten years? How old are you, anyway?"

Patrick laughed and leaned in to kiss her, avoiding the question.

She leaned back. "No way, you can't just kiss me. Answer the question."

"Age is just a number."

"And I want that number."

The woman was exasperating. "Forty-one. There, you happy?"

"Forty-one! You're twelve years older than me? I was way off. I thought ten, tops. You really look amazing—"

He zeroed in on her moving lips and cut her off. "Becca, I'm going to kiss you now."

"Okay," she whispered. "I would like that."

Patrick pressed close, pulling her closer. He placed his lips gently on hers and reveled in her sweet and salty taste. He turned his head to go deeper.

Suddenly, Becca was slapping him on the back and trying to pull away. In a daze, he let her go, not understanding what was happening now.

Then he heard a sweet voice from a few feet away on shore.

"Daddy? What are you doing to Becca?"

The two of them stared at each other, unsure of how to answer the child. This was a first of these kind of predicaments for him. Becca shrugged, also having no idea what to say.

Without taking his eyes off her, he said, "I'm loving her."

Instant tears sprang to her eyes, pooling up like the waters that surrounded her.

"You're loving Becca?" Jenny asked, excitement growing in her voice. She ran into the water, spraying it everywhere as she ran up to them. Each of her little arms wrapped around their waists, joining them all together. "Oh, Daddy, you have made me the happiest girl on earth!"

Patrick stared into Becca's eyes, wondering if she thought him nonsensical.

"You'll have to wait in line, Jenny," Becca said as she reached up to caress the side of his face. "I think I have first place for the happiest girl on earth right now."

The heavy weight of rejection lifted off him in an instant.

Now all he had to do was convince her to stay with him forever.

Chapter Five

"If this is a dream, I don't ever want to wake up," Becca said from the passenger side of a van. "How did they ever find you a van you could drive in your wheelchair, with raised pedals? Everything is so perfect." She faced Patrick in the driver's seat. "How did it even get to the cove?"

"Daddy!" Jenny yelled from the backseat. "Can I please tell her now?"

Patrick smiled and glanced at his daughter strapped in behind them. "Go ahead, squirt, she's about to find out anyway."

"Tell me what?" Becca looked back and forth between the two of them. "Please tell me I haven't been kidnapped, never to be seen or heard from again?"

Jenny giggled. "No, silly. Daddy doesn't kidnap people."

"Then don't make me wait. Tell me what's going on?"

Patrick took the next turn onto a sand-covered road that didn't look like much traffic ever traveled over it. Maybe she was being kidnapped after all.

"This is Daddy's van on the island."

"Of course!" Becca exclaimed as it all became clear. "You did say you come to Barbados often. You keep a van here for yourself. That's brilliant, and so freeing for you not to have to depend on other people for transportation."

The road opened wider and the terrain changed to concrete. The road curved, and as soon as it did, an open gate led way to an enormous home.

Patrick entered through and followed a roundabout around a three-tier fountain spouting water. He came to a stop beside the home's front arches.

"What is this place?" Becca asked. "It's so old and...eerie, but yet, in a beautiful way."

"That's exactly how I felt too, when I first saw it." He nodded to the open sea behind it. "I first noticed it when I was out on the water. Back then, it was in total disrepair. It was an old manor house of a plantation, left to rot. It reeled me in."

"Wait." Another realization occurred to Becca. "Are you telling me you bought it and fixed it up? That this is your home?"

Jenny giggled. "I tried to tell you we lived here. But Daddy wouldn't let me."

Patrick eyed his daughter in the rearview mirror again. "No reason to throw me under the bus, kiddo."

"What bus?" Jenny asked, looking out her window in confusion.

"Why, Patrick?" Becca asked.

He shrugged. "I'm a pretty private person. We didn't know you. I don't go around boasting. I don't know why, I guess. Maybe I just wanted you to like me for me." He scoffed. "That sounds so pathetic."

Becca reached for his hand. "Not at all. And honestly, all you had to say was it was none of my business." She turned to look at the home—*his* home. Yellow-painted brick and white trim gave a breezy feel to the seaside manor. New cobblestones led up to red double doors beyond the white archways. A glance at the van's digital clock showed she only had two hours before the liner set sail again. "May I see the inside quickly? We don't have much time left."

A strange sadness clouded his blue eyes to gray, but he nodded and waved to someone. The next moment, two men in billowing white shirts and khakis came out and opened the car doors. Becca had no idea other people were there. Apparently, Patrick kept a hired staff to watch over the place when he was gone and help him when he was on island. The man could buy anything he wanted.

Then why was he spending time with her?

The thought flitted through her mind, but she squashed it. This trip only had three more days left. Come Saturday, she would wake up from this dream and face the music of everyday life back in Seattle. For now, she would let the fairytale unfold.

One of the men helped her from the van. He introduced himself as Sam. The other attendant went around back. She started to walk up the steps but noticed the ramp on the side. She stopped and waited for Patrick to use the lift on the side of the van. When he came around the front, Jenny was back in his lap, a family of two who adored each other. Becca took a mental picture to remember them always like this. She swallowed the start of tears brewing and resolved herself to enjoy the last few days with them. At the ramp, she joined them to walk up with them.

Patrick talked about the history of the place and the architecture. She forced herself to remember the sound of his voice and how its timbre soothed her. When the three of them made it to the entrance, the doors opened wide, startling her.

"You'll get used to it." Patrick chuckled.

Becca wasn't sure that would happen in the hour or so that she was here, but she appreciated everyone's effort to help Patrick. One of the men scooped up Jenny and took her somewhere for a treat. "You have a lot of help."

"I appreciate each and every one of them." He waved for her to go before him. Always the gentleman.

The main hall extended through to the rear of the home. "Cavernous," she whispered, her sandals tapping lightly on the marble floors.

Patrick moved up beside her. "It feels that way because it's still so sparse. Many of the rooms are still untouched and empty. In my travels, I try to bring items back to fill them, but it will take some time."

"It's a beautiful home, Patrick." Becca walked around an ornate round table with a full floral arrangement of tropical flowers. She touched the petal of a large red hibiscus, rubbing it between her thumb and finger. Straight down the hall, the other set of double doors opened to a veranda that overlooked the sea and swaying palm trees. "With both doors opened on each end, the breeze is wonderful through here," she said, and she walked to stand on the threshold. Lifting her face to feel the sea air, she breathed in deeply. The thin, cotton fabric of her sundress whipped around her legs. She closed her eyes and committed the view and feel to memory.

"You are so lovely." Patrick spoke from her left side, his voice low. He took her hand. "Stay with me. With us."

She jerked at such an absurd idea. Had she heard correctly? "How—what—you can't be serious." Looking down at him, she turned to face him, their clasped hands between them. "I have a life in Seattle. I have responsibilities. A business to run. *You're* a businessman. You must understand responsibilities."

"None of those reasons have to exclude me. We can make both our businesses work. I could help you in building your interior designing business. We would be amazing together. A power couple, helping each other be the best we can be. Think of the future we would have."

Becca shook her head. "Like I said in the van. This all feels like a dream. It's not real. It will end."

"I disagree. I know I have never felt this way about anyone else. No one. I constantly want to be near you, to touch you. To be touched by you. You see me. *Me*! Not some head in a wheelchair. Have I been wrong in thinking that?"

"No, of course not. I feel it too, Patrick. And I *do* see you. And trust me, I love what I see. And not just in your looks, but how you treat the people who work for you. How you adore your daughter. That says so much about you." She came to the front of him and knelt to be at his level, their hands still clasped. "But you have to understand. How can I trust all this...what we have, when last week, I thought I had it with someone else? How can I trust that this is all real and not a fairytale that will come to an end in an instant? I know what it feels like to be left at the altar. Brad literally walked out of the church, leaving me to face everybody alone. *That* is reality, and I can't do it again. I won't."

Patrick leaned forward and pressed his forehead to hers. "I am so sorry he did that to you. If I had been there, I would have gone after him to make him pay. No. That's not true." He lifted his head a bit, stared straight into her eyes. "If I was there, I would have raced to the altar to take his place. Marry me."

"This is crazy. *You're* crazy." She tried to pull away to stand up, but he tugged her hand back.

He looked down at her hand and lifted it to show the ring. "Is that why you can't take this off? You still want that fairytale with Brad?"

A glance of the engagement ring still on her finger had her pulling her hand away to hide it in the folds of her sundress. She stood and backed away. "I don't know why I can't take it off." She sighed in frustration and dropped her forehead into the palm of her hand. "I didn't come on this trip to fall in love with another man. I came to start my life over. On my own. A table for one is my future, and I have to accept that."

"Why? I'm offering you a table for three. A family of your own. We need you just as much as you need us."

She grabbed fists of her cotton dress but stopped short of stomping her foot. "That's just it, Patrick. I can't *need* anyone. It hurts too much when you're left standing alone."

He huffed and looked out to sea. "And since I can't stand beside you, you would be left to do that a lot."

"That's not what I meant."

"But you also don't believe I will. Same thing." He backed up his chair and turned it. "I'll have Sam bring you back to the port."

"You're not going back on the ship?"

"I never was. I was only traveling to here. You'll be free to have your table for one for the rest of the trip. I wish you all the best, and more, Rebecca."

She cringed at the use of her full name, knowing he was mad at her. He moved away, her last glimpse of him when he turned a corner to some unknown place in his home.

He didn't even look back.

Just like Brad.

"She didn't even say good-bye!" Jenny wailed, pushing her face into her pillow. Her next words were muffled, but they resembled something about wanting Becca to stay forever.

Patrick finger-combed his daughter's damp red locks from beside her pink, canopied bed. He tried his best to soothe her when he himself wanted a pillow to push his face into too. "Sometimes things don't work out the way we want them too. Daddy has lots of business deals that don't come together. Sometimes I can fix them and sometimes I can't."

Jenny lifted her puffy, wet face and looked at him. "Is Becca a business deal?" She sniffed and rubbed her dripping nose.

"No, she's not." Patrick tried to think if at any time had he treated her as such. He didn't think so, but maybe somehow, something came across that way. He could be pushy when he wanted something bad enough.

And he wanted Becca badly.

But that was not to be so. And as always, he had his daughter to think of.

He turned to the nightstand to grab a tissue from the box. "Come here," he instructed and lifted Jenny into his lap. Cleaning up her face, he wiped the tip of her nose. "We're going to be okay. We do well, the two of us, don't you think?"

Jenny blew her nose—or tried to. Something they were still working on. She gave him back the tissue. "Thanks," she said. Patrick laughed to himself. At least the manners lessons were kicking in. He leaned down and kissed his daughter's sweaty forehead, closing his eyes and breathing her innocence in.

Off in the distance, the horn of the cruise ship blew. Thirty minutes and Becca would be gone from their lives forever.

"You told her you loved her, right?" Jenny spoke with the side of her head resting on his chest.

"Um...I think so." Patrick tried to remember. "I asked her to marry me." *Love is implied, isn't it?* "Maybe I didn't actually say it."

Jenny lifted her head and gave him her best disappointed face. *Is that what I look like when I give it to her?* He made a mental note to work on toning that down. She crossed her arms. "What am I going to do with you? *Duh*, everyone knows you have to say 'I love you' when you ask them to marry you."

"They do?"

Jenny nodded her head forcefully. "I saw it in a movie."

"What movie? Who's letting you watch this stuff?" *Parenting gets harder every day.*

"You have to go tell her, Daddy. Right now." Jenny hopped off his lap and ran to the back of his chair. "Come on, Daddy!" She started to turn him around and head to the door, pushing with all the might of her little legs.

Patrick twisted in his chair. "Jenny, stop. There's no time. You just heard the horn. I would never make it there that fast."

She stopped pushing. "We'll run. I'll get your running legs!" She ran out of the room, and Patrick followed to stop her.

"Jenny, Becca made her decision. She didn't want to stay. We have to honor that. We can't make people do things they don't want to do."

"But she doesn't know you love her," Jenny whined.

Sam came down the hall, keys in his hands. "Miss Becca has been dropped off at the port. Will there be anything else?"

"Yes!" Jenny yelled.

"No." Patrick said.

Sam raised his hands with a smile. "I'm not sure who I should listen to here."

"You need to bring Daddy to the ship. He has to tell Becca he loves her. Can you drive fast?"

"I sure can. I'll make it in ten minutes or less."

"I'll get Daddy his legs. He'll be able to run real fast." She was gone in a flash.

"Sir? If this is not something you want, you just say the word, and I'll explain it to the child."

It was a moment of honesty for Patrick. "What if it *is* something I want? More than anything in the world."

Sam chuckled. "Then we got to fly." He ran up behind the wheelchair and raced down the hall and out the door. He helped Patrick into the Mercedes's passenger seat just as Jenny came out with the prosthetic legs. She jumped in the back and passed them through to the front.

"We've got a boat to catch!" she yelled, strapping in. The sound of the ship's horn blared again, and they all sat in silence for the moment. It was an impossible feat ahead of them.

Then Patrick yelled, "Go, Sam, go!"

Becca made her way to her cabin while she also made plans to order in for dinner. Going down to the dining room didn't feel possible. She knew she would spend the whole meal looking for Patrick and Jenny, and they wouldn't be there. If she had known they weren't returning to the ship, she would have...what? It wasn't like he didn't give her a chance to prolong their time together. She could have stayed in Barbados and flown home in a couple days.

But the fact was she would still be going home.

Returning to the ship was her only choice. She clicked open her door and stepped inside. That's when she heard the television on.

Becca backed up to check the number on the wall. It was her cabin. But she knew she hadn't left the TV on. She didn't remember even turning it on that morning.

But maybe she had?

She remembered being in such an excited rush to spend the day with Patrick and Jenny on the catamaran and at the cove, she raced to meet them when they knocked on her door. She could have done without the catamaran, but their time at the cove would forever be a beautiful memory. She touched her lips and remembered Patrick's passionate kiss. Her eyes closed to hold it longer.

"Beccs? Is that you?"

Her eyes flew open. A man was here. At the end of the hall. In the lounge area. And not just any man. The only one who called her "Beccs."

She pulled her hand away from her lips and looked at her engagement ring. Brad's engagement ring. She lifted her gaze, and there he was, standing at the end of the hall, shirtless with a pink and orange striped swim trunks.

"Brad? What are you doing here?"

"Honey, I'm so sorry." He walked forward. "I took a plane down to meet you at the port."

"Stop, right there," she told him.

He raised his hands in front of him. His curly blond hair shook in his eyes.

So childish, she thought.

"Look," he said. "I know you're hurt. I don't blame you. I don't know what came over me. I got scared, that's all I can say. Please, you have to forgive me. My parents are so mad. They will never let me live this down. They can't believe I did something like this."

"*I* can't believe you did something like this. I thought I knew you, Brad." *Had she ever?*

He took another step but stopped at her glare. "You do know me, better than anyone else in the world. So you have to know I have trouble with change. What we had was so great. I didn't understand why it had to change."

"Because when you love someone, you want to spend the rest of your life with them."

Marry me.

Becca covered her mouth. "Oh, what have I done?" she said aloud.

"You see, I *knew* you would understand," Brad moved closer. She didn't stop him this time, and suddenly he stood right before her. "I forgive you."

She stared up at him, but his words didn't compute. "I'm sorry, did you say you forgive *me*?"

"Yes, for pushing me to commit to marriage. Maybe someday." He lifted her hand with the ring on her finger and kissed her fingertips. "For now, keep it on."

"So everyone will know I'm taken?"

He leaned in to kiss her just as a knock came on the door.

"Room service," the person announced.

"Leave it," Brad shouted over Becca's shoulder. He looked to her lips. "Now, where were we before we were so rudely interrupted?"

"She was just doing her job," Becca said, vouching for the crew. "You could have been a little nicer, more appreciative. She was doing you a favor."

"Why? She gets paid."

Patrick would be appalled by Brad. He would probably try to teach him the same manners lessons he taught his daughter.

A giggle bubbled up at the back of Becca's throat at the image that came to mind. Brad slouching in a classroom desk, and Patrick shaking his head in disappointment at the chalkboard.

But Becca wouldn't let herself off so easily. After all, she had loved this man before her. She had loved the fun they had. She glanced down at his trunks and asked, "What did you do all day at port?"

He shrugged. "The usual. Went jet-skiing, played a little water polo with some guys I met on the shore. They were cool. We're going to meet up with them later. They'll be bringing their girls too."

Suddenly, Becca saw her future begin to resemble her past.

Fun parties...wild times.

In other words, inconsequential.

We would be a power couple. Think of the future we would have.

The ship's horn blew right outside her cabin. Brad looked back down the hall to the window.

"Looks like we're heading out. This is a sweet upgrade, by the way. How'd you manage it?"

"A friend made the arrangements," she mumbled.

"That's some friend. Keep her around." He turned back and flashed his dazzling smile that had always curled her toes.

"Him," she corrected a little louder. Her thumb twirled her diamond ring, pushing it up her finger, little by little.

"What was that?" Brad asked in confusion.

The ring passed over her knuckle. "My friend is a man. A very kind and considerate man. He's an amazing father. So patient and dedicated and smart. He's also handsome. Beautiful, really."

Brad's eyes narrowed. "What are you saying?'

She took Brad's hand and turned it palm up. The ring fell off the rest of her finger onto his hand. She folded his fingers over it. "I'm saying I'm in love with someone else." She laughed at how freeing it was to admit it. "Good-bye, Brad. And thank you. You've actually given me the best wedding gift. Now God can give me my hope and future. And that's with Patrick and Jenny."

Becca turned around and opened the door. She stepped over the tray, calling back, "Enjoy your table for one!" She had a table for three waiting for her—*if* she could get off this ship in time.

She picked up her feet as she heard the final horn and announcement. The first deck to the exit was so far down from here. How would she ever make it in time? Her sandals wouldn't let her run. Two kicks and they were off.

Barefoot, she took the stairs two at a time before she finally hit the lower deck. Her college track race times would be beat today. Ahead, the gangway started to be pulled away.

"Wait!" she yelled as her feet hit the steel walkway. The non-slip paint gave her added traction. "I need to get off! Wait!"

"Wait!" she heard someone else yelling. "Let me on!"

"Patrick?" she called, recognizing the voice she had committed to memory. She scanned the port. "Where are you?"

"Becca!"

She found him. He was running down the walkway toward the gangway that was already disconnected and turned sideways. He ran up to it.

"Don't jump, Patrick!" She shouted. It wasn't worth getting hurt. "Let me come to you!"

He stopped at the closed gate.

She stopped at hers. There was no way either of them could get to the other side. "I'm sorry, Patrick. I ran as fast as I could."

"I love you!" he shouted. "I— I didn't tell you, and I should have. I just want you to know that, okay?"

Becca smiled with tears filling her eyes. "I love you too, Patrick! I love you so much, and I'll come back to you. I promise."

"No, I'll come to Seattle. You shouldn't have to give up your life."

"Hey! What's going on?" a crewman bellowed from down the port.

"I need to get on," Patrick said.

"I want to get off!" Becca shouted.

"Well, which is it?" the man asked.

Patrick looked across the divide to her. "Are you sure?"

Becca nodded. "I've never been surer of anything in my life. Let me off!"

The man radioed to someone, and soon the gangway was being turned back to connect the ship to the port again. As soon as the gate was opened on her side, she ran across and reached over the gate to touch Patrick. She wrapped her arms around his neck, and he pulled her closer.

"Hold on, you two," the man said as he slid open the gate. Once she could get through, Patrick pulled her against his chest, finding her lips. She lost herself in his embrace, and the world around them ceased to matter. "May I close the gate?"

Neither were able to answer.

Becca felt someone tapping on her shoulder. "Excuse me, I hate to interrupt, but are you staying in Barbados?"

Patrick lifted his head, his piercing blue eyes studied her face, waiting for her answer as well.

"If you'll still have me," she said.

A smile grew on his face. "She's staying. She's going to be my wife. And I'm going to love her forever."

The crewman slapped his thigh and congratulated them. "I wish you many years of happiness." He left to complete the departing process.

Patrick touched her cheek, rubbing the backs of his fingers along her jawline. When he reached her lips, she kissed his fingers. "If this is a dream, I don't ever want to wake up."

Becca pressed her lips to his. "It's a dream come true," she said.

"Daddy?" Jenny's voice called from down the port walkway. She stood with Sam's hand in hers. "What did she say?"

"Yes!" both Becca and Patrick shouted.

"Yay!" Jenny jumped up and down. She hooted and hollered while Becca couldn't peel her gaze from Patrick's.

"I love you, Patrick," she whispered. "I will never doubt us again."

He buried his fingers through her hair and lowered his forehead to hers. "Trust me, my love. I don't plan on ever giving you a reason to." And with that, they went to gather their daughter and begin their family of three.

Katy Lee is a Publishers Weekly best-selling author of eighteen novels full of intrigue, romance and inspiration. Romantic Times Book Reviews stated, "The action is intense in Lee's character-driven suspense." A native New Englander, Katy loves to knit warm woolly things and enjoys traveling around the globe. She is a two-time RITA® Award nominee for excellence in romance and a two-time Daphne du Maurier award nominee for excellence in mystery and suspense. She also has multiple award wins for the Inspirational Reader's Choice Award and the Selah Award for her romantic suspense *Blindsided*. Her website is KatyLeeBooks.com.

Latest 2020 Releases: Amish Sanctuary:
https://www.amazon.com/Amish-Sanctuary-Love-Inspired-Suspense-ebook/dp/B082P4W7PZ

Amish Country Undercover:

https://www.amazon.com/Amish-Country-Undercover-Inspired-Suspense-ebook/dp/B07V9P2H7W

Framed in Amish Country: A Novella :

https://www.amazon.com/Framed-Amish-Country-Inspirational-Romance-ebook/dp/B07TL8HGL2

Amazon Author Page with other Book Links:

https://www.amazon.com/Katy-Lee/e/B007UIVJR8

Partner in Crime

by

Melee McGuire

Chapter One

One thing was certain, she was getting royally screwed. Darling Fiori pulled her cellphone from the depths of her Coach satchel. She scrolled through the three names listed in her favorites to land her thumb on "Partner in Crime."

The phone rang twice before Penny picked up. "Hi, D. Everything okay?" Darling could hear her best friend's mouth chomping away at something. Knowing Penny, it was probably calorie-free, meat-free, taste-free, and probiotic.

"No. He arrived." Darling glanced over her shoulder at the man leaning against the bar in Seattle-Tacoma International Airport's Alaska Airlines first-class lounge. Rich, mahogany skin contrasted against his crisp, white button-down. He smiled at her before glancing back to the menu in his large hands. Damn it. He had a dimple. And beautiful teeth.

"Is he awful? I mean, he's government, so he has to be awful. Let me guess. Beer belly, combover, ill-fitting jacket and pants?" Penny's description of the agent veered comically far from the mark. Darling wasn't laughing. Her skin felt hot and prickly. Temper strained on a tight tether. The last thing she needed was an attractive distraction.

"I haven't spoken to him yet. I can't believe we're being forced into this." Darling tried to keep her voice calm. She glanced behind her again. He sipped his drink. Dark and stormy. The man, not the drink.

"Look, we got cocky on our last job, and we got caught. Joining forces with the CIA is not as bad as cooling our heels in some high-security prison, right?" Penny always saw the glass half full.

After ten years of killing some of the worst examples of human cruelty, Darling often didn't even see a glass. "Easy for you to say. You still get to work solo in the office."

"Not exactly. They have someone assigned to watch me here. She's pretty hot, though, so I'm not complaining." Penny purred like a kitten.

"Reel it in, Penny. Sleeping with the enemy is never a good plan." The line went quiet. "Penny, are you there? Did you hear me?"

"Yes, sorry. I got distracted by the optics."

Darling contained a snicker and tightened her grip on the phone. "You are shameless. Tell me we're going to get through this job."

"C'mon, Darling. You just killed a Guatemalan drug lord on his own private Caribbean island with nothing but tweezers and dental floss. Granted, that's what put us on CIA's radar, but no one is perfect. I think you can handle some government schlub."

"Does the schlub have to look so much like Idris Elba?"

"Seriously? Idris Elba? Where is the CIA recruiting their people? My chic could be a stunt double for J-Lo. Hand on my heart, and hopefully later, her ass."

"Focus, Penny!"

"Right. Sorry. Listen, Darling, we do this, pay our dues, and walk away with a little less soul, but no jail time. Remember, we are helping to save all the little Pennys and Darlings out there from the kind of horrific childhood we experienced. We can't do that if we're locked up."

"That's true."

"Just think about the epic contributions we could be making to society if we hadn't been so corrupted in our youth. Our ability to assassinate all the lowest, most evil, vile, dregs of society is creating a safer, brighter world, Darling."

Depressing, but inescapably true. "Damn it. You're right. I can do this. I'll play nice with the CIA, and they will look the other way while we kill all the pedophiles, sex-slavers, drug smugglers, and generally disgusting shit-heads that seem to escape the not-so-long arm of the law." Darling forced her shoulders back and took a cleansing breath. What she really wanted to do was to sink into the plush, leather captain's chair next to her and take a nice, long, dreamless nap.

Penny brought her back to reality. *"Bam!* We're our own bosses again, deciding the marks, making the world a better place one asshole assassination at a time. Besides, you need a date for this next job. The wedding invitation is for Mr. and Mrs. Jones."

"I know." Darling switched her cellphone to the other ear, shoving her wild black curls out of the way.

"And we would have taken this job regardless of the government mandate. The mark is a total douche."

"I know."

"And this CIA operative is a trained professional."

"I know."

"So you'll be fine."

Darling sighed. "He's coming over. I gotta go."

"Good luck killing the senator." Penny's annoyingly cheerful tone only heightened Darling's frustration.

"Luck has nothing to do with it." She ended the call and shoved her phone back into her leather satchel. Forcing her mouth into a tight smile, she tracked the far-too-handsome man as he collected his carryon and skirted around a couple drinking champagne. He strode toward her with the latent power and grace of an athlete. Or a killer.

"You must be Darling." His voice was smoke and gravel.

Darling ground her teeth and ordered the shivering in her belly to cease immediately. Attraction, like all other things in her life, needed to be planned, controlled, and executed with precision. This hormonal reaction was a rogue wave threatening to sweep her away in its chaotic frenzy of froth and foam. She dug her heels into the plush carpet and hardened her resolve.

"And you are Agent Sylas Johnson. Nice to meet you." Darling stuck out her hand. He stared for a moment, his lips twitched in the hint of a smile. Putting down his luggage, he encompassed her extended hand in a warm grip. She refused to notice how small her hand was in comparison to his wide palm and strong fingers.

"That's a firm handshake you have, Darling. I suppose you need to reassure men that small doesn't mean fragile."

Darling blinked twice and pulled her hand away. "Sometimes the most dangerous things are fragile. Bombs, glass shards, men's egos."

Sylas rocked back on his heels and chuckled low and soft. "Strong handshake and sharp wit. It's a pleasure to meet you."

Darling raised an eyebrow. "This is not about pleasure. If this had anything to do with pleasure, you would be writhing on the floor in agonizing pain, and I would be walking away a free woman."

"Sounds like most of my relationships." Sylas's lips twitched.

Darling refused to let his humor soften her resolve. "Sounds like you have relationship issues. You might want to work on that. Let's try to keep this professional, shall we?"

"Of course." Raising his glass to his lips, he sipped. Darling grudgingly noted the amber liquid was a few shades lighter than his eyes and equally intoxicating. If someone was careless, they might get drunk on a gaze that heated. Thankfully, Darling was a very careful woman. In the business of relationships and assassination, caution kept her alive as often as skill and planning.

A man in a pilot uniform interrupted them. "If you're ready?"

The pilot took Darling's bag and Sylas put down his glass and picked up his carryon. They followed the pilot out of the first-class lounge to a motorized cart. Whooshing through the airport, the pilot expertly maneuvered the glamorized golf-cart around lines of passengers waiting to file through customs. They took a ramp down to the runway reserved for charter and private planes.

The perks of working with a government agency included top-level resources Darling didn't have to pay for. A silver lining to the shit-storm of being caught mid-assassination by the CIA. Next time she would avoid druglords on the CIA's most-wanted list and focus on the sleaze balls the government chose to ignore.

The senator was a great example. The government couldn't be linked to the kill given the mark's status. He was far too well-connected to several high-level political leaders who didn't mind his ties to Russia and would adamantly oppose any actions being taken against him. Especially fatal ones. But the CIA knew he was a huge liability. Which put them in a sticky situation. Enter Darling.

The agency couldn't take the senator out themselves, but they had no qualms about forcing Darling's hand in the matter. If things went to hell, the agency could lay all the blame at her feet and walk away squeaky-clean. If things went to plan, they would be rid of a senator leaking secrets to Russia faster than a cracked pipe and avoid any pesky questions regarding who was responsible for his death. So, win-win for good ole Uncle Sam.

It would be a short trip from Seattle to Sequim. They could have taken the ferry and driven to the small town perched along the Strait of Juan de Fuca, but the government never did anything by halves, even when working incognito. As their pilot unfolded the steps to their plane, Darling was determine to enjoy the flight on the Cessna P206 and ignore her forced partnership with tall, dark, and frustratingly charming.

Chapter Two

"You received the dossier and are familiar with the particulars of this mission?" Sylas and Darling were both wearing headsets to cancel the noise of the prop, but she could hear his rough voice clearly.

He removed his jacket and unbuttoned his cuffs, rolling up his sleeves to reveal powerful forearms. Ropes of muscles flexed and shifted as he adjusted his seatbelt. The Cessna had two captain's chairs in the front. The pilot sat in one and Darling had hoped Sylas would take the other. No such luck. He sat far too close to her on the one bench seat in the back of the plane. While the information she received from the CIA stated the plane was fit for five, including the pilot, Darling didn't see how they could squeeze anyone else into the small cabin. Sylas seemed to take up all the available space. She turned away and focused on tucking her satchel behind her in the cargo bay, ignoring the pressure of his hard thigh pressing against her leg.

Sometimes it was best to face a problem head-on. She would defeat her attraction through immersion. Turning, she straightened her spine and faced him. "We're a married couple flying in from New York. Friends of the groom's family. You are an investment banker, and I am a happy little housewife making our Manhattan apartment an oasis from your hectic and stressful life."

Sylas raised his eyebrows and the corners of his mouth tipped up in appreciation. Darling ignored his approval. She didn't need it. She continued reciting the information gleaned from the CIA's dossier on their mission. "We'll blend into the wedding celebrations, and I'll get the senator alone. It needs to look like an assassination by his Russian handlers to send a message to any other sleeper cells, make them start to question whether they can trust the Russian government, so I'll make it messy. You'll stay clear of the scene and if anything goes wrong, hang me out to dry." Darling stretched her lips in a treacly smile and blinked slowly.

Sylas's jaw clenched, the only sign her little barb struck a soft spot. "I don't make a habit of leaving my partners behind."

"But I'm not your partner, am I? Just a rogue assassin who got caught by your agency and is being forced to do your dirty work." Darling let anger seep into her voice. God, it felt good to express an honest emotion. She leaned closer to him, the armrest of her seat digging into her side. She was within jabbing range. Her hands clenched, and she willed herself to remain calm.

Sylas narrowed his gaze. His whiskey eyes sparked with heat. Striations of chocolate brown blended with the lighter amber. "It's not my fault you got caught by the CIA. But I'll make damn sure it doesn't happen again. I didn't ask for this assignment, but I also don't leave my partners out to dry. Like it or not, for the next two days, we're in this together. So it will be my mission to guarantee you don't make any mistakes."

She wasn't the only one throwing verbal ammunition, and he hit her in the sensitive center of her self-doubt. It was Darling's fault she and Penny got caught. She was overly confident and careless with the druglord. If she had been sharper, she would have spotted the undercover CIA agents. She could have aborted the mission or been more subtle in her hit. The tweezers and dental floss were a flex, and she knew it. Now she was in this mess and letting her emotions saturate her reason. Unacceptable.

Darling took a calming breath but only inhaled his scent. Spice and leather. Her skin felt tight, and she was torn between wanting to smack his jaw or lick him like a cat. The stubble on his cheek would scratch against her softer skin and leave a trail of sensation both rough and sweet. Damn hormones. She forgot how quickly the heat of anger could amalgamate into something darker and more delicious. Sylas was reminding her.

"I think I should look over the dossier again." Darling pointedly muted her headphones. Retreat was sometimes the smartest move. Disappearing behind the dossier was her best option in the tight cabin. This forty-five minute flight to Sequim suddenly stretched into eternity.

Sequim Valley Airport boasted one runway, a full hangar, and no terminal. Their pilot helped Darling down the steps. Late July sun streaked across Darling's face, making her squint and shrug out of her suit-jacket.

Summer came late to Washington, but it came with passion.

The pilot shook Sylas's hand. "You have my number. Call me an hour prior to your desired departure and I'll have the plane ready and waiting for you."

Sylas nodded, then gallantly crooked his arm for Darling. She stared at him with eyebrows raised and mouth slightly open.

"Are you kidding?"

"We are a happily married couple, Darling. Shouldn't we act the part?"

"I can't tell if you're saying my name, or creating some pathetic term of endearment."

"You wound me, my little love muffin." He winked at her and showed off those beautiful teeth. His parents must have paid a fortune in orthodontia. No one's teeth were naturally that straight.

"I will wound you if you don't knock it off. Friendly fire is a real concern on this mission."

He snaked his arm around her before she could sidestep him. Steel-banded muscle flexed against her ribs as he pulled her into his solid chest. "If it appears like you hate me, people will notice. We don't want that, do we?" He leaned closer to her, his hand sliding up her back and settling between her shoulder blades. His palm was a large warm pressure pulling her closer to his mouth.

Holy shit-balls. He's moving in for a kiss.

But when his mouth was only a bullet's width away, he tilted his head and his lips nearly brushed her cheek. His breath tickled her ear. "Hate me if you must, but try to make it look like love, Darling. I'm sure it's not the first time you've lied to a man to get what you want."

Darling's hands pressed flat against his chest in an instinctively defensive gesture, but she let her right hand relax, skimming it over the impressive swell of his shoulders, her fingers teasing the tender skin where his firm jaw met a strong neck. His body hardened. He growled in her ear, a sound of animalistic approval. The answering quiver in her belly turned into a pool of heat, creating tingles in odd places. The backs of her knees. The arches of her feet. Her lips. She grabbed his ear in a vicious grip, twisting hard as she wrenched his head down. Clamping her free hand on the back of his neck to bend him over further, she shifted her weight onto her left leg and slammed her right knee into his stomach. His growl turned into a groan.

"I don't need to lie to get what I want. I take it. And I want *nothing* from you." Her body vehemently disagreed. Darling ignored the ache of need echoing through her and pushed Sylas's hunched body out of her way. She stiffened her back, straightened her shoulders and turned toward the rented Audi waiting in the gravel parking lot. "I'll drive."

Sylas recovered from her assault remarkably well. Most men would be pissed, or sulky. He appeared to be annoyingly chipper. Sitting in the passenger seat, he tapped his fingers on his knee to the beat of the radio.

Canada was only a two-hour ferry ride away and the station playing alternative rock was broadcasting from Victoria, BC.

"I guess you prove the theory right." Sylas's deep voice vibrated around Darling in the plush, leather-covered interior of the Audi.

He was baiting her. She wouldn't play his game. He wanted her to ask him to explain himself. She wouldn't.

"I mean, I always thought it was a coincidence, but after that ear twister, maybe they're onto something."

"Fine. I give. What are you talking about?" Irritation tightened like a vise against her temples. She was reminded of an unfortunate afternoon spent in an Italian basement with her head in an actual vise. Of course, her torturer ended the day with a switchblade in his throat, but he left her with a headache that lasted for weeks.

Sylas shifted his big body in the small space and angled toward her. "I knew you couldn't resist." When he smiled, his eyes lightened a shade, like amber struck by sunlight.

"Shut up. Never mind. I don't want to know."

His chuckle rumbled from deep within his chest. Darling never understood why cats purred until that very moment. She wanted to arch her back and rub against him. Which was ridiculous. Because she hated him.

"You want to know. Don't deny it. Or do. I'll tell you anyway." He cleared his throat dramatically and paused for effect. "The theory postulated by every woman I've ever been in a relationship with is that I drive them to violence. I have an innate ability to turn a sweet woman sour. On me, at least. One hundred percent of the time. It's actually pretty impressive accuracy."

Darling snorted. Then she tried to cover it with a cough. "Maybe it's your personality."

"That's a leading hypothesis. Feel free to add to the growing pile of evidence this weekend with your own experiments."

"You wouldn't survive my techniques." Darling winked before she could stop herself.

Double holy shit-balls. I'm flirting. With a CIA agent. Whom I hate. This has got to stop.

"And there it is. You just pressed your lips together and straightened your back. Like you remembered that fun is a threat to this mission." Sylas crossed his thick arms over an equally thick chest.

"It is. We need to focus, and this has to stop. I don't like you. And you don't like me." Darling said it as much to convince herself as Sylas.

"Well, you're half right. You definitely don't like me." He reached up and touched his ear.

"Okay, enough. Let's get back to the business of killing. Well, actually, I'll do all the killing. You stand around and chat with some rich politicians."

Sylas glared out the window and stayed silent long enough for Darling to glance at him. His profile was hard angles and sculpted planes. He could have been carved from marble and left brooding on a stone bench. Maybe she should stop poking the CIA agent. Except it was kind of fun.

"I meant what I said, Darling. We are partners on this mission. I won't leave you hanging." His voice was soft, but it carried in the confines of the car.

Darling swallowed. She swung her gaze back to the road. Trusting someone else was never wise. Penny was the only person she could count on to remain loyal to the end. A lesson painfully learned early in her career. "Let's go over the plan when we arrive. The wedding is happening at Green's Marsh tomorrow, with a cocktail party tonight to kick off the festivities."

"Affirmative. Green's Marsh is a huge farm backing up to the strait and owned by the senator. Or at least, his family. Old money, deep roots. Of course he went into politics." Sylas shook his head in disgust. Darling agreed with his sentiment. Deep pockets and powerful connections never guaranteed honorable leadership. Rich people wanted to stay rich. Powerful people wanted to stay powerful. Poor people never seemed to figure into the equation.

"We have to make the hit tonight, because the Russian delegate we're hoping to pin this on isn't going to stay for the wedding tomorrow." Darling tried to keep the strain from her voice. She was worried. She couldn't mess this up. She and Penny needed to be clear of this contract and back to controlling their destinies. She was already missing out on a perfect opportunity to eliminate a

Slovakian crime syndicate boss before he could raid any more orphanages to staff his prostitution ring.

"Security will be tight, but we've got a man on the inside with the catering crew. He will have already disabled the security cameras in the senator's office and be able to offer some assistance tonight, though it will be limited."

"It's a sprawling mansion." Darling could see the blueprints in her mind as if they were spread out before her. "The senator's office won't be open to the wedding guests. There should be enough privacy for me to eliminate the target with no collateral damage."

"I'll keep his security at bay, and you'll get him alone in his office."

Darling nodded. "The senator has been married for over thirty years, but he still likes to get his pickle tickled by pretty, young things. Hopefully I can work my seduction skills and entice him away from the crowd. If not, there's always threats and blackmail." The CIA provided Darling with several fairly graphic pictures of the senator during his last visit to the Kremlin. He was extremely naked with three underage ladies, a truckload of cocaine, and enough vodka to keep a sorority partying for a year.

"Don't worry. I doubt you'll need the pictures," Sylas murmured.

Heat climbed up Darling's neck and spread across her cheeks at the veiled compliment. Damn it. She was blushing. It was an unusual occurrence for her. Innocence and embarrassment had been replaced by cynicism and cunning a lifetime ago. Ten years of seeing and doing the worst things for the most honorable of reasons changed her from an idealistic young woman into a hardened assassin. Sometimes to kill monsters, you had to become one.

At thirty-one, Darling was too old and too wise to let Sylas's comments rush her back to a more innocent self.

"The cottage we're renting is only ten minutes from Green's Marsh, right?" Darling tightened her grip on the wheel and commanded her blood to retreat from her face.

Sylas laughed again, the warmth of it washing over her like water. "This town only has six thousand people in it. I would imagine it takes ten minutes to drive from one end to the other. So yeah. We're pretty close. We have it for the next two nights. If anyone checks, it looks like we're staying for the whole weekend. If things go well tonight, there won't be a wedding tomorrow, and we'll be on our way back to Seattle."

"If things don't go well, I'll be dead or arrested, and you can enjoy the area all by yourself. So win-win for you, hey?" Darling didn't miss how Sylas's jaw clenched. He really didn't want to be left out of the dirty work. She grudgingly admired his ideals, but intentions and actions often conflicted when someone's self-interest was at stake. If push came to shove, Sylas would follow his mission's directive and leave her to the wolves before risking his career, or his life. Maybe that was what was getting under his skin. Realization of his own compromise.

Darling followed the directions from the Audi's mapping system, which led them north, toward the water. They drove past lavender farms, fields dotted with cows, copses of pine, and three golf courses. White clouds chased each other in the cerulean sky, and while it was only in the seventies, it felt warmer. "People must like to golf around here," Darling mused aloud.

"Sequim is a retirement town. Lots of people with nothing better to do than swing their clubs. It's also the lavender capital of North America. There's a festival in July. Located in the rain shadow of the Olympic Mountains, it gets far more sun than most places on the Peninsula, earning it the title, 'Sunny Sequim.' "

"Aren't you full of useless trivia? Do you get paid by their tourism department?" Darling relaxed a fraction, grateful Sylas had shaken off his momentary melancholy. She may not like him, but she didn't want to see him miserable either.

"I like to do my research. Places. People. Partners. I come prepared."

Her momentary relief was replaced by alarm. Adrenaline spiked and her smile hardened into something sharper. "You researched me?"

"Looks like we're here." Sylas nodded his head toward a cottage with cedar shingles and white trim. The tidy little house could have been sitting on the coast of Maine instead of Washington. Crushed sea shells created the driveway, crunching under the tires. A porch wrapped around the entire cottage, creating a wide deck at the back, which faced the ocean. The day was clear, and Darling could see across the strait to Canada.

She clenched her teeth in frustration and parked the car. He wasn't getting off so easy. She needed to know what information the CIA had on her, and Sylas was going to tell her. He opened the door and briny sea air filled the car. Before she could demand an answer from him Sylas jumped out, ducking back in to snag his bag from the back seat.

"C'mon. We only have an hour before we're expected at the cocktail party. I call dibs on the shower first." Sylas winked at her. The nerve.

The house had several problems. One bathroom. One bedroom. One bed. In lieu of a couch, two plush armchairs sat facing a window overlooking the back deck and water views. Unless Darling wanted to sleep on the hardwood floor, she was going to have to share a bed with Sylas.

Blazing shit-balls in a bag. It was only one night. She could handle one night.

Sounds of the shower reached her in the kitchen. The house was under a thousand square feet, so privacy would be an issue. If she thought too hard in the kitchen, he would probably hear her in the bedroom. This might be the only time she could talk to Penny without a pesky eavesdropper.

Darling plugged in her phone and tapped on her recent calls. The phone only rang once.

"Hey, D. You doing okay? Survive the flight?" Penny yelled over the background noise of a bar.

"Yeah, I'm fine. Where are you?"

"Oh. Yeah. Well..." Penny's voice was suspiciously high.

"Penny, where are you? Better yet, who is with you?"

"Darling. Come on. It's happy hour and even CIA agents have to eat."

"You took her out? On a date? The enemy?" Darling tried to keep her voice low.

"Marilyn is not the enemy. She is a very nice woman with beautiful eyes, a great sense of humor, and an ass that is sheer magnificence."

"You are terrible. Really. The worst." Darling tried not to let the humor leak into her words. Penny fell often, hard, and usually for the wrong woman. Her love life followed the trajectory of an amusement park ride. Ups, downs, dips, turns, and often leaving her vacillating between exhilaration and nausea.

"Look, just because you refuse to engage in a game of nocturnal naughty-or-nice doesn't mean I have to strap on the old chastity belt."

"I could play naughty-or-nice if I wanted to." Darling's emotional hackles bristled at her friend's too-astute comment.

"Yes, but you never seem to want to. I wonder what that's all about," Penny said.

"Maybe it's the same reason you seem to only want to play games instead of engaging in a relationship that lasts longer than a bottle of milk." Offense was the best defense. Darling's weapons were far stronger than her shields.

"That's why I don't drink milk. Plus it's super-gross. I mean, really. Who wants to ingest breast milk designed to provide sustenance to a cow? We get freaked out when people over a year old drink human breast milk, but we're totally fine chugging cow breast milk well into old age? Why not cat milk? Or deer milk? It's madness." Penny was the only person who could stir Darling up, and calm her back down again. Or at least distract her with a long-winded argument examining milk's levels of disgustingness. "Listen, Darling, don't worry about me and Ms. ClAss-to-kill-for. How are you feeling about this mission?"

Darling huffed out a breath. "Not great. There's only one bed."

Penny drew in a dramatic gasp. "Oh my God. What will you do? How can you possibly survive such an unbearable situation?"

"Shut up. I'm just saying."

"So you have to share a bed with the guy. Big whoop. Unless he snores. Or you jump his bones in the middle of the night. Which is impossible because you'd have to find him attractive. And you hate the guy, right?"

"Hating someone and being attracted to someone are not mutually exclusive." Darling immediately regretted her honesty. But if she couldn't tell Penny what swirled and spun in her brain, she would go crazy.

"Oh. My. God. You *are* attracted to him? Darling, do you know what this means?"

"That I'm an idiot."

"No. That your lady-bits haven't actually atrophied from lack of use. I thought for sure you were turning into a modern murdering nun."

"Fuck off."

"Now, now. What would mother superior say about such language?" Penny dissolved into giggles.

"I'm hanging up now. You've been a big help. Really."

"Hey, Darling, in all seriousness...maybe this is a good thing. Peter-the-douche happened years ago. It's time to move on to bigger and better things. And when I say bigger, I mean his junk. And when I say better, I mean your sex life. Just to be clear."

"It's a good thing I love you, Penny."

"You're the only one."

The shower turned off, and Darling could hear Sylas moving around in the bathroom. "I gotta go. Please be careful with Agent Sexy-Ass. Your heart is far more fragile than you seem to realize."

"Yeah, yeah. And maybe you could stand to be a little bit careless with Double-O-Smolder-Pants. A fling isn't going to kill you."

Darling ended the call as the bathroom door opened. Sylas emerged, wearing a towel slung low around his hips.

Daaayyyuuum.

He had muscles Darling had only seen on movie stars. Her mouth went dry, moisture flooding to other, lower regions of her anatomy.

"Shower's free if you want to jump in." Sylas smirked at her. He knew she was staring. The jerk probably left his clothes in the bedroom on purpose. Sneaky, smoking-hot, ripped as sin, infuriating man.

Darling was quick in the shower but spent some time with her makeup. She didn't usually wear a lot of cosmetics, but this mission required her to make an impression on the senator. She slicked on dark red lipstick, shimmering eyeshadow, and a hint of color on her cheeks. By the time she exited the bathroom in a simple black cocktail dress, Sylas had found slacks and a shirt. Thank god.

"Wow. You clean up nice, Darling." He did a slow sweep from her prized Jimmy Choo stilettos to her hard-won casual upsweep. It was ridiculous that a hairstyle designed to appear careless took so much time and effort. It didn't help that Darling's black curls were as dense and tangled as the vines in an Amazonian jungle.

"Thanks. You don't look awful either." She tried to keep her eyes from wandering, but holy hot peppers on a flaming grill, the man could fill out a pair of slacks. His dress shirt covered all the muscles she'd seen in tantalizing clarity after his shower, but she knew they were there. Rippling and bunching under his shirt every time he moved. Highly distracting.

"I'll take that as a compliment. Now, take off your dress."

"I'm sorry, what?" Darling's eyes widened and tingles reappeared in those odd places where her skin was most sensitive.

"I need to mic you up. I've already done me. With only two of us on this mission, we need to make certain we can communicate when you're in the office and I'm distracting security." Sylas lifted his left eyebrow. "What? You thought I had other intentions?"

"No," Darling responded quickly. Too quickly.

"I am a professional, Darling."

"Yes. Of course."

"And as a professional, I solemnly swear to keep my hands and eyes focused on the parts of you needing to be wired. Although I must warn you we usually hide the pack on women in their bras. I'm not trying to get fresh, I just want to prepare you." He pulled a small transmitter pack and earpiece from his pocket.

Darling took a shallow breath. "Um...I'm not wearing one." She turned so he could see the back of her halter dress. Or more accurately, the backlessness of her halter dress.

"Right." Sylas cleared his throat, and Darling noticed his hands were less steady than before. "Your underwear, then?" His voice deepened with a defined rasp.

"Okay. Maybe we can hook it in the back so the skirt covers it?"

"Yeah. Sure. You want to..." Sylas handed her the transmitter and kept his eyes focused on the ceiling as she flipped up her skirt and twisted awkwardly to clip the transmitter to her lace G-string.

"Nice hardware."

Darling whipped her head around and caught Sylas admiring her thighs. Or the snub-nose thirty-six strapped high on her right leg and the switchblade attached to her left. "You said you would keep your eyes focused on the parts needing to be wired."

"I did say that. Yes. But then you pulled up your skirt, and I realized I would be remiss if I didn't inventory exactly what weaponry you're taking into this mission. As your partner, and for purely professional reasons, I had to look."

Darling didn't want to smile. It would only encourage his behavior. But his expression killed her. A smile of wide innocence undermined by eyes gleaming with trouble. "You are terrible."

"And you are dangerous. I pity the idiot who crosses you."

"That may be the nicest thing a man has ever said to me."

Sylas's smile faltered. "Really?"

Darling's internal alarm bells began ringing. She didn't mean to reveal anything so close to the truth.

"A man's never told you that you're beautiful? Or wicked smart? Or funny?"

She wanted to shrug off his words as a joke, but his voice echoed with earnest disbelief. Meaningless repartee had become treacherous as they danced dangerously close to honesty. "No. Of course not. Men pay me compliments all the time. I was just...never mind. We should go."

"When you lie, your left shoulder hitches up. Just slightly."

"I'm not lying," Darling lied.

"Sure. Of course." Sylas offered his arm to her. His smile returned, but his eyes no longer sparked with mischief. They darkened with something more intense. "You deserve to hear real compliments. But I guess you do. All the time. Shall we?"

It would be petty not to oblige him, so Darling rested her hand lightly on his arm, noting the hardness beneath the smooth fabric of his shirt. He smelled like spice, leather, and sin. Maybe Penny was right. Would it kill her to indulge in a little harmless canoodling with a man who said she deserved to be complimented? Quite possibly.

Chapter Three

Darling let Sylas drive to Green's Marsh. Mostly because it would spark comments if the patriarchal idiots attending the cocktail party saw a woman driving; the same morons who would raise their brows at a black man marrying a white woman. Money couldn't buy intelligence, but it could fund careers and swanky parties. Darling swallowed her anger and focused on the mission ahead.

The senator's farm was protected by miles of fencing. They had to show identification at the gates. Hers was a driver's license for one Diane Jones. Darling would have killed in high school for a fake ID as realistic as the license she flashed for Diane Jones. Of course now, it was the fake ID that helped her kill. She controlled her impulse to laugh as the guard glared at her identification.

Once admitted, they drove along a gravel road flanked by ancient oak trees on either side. Eventually, they came to a massive circular drive and passed a carriage house large enough to fit three of Darling's apartments within its white walls. But that was nothing compared to the main house. A uniformed valet waited at the steps of a grand stone staircase. He helped Darling out before he drove the car away to a separate parking area.

"Jesus. This place is massive." Darling tilted her head back to take in the six huge columns spanning the front of the three-story mansion. An east and west wing extended on either side of the house, and the stone steps led up to the expansive porch. Servants waited at the front doors with trays of champagne glasses.

Sylas offered his arm once more, and Darling leaned against him as they traversed the stairs. She took a crystal flute of champagne and amped up the wattage of her smile as she looked up at Sylas. Clinking her glass against his, she leaned closer to murmur in his ear. "Here's to a successful evening, Mr. Simon Jones."

"Here's to never treating my partner like laundry, Mrs. Diane Jones."

Darling quirked her brow in a silent question.

"Never leaving you out to dry." Sylas's lips curved into a smile and his whiskey eyes glinted.

Darling laughed in spite of herself. She sipped her champagne as they followed the sounds of music and voices.

The "intimate" cocktail party of family and close friends to the bride and groom numbered nearly three hundred people. Given the beautiful weather and long days, the party spilled from a large ballroom out onto a massive stone deck and down a double stairway to the perfectly landscaped garden. Though it was six in the evening, the sun shone bright in the sky, sunset still hours away. A white tent invited partygoers to freshen their drinks at the open bar. Finely dressed guests snacked on canapés, crab-stuffed pastries, caviar, lobster, and an endless variety of treats being circulated by uniformed serving staff. A dance floor was constructed within the tent, and couples spun around in graceful circles to a string quartet playing a mixture of classic waltzes and more popular hits.

Darling and Sylas spent the first hour surveying the crowd, learning the lay of the land, and homing in on the senator.

"Darling, shall we dance?" Sylas glanced meaningfully at the group of couples dancing. He had an advantage of using her real name without betraying the alias she'd been given. Anyone who overheard Sylas would assume it was a term of endearment.

Darling followed his gaze and saw the senator and his wife moving sedately across the floor. "That sounds lovely, love muffin." She raised an eyebrow and smiled. "Dare I hope you know *how* to dance?"

Sylas took her hand and swept her onto the floor. He created a solid frame with one arm gripping her waist and the other holding her hand out. It was startlingly vulnerable to have her arms spread wide, her body not quite touching his, but close enough to feel the heat emanating from his chest. She had danced before, but never with a man who created such a storm of reaction within her.

"You said you liked to research. So what did you find out about me?" Her heart raced as he led her into a smooth waltz. She shouldn't have worried about his skills on the dance floor. His athletic frame moved with the grace of a classically trained dancer.

"What do you think?" He leaned closer to her, his breath whispering over her cheek.

"I don't know. Probably not anything good." Darling hated how fear crawled up from her chest, wrapping around her throat. The past was behind her. It shouldn't have the power to hurt her now. It shouldn't matter if he knew the sordid details of her history. She didn't care what he thought about her. But there were crimes buried deep. If uncovered, they would be another link in the chain binding her to this government contract. One job might be turned into more with the proper leverage.

"I found a girl who was brave. Fearless. An orphan put into foster care at twelve, only to be removed a few years later when reports of abuse surfaced." His hand glided up her back and stroked down again, creating a soothing contrast to his words as they ripped open old wounds.

"The reports never went anywhere. My foster father was never formally accused of a crime."

"And his other child, the one he legally adopted, was never removed from the home. But you kept in touch with her. Penny? Your partner?" He gave a gentle push against her hip and extended an arm, spinning her into a perfect twirl before pulling her body back against his.

"I thought you were my partner." Darling tried to laugh, but her throat squeezed too tight to exhale and her mind still spun from the dance or memories long buried.

"I am. Tonight, I'm your partner." He pressed his hand against the small of her back. His thumb made slow, distracting circles she could feel through the silk of her dress.

"Is that all you found out?"

"No. Your foster father disappeared. Right around the time you turned eighteen. When you left the group home."

"You can't stay after your eighteenth birthday. Even if I was in foster care, they would have removed me." Darling wished she hadn't asked him what he knew.

"Your foster father somehow got around that rule with Penny. Interesting, isn't it? He went out for drinks one night with his buddies, but didn't return. They found his car abandoned in the woods, twenty miles from the bar. His body was never recovered. The police investigated, but couldn't turn up any leads." He breathed the words against her temple. Anyone watching would assume they were love words whispered from husband to wife, and not the ugly truths of her past being spilled onto the floor like black waters from a fetid pond.

"He liked to drink too much. Maybe he wandered off into the woods to take a piss and found himself a bear instead. There's a lot of wilderness in the Pacific Northwest. Easy for people to get lost." Darling kept her voice steady while her heart pounded. Sylas leaned her back against the strength of his arm in a daringly low dip.

Darling gripped his shoulder as he pulled her upright. Without a pause, he deftly led her in complicated steps, guiding her around other dancers as he spoke. "Then Penny moved in with you, and a few years later you started a consulting company for 'businesses seeking fiscal efficiency and profit enhancement.' "

"That's what the business license reads." She tried to keep the strain from her voice.

"You had a third partner. Peter Snell. He left the business five years ago. He disappeared from the Seattle area but is listed as a silent partner. Still receives a third of your profits. That seems odd." Sylas's words were clipped.

Darling pulled away from him to see his face. She wanted to read the expression in his eyes. He seemed angry. Odd that of all the information he discovered about her, it was Peter who struck a chord of angst within Sylas.

She didn't owe him an explanation, but she offered one anyway. "Information is often more valuable than money. Peter knows a lot of things. It's easier to pay him off than deal with the fallout. Money isn't everything. But freedom is."

Peter took her money, broke her heart, and reminded her that trusting the wrong person invited destruction and misery. A lesson she needed to review as she struggled not to become lost in the varying chocolate and amber of Sylas's eyes.

She was free of Peter now, except for the check she cut him every month. A price she happily paid to keep the lying bastard far away from Seattle. "Look, I would appreciate you keeping any theories you have about my foster father to yourself. I'm paying my dues with this contract, but I don't need any more debt to the government. Penny and I have worked hard to control our own company. Our own future."

Sylas spun her away from him again, then tugged her back. His proper dance frame disintegrated as he held her flush to his body. Sylas's hard chest pressed against her soft breasts. His right thigh nudged between her legs as they stepped in time to the music. The sinews and muscles of his body flexed and strained against her as he glided them across the floor. For a mad moment, firm lips nibbled her neck before he pulled away. "I would never take your freedom from you. Or your power. You have a right to control your own destiny. I respect that. I respect you."

"You don't know me." Darling wanted to lean into him. To let him bear her weight for a moment. To borrow some of his strength.

"I know about you. I'd like to know you. I'd like you to know me. And hopefully not be inspired to acts of violence from the effects of my personality." His chuckle vibrated out from his chest and into hers, dissipating the tension. Allowing her to share his joy.

The music paused, and they separated to clap politely.

"Although," Sylas leaned down to murmur in her ear, "I might be inspired to a few acts of violence against this Peter character. Just saying."

Darling couldn't stop the burst of laughter that she quickly muffled by covering her mouth. They had been ensconced in their own personal bubble that popped when the music stopped. Scanning the crowd, she noticed the senator and his wife were only one couple away.

Glancing back at Sylas, she nodded. Back to the business of killing.

Sylas escorted her toward the senator and his wife. He tapped the gentleman on his shoulder. "Excuse me, sir, I'm a friend of your daughter's fiancé. My name is Simon Jones. My wife and I flew in from New York, and we are so honored to be here to celebrate this wonderful occasion."

Darling smiled and forced a throaty laugh as she extended her hand to the senator. "Pleasure to meet you both." She kept her eyes focused on the senator and executed a well-practiced smoldering gaze as she squeezed his pudgy fingers.

"May I steal your beautiful wife for a spin on the dance floor?" Sylas was all charm and finesse. He lifted the senator's wife's hand to his mouth and pressed a gallant kiss to her knuckles.

"Please, call me Karen. Any friend of Thomas's is a friend of the family. He is such a sweet young man. We couldn't be happier with our daughter's choice." The senator's wife gushed the words, and her cheeks grew pink with pleasure at Sylas's lingering kiss. Karen was pushing sixty but had the well-kept skin of someone professionally pampered on a regular basis. Darling hated to think how much taxpayer dollars were funding her esthetician bill.

Karen's flowing, pale lavender gown showed off her trim figure and surgically enhanced cleavage. In comparison, the senator was not aging well. His eyes bagged with fatigue or excess alcohol. An expensive suit, tailored to perfection, didn't hide the paunch overflowing his belt. Feather-thin hair was sprayed into an aggressive comb-over that highlighted rather than hid his bald spot. The fact he was schtupping other women when his own wife was so far out of his aesthetic league only highlighted the draw of power and money.

"Simon, I'm sure the senator would prefer to dance with his own wife." Darling angled her body slightly so her hip pressed against the senator's. She rested her hand lightly on the senator's arm. It was like touching a raw ball of dough left too long in the proofing drawer.

"Nonsense. Poor Karen has put up with both of my left feet all evening. It would be the pinnacle of her night to dance with someone who isn't stepping all over her shoes." The senator smiled at his wife while his hand found its way to the small of Darling's back and headed determinedly southward. Lovely. Darling had to school her features into a pleasant smile to avoid gagging.

Sylas thanked the senator and swept his wife onto the dance floor. Darling could hear Karen's delighted giggle as Sylas dipped her. She could also hear Sylas's voice in her earpiece as he complimented Karen's graceful dance steps.

"Perhaps you could show me more of your lovely home? I'm working on renovating our apartment, but I don't have the style and taste to match a place as stunning as this. I promised Simon I'd create an office space for him, but I'm hopeless with masculine touches." Darling leaned forward enough to deepen the senator's view of her cleavage. She glanced back at Sylas, meeting his gaze across the dance floor. He could hear her as clearly as she heard him. Having Sylas's voice in her head and knowing he was listening to every word she spoke was disconcertingly intimate.

The senator pulled her focus back to the task at hand. "My pleasure. I would love to show you some of the more private spaces. I'm sorry. I missed your name. Or should I just call you 'Beauty'?"

Barf-o-rama.

Darling faked a giggle. "Hardly that!" She tapped him playfully on the arm as he escorted her away from the tent and toward the house. Two security guards fell in step behind them. "I had no idea a cocktail party could be so dangerous." She looked pointedly over her shoulder at one of the guards.

"Don't mind them, my dear. Hazards of being rich and powerful. Never can be too careful."

"I hope you aren't worried about me causing harm. I can't even squish a spider. I make Simon do it for me." She giggled and leaned her body against the senator as he guided them through the house, toward an internal staircase on the western wing. "I've always found powerful men to be so attractive. There's something quite virile about wielding that much responsibility. Simon is a wonderful husband, but I sometimes wish for an older man who is a little wiser in the ways of the world. I suppose you get that all the time." Darling lowered her tone to a breathy purr.

Sylas's rough voice crackled through the tiny earpiece hidden by her hair. "Dance is over. I'm making my way to the house. I'm right here if you need me. You're laying it on a little thick with the senator, wouldn't you say?"

Darling smiled, letting the senator think it was for him.

"Gentleman, I think I'll be quite safe with this one. Stay here." The senator glared at his security then unlocked the door to his study, ushering Darling into the darkened room. "I believe you'll find the masculine touches in here quite something." He leaned close to her ear, and his damp breath brought a shiver of revulsion she disguised as desire.

When the door shut behind them, Darling was ready.

The senator wasted no time pushing her against the wall and clamping his pudgy hands over her breasts. He mashed his mouth against hers. Darling fumbled with her skirt. Her gun didn't have a silencer, it made the weapon too bulky under her clothes. With two guards standing directly outside the door, it would have to be the knife.

She pulled the blade free and turned her head away from the senator's sloppy kiss. Shoving him hard, she gained space. This man was selling out American operatives in Russia. Men and women died because of the information he willingly handed over in return for money and favors. She arced the knife through the air, slicing a clean line across his throat.

His eyes widened. He opened his mouth to scream, but the sound came out as a wet gargle. Stumbling backward, the senator slapped a hand over his gushing throat and fell hard against the desk. A Tiffany lamp toppled over, slamming against the floor and smashing into a thousand pieces of broken glass.

Shitty-shitting bloody blazing shit-balls.

"What's going on? Do you need help?" Sylas was in her ear, but Darling didn't have time to respond. She barely had time to spin around. The security guards burst through the office door. She dropped down and threw her knife. The blade landed in the first guard's forearm. He dropped his gun and grabbed his wounded arm.

The easiest option would be to pull her gun and shoot both of the men, but that would blow her cover and bring a crowd. Cursing her poor luck, Darling swiped a paperweight from the senator's desk and hurled it at the second guard, catching him in the temple. She leapt for him, grabbing his nine millimeter by the barrel and twisting hard, breaking his hold on the weapon. The first guard pulled the knife free and fumbled for his gun. She put the second guard into a chokehold, angling his body to be a human shield. She couldn't take out both guards without being discovered.

"I'm fucked. Get out of here," she told Sylas.

"We're not going anywhere." The second guard gasped as she increased the pressure on his windpipe. He misunderstood. He thought she was talking to them. That she was alone.

Maybe the guard was right. If Sylas was smart and followed orders, he would exit the party, call the pilot, and be on a flight out of there before the senator's blood congealed. And Darling would be alone.

She stiffened her back and pressed her lips together. She was used to being alone.

"If you shoot me, you'll end up hitting your buddy," Darling said to the first guard, using her only bargaining chip.

The first guard held his gun steady despite the blood dripping from his arm onto the carpet. The cleaning crew was going to have a helluva time getting all those bloodstains out of the senator's rug.

"The thing is," the guard said with a shrug, his gun shifting with the movement, "I don't even know that guy." He smiled and pulled the trigger three times. The silencer chirped like an angry bird. Darling felt the impact of the bullets hit the man she was holding. He turned into dead weight, and she was forced to let him go or be dragged to the floor with him.

Motherfu...

Another bird chirped behind her. The first guard's head snapped back. He fell to the ground. She turned around slowly, and Sylas lowered his gun.

"You're still here." Shock flavored her words. Disbelief and hope mingled, creating a confusing blend of light and dark within her. He stayed. With her. She wasn't alone.

"Of course I am. We're partners."

Darling let out a shaky laugh. "Yeah. That's what you said. Partners."

Sylas pulled her closer on the dance floor, and they swayed to the strains of "Halo" from the string quartet. For a brilliant moment, she gave into temptation and sunk into him, marveling at how easily he held her, as though she were weightless.

"Did you slip your knife into the Russian's pocket?" He crooned against her ear, then nuzzled her neck.

Darling was quite breathless. "Yes. Did you get our inside man to plant the gun in the Russian's room?"

"Already done. I'm all over it." Sylas's hand drifted lower on her back.

"You're all over me." Darling brushed her lips against his stubbled cheek and savored the rasp.

"I think we're about ten minutes away from his body being discovered. Wanna get outta here before this party goes downhill?" Sylas nibble his way up her neck and bit her earlobe.

Darling's belly filled with sparkling fireflies. She moaned softly. "I think, maybe...yes."

Sylas took her hand, and they passed the soon-to-be bride and groom swaying together on the dance floor. They were a beautiful couple.

Darling stumbled. It wasn't fair. The senator's daughter didn't deserve to have her wedding ruined, to face the gruesome death of her father, on what should be a night full of hope and promise. She tightened her grip on Sylas's hand.

"It's not your fault," Sylas whispered.

"I know." Darling's words tasted like ash. "But she doesn't deserve to suffer because of her father's sins."

"Neither do all the other men and women he was selling out. Her pain tonight is one more crime heaped on the senator's plate. This is his fault. Not yours."

Darling leaned into Sylas. "I know."

"But you still feel responsible. You're not." His deep voice washed over her, the benediction of a fellow warrior. What they did was cruel, and terrible, and necessary. Sylas understood that.

While they waited for the valet to bring their car around, Sylas wrapped his arms around Darling, pulling her back against his chest. She closed her eyes and rested her head on his shoulder, feeling the bobby pins from her casual up-do pressing against her scalp. Lifting her chin, she gave him access to the vulnerable curve of her neck. Sylas didn't waste the opportunity, pressing his firm lips against her wildly beating pulse.

"So, Sylas, do you snore?"

Sylas's lips curved against the sensitive flesh of her neck in a smile she felt, but couldn't see. "No. Why?"

"There's only one bed. Which wouldn't be a problem as long as you don't snore, and I don't jump your bones in the middle of the night."

"Huh. Well, thank goodness you have no intention of jumping my bones, and I don't snore. No problem, right?" Sylas tightened his arms around her.

"Oh no." Darling turned within the circle of his embrace to face him. "It's going to be a big problem." She pulled his head down and pressed her lips against his, testing the seam of his mouth with her tongue. Breathing his air.

Sylas gripped her hips, pulling her close. "I've never been scared to tackle a problem head-on." He covered her mouth with soft kisses, then delved deeper, tangling his tongue with hers, biting her bottom lip hard enough to heighten her pleasure with a hint of pain.

"I have a new theory about you inspiring acts of violence," Darling sighed.

"I'm intrigued." Sylas voice was a hungry rasp.

"Maybe the women you dated couldn't channel all that energy."

"But you can?"

Darling smiled. "We're going to find out."

The valet arrived with their car.

"You drive." Sylas winked at Darling.

"Penny's going to be pissed." Darling shook her head.

"Why?" Sylas asked.

"She's used to being my only partner in crime."

Sylas's laughter filled the car as Darling drove into the warm summer night.

Melee McGuire is a high school counselor who grew up in New Zealand but happily settled in the Pacific Northwest six years ago. She has a short story published in an anthology of Pacific Northwest authors, and her writing won the mystery category of the Pacific Northwest Writers Association in 2017, was a finalist in the romance category in 2019, and is a finalist in Contemporary Romance's 2020 Stiletto Competition. Melee is actively seeking an agent for her new book, *The Assassin's Guide to Internet Dating* and is working hard to make her dreams of becoming a full-time writer come true. She loves writing about fierce female assassins who dodge bullets, but never seem to escape Cupid's Arrow.

Connect with Melee: While Melee has accounts on multiple medias, she is most active on Instagram. Please feel free to follow her on the following accounts:

Instragram: meleemcguire

Twitter: @MeleeMcGuire

Facebook: Melee McGuire

Love Unexpected

A Wilding Point Romance Short

by

Joleen James

Chapter One

The Rehearsal Dinner

"When did you say Sean's family is arriving?"

Julia Sterling opened the French doors in her bedroom to let the salt air in. Ah, July, warm beach weather. She loved this time of year, the sun, longer days, summer sunsets. She inhaled deeply before walking to her daughter, Kate, who sat at Julia's vanity table, fussing with her hair. Julia smiled. Kate. Her beautiful girl, getting married tomorrow. She'd always known this day would come, but she'd thought Kate would be older, not a tender twenty-four.

"I think Sean's dad is here now." Kate set the comb down. "His mom comes in around four. Sean is going to pick her up and meet us at the restaurant."

"Got it," Julia said. She knew from Kate that Sean's parents barely tolerated each other since their divorce. She hoped for the kids' sake that the parents could put their differences aside for the wedding. At least Sean had both of his parents. There was definitely a void in her family. She placed a hand on Kate's shoulder. "I wish Daddy could see you now."

Kate's eyes filled with tears. "Me, too. I miss him so much."

Julia hugged Kate, her own heart heavy in her chest. It had been a year since Robert had passed away, the cancer, brutal and unforgiving, eating away at him until he had nothing left to give.

"Your dad would be so proud of you." Julia smoothed her daughter's thick, dark hair. "Look at you. A college grad. You've started your own business at twenty-four. You're in the process of buying a condo. You are getting married." Julia smiled. "You've made us proud, honey." She passed Kate a tissue.

Kate blotted her eye makeup. "Thanks, Mom." She blew out a breath. "No more getting emotional, okay? It's ruining my makeup. Let's enjoy the weekend. My wedding weekend!"

"Deal." Julia checked her own reflection in the mirror. Wanting to lighten their conversation, she said, "Can you help me do something with my hair?"

Kate laughed. "You know I can." She stood, then pushed Julia into the chair at the vanity table. "And maybe a touch more makeup than you usually wear? I mean you always look great, Mom, but I can make you shine."

"Okay," Julia conceded, "maybe just this once." She was a mascara and lip gloss person. No fuss. Her shoulder-length dark hair was thick and straight, and she wore it pulled back in a low ponytail most of the time. She knew she was a little too boho for her daughter, but that amused Julia. What was wrong with natural beauty?

Julia's eyes closed as Kate dragged the brush through her hair. She'd hold this special moment with Kate close to her heart. Things were changing between them. Soon, Kate would have a husband, someone other than Julia to lean on. Julia liked that Kate had someone special, someone she loved.

"Thank you, Mom," Kate said, meeting Julia's eyes in the vanity mirror. "For the wedding."

The melancholy in her daughter's tone caused Julia to swivel around. "You're welcome, Kate. I've dreamed of this day as much as you have. You only get married once."

"I hope so," Kate said, and Julia sensed hesitation.

"You're certain Sean is the one?" Julia asked. "If you're not sure—"

"I'm sure," Kate said with confidence. "Really, Mom. I'm just feeling sentimental. I keep thinking about Dad. You were happy, right?"

"Of course we were," Julia said, the lie bitter on her tongue. "Why would you ask?"

"Not many parents stay married, not as long as you and Dad did," Kate said. "It seems the odds are stacked against me and Sean, but I love him so much, I'll fight the odds to be with him. He's everything to me."

Julia prayed Kate's love for Sean would last a lifetime, but deep down, she knew that love faded, that people made mistakes. Mistakes Kate would never know about. Mistakes Julia would take to her grave.

"Come on now," Julia said, her tone much happier than her sudden flashback to a time she didn't want to remember. "Finish my hair. Make me pretty."

"I love you, Mom," Kate said as she resumed brushing.

"I love you, too, baby. So much."

Ben Delano hated crowds, tight places, and weddings. He paused outside the restaurant where his son, Sean's, wedding rehearsal dinner was being held, waiting for his daughter, Madison, to exit the car.

Dellinger's On The Point. The place looked expensive. He'd agreed to pay for the rehearsal dinner, and he was happy to do so, but a gathering like this made him uneasy in his skin. He loved Sean, would do anything for his son, so he'd shed his usual jeans and T-shirt, trading his old friends for charcoal gray slacks and a light blue button-down shirt, that Madison had told him "made his blue eyes 'pop,'" whatever that meant.

"Come on, Dad," Madison said. She linked her arm through his. "You can do this. Take a deep breath of the clean salt air." She inhaled, then exhaled. "I love the scent of the beach. There's nothing like it."

"Sure there is," he said as they made their way inside. "How about the smell of the river?"

"I guess." She shrugged. "Different scent, more of a fresh-water smell, for the lack of a better way to describe it. This place smells like possibility to me. River water smells like Montana."

Man, he hated to hear her say that. He was losing both of his kids to the Pacific Northwest. Montana was his home, their home, where they were born and raised. Lately, he'd done nothing but think about what his life would be like if both Sean and Madison stayed in the Seattle area.

His life would be sad, pathetic, lonely.

Inside the restaurant now, he scanned for his son, wondering if they'd beat Sean and Amanda here. Parts of this wedding weekend would be endured. Seven years had passed since he'd caught Amanda in bed with one of her co-workers. The bitter divorce that followed, and the effect it had had on their kids, had left him irritated and on edge when it came to his ex-wife. She wasn't his favorite and the kids knew it, even though he worked hard to keep his sour feelings to himself.

"I see Mom," Madison said with excitement.

She tugged on his arm, leading him into what appeared to be a private banquet room on his right.

"Mom," Madison cried, waving.

"Honey," Amanda said, her eyes lighting with pleasure. She broke away from the circle of people she'd been chatting with and walked to meet her daughter. Her blond hair was up in a high ponytail, her makeup perfect, her lips that sexy shade of pink she liked. Amanda was a beauty, a fact she never let him forget. Men loved her.

"Hi, honey." Amanda hugged Madison. "I've missed you."

"I've missed you too, Mom." Madison leaned back to look at her mother. "You look great."

"I feel great," Amanda said, the words full of energy.

Ben was struck by the resemblance between the two women, both blondes and beautiful.

Amanda brought her attention to him. "Ben. Hello."

She stepped forward, giving him no option but to hug her.

She smelled the same, like jasmine. He waited for a jolt of lust, but none came. He really was over her. He smiled perfunctorily. "How are you, Amanda?"

"Great. Fantastic," she said, but her tone told him otherwise.

"Good." He knew her well enough to know when she was lying. She was playing a part right now. Something she did well.

"Dad," Sean said, joining them. "Come with me. You have to meet Kate's mom."

"Sure," Ben said, glad to make his exit. "Excuse me."

"Of course," Amanda said coolly before turning to Madison and saying, "There's an open bar. Let's get a drink, shall we?"

Ben followed Sean. His son, unlike his daughter, looked just like him, with dark hair, blue eyes. Well, his own hair wasn't exactly dark now, but more silver. It sucked getting old.

"Kate's mom and grandparents are over there." Sean pointed to a group of people.

Ben found Kate easily, then moved on to the woman standing beside her. Whoa. That was Kate's mom? They looked like sisters. She wore a short-sleeved midnight blue dress that hugged her body in all the right places, and strappy high-heeled sandals that instantly reminded him he wasn't dead inside.

"Kate," Sean called as they approached.

Both Kate and her mother turned.

Kate smiled. "Mom, this is Sean's dad, Ben Delano. Ben, my mother, Julia Sterling."

Julia extended her hand. "Nice to meet you."

"You, too," Ben said. Her hand was soft in his, her grip firm.

"You're going to be in-laws," Kate said with delight. "How great is that?"

"It's pretty great," Julia said, laughing. "Right, Ben?"

He had the feeling she was humoring her over-enthusiastic daughter. He grinned. "Sounds good to me."

"You two have so much in common," Kate said. "Mom owns a store too."

"Really," Ben said, finding Julia Sterling more interesting by the minute. "What kind of store?"

"Home décor," Julia replied. "You?"

"Outdoor sporting goods," he told her. "It's called Delano's Outdoor. "

"Mine is Sterling's Home Décor." She smiled again.

Something inside Ben shifted, as if he was making room for her near his heart. "Can I get you a drink? I'm buying." He winked.

She chuckled. "Yes, you certainly are."

He didn't miss the amused look Sean and Kate shared. Did they think it was funny that their parents were flirting? Or were they slightly repulsed? He didn't care what they thought.

On the way to the bar Julia introduced him to her parents, and to her late husband's mother. They also said hello to several more relatives, but Ben couldn't remember any of their names when they finally ordered their drinks: a white wine for Julia, a beer for him.

"I'm sure this is a little overwhelming for you," Julia said. She sipped her wine.

"I'll admit I'm a bit of a hermit," Ben said. "Sweet Rose, Montana, is a small town. Not many surprises there, or strangers. And don't get me started on the traffic here."

"Believe it or not, Wilding Point is considered a small town." She fiddled with the stem of the wine glass.

He remembered the softness of her hand and shifted in his seat. "You're kidding?"

"Nope." She smiled again. "Can you believe our kids are getting married?"

"Seems like they were just born," Ben said, a sudden sharp longing for those early years with Sean filling him. "I'm not sure I'm liking the empty nest thing."

"Me either," she said wistfully. "I knew it would happen, but I guess I thought I'd be older."

He wondered how old she was. Late forties? Younger than his fifty-two years, for sure. He wracked his brain trying to remember what Sean had told him about Julia's late husband. He'd been an attorney. He'd died of cancer. He'd left her pretty well-to-do. Had her marriage been a great love story?

"Mom."

Kate came toward them. "Time to take our seats. Both of you are at the head table."

"Lead the way," Julia said, wine glass in hand.

Ben followed the ladies. At the table he was disappointed to see he and Julia were separated by several people. Ben made the best of it, talking with the grandparents, the best man, all while keeping one eye on Julia Sterling.

Julia took a bite of key lime pie, Kate's favorite dessert. She glanced up to find Ben watching her—again. He gave her a small smile, a smile that warmed her all over. Wow. What was happening here? She couldn't remember the last time any man had caught her eye. Why hadn't Kate mentioned how handsome he was? And those eyes—so blue, like the shade of aqua found only in pool water.

"Did you hear me, Mom?" Kate asked.

"I'm sorry, what?" Julia said, embarrassed to be caught daydreaming.

"I reminded you that hair and makeup start at 9 a.m. tomorrow," Kate said.

"I know, honey. I remember." Julia indulged in more pie. "This dessert is great."

"Delicious," Kate agreed. "It's so awesome that Sean's dad sprung for this place. It's my favorite on the waterfront."

"Yes," Julia agreed. Everything was first class. The perfect kickoff to the wedding weekend. A waiter stopped by and refilled her coffee. "Thank you."

Toasts had been made. People were finishing up their dessert and coffee. Some were up and moving about the room, visiting.

"Where are Sean's parents staying?" Julia asked, suddenly wanting to know more about the Delanos.

"The Marriott," Kate said.

Julia thought that Ben would probably hate the sterile hotel environment. However, Amanda would probably love the amenities there. It was hard to imagine Ben and Amanda ever being married. They were so different—Ben simple and humble, Amanda bigger than life, flashy. Julia wondered if people had thought that she and Robert had been wrong for each other. If they had, they would have been right.

She'd been the last one to realize how truly wrong for her that Robert had been.

"I'm going make my rounds," Julia said to Kate. "Looks like people are getting ready to leave."

"Me, too." Kate pushed back in her chair.

They rose and separated. Julia went to each guest and made small talk. She escorted the grandparents to their cars. She made her good-byes until the only people left were Sean, Ben, Amanda, Madison, Kate, and herself.

Ben was settling the bill when Amanda approached her.

"It was a wonderful dinner," Amanda said.

"Yes, a big thank-you to you and Ben," Julia said. "Tonight was perfect and so generous."

"Of course," Amanda said. "We would have it no other way."

"So we will see you tomorrow morning, 9 a.m. at my place for hair and makeup?" Julia asked.

"Absolutely," Amanda replied. "I wouldn't miss it." She yawned. "Oh, I'm sorry. The day is catching up with me. I'm going to head back to the hotel. I'm exhausted."

"I know what you mean," Julia said with a smile. "See you tomorrow."

"Yes." Amanda walked to Ben and said something to him. He frowned. Amanda left.

"Ready to go, Mom?" Kate asked.

"Yes." She glanced at Ben. "Let me say thank-you and good-bye to Ben."

"I'll meet you at the car," Kate said, Madison and Sean following her out of the restaurant.

Ben met her halfway.

"All set?" Julia asked.

"Yes. Kids go out already?"

"They did," Julia told him. "Thank you so much for the fabulous rehearsal dinner. You made big points with Kate."

He grinned. "My pleasure."

They walked outside together.

"Until tomorrow," Ben said, the words soft.

"Until tomorrow," Julia echoed.

Their eyes met, and sparks flew. She wasn't imagining his interest in her. She felt the flame deep in her gut.

And heaven help her, the feeling was mutual.

Chapter Two

The Wedding

"I think Sean is having second thoughts," Kate said. "He's not even here yet."

They'd just arrived at the church to find no Sean. "He's just running late," Julia said, "that's all."

"You know he's never late," Kate said as she unzipped the garment bag holding her wedding dress. "He said something last night, something about his parents' marriage and how awful it had been."

Julia helped Kate free the wedding dress from the garment bag. "What did he say?"

"Something like, he'd seen the dark side of love," Kate said, "and I had the feeling he didn't like it." She caught Julia's gaze. "What if he doesn't want to marry me now? What if he thinks I'll be just like his mom and he'll be left all alone like Ben?"

"First of all," Julia said, "you are not his mother. You would never hurt Sean that way, and deep down, he knows that. And second, I think Ben is doing just fine."

Kate sniffed.

Julia passed her a tissue. "Fix your makeup."

Kate went to the mirror. Her eyes went wide with horror. "Oh, no, I've made a mess."

"Nothing that can't be fixed." Julia retrieved her emergency makeup kit, producing makeup remover towelettes. "Let me see." She wiped the makeup from under Kate's eyes, then found mascara, fixing her lashes. "There. Good as new."

Kate nodded. "I'm scared, Mom."

"Of what?" Julia asked, wondering what was really going on here.

"Of losing Sean like we lost Dad."

So this was about Robert? This Julia could handle. "Sean is a young, healthy man. You are worrying about something that most likely will never happen. Think happy thoughts today. It's how I get through every day."

Kate's eyes softened. "I know how much you loved Dad."

Julia's heart took a hit. If Kate knew her true feelings for Robert, she'd be destroyed. Their life had been built on lies and betrayal. "Your dad and I had our time. This is your time, Kate. Please, don't worry about me. I'm fine, happy and optimistic about the future. Life doesn't come with guarantees. We need to latch on to all the happiness we can find. Sean makes you happy."

"It's so like you to be an optimist, Mom," Kate said, giving Julia's hand a squeeze.

A car door closed outside.

"Sean." Kate flew to the window. "No, it's Ben."

"Let me see." Julia peered out. Ben strode to the church. Dressed in a gray tux, the color set off his silver hair, complimented his tan. He glanced up, waving.

Julia's pulse revved. What was she? Sixteen? Or was she merely starved for a man's attention, his touch?

"Mom, go ask Ben where Sean is," Kate said. "Please."

"Of course," Julia said, willing to do anything to ease Kate's mind.

The door to the dressing room opened and the bridesmaids entered, all four of them talking at once. They wore long, light blue dresses that hugged their slender bodies. Beautiful girls, carefree, excited.

Julia loved their innocence. "Girls," she said. "Kate needs help dressing."

"Of course," said Michelle, Kate's best friend and maid of honor. "We are on it, Mrs. S."

"Thanks," Julia said. "I'll be back."

As she left the room, she heard Kate say, "Sean isn't here yet."

Julia closed the door. Was Sean missing? She prayed not. She walked briskly down the hall to the stairs. Ben stood at the bottom of the staircase. He noticed her, watched her as she descended, each step bringing her closer to him.

"Hi," he said warmly.

"Hi," she replied, very conscious of her professionally done hair and makeup, and the gorgeous silver satin dress she wore.

"You look great," he said, the words holding the right amount of appreciation.

She smiled. "Thanks. So do you."

"How is the bride?" he asked.

"Not good," Julia admitted. "Kate seems to think Sean's got cold feet. He said something to her about marriage not always working out last night."

Ben frowned. "I guess the kid knows that from experience."

"Do you know where Sean is?"

"Right behind me," Ben said. "He stopped to pick up his wedding present for Kate. He's head over heels for her. He had a diamond necklace made for her of her favorite star, Vega. Told me he wanted to give her the stars."

Relief filled Julia. "Oh, that's so sweet. She will love it. She and her dad used to stargaze. It was their thing. I'll go tell Kate he's coming."

She started for the stairs, but Ben caught her arm. She looked at him expectantly.

"Save a dance for me," he said, the words low and sexy. "Save all of them."

The heat in his eyes, the way he looked at her as if he couldn't wait to have her, left her weak with desire. A desire she didn't think she was capable of feeling anymore.

Never had she wanted a man the way she wanted Ben Delano.

Not even Robert.

"You may kiss your bride," the minister said.

Julia dabbed her eyes as Sean planted a serious kiss on her daughter. And just like that, they were married. Kate didn't belong to her anymore. She had to share her with

Sean now. Sean. A sweet guy who had given her daughter the most thoughtful wedding gift. Kate had practically melted with love when Sean had given her the diamond necklace. Julia felt pretty sure Kate was certain of Sean's love for her now and all dark thoughts of marriages gone bad had faded away.

Julia glanced at Ben. He sat across the aisle from her, his eyes on the newlyweds. Around her everyone erupted into applause. Sean and Kate linked hands then held them high above their heads in a show of victory, their beaming faces saying it all.

The newlyweds started down the aisle, followed by their wedding party. Julia met Ben and Amanda in the center aisle. Amanda clung to Ben's arm, and Julia's new feelings for Ben took a hit. Ben and Amanda had a fiery history. Did that ever wane? Some people fed on that kind of drama.

"They did it," Amanda gushed, her smile wide. "My baby is married."

"Mine, too," Julia said.

Ben held her gaze for the barest second, long enough for Julia to know that she mattered to him. Amanda tugged on his arm. The three of them filed out of the church and into the sunshine. The reception was being held at Julia's. It had always been Kate's dream to have her wedding reception at home, Julia's too. The beach was the perfect setting. Tables had been set up on the lawn and the deck, the wedding planner and caterer taking care of everything. All they had to do was show up.

Kate and Sean had started a reception line, and Julia took her place next to her daughter, with Ben and Amanda on the other side of Sean. They spent the better part of the next hour greeting each guest, sending them on to Julia's house for cocktails, followed by a summer seafood boil, complete with fresh scallops, prawns, crab, and lobster.

By the time Julia reached the house, she was happy to accept the glass of white wine the waiter offered her. She stopped by the kitchen to check on the caterer before making her way outside.

"There you are," her best friend Sophia said, taking her arm. "Have you seen the father of the groom? Holy cow. I hope you're on that."

Mortified, Julia said, "Sophia, really?"

"What? It's time you had some fun." Sophia winked. "Even if it's just for one night. That's what weddings are all about. People always hook up."

"I am not a one-night-stand kind of girl," Julia said, even though she wasn't completely sure that was true anymore. Life was too short. If she'd learned anything from Robert's death, she'd learned that.

"Even with him." Sophia nodded to Ben. He was chatting with Julia's parents, laughing at something her dad said.

"Let's change the subject," Julia said, not wanting to discuss Ben with Sophia. "I need to circulate."

"Okay, okay." Sophia grinned. "Let's mingle."

Julia took her time, enjoying herself. There had been one hundred and fifty RSVPs. Not a big wedding, but big enough. No matter her problems with Robert, she did wish he was there. She missed his take-charge attitude, the way he took care of her and Kate. Robert might have been a snake, but he didn't deserve to die so young, didn't deserve to miss his daughter's wedding. Suddenly sad, Julia removed her shoes and took the short path to the beach. Once there, she breathed.

Her life was about to take a new direction. She let the good vibes fuel her body. She could do this, let her daughter go, embrace a new life, maybe take more time for herself.

"Hey."

She turned. "Hi." Ben came down the path toward her, a ridiculously happy grin on his face.

"Hiding out?" he asked when he reached her.

"No, taking a breather," she said. "The hard part is over. This is easy."

"They are getting ready to serve," Ben said. "Kate sent me after you."

"Right." Together they headed to the house.

"Your place is nice," he said.

"What's your house like?" she asked.

"More of a cabin," he told her. "But it's on a river. I can literally step out my back door and fly-fish."

"Sounds perfect," she said, and she could picture him there. The setting fit the man.

"For me." He shrugged. "Amanda hated it."

"Really? Why?"

"She'd rather have something like this," he said. "This is where she'd fit best. She never worked in Montana."

Julia wondered if he thought she wouldn't work in Montana either.

"There you are," Kate said when she spied them. "Come on."

Guests were locating their place cards and taking their seats. Julia knew that she and Ben were at the same table, courtesy of Kate, as was Amanda. Her daughter thought it would be nice if the in-laws got to know each other better.

Julia slid into her chair. Ben sat between her and Amanda. What a triangle! Julia made it through the dinner, the toasts, the cake cutting. Ben turned out to be an engaging dinner partner, Amanda an amusing one, in an over-the-top way.

When it was time for the father-daughter dance, Julia's dad filled in, dancing with Kate. The sight brought tears to Julia's eyes. She ached for Kate, knowing how much she missed her dad. Julia had her own dance with Sean, then the dance floor opened for all.

"My turn," Ben said, his hand on the small of her back.

She came alive. Wanted more of him. "Lead the way."

He guided her onto the crowded dance floor. A slow song played, and Ben held her close, but not too close.

His clean scent, probably soap and water, drew her in, made her ache to press her nose against his neck and inhale. All too soon the dance ended. The regret she saw in his eyes echoed her own.

Again, she became the mother of the bride and she finished out the event playing hostess. Sean and Kate departed to bubbles and rose petals. Guests left until it was just her, Ben, and the caterers. Ben helped take the tables down. Everything was loaded up, then they were alone.

"That's everything," Julia said as the last truck rolled away. "Thank you so much for staying to help."

"What do you want to do now?" Ben asked, a mischievous note to the words.

Julia's answer was a smile.

Chapter Three

After the Wedding

Ben shed his suit jacket, tie, then unbuttoned the top button of his white dress shirt. Ah, he could breathe again. The wedding had gone off without a hitch. Sean was married. Amanda and Madison had left together, going back to the hotel for girl time. He was free until the brunch tomorrow morning.

Upstairs, Julia was changing into something more comfortable. The thought alone filled him with possibilities.

Optimism fueled him as he headed to the kitchen. He grabbed a bottle of leftover wine and two glasses before going out to the deck. All of this was impulsive for him. Everything. The setting, the event, the woman. Yet a raw excitement sizzled in his veins. He couldn't remember the last time he'd felt so stoked about another human being.

"I feel ten times better," Julia said as she joined him. She smiled and took the seat closest to him at the outdoor table.

She'd dressed in black yoga pants and a Bon Jovi T-shirt. Not exactly romance attire, but on her, the look worked.

The sun had set, leaving a pink glow above Salmon Island. Overhead, a bright star twinkled alone in the lavender sky. Vega, Kate's star? Salt air filled his senses, setting a sultry backdrop for them.

"Wine?" Ben asked.

"Yes, please." Julia made a sound of contentment. "This is nice, peaceful."

"I agree." Ben passed her the wine.

She drank before setting the wine on the glass table. "So much planning." She grinned. "So much angst, and poof, it's over."

"To us." Ben raised his glass. "The hard-working parents."

Julia lifted her glass. "To us." She touched her glass to his. "How soon do you leave?"

"Tomorrow night," Ben said, regret already an emotion he wasn't ready to acknowledge. "Too soon."

"Yes." Her tongue came out to wet her lips.

Lips that he imagined would taste like wine. "I feel like I just got here. I never expected to like it here...or like you as much as I do."

If he'd embarrassed her, he couldn't tell. Purple twilight hid a lot.

"Are you hitting on me?" she asked, but she didn't sound upset. Not at all.

"Yeah," he admitted. "And I'm out of practice. Is it too soon? I know your husband hasn't been gone long."

"A little over a year," she said. "But it's not too soon. I'm afraid I have something of a secret. My marriage wasn't as happy as Kate thinks it was. Robert and I weren't getting along before he got sick. We were on the verge of separating."

"I'm sorry," he said. He didn't wish an unhappy marriage on his worst enemy. "I had no idea."

"No one does." She took a sip of wine. "And I don't want Kate to ever find out. She adored her father. Robert was a good dad, the best. Kate was away at college when the trouble started between us. She never suspected." She blew out a breath. "I'm not sure why I'm telling you this. My sad story is a mood killer for sure."

"Not for me," Ben said. "I'm honored that you'd share your past with me."

"How about your marriage?" Julia asked. "Any sparks left there?"

"None," he said. "I feel bad for the kids, but Amanda and I are too different."

"You and I are different," Julia said.

He considered her words, then replied, "I don't think we are. We may live in different states, but I'd bet we'd agree on a lot of things."

She laughed. "Such as?"

"The kind of life we'd want," he said. "You have a beautiful home, and obviously Robert left you well-off, but I'd bet that money isn't everything to you."

"You'd win that bet," she replied, the words filled with enough heart he instantly knew he was right about her. "I love this town, but if Kate relocated and asked me to go with her, I'd go. Home is wherever the people you love are."

He nodded. "I agree, and my two kids have relocated here and it seems they plan on staying."

"Are you saying you're open to moving this way?" Julia asked.

"I've been thinking about it for a while now," he admitted, "but I'm waiting to see how things shake out for Sean and Madison."

Julia smiled.

He smiled back, feeling alive and open for anything.

"How about a walk on the beach?" Julia suggested. "I have a basket of flip-flops, all sizes, that I keep on hand for guests. You're welcome to a pair."

"Sold," he said, rising. He followed her inside to her mudroom area, found a pair of flip-flops in his size, and put them on. Together they left the deck, taking the short trail to the beach.

The beach in Wilding Point was not soft sand, like an ocean beach, but more of a mix of sand, small rocks, and ground-up shells. *Rustic* was how he'd describe it. They walked to the shoreline, then turned, staying close to the water.

Ben found her hand. "This okay?"

Her hand closed around his. "Yes. I don't remember the last time someone held my hand. I like it."

He chuckled. Her hand felt so small and soft in his, and a surge of protectiveness for this woman blindsided him. Never had he experienced this kind of chemistry with another person. He felt high, he felt fear. Intense emotions were so not his thing, but they were with her.

"You're easy to be with," Julia said.

He squeezed her hand. "Ditto."

Along the shore the houses of Wilding Point were lit, reminding Ben of sparkling jewels. They walked for a while, then stopped to admire the crescent moon.

"I love the stars," Julia said, her gaze on the sky.

"Lady, you need to see Montana stars," Ben told her, "so thick and glittering in the sky there's no end to them. I never take the stars for granted. There's nothing more magical."

"I'd love for you to show them to me." She brought her gaze to him.

"I will. That's a promise."

Time stopped. Julia's lips parted. Ben framed her beautiful face in his hands, his mouth taking hers. She moaned softly, letting him in, and he was lost in her taste, in the feel of her skin under his hands, lost in the softness of her body pressed to his.

Her hands touched his chest before moving around to circle his back. His nerve endings buzzed, exploded, and he knew that kissing her would never be enough.

"Julia," he said, her name a caress. He saw the passion in her eyes, felt it in her touch.

"That was some kiss," she said with awe. "In fact, I don't think I've ever been kissed like that. So completely."

Her words pleased him. "I could kiss you forever."

"You barely know me," she said, as if trying to become the voice of reason where no reason existed.

"I'm all ears," he said.

She started back the way they'd come. "Let's go back, and I'll let you ask me anything, if I can do the same to you."

Ben smiled. "I'm an open book, baby."

Julia laughed. "We'll see, Ben Delano. We'll see."

Julia stretched out on the lounge chair.

A small glass table stood between her chair and Ben's. A good buffer between her intense feelings for him and the man himself. Clearly, she had no self-control where Ben was concerned.

In the back of her mind she kept thinking that it could never work between them. He was the father of her daughter's husband. But even weirder than that, she was afraid Kate would never accept Ben or any other man in her life this soon after Robert's passing. Yet, spending this time with Ben felt right to her. And she couldn't help but think she'd been waiting for him all her life.

"Okay," Ben said. "Ask me anything."

"Hmm, let me see. Well, there's the obvious. What's your favorite food?"

"I like a good steak, and I mean good, high-quality beef, and I'll pay top dollar for it."

Julia laughed. "You know I barely eat meat, right?"

"To each his own," Ben said good-naturedly. "What's your favorite food?"

"You'll probably think this is weird, but it's blue cheese."

He smiled. "Not weird. I like blue cheese too. It's great on steak."

She stuck her tongue out at him. "What's it like where you live?"

"In a word—stunning," he said. "I live on the river in a two thousand square foot log house I built myself. My deck is my favorite place."

"I understand that. I love my deck too."

"I'm an outdoor person," he said.

"So am I. I have heaters out here in the winter." She smiled.

"I like that." He reached across the table, his hand finding hers. "I don't think you can scare me away."

"I don't want to," she said, hoping her tone told him how much she liked him.

He let go of her hand and stood. He moved the small table out of the way and pushed their lounge chairs together.

This was intimate, almost like a bed, and possibly a mistake, but Julia was way past caring.

Ben climbed back on his chair and scooted close to her. "I want to kiss you again."

"I want that too." His hands found her body, urging her closer. Julia melted into him, her mouth finding his. He tasted so good, like wine and promise. His hands found their way under her T-shirt. It had been so long since she'd been touched like this. She wanted to strip her clothes off and have her way with him, but she held back. This was too new; the stakes were too high. They had to consider the kids, put them first, didn't they?

"Too much?" he asked, as if sensing her hesitation.

"I want this, I do," she said, "but can we slow down a little?"

"You take the lead," Ben said. "Slow or fast, I want to be right where I am."

"Me, too."

The air had cooled considerably and she'd had the foresight to bring out blankets.

Ben spread the blankets over them. "How's this? Just let me hold you."

"I'd love that."

Julia snuggled into the crook of his arm, her head on his shoulder, her eyes on the stars. The blanket and his body heat warmed her. Exhaustion made her limbs heavy.

"This feels good," Ben said.

"I didn't realize how tired I am until now." She yawned.

"Me either," Ben said. "Brunch is at ten?"

"Ten," she said. "It's all done, really. I had the food catered from the Main Street Bakery. I have an assortment of croissant breakfast sandwiches, fruit salad, pastries, coffee, and mimosas."

"Sounds great," Ben said. "I should probably go so you can get some rest."

"Not yet," she said. "This is heavenly. Stay a little longer."

"I was hoping you'd say that."

Julia snuggled against him. Ben stroked her back. He pressed his lips to her hair. She closed her eyes, savoring the moment, savoring Ben Delano.

Chapter Four

Brunch

"What the heck is going on here?" Kate cried. "Mom!"

Julia snapped awake. "What?"

"Mom," Kate said. "Are you kidding me?"

"Kate," Julia said, realizing all at once where she was and who she was with. They'd fallen asleep, outside in the lounge chairs. Beside her, Ben sat up, looking as dumbfounded as she felt. "I can explain."

"How could you, Mom?" Kate whirled away, running into the house.

"Kate!" Julia threw the blanket off and jumped up. "Wait."

"I'm sorry." Ben stood.

"It's not your fault," Julia called over her shoulder. She met Sean at the door.

"What's going on?" Sean said, then when he saw Ben, "Whoa, Dad, seriously?"

"Shut up," Ben said, sounding grumpy.

Julia found Kate in the kitchen. She sat at the island, crying.

"How could you, Mom?" Kate said, her tone heavy with accusation.

"Kate," Julia said, unsure of how to make this situation better. "We were both exhausted. We fell asleep."

"With your chairs pushed together," Kate said, between sniffs. "That looked deliberate, Mom. Your head was on his shoulder. I mean, it's Sean's dad. That's gross."

Julia bit her tongue. There was nothing gross about it. "I'm sorry you're upset, but it was innocent." She glanced at the clock. 9:40. "I can't believe I overslept. Look, I know we need to talk about this, but everyone else will be here in a few minutes. I'm going to run upstairs and change. Will you please pull the food out of the fridge and start setting up? I'll be right back."

"No," Kate said as if Julia were an idiot. "You've ruined everything."

Sean and Ben came into the kitchen.

"Nothing is ruined," Julia said, feeling worse than ever. "Kate, come on. I'm sorry we feel asleep, but it's hardly a crime."

"What about *Daddy*?" Kate asked, and Julia instantly heard Kate's little-girl voice.

Julia's heart sank. She didn't know what to say. Anything would be inadequate. Maybe she'd been wrong to keep the truth about Robert from her daughter, but it was too late now.

"He's gone, honey," Julia said sadly, her entire body weighted in regret for her actions last night.

Tears filled Kate's eyes again. Sean rushed over to comfort his bride.

"Take care of her," Julia said to Sean. "I'm going to change."

"I'm heading to the hotel and changing too," Ben said. "I'll be back."

They left the kitchen together.

"Man, I'm sorry," Ben said, running a hand through his messy hair. "I should have set an alarm."

"It's too late now," Julia said. "Let's just get this brunch over with."

"Wait." Ben touched her arm. "You don't regret last night, do you?"

Julia shook her head. "Right now, I'm not sure what I feel. I just know my daughter thinks I betrayed her, and maybe I have."

"Julia," Ben said.

"Just go, Ben, please."

Hurt filled Ben's eyes, but he turned and walked away. He didn't look back.

Sucking up her hurt and regret, Julia headed upstairs.

Somehow Julia changed and was downstairs in time to get the food out before everyone arrived. Kate and Sean had disappeared, and she feared they'd left, but a peek outside told her their car was still in the driveway. She assumed they'd gone for a walk on the beach, no doubt to talk about their loser parents.

Julia put on her big-girl panties, pasted a smile on her face, and welcomed the guests as they arrived, her parents first, followed by Robert's mother, then Madison and Amanda.

Still no Kate, Sean, or Ben.

Ben.

What on earth was going through his mind? She'd frozen him out when that was the last thing she'd wanted to do, but her child came first. She couldn't lose Kate. She'd die.

She was in the process of serving up mimosas when Kate and Sean returned from their walk. She prayed no one would notice Kate's red eyes.

"There you are," she said cheerfully when the two hit the deck.

"Hello, everyone," Sean called out, waving. Kate smiled, but Julia could see she was still upset. This was sulking Kate. Julia knew her well. All was not forgiven.

Thankfully, no one seemed to notice that Kate was upset. Sean brought Kate a mimosa. Smart man.

"I can't imagine what's keeping Ben," Amanda said, on her second mimosa now. "I'm so sorry. I tried to call him, but he's not picking up."

Julia's gut ached. Was he even coming?

What a mess.

She had just announced that brunch was served when Ben came up the deck steps. Dressed in well-worn jeans and a black T-shirt that hugged his muscular chest, Ben stole her breath. Physically, he was the one for her, no doubt about it.

"Finally, Dad," Madison said, going to her father and leading him over to the group. "Where have you been?"

"Overslept," he said. "Sorry."

Ben greeted everyone as they made their way inside to go through the brunch line. Julia waited by the door.

"I'm sorry," she said as he passed.

"How are things here?" he asked.

"Kate's not speaking to me," she told him. "Sean is trying to keep the peace by making sure Kate is swimming in mimosas."

"Hang in there," Ben said, giving her hand a brief squeeze. "We will get through this."

Julia nodded, then left him to see to the food. She spent the next hour eating and smiling until her teeth hurt. Thankfully, Kate and Sean had a plane to catch and had to make an exit.

Julia saw Kate go into the bathroom and she followed her, waiting outside the door. She couldn't let Kate leave like this, with things strained between them.

Kate opened the door, stopping short when she saw Julia. "Not now, Mother."

"Now," Julia said, giving Kate a gentle nudge back into the bathroom. Julia stepped inside and closed the door. "I can't let you leave angry with me, when there is really no reason to be."

"I saw you," Kate said in an accusing tone.

"You saw two exhausted, fully clothed people sleeping after an exhausting day," Julia said. "Nothing more. I promise."

"Really?" Kate said.

"Really," Julia lied. "I barely know Ben. I met him two days ago. We had a drink after the clean-up and passed out."

Relief filled Kate's face. "I want to believe you."

"You can," Julia said. "Honey, I want you to have so much fun on your honeymoon. Please don't even think about this again. There's no need."

"You really promise?" Kate asked.

Julia crossed her heart. "I promise."

Kate threw herself into Julia's arms. "Thank God. I couldn't stand the thought of you cheating on Daddy."

"I would never do that," Julia said, meaning it. It wasn't a lie. She wasn't cheating now. Robert was dead.

"I love you, Mom," Kate said.

"I love you, too, Kate, so much." They embraced again. "Now, come on, let me see you off on your fabulous Hawaiian honeymoon."

Kate nodded, all smiles now.

Back in the kitchen, Kate went to Sean, whispering in his ear. The look of relief on his face was comical. He'd probably thought the sex had been cut from his honeymoon. If Julia wasn't so dismayed, she'd find his relief funny. Instead, the promise she'd made to Kate—that there was nothing between herself and Ben—caused a deep sorrow in her chest, an ache she knew would take forever to go away.

She couldn't lie to her daughter. Ben would have to be out of the picture from this point forward. She prayed he'd understand, when she didn't understand herself.

303

Ben left the brunch at Julia's when everyone else left the brunch, but he doubled back. After brunch, he'd noticed a change in Kate. She'd become happy again, no doubt due to something Julia had said to her. Had she simply convinced Kate that nothing had happened between them, or had she promised something more?

The latter terrified him. He didn't want to give Julia up. Last night he'd gotten a taste of his life with her in it. A life where he lived nearby, close to his kids, close to Julia.

It was a future he wanted more than anything. A future he'd leave his beloved Montana for.

He pulled into Julia's driveway and cut the engine.

She sat on the front steps, looking like she'd collapsed there after the last guest had left and didn't have the strength to get back up.

Ben walk to her. "Julia."

She gave him a small smile.

"Are we okay?" He sat beside her.

She shook her head. "No."

He heard resignation in that one, tiny word, and his gut twisted. "What happened?"

"I told Kate there was nothing between us, that we were exhausted and fell asleep," Julia said. "I promised her there was nothing going on. I have to keep that promise."

"That's insane," Ben said, realizing he was losing her. "We've just begun."

"It's over." Tears filled her eyes. "Kate will never accept us. It's my fault. She idolized her father, loved him so much, and she believed I loved him, too. Apparently, I'm a very good actress." She scoffed. "If I'd leveled with her, told her the truth, that he was a lying, cheating snake, and had been for much of our marriage, maybe she would have been able to accept us—even though she thinks we *are* gross."

Ben swore. "Wouldn't she want you to be happy?"

"I don't know, not if it doesn't suit her version of what happiness is. I'm afraid I may have raised a self-centered girl. But she's also a girl who's already lost a parent at age twenty-four, and that's not fair either."

"I don't want to let you go," Ben said.

She touched his face. "I don't want to let you go either, but I have to. That's what being a mother is all about, making sacrifices for your children."

"I disagree," he said. "Kate's a big girl. She's a married woman now. She will come around."

"She won't," Julia said. "She'll freeze me out, like she did today. I'm not strong enough, Ben. I need her like I need oxygen."

He understood the parent/child bound, had one himself. What choice would he make if faced with the same problem? He didn't know, and that was answer enough for him. He had to support Julia in this—for now. Things would calm down. Sean and Kate would start their life. The wedding drama would fade, and the hard work of marriage would begin.

"Okay," he said, willing to give her the space she needed. "For now."

"For now?" she questioned. "What does that mean?"

"It means, I'll respect your wishes. I don't agree, but I understand." He threaded his fingers through hers. "We've got something, Julia, you and I. At some point I think we need to put our happiness first and find out how good it can really be between us."

She pressed her lips together.

He stroked her cheek. "You haven't seen the last of me. I guarantee it."

Ben kissed her, thoroughly, putting his want for her into that kiss, and when they parted, her eyes told him everything he needed to know.

He'd go for now, but he'd be back.

And when he saw her again, he wasn't about to take no for an answer.

Chapter Five

Thanksgiving

Julia took the turkey out of the oven, placing it on the stove to rest. Nothing smelled as good as roasted turkey, stuffing, and pumpkin pie. Outside, a storm brewed, sheets of rain pelting the windows—Puget Sound choppy and steel gray. Inside, it was toasty warm and cozy. Everyone she loved was here—Kate and Sean, her parents, her best friend, Sophia. Everyone but Ben. The thought left her feeling flat.

"Oh, Mom," Kate said, as she came into the kitchen, "the turkey looks beautiful."

"It does, doesn't it." Julia tested a potato. Just right. "You know Thanksgiving is my favorite holiday."

"I know," Kate said. "Food, family, and no gift hassle."

"Right." Julia drained the potatoes. "Does anyone need anything out there? It will probably be another forty-five minutes before I get everything on the table."

"I was coming for wine." Kate picked up a bottle of chardonnay. "Grandma sent me in for this one."

"Oh no," Julia said with a shake of her head. "How much has she had?" The last thing she needed was tipsy grandparents.

"Two glasses."

"Ugh, go easy on the pour and help me make sure she drinks a lot of coffee after dinner," Julia said.

"Will do." Bottle in hand, Kate left the kitchen.

Her daughter had done a one-eighty since returning from her honeymoon. It was almost as if she'd never caught Julia and Ben together. They'd never spoken about it again. And true to his word, Ben had not called her. The fact stung a little, but he'd said he'd respect her wishes, and he had.

That said something about his character. Still, she'd secretly hoped he'd find a way to fight for her. She knew from Sean that Ben was spending Thanksgiving in Montana and that Madison had gone home to be with him. She was glad he had someone to spend the holiday with. She wouldn't have been able to bear thinking about him being all alone.

Just under an hour later, Julia had all the food on the table. Everyone took their seats.

"Let's give thanks," her mother said, taking Julia's hand. "I want to thank my daughter for this wonderful feast. I'm thankful to be here with family and friends." She smiled. "Let's eat."

"Amen," Sean said with gusto. "I'm starving."

The next minutes were a food fest, with limited talking. As they finished up, Julia took a minute to savor everything—the food, the people, her life. She was blessed in so many ways. All of this should be enough for her, but deep down she knew it wasn't. She'd glimpsed a brighter future with Ben, and she had no idea how to make that future a reality. In fact, she felt guilty for wanting more when she already had so much.

"You okay, Mom?" Kate asked. "You seem quiet."

"Do I?" Julia said. "Just reflecting a bit. Thanksgiving always reminds me how lucky I am."

Kate gave her a quizzical look, but didn't comment.

Had she done the right thing, keeping the truth about Robert from her daughter? She didn't want Kate to think her entire life had been built on a lie. She didn't want Kate to question everything Robert had said, done, or not done.

If giving up Ben, and a possible romance with him, made Kate happy, she'd do it gladly. The thought gave her some peace.

Sean and Kate cleared the dishes, leaving Julia to chat with her parents and Sophia. She sipped her wine, her mind on Ben. Restless, she excused herself to get dessert started.

"Hey," she said, smiling at Sean and Kate. They worked side by side at the sink, taking care of the dishes. "Thanks, you two. I love having help."

Sean finished drying the last pan. "All done."

On her kitchen island three pies waited: pumpkin, apple, and cherry, the last one baked in honor of Robert by Kate.

"You good?" Sean asked Kate.

"Yep."

He left the kitchen. Kate brought her the stack of dessert plates.

"I'm just going to set everything out and let people help themselves," Julia said. "Can you get the whipped cream out of the fridge?"

"Sure." Kate brought over the bowl of freshly whipped cream. "Mom, can I say something?"

"You bet." Julia began cutting the pumpkin pie into slices.

"I'm sorry about the way I behaved toward you and Ben," Kate said. "It was immature and selfish."

Julia set the knife down. "What?"

"I had no right to treat you or Ben like that," Kate said. "Sean and I have talked about it a lot. We think both you and Ben are unhappy."

"No," Julia assured her. "I'm fine."

Kate shook her head. "You're not. You're lonely, and this is all my fault."

"Sweetie, no," Julia said, not wanting Kate to feel bad.

"I know, Mom. And I know you know."

Julia didn't understand. "You know what?"

"I know about Dad, about the affair."

Julia's stomach dropped. Her hand went to her chest, pressing against her beating heart.

"I caught him with her once—Tiffany. And I heard you and Dad arguing about her."

"Oh no," Julia said. "Honey, I'm so sorry. I'm sure you were devastated."

"I was," Kate said, the shine of tears in her eyes, "but most of all, I was devastated for you."

Julia reached for Kate, hugging her daughter, wishing her pain away, pain Julia understood all too well. "Why didn't you say anything?"

"Why didn't you?" Kate asked, pulling back to look at her mother.

"I couldn't," Julia said. "I would never spoil his memory for you."

"But you weren't in love with him anymore, right?" Kate asked. "I mean, you hid it, but I sensed a change."

"We had agreed to separate, right before he got sick," Julia said.

Sean poked his head in the kitchen. "How's that pie coming?"

"Almost ready," Julia said. "Give us a sec."

Sean's gaze bounced between the two women, and he made a hasty retreat.

"You are strong, Mom," Kate said. "So much stronger than I am. When I saw you with Ben, all I could think about was that I couldn't lose you too."

"Honey, I barely know Ben," Julia said.

"I know, but I took that chance away from both of you," Kate said. "Ben is miserable. Sean told me. He likes you, Mom."

Julia smiled. "I like him, too."

"Then go and get him," Kate said, as if it were the easiest thing in the world. "I want you to be as happy as I am."

Julia embraced her daughter again. "You have grown up, my girl."

Kate nodded. "It's about time."

"How about that pie," Julia's dad called from the other room. "And your mother needs coffee."

Julia and Kate laughed, wiping away their tears, tears born of love, of healing.

"Go on," Julia said, "wave them all in here."

Kate smiled. "I love you, Mom."

"I love you too, Katie." She needed time to process all Kate had said. Hope beat in her belly. Was she really free to see Ben?

"Come on in, everyone," Kate called. "Dessert is served."

The group shuffled into the kitchen, talking, laughing. The doorbell rang.

"I'll get it," Julia said, squeezing past her father, who was serving up a big slice of apple pie.

She opened the front door.

Ben stood on the porch, as if she'd wished him there. His hair was wet, his coat dotted with fat raindrops. Julia's knees went weak. He looked so good, handsome, and those blue eyes...she'd almost forgotten how gorgeous they were.

He smiled. "I hope I'm not too late for dessert."

"You're just in time." She held the door wider. "I thought you were having Thanksgiving with Madison."

"I sent her to Amanda's," Ben said as he removed his jacket. "Tell me it's okay that I'm here, Julia."

She smiled. "It's more than okay."

"I can't stop thinking about you." He closed the gap between them.

"Me, either," Julia said.

He reached for her, framing her face with his hands. "I want to kiss you."

Julia raised her mouth to his, kissing him, drowning in him, his scent, the way his lips felt under hers, the hard planes of his back under her hands.

"Mom," Kate said with surprise.

Ben broke the kiss, mouthing, "I'm sorry."

"It's okay," Julia said, happiness filling her. She linked her arm through Ben's. "Come on in and I'll explain. Boy, do I have a lot to be thankful for this year."

"I don't know what's going on," Ben said, grinning, "but I'll second that."

Julia kissed him again, right in front of her daughter, a soft kiss born of hope. "It's our time, Ben. Whatever this is, we will find out together."

"Come on, you two," Kate said, in a teasing tone. "Let go eat pie."

Julia laughed, as she and Ben followed her daughter to the kitchen, to a new beginning for them all.

Joleen James is the author of The Wilding Point Romance Series, The Hometown Alaska Men Series, and several stand-alone contemporary romances, including the award-winning UNDER A HARVEST MOON. Currently, she's working on ONE WILD KISS, book 5 in the Wilding Point Romance Series. LOVE UNEXPECTED is her first romance short set in Wilding Point. Visit Joleen James at www.joleenjames.com, or look for her on Facebook and Twitter.

Also by Joleen James

<u>WILDING POINT ROMANCE SERIES</u>

WILD ABOUT RAND
WILD ABOUT LUCKY
WILD ABOUT CAM
ONE WILD CHRISTMAS
ONE WILD KISS – Available Fall 2020
LOVE UNEXPECTED, A Wilding Point Short

<u>HOMETOWN ALASKA MEN SERIES</u>

HOMETOWN STAR
HOMETOWN HERO
HOMETOWN HEARTBREAKER
HOMETOWN CHRISTMAS, A Novella

COWBOY, I'M YOURS

LOVING GLORY

UNDER A HARVEST MOON

FALLING FOR NICK

HOSTAGE HEART, A SHORT STORY

Not a Small Town Girl

By

Teresa DesJardien

"Ashton" is a real place. However, names and some details have been changed to protect my innocent relatives, and in order to have fun shaping the story.

Chapter One

"You know, the paint won't unpeel no matter how long you stare at it."

Ashley Collins nodded, her mouth turning down. "True."

She'd heard the man approach, and seen him out of the corners of her eyes. She didn't know him, but they stood on a sidewalk in bright afternoon sunlight. He stayed a polite four feet away, his hands in his faded jeans pockets, also gazing at the tattered house before them. Anywhere but in this tiny town, she might have been more concerned to be approached by a stranger.

She unfolded her arms and shook her head, not at their brief conversation but the condition of the old house.

"Thinking of buying it?" he asked, rubbing the back of his neck with one hand.

She slid him a look—he was nice-looking, about her age of thirty, slim, maybe six feet tall—before she looked back to the house. "Not exactly."

He put a hand to his heart. "Whew! For a second there I thought it was going to sell out from under me." She raised her eyebrows, and he elaborated. "I've been eyeballing this house for a while. I'm very close to being able to afford it. Well, halfway. A third." He started over. "There's so much I could do with a house like this. It *is* going on the market, right?"

"Probably," she said. She raised a finger toward the front of the house, which, like all the homes on this side of the street, stood about five feet higher than the sidewalk. Cement steps urged the traveler to seek the elevated front door. "You love it?" Her doubt was in her tone.

He gave a lopsided grin. "I know what you mean. The place is creepy. Dark colors, dark interiors. Very 'haunted house.' And there's the weird gingerbread trim that's somehow wrong instead of charming."

"I always thought so."

His grin slipped. "Oh geez. You know this place? Are you related to old lady Lewis?" Twin red spots bloomed high on his cheekbones, good cheekbones that made his face angular and interesting. "I mean Hannah Lewis."

"Guilty," Ashley said, turning toward him. She took half a step toward him and put out her hand. "I'm Ashley Collins. Grandma—that is, Hannah—was my mom's mother."

He took her hand and shook it, still flushed. "I'm Liam Harcourt."

To spare him the awkward apology that seemed to be forming, she spoke instead. "I don't recall the name 'Harcourt.' Have you always lived in Ashton?"

"Nah. Grew up in Prosser. I've only lived here about eight years."

Prosser? Another small town on the farm-dotted Palouse in eastern Washington. That explained her not knowing his surname. She was probably literally related to a third of the population of Ashton. She'd have heard of the Harcourts if they'd been here for years.

She pointed at the house. "Do you really like this place? I just inherited it, and...well, I'm trying to decide what to do with it."

He looked into her face, back at the property, and then into her eyes. He had an open expression, making her feel even less inclined to worry about him. "I'd love to buy it." He rubbed his neck again. "But there's a little problem in terms of affording it just now."

Ashley shrugged. "Ah. Well, there's no hurry. Yet. I've got two weeks off work. I'm going to stay here, and let my gut tell me what to do with the place." She shrugged. "But it's highly likely I'll put it up to sell."

He gave a short nod. "So, there's little chance you'd want to live here?"

Her laugh was dismissive. "No. I've got my condo in Seattle. My job's there. Well, it could be anywhere, I work from home most of the time. But no, I can't imagine staying here in Ashton." She realized she was quasi-insulting a town he presumably lived in. "I mean, it's pretty here," she went on. "It's quiet. It's got charm."

She glanced around, silently acknowledging that coming back here as an adult had given her different eyes with which to see the town's clean streets, well-kept homes, and so many old trees. The place had an easy-to-spot grace that a child's eyes hadn't been able to see. Back then she'd only known there was too little to do, and she'd smelled too much of the cattle that wandered the part of the hills around the town that weren't planted with wheat. Despite the new data, she gave a tiny shake of her head. "I'm used to suburban living. Lots of restaurants. Movie theaters. More than one bowling alley."

"Our alley has four lanes now," he said as he held up four fingers. His twinkling brown eyes inviting her to laugh. He folded down two of the sun-browned fingers. "Only had two until about three years ago."

She smiled at him. "I know. I bowled there as a kid."

"Oh. You lived here, or just visited your grandma?"

"Visited Grandma, now and then. Grandpa was already dead by the time I was born. But you live here in Ashton, I presume, Liam?"

He hitched a thumb over his shoulder. "Twelve miles out. Ashton's Corner."

Without allowing her lips to part, she let her chin drop, showing her surprise. "Let me guess. You're working on the old Cantrell place?"

His grin renewed. "You know it?"

She nodded. "The house there is gorgeous. Stately." She turned back to Grandma Hannah's place. "Not eerie like this."

He gave a half-shrug, acknowledging the truth.

"Does your wife mind living out of town?" There were only two houses out in Ashton's Corner as far as she knew, one of them attached to a gas station, the other Liam Harcourt's home. Such isolation would drive her nuts.

"I'm not married. Never been."

"Oh. Me neither," she said. She gave a little frown. "You're in that big old house alone?"

"Yep."

"You work the fields all by yourself?"

"Nope. The Cantrells aren't growing crops anymore. I just have a big kitchen garden that I keep, and a few cattle and chickens. I'm a half-farmer, for now."

Her mouth slanted up at the term she'd never heard before, "half-farmer."

"Mostly I'm there to keep the house up. It was starting to go to ruin, and Miss Clara and Miss Marie wanted someone staying in the place. Making repairs. I hope to buy the spread from them one day. I've got half the money saved. Well, a third."

Her lips twitched.

He made a face. "Maybe I've got more ideas than money."

She politely chose not to nod. "Are you telling me the Cantrells are still alive? Those ladies were ancient when I was a kid."

"Yep, still alive. Miss Marie's in a retirement home now in Milton-Freewater, but Miss Clara still lives in the family home, with a helper who comes in."

"Wow," Ashley said. This news was proof she hadn't been back in some ten years, long since before Grandma Hannah had come to Seattle to live with her daughter, Ashley's mom.

"You going in the house?" Liam asked, glancing at the black front door.

A black door on a dark gray house, with black dentine, scrollwork, and other gingerbread designs for which Ashley didn't know the name. Who chose black for a front door? For the detailed decoration? In an urban environment maybe, sure, but in small-town eastern Washington? Every other door on this street was made of wood or painted white. Granted, those were town houses, not farm houses, but...black? In Ashton? Come to think of it, though, Grandma had worn a lot of black. Her fanciest clothes had always been a variation of black, maybe with touches of white or gray. She must have liked it.

"Yeah, I'm going inside." Ashley paused a moment, then made a decision. "Want to come in with me?" The truth was, she'd been standing there, trying to work up the courage to go in. She'd welcome another's presence. *He's absolutely right, this place is creepy. Always has been.* "Or are you busy? I don't want to keep you...?"

He rubbed his hands together. "I confess I've looked in the windows, but I've never been in. Heck yeah, I'd love to go in with you."

"Okay," she said, trying not to sound relieved as she dug from her pocket the key the lawyer had given her.

Chapter Two

As interested as Liam was in the architecture of the spooky old house, it was to Ashley Collins that he looked when they crossed over the threshold. Her expression was tight, as if she held her breath. Well, it wouldn't be emotion-free to go into your deceased grandma's old house.

Being midday, the windows, complete with creepy yellowed lace curtains some Hollywood horror set designer would have chosen, provided some light. All the same, Ashley reached to turn on the front room's single overhead light. As she looked around, Liam belatedly did, too. The furniture was gone, every surface was dusty, and the dark wallpaper, patterned in dim and dimmer shades of green, might have been chosen for Halloween.

His gaze rose to near the ceiling. "Whoa. Twelve-foot ceilings. And look at the moldings. I don't think those are layered. I think they were cut from single planks of wood. You don't see that much anymore. They're usually pieced together these days."

She raised her eyes to the ceiling edges as well. "Why'd they make everything so dark? Dark green paper, going so dreadfully with trim that looks like brownish dried blood. It'd look so much better in here if the wallpaper came down and everything was painted white."

He cocked his head. "I'm all for preserving styles of the past, but, yeah, when you're right, you're right. This room could be fantastic if it were just brightened up. Maybe a cream?"

Ashley didn't respond, instead striding across the room to a closed door. She hesitated for a long moment, then twisted the old-fashioned dark metal knob and pulled the door open. She sucked in a sharp breath. "It's still there," she stated, her voice gone strangely flat.

Seeing her shiver, Liam moved to her side, looking up a staircase leading to the second floor. "What? That coat rack?"

The flat expression melted away, and a wry look crossed her face as she stared up at the offending object on the landing. "It terrified me when I was a kid. I'd come out of my bedroom for the bathroom, and there'd be this 'man' standing here. Made me jump every time. I tell you, I ran to the bathroom, and then again back to bed. Every time." She tilted her head, measuring the rack with narrowed eyes. "The coats are still here. But the hat is gone." She glanced at Liam, flashing a brief half-smile. "It used to always have my deceased grandfather's hat perched from that knob on the top."

"I can see how that would make it look even more like a man," Liam allowed.

She turned away. "Let's check out the kitchen. It has a serial killer sink in it."

Liam didn't know whether to laugh or not. He followed Ashley to the room opposite the stairway door. As they moved, he decided Hannah Lewis's granddaughter was pretty, maybe not beautiful, with a nose that was a tad small and a mouth that was a little wide. She had shoulder-length sandy brown hair with a bit of curl to it. And her rear view...well, it wasn't bad either. He'd always appreciated a nicely shaped keister, and Ashley had one. Truth was truth.

She was also right. It was a serial killer sink. "It's huge," he said, amazed by the size of the farm-style sink.

"I once saw Grandma cleaning fish in that sink. I was little, and I didn't know anything about serial killers, but I remember the fish blood and that Grandma wasn't squeamish at all." She shivered again. "Why do you think they made it so big?"

"For bathing critters? Kids?" Liam suggested.

Ashley gave a little nod. "Well, they did raise both."

Liam circled slowly. "High ceilings again. Nice. Those curtains are criminal, though. Bet they'd fall apart if you touched them. And these cabinets are so basic I wonder if your grandfather maybe built them? No insult intended to your grandpa."

"I never thought to ask, but I think you might be right." She shook her head, and pointed to the copper hinges and cabinet knobs. "I think Grandma must have kept those pulls up, because they were bright in her day. This tarnish is kind of sad to see."

"She hadn't lived here in...?"

"Four years. She couldn't maintain it anymore, and moved over to the west side of the state to live with Mom."

"I mow the lawn, but this place hasn't gotten any other love since. When a house sits..." He let the comment hang, not needing to complete it.

She turned to him. "You mow the lawn? Why you?"

He hitched his thumb over his shoulder again, pointing out the kitchen window behind himself. "My buddy, Mike, lives next door. He lets me stay at his place sometimes when I need an overnighter in town, so I mow his lawn and this one."

"Wow. That's really nice. Thank you."

"Civic duty," he said, and at her questioning look, he was sure a sheepish look crossed his face. "I'm the mayor. We want things to look nice around here, you know?"

Her lips parted. "The mayor? Of Ashton?"

He nodded. "The voters thought it was all right since I live in Ashton's Corner. Maybe they prefer that I'm usually not underfoot." He shrugged. "Or nobody else wanted to be mayor. I ran unopposed."

"So, let me get this straight. You're a mayor, a small-time farmer, a local mower, and a real estate enthusiast. Anything else?"

"I do this and that. But don't be impressed by the 'mayor' part. It only pays a thousand dollars a month."

She made a face. "Yikes. But I believe you. Ashton is pretty small."

"It's just right," he said, feeling his grin broaden.

"For you, maybe. As I said, not for me. I'm not a small-town girl."

"No? They say home is where the heart is," he said.

She looked as if she could make several replies to that, but instead she waved to a door behind him to his left. "That leads to a screened-in porch." She wrinkled her nose. "I hope there isn't a full freezer left unplugged and rotting out there."

"You'd be smelling it. Besides, I've looked through the screening. There's just a folded-up card table."

She led him back into the front room, pointing to two more doors, one on either side of the stairway door. They were open, the rooms dark like the rest of the house. "The one on the left was Grandma's room. The right is a kind of parlor, I think." She moved toward the latter. "Yeah. I remembered it right. Maybe the creepiest room here."

Liam came behind her, nearly touching her shoulder where she blocked the doorway as he leaned in to take a look. "Whoo. That wallpaper. Are those...birds? Angels? Anyway, its vibe is Early Gothic Funeral Home."

Ashley eyed the patterned dark-blue wall covering. "I suppose it was fashionable once upon a time. I'm coming to understand Grandma liked dark colors."

Liam knelt, caressing the floor with one hand, leaving finger streaks in the dust. "Under that dark stain I think that's oak. These floors could be sanded and saved."

"That's right, you're also a handyman. You know about fixing up houses."

He stood, dusting his hands together. His face seemed to brighten as an idea occurred to him. "Hey, want to hire me? I could do a few things around the place, like these floors. I'd be improving it for whoever ends up buying it—or for you, if you decide to keep it."

"Oh, I don't know. I'm not sure I want to get tangled up in house repairs. I'm only here two weeks, tops—"

"Well, maybe not the floors now, then. But I could clean and paint? Some of the interior anyway. Let you see the place looking a bit shined up?"

He watched her gaze circle the front room. It was easy to guess her thoughts: should she bother to update it? Even a little? But then again, why not have it show better?

"Give it a chance to charm someone?" she said, more to herself than to him. "I've got some savings. I can afford a few fixes?" she said the last as a question, weighing the options.

"Twenty-five bucks an hour?" she finally ventured. "Plus materials. You could work half days so it doesn't interfere with your other work?"

Liam grinned, and thrust out a hand. She took it, shaking it.

"Start thinking about colors," he said as he let her hand go. "How about I come back tomorrow at ten? You can show me the upstairs. I'll bring a clipboard so I can take some measurements, look for problems, all that kind of thing."

"Sounds good."

"Yeah." He clapped his hands together. "So, I'm going to go now. Can I stop by the utilities department and get the water turned back on for you?"

"That would be great. I'd wondered how bathroom needs were going to work." That seemed to embarrass her a little, so she quickly added, "I knew the electricity is still on, to keep the baseboards running during the winter. Mom has been paying the bill for the last year or so."

He nodded. "I'm off, then. Before I am, though, do you need anything else? Can I carry anything in from your car for you?"

"No, thanks. It's just my suitcase, pillow, and a sleeping bag."

He winced. "Ouch. Fun night sleeping on these hardwoods. But what about the coat rack? You want me to take that away?"

He watched her cross her arms, waited for her answer as she thought a long moment. He saw discomfort, and something that made him think she was pondering if she'd look foolish if she agreed.

She gave a sigh, and nodded. "Yep. Yes, please, that needs to go somewhere I can't see it."

He carried it out, coats and all, ratty old things that hadn't merited being taken away.

As he stashed it on Mike's back porch next door, he grinned, knowing the moment she decided to give in to a childhood fear, to let him see her do so, was the moment he'd decided he liked Ms. Ashley Collins.

Chapter Three

Retrieving her things from her car, Ashley elected to leave her work bag and laptop in the trunk. She wanted to truly be on vacation, so for now work could wait. She had little doubt that in Ashton her computer bag would be safe in the trunk.

As night deepened, she noted that only two lightbulbs on the house's ground floor were burned out. Still, she wished she had some lamps to help lighten this front room's dismal interior. She'd bought food, supplies, and lightbulbs at the town's only grocery store, but hadn't thought about needing a ladder in order to replace the bulbs twelve feet up. Maybe Liam could do that tomorrow? There was a tiny hardware store next door to the grocery, but would they have a tall-enough ladder? Or would she have to drive for more than an hour one way to Walla Walla to buy one? No, wait, she was thinking like a city dweller. Surely she could borrow one from a neighbor or a relative? Heaven knew she had dozens, if not hundreds, in town.

She sat on the floor a while, just looking at the house's front room. The heavy doorjambs. The intricately paneled stairway door that totally didn't match the plain bedroom doors on either side. The darker spot on the floorboards near the front door that indicated a mat had once lived there. She thought to herself, as she had a dozen times already, that this house was a strange place to choose to visit, to spend two weeks of precious vacation time on.

Why had she?

Truth was, it was a place to go. A thing to see. A memory that needed confirming.

But much more, she knew she wanted...something. Not a husband. Not kids. Not necessarily. If she never had either, she'd be okay with that. Not that she wasn't dating, trying to find someone to love and cherish. Not that she rejected marriage or kids or tradition. However, what she really felt was the lack of *change*. The getting of an education was behind her, the good IT job acquired, the condo bought and more than half paid for already.

Her tech work was challenging. She'd lately cut back on the perpetual demand to work the fifty or sixty hours per week that was the norm as a programmer. She'd thought about taking more classes to advance at work— but she hadn't signed up for them. She'd learned to crochet. She'd discovered she was a lousy photographer. She'd learned to waterski; that had been fun, but she didn't know anyone else who skied or owned a boat. The truth was, the zeros and ones that made up her work, the pattern of her days, had gone stale on a certain level. Lost color. Had become...expected.

She was being called to a search. An exploration. What was next? What goal waited out there for her? Did she need a goal? Why was she restless? Why did "something" call to her?

She glanced around again, and shook her head with a small smile. Yeah, this house was "something," all right. But there was no way this house, this town, this seven-hour drive from Seattle was the future, the change, the "new" she sought.

Night had firmly fallen by the time she rose to make a dinner of canned chili. She added some pre-grated cheese and crumbled saltines. Holding a filled paper bowl on paper towels to block the heat from burning her hands, and tucking a four-pack of toilet paper under one arm, she began making her way through the house, particularly intent on exploring the upstairs. As she walked, she blew on and took spoonfuls of chili for which she was suddenly very hungry.

She switched on every functioning overhead light as she went—only the fourth bedroom's switch produced no result. That was ironic, since it'd been the bedroom she'd slept in the most as a kid, the one that had made her fleeing retreats from the coat rack "man" as far a trek to safety (and the somehow rescue-filled bed covers) as possible within the house. And now it stood dark.

She left burning every working light as she advanced through the sleeping quarters. Looking at each room, closet, and built-in cupboard, she was half prepared to find mouse droppings, or some of the smallish local bats hanging from curtain rods. She found none, much to her surprise. Well, maybe there'd be something in the attic? But she wasn't going up the pulldown ladder in the biggest bedroom to find out. Nope! Not at night. Not in her grandma's sort-of haunted house.

Really, though, the place did have great bones. She could see it as she made herself look beyond old impressions and unfortunate color choices. She even felt a little buzz of excitement as ideas for improvement teased her brain. It could be a fine house for some young couple. With the evil coat rack now and forever banished from the second-story landing, it could even be a good house for kids.

She used the upstairs bathroom, the only one in the house. She'd first made sure the water had indeed been turned on, sending up a silent thank-you to Mayor Liam Harcourt. The tap had sputtered out a little bit of copper-colored water for a few seconds before it began to run clear, and even produced hot water. *Nice. Hmm, I wonder where the water heater is? Maybe on the back porch?*

Shaking her hands to dry them, she made a face at having forgotten to bring a roll of paper towels up. Not that the room had a wastebasket anyway. As she did so, she had time to notice the wallpaper. *So much wallpaper in this house.* It was a far friendlier choice than those used downstairs. It had been white, though now yellowed by age, with a repeating pattern of tiny roses winding every twelve inches apart, marching from ceiling to floor, on all four walls.

Turning to see more, she half-smiled, half-grimaced at the old clawfoot tub. As a kid she'd imagined being in the "belly of the beast" when she'd bathed there, or she'd played a more upbeat mermaid in its voluminous depths, depending on whether she was in a creeped-out mood or a happy one.

And there *had* been good times here. In fact, most of her memories were happy enough; it was just that the house design had been too much for a little girl with a fertile imagination. That had not been improved by cousins who'd told her ghost stories the handful of times they'd all stayed there together.

She lifted her chin. "You couldn't help it you were a bit scary with your eagle talon feet," she assured the tub. "It's unlikely I'll replace you." She even reached out to give the high rim a pat. After all, some people loved claw-footed tubs. "You're a selling point, right?" she threw over her shoulder as she moved to return downstairs.

She opened the box of garbage bags she'd left among the bags on the counter in the kitchen. She snapped one open, and tossed in her used paper bowl, plastic spoon, and paper towels. She'd have tossed in the cheap skillet she'd bought, too, she supposed, if she hadn't had running water. Which raised the thought. What was she going to do for meals while she was here? There had been one restaurant in town when she was a kid. Was it still open? She'd passed it on the way to Grandma's street, but there'd been no cars in its parking lot, no flashing "open" sign. Maybe she'd need to buy a microwave? She could leave it here once she went home, a gift to any future homeowner. Or just keep on using the stovetop? Either way, now she retrieved shampoo from her bag to wash the skillet out.

"The dishes" done, she settled against a wall, digging her phone out of her purse. She thought about watching videos, but chose tunes instead as she wandered from room to room, thinking about changes that could be made.

A half hour later, she thumbed off the music, thinking about sleep even as she noted it was only 8:15. *Sheesh.*

She decided to bed down anyway, despite the early hour. Suitcase in hand, she moved into Grandma's old bedroom, now utterly empty of anything but lacy curtains that matched those in the rest of the house. Had Grandma made them? Or were they precious Irish lace? Nah, if they had value, they'd have been removed. They certainly had grown dingy. Since the room didn't look onto anyone else's property, it suited for her to change there into a cotton nightgown covered with pink and red hearts. It went down to mid-thigh. She left on her socks, concerned she might get cold despite her sleeping bag. Maybe she ought to have brought PJ bottoms?

It felt a bit weird to bed down in Grandma's room, so Ashley chose the corner of the front room nearest to it. She brushed her teeth in the kitchen, then went quickly through the house, checking all the window and door locks. When she'd been a kid, Grandma had seldom bothered to lock up. But not her, not in a barely familiar old house.

Next, Ashley spread out her sleeping bag and pillow, then went around to turn off some of the lights. She left the hideous parlor's light on, with the door mostly closed, and all the ones upstairs burning still, but she turned off the light in Grandma's room, the kitchen, and the front room. The light spilling down the stairs bothered her a little, but she knew she'd sleep better with it than without it.

She retrieved her phone, and squirmed into the sleeping bag. She propped herself up on one elbow in order to read a book she had stored on her cell.

She expected the inevitable weird house noises and the hardness of the floor. But she'd forgotten that the cattle dotting the rolling hills around Ashton sometimes mooed at night. *Yeah, that's a cow, not a moaning zombie at all,* she told herself, shivering despite the sleeping bag.

With an effort, she forced her attention back to the book. She hoped it would relax her into feeling tired. It wasn't even 9:00 yet. She'd never get to sleep...

Chapter Four

A scream dragged Ashley from some dreamworld to wakefulness in an instant. It took her half a second more to remember where she was, and another to press the on button of her phone with an unsteady hand. Three forty-six. She was instantly grateful that house lights she'd left on still shone. If she'd woken in total darkness to that unholy sound...

The sound she'd begun to think she'd dreamed came again, high, weirdly short, like a woman trying repeatedly to scream while being strangled. "Oh, crap," she said aloud as she scrambled out of the sleeping bag. She stood in the center of her grandmother's eerie house and listened hard, shivering from the night's chill and a bone-deep alarm.

Flashlight! She had a flashlight on her phone. She backed up to where it was plugged in near her sleeping bag, as if turning her back to the front door would somehow allow the dying woman to plunge through that portal, trailing ropes and blood and a crazed killer behind her.

The flashlight switched on, but Ashley found it did absolutely nothing to help, gave her no idea what to do next. She was frozen, even though it belatedly occurred to her she could have just switched on more lights.

That terrible sound came again, closer.

The dark outline of a man passed the outside of one of the front windows, his silhouette coming through the lace curtains. Ashley gave a very tiny *"Urp!"* the closest thing her tight throat was able to form as a scream. She literally jumped an inch off the floor when there was a sudden knock on the front door.

"Ashley?" came a male voice. "Ashley, it's Liam. From next door?"

Somehow her feet moved forward, but she made sure the door she pressed herself against blocked her from the view of the man outside. She switched off the phone's light, as if that would make it harder to spot her if he somehow managed to peep in through one of the windows on either side of the door.

"What do you want? What is it?" she asked, each word a little louder than the one before it, as her mind struggled to act like a grown-up.

"I wanted to tell you about the noise."

"The...the noise?" she said through the door.

"I forgot to warn you."

So the house is haunted after all, she thought, nodding too much.

"It's a vixen."

She frowned. "A what?"

"A fox. A female fox. It's mating season. They make a terrible noise, like a woman being murdered."

Ashley remained still, but then the sense of it all came through and she felt her shoulders drop, and a blush stole over her face. She knew there were foxes around here.

A little surprised she'd managed to find a thread of composure, she watched her hands unlock the door and pull it open. Her rational mind remained just a bit eight-years-old at the moment, though, as she was even more relieved to see it was indeed Liam and that he didn't lunge at her with a butcher knife. He wore striped pajama bottoms and a white T-shirt that accented a muscled chest and arms.

"It's... I... Seattle doesn't have a lot of foxes. I've heard peacocks before. They make a terrible sound, too. I..." She stared into his sympathetic expression, and suddenly blurted, "If you've got rum, I've got cola."

They sat on her front stoop in the cool dark, the porch light switched off, inviting the night into their impromptu assembly. Grandma had called the stoop a "porch," but it barely had room for the two lawn chairs Liam had carried over from his buddy's property. If either of them rocked back, there were no railings to keep them from tumbling off, against any kind of code that would have been enforced anywhere but Ashton.

Liam's bed attire was covered now by two plaid blankets, and Ashley's by her sleeping bag, pulled up to her shoulders. She held it in place with one hand, while the other held a rum and off-brand cola near her chin.

As the cries of mating foxes faded, and in low voices meant not to disturb the neighbors, they'd already talked about the weirdnesses of mating animals, the stunning clarity of the night sky far from big city lights, and how a person seemed to notice the scent of flowers more keenly at night.

Ashley had learned that Liam had even more jobs than she'd already discovered. He brought dead animals found on the freeway to a special composting center. Live ones were returned home if they had collars or ID chips, but otherwise went to the Humane Society in Walla Walla. He sawed rounds and split wood, selling bundles to campers or cords to locals. Everyone knew to bring downed trees to him.

"Wow. You work every hour you're awake. I'm now convinced I am incredibly lazy," Ashley said, tipping her red plastic cup an inch his way in salute.

"Nah. Probably just smarter than me," Liam said. "You've got a good-paying job." She'd told him about the internationally known company she worked for. "I have to work a dozen jobs to make a living," he pointed out.

"Why'd you leave Prosser? I assume your folks are there? No jobs?"

He shrugged. "Yeah, my folks are still there. They have a farm. Potatoes. They do okay. And, yeah, there's a lot of manual work to be had in Prosser. Cherry-picking. Apples. Bell peppers. Lots of fruits and veggies. But by the time I graduated high school, I'd had my fill of potato farming. I wanted to try anything else." At her encouraging look, he went on. "I left Prosser to go to Washington State."

"Oh. Okay." She nodded. "I went to the U of W."

"A Husky, eh? I forgive you."

Her mouth slanted. "What'd you study, Coug?"

He rubbed his upper lip. "That's the problem. I didn't. My college grades were 'not superior.' I didn't know what I wanted to study, what I wanted to do. Turns out I'm good with my hands. So I decided to work with them instead of studying. So much for not being a farmer, right?"

She shook her head. "You've got to do what suits you. Follow your bliss."

He laughed softly. "Is Ashton bliss?" He resettled in the lawn chair. "But I like it. I like keeping busy. Variety. You wouldn't think a tiny town would provide variety, but it's there to be found." He nodded, confirming his opinion. "I guess it, and the Corner, fit me."

Ashton's Corner. A mere crossroads. Amazingly, a place smaller than Ashton itself. Ashley gazed outward. From the rise of the porch she could see only three streetlamps total. Who needed more aspects of protection in a place where you could call out a drunk or a window-breaker by name?

The place was surrounded by low hills and rolling fields, with very few trees beyond town; there was little to break up the wind. She remembered there was always a breeze here, if not outright gusts. Now the softly moving air carried the faint and often present odor of cow dung. The breeze danced through someone's nearby windchimes, playing a pleasantly discordant tune. Scents of cut grass and hay reached her nose, too—but there were not-yet-harvested fields nearby as well. She could hear them.

Without the daytime noise of town, you could hear the subtle song of wheat stalks rustling on the close-in hills. It was a sound she hadn't known she recalled, this sigh of sound, and hearing it again gave her a weird sort of gentle ache somewhere deep in her core.

"I remembered this place like a kid does," she said.

Even in the dim light she could see his eyebrows lift, inviting an explanation.

She was glad it was dark and that he probably couldn't see if her face colored. She hadn't meant to say the words aloud, but now she felt obliged to go on. She tilted her head back, indicating the house behind them. "The house scared me."

"I kind of picked up on that." He sipped his drink.

"I thought that was the sum of my experience here. But I guess I didn't realize the impression the rest of the town had made on me. There are things that...stuck. Sounds. Smells." She looked down, a little embarrassed.

When she looked up again his teeth showed in a smile, even in the meager light. "You're falling for old Ashton? Turning into a small-town gal after all?"

"Hardly. I need a bookstore. And a movie theater, or three. Live theater! More than one restaurant. More than one grocery store, for Pete's sake."

"But here you get fresh air. Good dirt—"

"Good dirt?" she echoed, laughing into her cup. "In Seattle I can buy good dirt at the nursery not even a mile from my condo."

He pretended to be offended. "But what about morel mushroom hunting? Can you do that in Seattle?"

"I don't know. Probably."

"Probably not. And there are crowds everywhere. So many people. So many cars. The traffic is..." he groaned as he searched for the words, "...simply amazing."

She could only agree. "Amazingly awful."

"A traffic jam here is four cars."

She laughed. "Okay, less traffic would be great, I admit it."

"And you can always drive from here to Seattle if you need some live theater. It's not that far."

"Seven hours away is not far?"

"Six hours."

"Okay, so you're also a race car driver, because it takes seven hours to get there for normal drivers."

"I'm not a grandpa, I think you mean."

"Are you saying I drive like a grandma? You don't know that."

He started to tease right back, but a porch light three houses away flicked on, catching the attention of them both.

"Oh, dang, I think we're getting too loud," she whispered, sinking down a bit more into her sleeping bag.

He lifted one side of his lip, a young boy unchastened, but all the same he rose and tossed a trailing end of blanket over one shoulder. "I've got to grab a couple more hours of sleep." He met her gaze. "Sorry I forgot to warn you about the foxes. I'm almost used to them myself now, though the first one every year still gives me a heart attack."

"Yeah. I don't think I'll borrow their 'love call' as a technique for my next date."

Liam cocked his head at her for a moment, but seemed to change direction when he said, "See you at ten?"

"That's fine," she said, also rising to dump out the last of her drink. She set the cup by her feet as she squirmed out of the sleeping bag. She felt silly, standing there in her nightgown and socks, so to cover over the moment, she reached to fold the lawn chair she'd been sitting in and hand it to him. "Hey, thanks for the rum."

He handed her his own empty cup. "Thanks for the cola. Sorry Mike didn't have any ice cubes."

"I understand. Small towns don't have fancy new inventions like ice cubes."

"Ha ha," he said dryly, but he smiled. "Good night."

"Good night," she echoed, smiling back.

Stooping to nestle her cup with his, she used the motion to watch him walk away out of the corner of one eye. *Nice build. Nice guy.*

She only realized she'd had no trouble going back to sleep when the alarm woke her four hours later.

Chapter Five

Liam was prompt, at her front door by ten straight up. Ashley had bathed—*that tub really is huge, even a guy Liam's size could stretch out in it...* She was dressed—*so I put on a little lip gloss and a touch of mascara, nothing unusual about that...*

"You shopped already? You chose a color?" she asked as soon as she opened the door, startled to see he carried a gallon of paint in either hand.

"'Course not. This is primer. I thought it was safe to go with white, since you said you wanted to lighten up this front room."

"All the rooms," she agreed, although she hadn't, until this moment, consciously made such a sweeping decision to invest so much effort here. She put out a hand, curling her fingers a couple times to indicate he should hand a can over. "You're right. These rooms are going to need priming. Do you have paint rollers?"

"Yep. In my truck. Just gotta fetch 'em," he said, handing her the two cans instead of one.

"Do we need to steam off the wallpaper first before we paint?" She made a face of distaste at the idea as she adjusted her fingers where they gripped the narrow can handles.

"Unfortunately, maybe," he agreed.

Lunch (peanut butter sandwiches) had come and gone. Ashley was aware she was panting a little bit, and that her arms were aching. From the seat she'd taken on the tarped floor, she looked up to Liam, who didn't seem winded by their work at all. *Some men look good when they're working,* she thought. His green T-shirt, streaked and dotted from other paint jobs, stretched very nicely when he reached to brush in a high corner. It had turned out that Liam's buddy had a tall-enough ladder.

From her seat, she reached to rest the paint roller on the nearly empty paint tray, and spread her arms to shake out the aches. She watched Liam climb down the ladder. "Dang!" she told him. "I can definitely say you're not a dilly-dallier."

"'Dilly-dallier'?" Liam fixed her with a skeptical look. "Are you sure you're not the one who grew up in a small town?"

She laughed, afraid it came out a bit of a twitter. "What do you mean?"

"I would have expected someone in the tech field to be more profane. A 'city woman.' To talk like someone who lives an urban life."

"What can I say? I swear. I do. Sometimes. I just never liked it much. I guess it's not me," she finished, feeling a bit lame. "Not everybody who lives in a city swears left and right, you know."

Liam took one more pass on the wall he'd just finished priming. "Don't get me wrong. I'm not judging. It just surprised me to hear 'gee whiz' and 'golly, mister' coming out of your mouth. Do you watch a lot of retro TV?"

She snorted. "I never said 'golly, mister.'"

"Didn't you?" He put his brush down in the tray, too, and extended a hand to her. He pulled her to her feet, and...did his hand linger? Just for an extra second?

They both turned in a full circle as if cued to a dance move, gazes flying to take in the whole of the front room.

"Wow," Ashley breathed, all at once struck by the work they'd done.

"Damn," Liam said, then whistled.

"It looks so much better," they said together. Eyes met, and flew away again.

It did look better. The coat of primer changed the very essence of the room. They'd even done the ceiling, a choice that Ashley could see helped to disguise the ceiling bowing that had formed with age. Gone was the dark brown of the trim that had looked like dried blood. They'd quickly discovered the wallpaper wasn't going anywhere, so Liam had used a compound to smooth a couple of rough areas, and they'd painted over the paper. She was thrilled to see it had worked.

"Cream," she breathed out, repeating a word Liam had said yesterday. "It's going to be matte cream on the walls, and semi-gloss cream on the trim."

He nodded slowly. "Yep." He gave another little nod of his head toward the door. "Then let's go get 'em."

"I'll get my wallet. But—" she stopped in mid-motion from sudden hesitation. "I don't think I can go with you.

You know what the color should be," she said, surprised to find she believed he would choose well without her input. "But I've got some relatives I need to visit. They know I was coming to town. I promised Mom. Do you mind? Or...I'll bet you need to do some work at your place?"

"I already watered the cattle this morning. Fed the chickens and gathered the eggs. That reminds me, I've got a half dozen for you in my truck. They'll keep for a couple weeks without refrigeration."

Her eyes widened. "You did all that before you came here?"

"Yep. The hardware store doesn't open until nine."

"Now I feel even more guilty making you sit up with me last night."

"Don't. You didn't make me."

A long moment passed, and his usual sidelong teasing smile seemed to take a second to form, as if something weighty held it back for a moment.

He blew out a breath, and ran a hand through his hair. "And, sure, I'll get the paint. No problem." He gave a small weave of his head, a motion that indicated a sudden uncertainty. "But I may have to drive to Lewiston to get the right paint."

"Lewiston? As in Idaho?"

He shrugged. "It's not that far."

It kind of was, in terms of a run to the hardware store. Ashley added gas money to the tab in her head.

"First, though, I'm going to replace your burned-out lightbulbs," he told her.

"That's great." She meant it. "Liam, you're awesome."

He made a dismissive gesture, so she was glad when he accepted the cash for the primer, supplies, and new paint. "Use that to fill your gas tank, too," she said firmly.

He nodded, then grabbed the ladder and pack of bulbs, and headed upstairs.

Ashley pushed out a breath of her own as she returned her wallet to her purse. She felt...weird. In a good way. Right? She hadn't made a new friend in a while. It seemed she was out of practice with the skill. He was a friend, right?

And she hadn't done much lately that was as physical as painting; programming could be creativity-driven, but of the mind rather than the body. This felt...different. Good. Refreshing. *Maybe this little "vacation" is less of a disaster than I feared it would be?*

When, including the ground floor, Liam pronounced all the bulbs replaced, he left a roughly cut half-carton of eggs on her front steps. He jumped in his faded blue truck, waved a hand out the opened driver's window, and drove off to get the paint.

She collected the thoughtful little gift, liking the eggs lightly speckled brown shells. Placing them on the kitchen counter, Ashley then did as she'd told Liam she'd do: she left the kitchen door and the porch screen unlatched. *Look at me, leaving doors unlocked.* She smiled at the unfamiliar choice, but he needed to be able to get back in if she was still gone.

While on the porch, she discovered the water heater was indeed there, in its own cupboard. *That needs insulation, how'd it avoid freezing up during the winters?* She shook her head. That would be the new owner's problem.

Gathering her phone and purse, she secured the front door and walked toward her first destination. Her mom's aunt, Gracie, lived just two blocks over. Her house was kitty-corner from the graceful, red-brick St. Sebastien's, a building wherein a younger Ashley had been both bored and a bit awed by saintly statues and tall stained-glass windows. Maybe she'd stop in there, if it was unlocked, for a nostalgic visit later. If Aunt Gracie, then the Prewitt cousins, and dozens of other possible relatives didn't keep her too late, that is.

And, well, too, she really ought to go back and help out Liam sometime before the end of the day...

Chapter Six

Ashley's first week as the prodigal daughter went by in a flash. It was great seeing A.J., Ingrid, and Dave again. It was fun telling these first cousins—not to mention a plethora of second and third cousins—that she was fixing up Grandma Lewis's house for sale, of which the relatives seemed to approve. It was entertaining to revisit their childhood tales of pranks, and ghost stories, and tadpole hunts with canning jars at the creek.

She was fed a lot of good food, dishes she'd half forgotten about, like mini-marshmallow dotted ambrosia, warm and vinegary German potato salad, bacon-wrapped meatloaf. Plates to take to the house with her were pressed on her, which she'd gratefully accepted. Earlier in the week she'd bought a microwave after all, and a mini-fridge, so she could keep milk for morning cereal, and eggs, and to keep a plate of food for Liam's lunch when he came to work on Grandma's place. He enjoyed the family's food as much as she did; it was fun to watch his eyes light up as he peeled back the foil and assessed the most recent offering.

Six days later, after a lot of scraping and painting and sweating in a growing summer heat, and with the last day of her vacation looming tomorrow, Ashley stood high on a ladder. She reached to press a piece of replacement fretwork wood to the right side of the house. She growled, tried it again, then hung her head in agitation. She'd measured it wrong *again*.

She came down the ladder to glare at the saw and miter box. "I am the leader of my team at work. I've dazzled clients. I've won awards. I *will* conquer you, you evil miter box," she told the tool, shaking a finger at it.

But it was an empty promise. She was leaving tomorrow.

At the weird feeling that came into her stomach at the repeating thought, Ashley sighed. She put down the supplies and moved down to the sidewalk so she could get another look at her grandma's house.

Only, no, not Grandma's house.

Her house.

She'd inherited it, and she was changing it.

The coat rack had been donated to charity. All the rooms had been painted a warm and comforting cream. The front parlor had an accent wall of rich blue that she was liking more and more, even imagining what kind of décor would look good in there. The tattered curtains had all been taken down; she was thinking of installing plain panels, maybe textured? The exterior had been pressure-washed, shedding its peeled paint. Some of the gingerbread pieces had been damaged in the washing, and Liam was trying to teach her how to replace those bits.

He'd promised he'd keep working on the place after she left. She'd given him more cash. He'd said he'd send inventories, and photos.

She frowned now. "Maybe I'll come back in a month to see how you're coming along," she told the house, and the weirdness in her stomach was another uncomfortable lurch. "Or in a couple weeks." She gave the miter box another scowl. "Or next weekend, so I can defeat you."

Now she sat on the front porch steps, a glass of iced tea held between her hands, another one dripping condensation where it sat beside her. It waited for Liam. He'd said he'd be back in town after noon today, and that was five minutes away. She knew she blushed, just knowing he'd be there soon.

Watching as an ant redirected its path around her left sandal, Ashley forced her thoughts back to Seattle. Last night she'd finally retrieved her computer bag from her car's trunk. She really ought to have checked in with work email before. And, sure enough, the Turner project had been moved up by a month. Cecily and Nick were working on it, but they'd each sent her a half-dozen messages, with an increasing number of exclamation points in the subject lines. She would no doubt soon regret she hadn't spent at least a little time each evening working on the scheduling and checking some of the code.

Too bad. I deserve to have enjoyed my time away from work. I deserve to do something different. To have learned how to fix broken gingerbread decorations.

Ah. The gingerbread trim.

Liam had talked her out of removing it from the exterior of the house. She'd always found the black décor to be so *dour*. But Liam had argued vociferously for the detailing to stay.

"They make the place look haunted," she'd argued back.

"But they don't have to! Look, let me paint the arch over the front door, just the arch for now, so you can see what it could look like."

"Are you talking like pinks, and purples, and electric green all together?" She'd shaken her head, unable to visualize such a thing in Ashton. She thought of the whimsical paint jobs in San Francisco. Maybe that was why Grandma had never repainted the house, to keep the unusual-for-Ashton trim from becoming too fanciful for its other residents?

"I'm talking any color combo you want. It's the color that offends you, not the fretwork, I bet."

She'd thought a long moment, but a sense of appeal, of daring, had risen. "Okay," she'd said slowly. "How about a couple shades of blue?" She'd held up a warning finger. "But nothing too dark."

He'd grinned from ear to ear. Two days later, he'd escorted her from where she was sanding the plain bedroom doors (to add trim to them, so they'd more match the staircase door) to see his attempt.

"Holy crud," she'd breathed out, very mild words for a very sudden and large feeling. "Liam, it's... It's fantastic." And it was: three shades of blue picking out the different woodwork details, magically making over what had been dismal into something whimsical and charming. In a flash, she was able to visualize the whole house like this, so unlike its neighbors in the most cheerful and eclectic way.

"The residents of Ashton will shit a brick," she'd breathed out.

"Ha! There's the swearing I've been looking for," Liam had said, laughing.

"But I love it."

She'd turned to—she wasn't sure—slug him in the arm maybe? But she'd missed her aim, falling into chest. His arms had closed around her, steadying her.

And then they were kissing. It had only taken one heartbeat for her to get over being surprised, instead kissing him back with—well, with delight. And something else. A new something. A welcome newness. A scary and already precious *change* that was growing inside her.

Now she waited with iced tea for him, hoping his arrival would bring with it a tenth kiss, or would it be their eleventh since that first? *Yeah, eleventh,* she thought, knowing her thoughts were giddy, and not minding.

His truck pulled up, and he climbed out with a wave and a smile, a simple greeting that made her heart flip over.

A hammer in one hand, a paint scraper in the other, Liam walked up to her. Two sides of the house's exterior re-trimming were already done, and he'd come armed to help her with the third. He set the implements down as Ashley crossed to him, handing him the glass of iced tea.

She turned to take in the house again. "So, when you're done, what do you think she'll be worth?"

"Twice as much as she was. Really." He hoisted the glass, acknowledging it. "Thanks for this." After downing half the contents, he ran his tongue over his teeth, then gave her an apologetic look. "Listen, uh, Ashley. I've got to tell you, I didn't get that sheet of quartz for the bathroom counter. It's just too expensive."

She studied his face for a moment, liking its look, liking the honesty he'd brought with him into the yard. She liked that the mayor of Ashton was hard-working, self-motivated, punctual, and she knew she wanted to learn if he was the open book he presented himself to be.

"I know," she said.

He shook his head, the rueful look on his face deepening. "It's the wrong product. Wrong investment. You're thinking like a homeowner, not like a home flipper."

She met his gaze and, in an instant, made the decision that had been taunting and teasing her since she'd woken. It was amazingly easy, and it was right. She slowly smiled. "I know."

He went to expand his argument, but stopped abruptly. There must have been a clear message in her face, because she saw understanding dawn across his.

"I've fallen in love," she declared, in her excitement her voice going higher than she'd meant it to.

He opened his mouth, and closed it. Color rose on his cheeks. One hand went to rub the back of his neck. "Uh..."

She spun to face the house. "I mean, just look at her! She's already halfway to fabulous. She just needed a bit of change. I can't sell her. I've got to keep her."

"Oh," Liam said. His hand dropped, and he nodded, perhaps a few times too many. "But...uh, what does that mean?"

Ashley turned back to face him. "She's going to be my vacation home. For now."

"For now?"

Ashley tilted her head, dividing her glance between Liam and the house. "I think... Maybe I could make this my home, and my condo my 'other place'? You know, if I were to stay here most of the time, I'd still need to go to Seattle once a month or so."

He looked at her for a long moment, then a smile slowly spread his lips. "Hannah Lewis's big-city granddaughter, are you telling me you might just be thinking about becoming a small-town girl?"

"Well," she said, trying not to smile back, but failing. "I'm willing to try. For now. For a while. We'll see," she said.

"We'll see," he repeated. "Good." The smile spread deep into his brown eyes, and maybe she saw the beginning of a change inside him, too.

There was a lot to be decided. Tried. Change to be met and adapted to. It'd take time, of course.

But, in the meanwhile, she was more than happy to lean in and share her eleventh kiss with a small-town boy.

Teresa DesJardien is the author of fifteen 19th century Regency Romances. Also of the highly useful research guide called: *Jane Austen Shopped Here*. A sometimes small town girl herself, Ms. DesJardien immensely enjoyed writing a modern tale set in Washington State, where she resides with her husband, kids, and grandkids.

Promo info for my works:

Regency Romances:

A June Bride – "In a marriage of convenience, love is not part of the plan."
ISBN 9780986212659/eBook
ISBN 9780986212604/paperback

The Marriage Mart – "Love is a nuisance for a lady in the market for a husband."
ISBN 9780986212666/eBook
ISBN 9780986212611/paperback

Haunted Hearts – "Even romance wears a disguise on All Hallow's Eve."
ISBN 9780986212673/eBook
ISBN 9780986212628/paperback

A Heart's Treasure – "It was a delightful adventure that could only lead to mischief...and love."
ISBN 9780986212680/eBook
ISBN 9780986212635/paperback

A Scandalous Proposa – "Attracted to the wrong man, will the right one find her?"
ISBN 9780986212697/eBook
ISBN 9780986212642/paperback

A Winsome Widow – "It's a simple wager, but all bets are off when it comes to love."
ISBN 9781945458002/eBook
ISBN 9781945458019/paperback

Love's Magic – "Can a wary heart by healed by love and a little magic?"

ISBN 9781945458026/eBook

ISBN 9781945458033/paperback

Borrowed Kisses – "All it takes is one borrowed kiss..."

ISBN 9781945458040/eBook

ISBN 9781945458057/paperback

Coming in August 2020:

Jane Austen Shopped Here – A fabulous and entertaining resource guide for the English Regency, London's confines, manners, marriage and beyond. Perfect for lovers of things Austen, British, Historical, and anyone who seeks more knowledge about the past.

ISBN 9781945458200/eBook

ISBN 9781945458217/paperback

ISBN 9781945458224/hard cover

The Beach List

by

Angela Ford

Chapter One

I sink into my favorite armchair, tossing my hospital badge on the table next to the white daisies. My gaze settles on their beauty as my eyes close. There's a kind of tired that needs a good night's sleep, and another that needs so much more. Drained, coping with life's storms and helping others, I need this time off and I don't care if I spend the next month in my chair. Though fun, friendship, and good times would be better. The past fifteen months have taken a toll on me. The pandemic. The breakup. *Todd.* His name slips through my thoughts, only causing my heart to shatter a little more. If possible. I thought he was the one. His Southern charm, those emerald eyes sparkling beneath long dark lashes—

"How was your shift?"

My peace is suddenly invaded by Sam Jenkins, my roommate and best friend. I open my eyes to his wide-eyed and unshaven face, munching his way through a mouthful of cereal. Next thing—*whomp!* Milk dribbles from his mouth as he tosses a brochure on my lap.

"We deserve this."

He's mistaken my calm for his readiness to take on more. "I can barely think about food," I argue as my stomach growls.

"Since when?" He wipes the dribble from his mouth, promising to feed me if I take a look.

"Cereal?" I tease, my senses having picked up the scent of his cooking the moment I walked through the door.

He walks away from me, stating the cereal is his appetizer. Sam always cooks unless he's working; then I have cereal or takeout, which we've had a lot of the past year. Our open-spaced loft makes it easy for him to ramble while he adds the finishing touches to what I know will be a gourmet meal. The man can cook. Another reason I love him. He keeps my food addiction in check.

It's been a long year. Endless shifts. And by the time we both had the same day off, we camped on the couch for a Netflix binge, ending quickly with Sam's snoring.

His head pops up from behind the fridge door. "Let's take the month and hit the beach."

I pick up the brochure. Beach. Sand. Sunsets. If there's one thing I love, it's the beach. A common factor with Sam besides food, movies, and of course our chosen careers in nursing. He's right. We deserve a real vacation. But this paradise looks beyond our budget.

"Can we even afford this?"

He walks around the kitchen island, chopping knife in hand, and that eyebrow raised. Grinning, ear to ear, waving that knife a little too much for my liking. He glances at it briefly and snickers, "Yes." Then waves it closer to irritate me in a fun way. "Aunt Jane's beach house is there and she's off to Europe. It's ours if we want it."

My so-called tired feet hit the floor, "Seriously?"

Sam smiles. "Would I ever lie to you?"

He never would. I trust him with my life. He loves me—I'm his best friend. Though we did kiss once back in high school. Well, I kissed him. He didn't kiss me back. I was crushed until he confessed, "I don't like girls."

"We haven't been there since—"

Sam finishes my sentence. "Graduation. Long overdue," he mumbles, looking in the fridge. "Iceberg or romaine?"

"Simplicity" sums up Sam. Easy-going, carefree, and drop-dead gorgeous. I'd kill for his hair. Just long enough for your hands to run through that silky mess of dark wavy locks. And his eyes. Let's just say, if there were bedroom eyes—Sam has them. I compliment him all the time as a best friend should.

Me, Rachel Lewis, never carefree. For twenty-seven years, I've been organized. Sam will tease that I'm anal about my skills. He has since I first lived with him back in high school. His parents took me in when my parents were killed in a car accident. His parents I've known my entire life, and they're family. Always will be. His mom always hoped we'd get married but when Sam came out, she realized why I'd only ever be Sam's best friend. His mom has been okay with his sexual orientation; however, his dad has taken some time and is still adjusting.

I am blessed with Sam, his parents, and a career I love. But one over the past year that has exhausted us. Sam is right, we deserve a month in a beach house. A couple hours up the coast will be perfect to relax and unwind. I need to get *him* out of my mind. Him being Todd. He cheated on me a month before the virus struck, which has kept me busy, but he still lingered in my thoughts.

"Rach." Sam's voice brings me back. "You still with me?"

Not wanting to admit I was thinking about Todd, I say, "I am. Just making a beach list in my head."

I lied. Sort of. I mentally organize too. Shaking his head, knowing damn well where my thoughts drifted to, Sam makes fun of my detailed-oriented way. "Seriously, Rach? A beach list."

After a year in a pandemic—on the front lines—in a mask, shield, extra layer of clothing. I know we're different, but a vacation requires some planning.

"What? you don't have a list?"

"Nope." He snickers. "Toss shorts in a bag and off to the beach we go. In hopes of great sex."

I shake my head at his happy-go-lucky nature. "Why are we best friends?"

Sam reminds me we love each other. Simple Sam. Yet this simple man has a wild imagination. I'm more— cautious. Especially since— No. I'm not going there again.

"Is there 'Find a man' on your list?" Sam playfully teases. I take a seat and notice his stare.

"What was the question?" Knowing it drives him crazy when I'm lost in my own thoughts. I chuckle inside as he repeats his question. "Is—there—find—a—man on that beach list of yours?"

"Um...ah... No!"

I had thought about dating after Todd and tossed the idea out to the universe for a sign. Then a pandemic hit.

"Todd is a pompous ass! Don't compare him to the rest of the world."

I know Sam's right. Not every man in the world is like Todd.

"My heart is on leave."

"We've all been on leave during the pandemic. Now it's time for an adventure."

Sam's wiggling of his hips tells me he has "Find a man" on his brain.

"I'm not as adventurous as you are, Sam."

"And what does that mean?" He raises that eyebrow, waiting for my explanation.

"I'm just saying—" I attempt to explain, and he cuts me off.

"I know what you're saying. All I'm suggesting is for you to live a little. Expect the unexpected. You never know what's out there for you."

"Well, I can tell you it's not a man," I sternly assure him.

There goes the eyebrow again. His next piece of advice is coming. Surprised? Never.

"So have a summer fling."

Sam made it sound so simple. I've never been spontaneous. Never.

Chapter Two

"Damn, girl, what's in here?" Sam lifts my suitcase into the hatchback of my Honda HRV.

I laugh. "Come on, you're a nurse. You move patients heavier than that." He blows a fallen dark lock away from his face and ignores my comeback. Inside I chuckle, daring not to crack a smile over his whininess and give any further attention to the situation. We were going away for a month. There are things a girl needs and probably doesn't. I packed for the just-in-case moments. I roll my eyes when Sam tosses in his bag. *How does he travel so light?*

It takes an hour to get through Seattle traffic, then two hours northwest along the coastline before I signal at the exit for Ocean Shores. The scenery is beautiful. For some funny reason, it hits me that Sam and I only visit this place as a reward. This time, not a graduation, and not sex as Sam so eagerly hopes for. This time is for the endless hours worked during the pandemic. The second wave last fall hit harder than the first in the spring. So many lives lost. It still saddens my heart to think about it. We barely saw each other, and we didn't see his parents for months. Thankful Sam and I never tested positive, nor his parents. But there were so many. Too many.

My GPS directs one last turn.

The majestic deep blue ocean instantly removes all worry. The golden sand dazzles from the sunlight, making it sparkle, like thousands of tiny jewels. I turn off the air and power down my window to take in that glorious salt air and listen to the waves crash against the shores. I slow to take it all in. "This is paradise." Looking at Sam, I see his eyes are fixated on the view.

"So calming," comes from his lips.

I had to agree. "You were right, Sam. We did need this."

He questions my statement. "When am I ever wrong?"

I swat his arm.

"Ouch." He whines like a baby. I didn't even slap him that hard.

"Such a wimp."

I tease and then continue along the shore road to what I remember of the two short weekends spent here—the mansion. Sam and I stayed in the guest home, which is no tiny cabin. It has two extremely comfortable queen-size bedrooms; a large open living area clad in beautiful pine timber on the internal walls and ceiling that makes it so warm and welcoming. I pass by it almost wanting to revisit but I knew I'd take a look at some point. This time, we have the entire mansion. Sam's aunt, a world-renowned author, jetted off to Europe to write her next bestseller. I have a few of hers packed, which accounts for the heaviness of my case. I picture myself relaxing on the terrace with one of her books, sipping red wine while marveling at the ocean. The rest of the world will melt away by the serenity of this beautiful location. I look at Sam. "It can't get any better than this."

"It could," Sam adds. I question his argumentative words, wondering what the hell anyone could possibly need above all this. He answers quickly. "A summer fling."

I tilt my head as the corners of his mouth curve into that boyish grin, making those cute dimples appear. "It's not on my beach list. Remember."

He laughs, "You may have not added it, but I did. It's just left unchecked."

"I'm not ready for any form of a relationship," I remind him for the umpteenth time.

Sam opens the door, ignoring me. I step inside the marbled floor kitchen. I love everything about this place. "Absolutely stunning." The words slip from my mouth, leaving Sam to carry in our bags. I love it, its setting, and the elaborate decorative fixings. Something you'd find in one of those home magazines. Passing through the kitchen to the living room, the view is mesmerizing. "I wouldn't have minded being in lockdown here."

"With a sexy beach body to take away any slight boredom?" Sam adds.

I turn, shaking my head. "Down, boy. Is that all you think about?" I make it sound like I don't. And trust me. I do. A lot. My heart may be broken, but all my female parts are quite alive anytime the resemblance of pure masculinity enters my vicinity. It's been a long time since I've been kissed, touched, or even thought of. Well, as far as I knew, not one man has thought about me.

"It is with *him* running along the shoreline."

Sam's focus is to the stretch of beach to the left. My eyes following his stare, I had to agree. Not that I'd admit it to Sam. Silence fills the room as we watch the tanned, ripped, shirtless man slow as if he notices us. Thankful the distance keeps him from seeing us drool in his presence. The mysterious god on the beach waves. Sam grabs my hand, pulling me toward the French doors leading outside, closer to what I fight to stay away from—temptation.

"Sam!" My frantic plea for him to stop is completely ignored.

"We can't be rude. Let's meet him. It's the neighborly thing to do."

Sam opens the doors and pulls me through. *Yeah, right.* He's just feeding his hormones with hopes that this beach god doesn't like girls either. I'll play along, part of me hoping the same. Then that need I feel between my legs will fade and I can read a book and sip on my wine like I plan.

"Hi!" Sam introduces himself and then me. I stand slightly behind Sam, hiding from my own desire to reach out and touch the forbidden fruit.

"Hi, I'm Lucas." His voice, oh dear God, why did he have such a sexy seductive voice. So deep, as if spoken from his chest and not his head. That only takes my eyes to his chest. Bare. Tanned. Toned. Beads of sweat dripping down his sculpted stomach, giving me that Christmas Day feeling. Moisture begins to pool between my thighs as I envision my finger tracing that bead of sweat dripping over his six-pack. It didn't help that he continued to speak.

"You must be Jane's nephew?"

Oh, thank God, he'll hold the conversation with Sam. I listen as he mentions Jane told him we would be occupying her house in July. Sam, eager and hopeful, continues to converse with Lucas. I remain speechless. Not sure why I find myself thinking about taking a stranger on the beach.

Both of them look at me when my phone rings. Embarrassed, hoping I'm not blushing from my recent thoughts, I excuse myself.

Within minutes I finish my call and Sam meets me on the terrace, reminding me we're on vacation.

"I know. Last call. I messaged Lisa to call before she began her shift so I could fill her in on a few things. She sounds refreshed after her vacation."

"We will be too," Sam promises, and his expression changes.

"What's wrong?" I touch his arm. The sadness in his eyes worries me. We know each other so well, like twins who feel each other's emotions.

"He likes girls."

"Who does?"

"Lucas."

I'd briefly forgotten about *him* once my mind went into work mode. The mention of his name brings back that throbbing action between my legs. Sam's comment brings a glimmer of hope. *No!* I harshly remind myself. I don't do flings, or one-nights, and I'm not ready for a relationship. And right now, my best friend needs my comfort.

"I'm sorry, hon." I wrap my arms around him and hold him tightly as he whispers in my ear.

"But he's definitely into you." *How quickly he recovered from that letdown*, I think and release him from our hug.

"Not interested." I start to make my way inside but turn back at the doorway. I have to ask. "And you know this because he told you?"

Sam follows me, smiling. "He didn't have to. As soon as you turned, he checked out your ass."

"That doesn't mean anything. I look at your ass." I laugh it off. I need to. Temptation is not going to win.

Like a lost puppy, Sam follows me inside. "When I'm trying on new jeans. Who else can I trust to tell me if I look good?"

"So who is this Lucas anyway?" I reach for my case, pulling it toward the elevator. Another reason I find it difficult to call this a house.

Sam hits the button, sporting his boyish grin. "Ah, you are interested?"

"Nope. Just being cautious that he's a concerned neighbor and not a plotting thief."

Yep, that's me. Always cautious. Not that Sam isn't. He's not gullible by any means. He's single because he can't commit. Sam tells me his aunt mentioned if there was any trouble with the house that her neighbor is a big help.

"So, he's just a hot neighborly kind of guy." Sam shrugs. "Sorry to burst your belief of him being a plotting thief." Laughter fills the hallway as we step outside the elevator. I stand there for a moment, wondering which way to go. I remember there being five bedrooms fully equipped with their own bathrooms and terrace.

Sam decides for us. "I'll go left, and you go right. That way you're getting closer to Lucas and that awesome sex he could provide."

"Ha!" I turn right without any further acknowledgment to Sam's bold statement. That doesn't stop him. He calls out, "Just think about it, Rach. Hot, wild sex with that body. My God, girl, let him fuck the Todd right out of you."

I smile because I know Sam can't see my face. Many would be offended by his words but not me. I'm used to him. I keep walking. "Love you. I need a shower and then food." I stop at my door and turn.

At the end of the hall, Sam has his hands settled on his hips. "Yes, I'll feed you. Love you too."

"Such a cooperative man." I turn the doorknob, hearing Sam state he knows another cooperative man— next door. "Not interested," I call out and disappear into my room.

I lie. I am interested.

Chapter Three

I feel as though I spent the past hour in a sauna and not a thirty-minute run along the shoreline. The breeze is strong but warm. At least it swirls around me in all directions as I slow in front of my neighbor's house. The perfect time to pace before reaching mine. Each stride on the pale yellow sand not only slows my heart rate but also my mind. The past year has been a roller coaster of emotions. Let down. Worry. Scared. Pumped. Excited. Then nothing. I always feel empty at the end of a tour.

I catch my breath and stretch. The sky above is a gorgeous light blue, with big white clouds, but the sun is fierce. The bead of sweat dripping from my forehead reminds me of its heat. Wiping my brow, I look up at the house and spot people watching me. I assume it's Jane's nephew and his friend. She mentioned they'd be staying at her place. I promised her I'd be around if they needed anything. She'd been kind to me since I moved next door.

The pandemic left Jane and me both sheltered from the world we sometimes fought to hide from. "Be careful what you wish for." I remembered her words when the pandemic hit. I could always talk openly with Jane. She knew how publicity could get to you and you need to take cover. I hadn't meant a pandemic, which canceled last year's tour, and hers. But we survived it like some and not like others.

Then my world switched back to a busy schedule. A successful one. I love what I do. Music has always been my passion. That's what keeps me going and not the fame it brings. The last few months became a blur. Living the life, burning the midnight oil left me exhausted. I need the next month to relax and simply enjoy life at the beach.

I lift my arm in a wave to my watchers and thought it best to do the neighborly thing—introduce myself.

I make my way toward them and Sam introduces himself first, and then his friend, Rachel. He seems more sociable than she does. Shying behind him, more focused on dipping her toes into the hot sand. My mind follows those toes up slender, tanned legs that seem to go on forever until reaching the frayed hem of her denim shorts. To me nothing is hotter than a beautiful woman not advertising how hot she is. Ones with attitude are pains in the ass. Good for eye candy and sex, but to date one is an enormous task not worth the reward. With my success I've encountered too many that bring nothing to the table except their looks, and those fade.

Still, hot sweaty sex with Rachel, the kind that leaves you exhausted and weak, enters my mind. Her phone rings and slams my mind and my cock back to the word "friend" attached to Sam's introduction, but leaves me wondering whether it's platonic or romantic. Polite, yet eager to escape, she excuses herself.

"I'm sorry, I have to take this." She has the voice of an angel. I wonder if she sings. A gust of wind blows her hair around her face and she struggles to contain it as it billows behind her. I want to reach out and touch it. Of course, the back view leads my focus to her ass, but Sam's chatting quickly brings me back to my senses. If their relationship is romantic then I'd just been a dick. I'd never cheat on a woman or with someone's woman. My mother raised me to be a decent guy. It just wasn't right.

Sam glances up at the terrace with concern. I hope the call Rachel received isn't bad news. I remember her name like I'm going to use it in my next song. "I should make my way to a shower. I hope you enjoy your stay and again, if you need anything, just call or stop by."

He thanks me and follows his friend. I start back toward my place, looking back to see her hand touch his arm. She takes him in her arms as he says something against her ear. She moves toward the door with a smile and he follows. *Yep. I was a dick.* I reprimand myself. She's his and it's not platonic. I turn, needing that shower. A cold one.

The early morning temperature turns out better for my run. With the bonus of not running into the honeymooners like the day before. A temptation to avoid. She belongs to him. Heck, I didn't even know this woman. It's just one of those instant attractions. The damage would be irreversible. Why do I even argue the effects of that possibility? That's not me and these feelings will pass. I have to get her off my mind and the cold showers weren't helping, so I do what I love—writing music. Before I know it, it's mid-afternoon, and my stomach reminds me I hadn't eaten since six.

Making my way to the kitchen I notice Sam on my terrace. He's waving two beers in his hands. She's not with him. Not that I need to see her, *she's his.*

I invite him in. "Hey, Sam."

He offers me a beer and I offer him a sandwich. He appears to have had a few already as he staggers inside. I ask how the vacation is going.

"Great. We've worked so many endless hours the past year."

Sam settles himself on a stool and finishes his beer. Normally, I'd offer another, but I think he's had enough and set a bottle of water beside the sandwich.

"Rach and I are both nurses." He rambles a few minutes about their work, their loft, and briefly about the pandemic. "We deserve this vacation. Rach even more than me."

The way he talks about her, I can tell he loves her. I agree with him about the pandemic.

"I hope we never experience another in our lifetime."

Sam cheers me with his empty bottle. "Got any beer?"

I push the plate with the sandwich closer to him. "As long as you eat something."

He agrees and confesses he loves to cook but when Rachel's on shift, he usually has cereal. I get the feeling she's not around or he would have had some food in his stomach to balance his beer intake. Sam finishes the sandwich yet he's still slurring so I offer to walk him back or call Rachel to come get him.

"She went shopping. I'll be fine."

Sam staggers to the door. "She's the best."

I nod. "I'll take your word for that."

He then asks if I'd like to get to know her better. With his tone, I hope it's the beer talking, or I should worry that I have neighbors looking for a ménage à trois. "Sorry, man, I'm not into threesomes."

Sam leans against the door frame. "Me either. I meant just you and Rachel. She's had a rough year and needs to get Todd fucked out of her system." Definitely the beer talking. At least I hoped. She seemed nice. I wonder if this Todd he mentioned had been a willing participant. Either way, I need to stay away from Jane's nephew and his friend, but I didn't want him staggering that close to the water. "I should take you home."

I love the small village of Ocean Shores. The few shops are quaint, and parking isn't a bitch. I pull into Jane's driveway as Lucas passes by and waves. He doesn't seem as friendly as the day before, but I shrug it off. It's better if he isn't friendly so my craving for him will stay a fantasy. And my theory that 99 percent of men are not worth my thoughts. I'm happy to have that one percent as my best friend. My stomach growls and I remind myself that one percent will feed me.

"Sam," I call out as I struggle to get my shopping bags through the door. I set them down on the kitchen floor and call out to him again. Did he go out? If I hadn't focused on Lucas I might have noticed if Sam was with him. No, he would have left a note.

I proceed with my search. I can smell him before I see him sprawled on the living room sofa. It appears he spent the afternoon drinking. "Sam," I abruptly announce my presence as his eyes barely open. "Drinking alone?" He quickly defends through slurred words that he'd been over to visit Lucas and then apologizes.

"For what?" I dare ask. Sam could never hold his liquor. I could easily drink him under the table. But when he drank, his lips became a little loose and his words a little bolder.

"I may have suggested that he fuck Todd out of your system."

"You *what*?"

Sam tells me he loves me and then passes out. Damn it! His heart is always in the right place. I think back to Lucas's expression and wonder what he must possibly think of me.

Chapter Four

"May I come in?"

I dare let her in after her boyfriend's outrageous offer. But she appears nervous, her tone apologetic. I should ask if everything is okay, yet Sam's suggestion that I bang his girlfriend weighs heavier in my thoughts. I'd stand my ground, no matter how tempting. I draw the line at fucking another man's woman. I open the door and her apology immediately follows.

"I'm here to apologize for Sam's behavior."

She seems frazzled, so I offer her a beer. Thanking me, she takes a long swig as I brace myself. Strangely, I pray this beautiful woman isn't about to hit on me.

"Sometimes Sam gets a little bold." She corrects herself. "No." She laughs and admits he's always bold, but after a couple of beers he says what's on his mind.

I listen as she struggles with her words. She looks at me and I see her eyes, not covered by sunglasses. Beautiful. Deep. The color of the ocean. So big and bright, I get lost. But I hear what I didn't want to. "Sam just, well, he just loves me so much. I guess that's why he said what he did." Her shameful expression tells me she wonders what I think of her.

"Look, I'm flattered. Really. I am. You are a beautiful woman. But I'm not into threesomes and I'd never even think of hitting on another man's woman." I assure her I didn't judge whatever the two of them were into. "Call me old-fashioned. I believe in monogamous relationships. And if one wants to move on to another, so be it. Just be honest."

Her eyes hold a certain acceptance, like she agreed. Maybe she did and she loves him so much she went along with it. Then she starts laughing, which I think is rude. Those were my standards, if not hers. When she catches her breath, she apologizes. "I'm not laughing at your morals. I'm laughing you think Sam and I are lovers looking for *a ménage à trois*."

Now I'm confused. "You're not?" Wishful. Hopeful. Wanting her again suddenly returns.

"Sam's gay," she blurts, explaining they'd been best friends since they were five.

"Gay?"

"Yes."

Lucas laughs. "I thought you two were an item and trying to get me to—I don't know—spice up the relationship." I confirm, again, I'm not into that and would never go anywhere near making problems that could hurt a relationship. To me, that's off limits.

"Oh God! That's what you thought? That's even worse than thinking I can't get a date and my best friend has to hook me up."

Rachel fills me in on her breakup with Todd and her beach list Sam jokingly suggested she add a summer fling to. I admit I'm pleased to be nominated. Her smile hits me right in the heart and awakens the temptation again. But her words knock my ego back down.

"It's not you. I'm just not ready for any type of relationship. Besides, I've never even had a fling before, or a one-nighter."

I can't agree with her. I've had a few too many. It's the relationship I couldn't do. My crazy life and schedule wouldn't be fair to another person. Besides the fact that any woman I'd been with had probably been with me because I was Lucas Locklin. Not one of them had wanted *me*—Lucas. That I came to accept.

Rachel finishes her beer and thanks me for my understanding. She's leaving, her words clear on the fact she didn't want me one way or the other. But her eyes tell me differently and I take the chance. "If you change your mind, I'd be willing."

Her stomach growls before she can answer. Blushing with embarrassment, she apologizes.

I remember Sam saying he did all the cooking and with his state, she may go hungry.

"Since it appears Sam won't be cooking, would you like to join me for dinner? I'm a fantastic griller." She hesitates, so I add, "Just dinner. No pressure and I promise to be the perfect gentleman. But if you do change your mind, you'll have to make the first move."

She nervously chuckles and asks if she has time to clean up and check on Sam.

I smile. "Seven on the terrace." She nods. "Okay, see you then."

Chapter Five

He offers me sex without strings, and I turn him down. *What the hell is wrong with me?* I think as the scent of my lavender shampoo lingers in the air, calming my overactive mind. I get into the music playing through the built-in wall speakers and finish my makeup. Just a touch of blush and gloss to enhance my tanned complexion. I look in the mirror, pleased, and tell myself, "Time to figure out what to wear." And I have no idea.

I find Sam standing in my room. His finger resting on his chin, that eyebrow raised, and he's staring at my wardrobe. "Tonight's outfit. It should be casual but sexy. Flirtatious yet not screaming out 'I haven't had sex in over a year.' "

I remove the towel from my head and swat him with it. "Thought you were passed out cold."

"Ouch! I get no appreciation." He teases and then admits he read my note on the kitchen counter.

"Thought you'd slip out for a little sex tonight, did you?"

Shaking my head, I reiterate what my note said. "It's just dinner."

He moves in closer. "You smell too good for dinner." His eyes travel below the hem of my robe. "And freshly shaven legs." His gaze moves upward to meet mine. "Dinner, my ass!"

I defend my answer. "He offered to feed me since you were passed out. You know how much I enjoy food." I wasn't sure if I was trying to convince Sam or myself. I collapse on the bed with hesitation racing through my brain. I remember Lucas's words: *If you change your mind. You'll have to make the first move.*

I'm safe. I'd never be that brave.

"Rach, are you being indecisive?"

I lift my head to find Sam holding a dress in each hand and I ask him which color he likes.

"I'm not talking about the color, Rach." His head tilts. "I know you're hesitating. No backing out now. The man is hot and into you."

Sam makes it sound so simple and I make it so complicated. "How do you do it?"

"You want specifics?" he teases.

"Ha! I know what to do. Just don't know if casual sex is me."

Sam asks me if I like Lucas. I nod.

"Does he make you horny?"

"Jesus, Sam."

"Talking to me is like talking it out in your head." He strangely makes sense, and what woman in her right mind would turn down Lucas's offer? Sam snaps his fingers to get my attention again. "I didn't *mean* for you to talk it out in your head. Answer me."

I follow Sam's movement as he lifts each dress in the air. "And if your answer is yes, then we need to decide on the color."

I grin. "I love you."

"Ditto. Now decide." His impatience makes me giggle and I decide on the blue.

I find Lucas at the grill dressed in khakis and a white cotton shirt enhancing that ripped physique of his. He glances over at me and I feel my cheeks grow red. His sincere and gentle eyes help start a conversation, break the ice, but his smile is a powerful weapon for seduction.

Just being in his presence makes me catch my breath and my skin tingle. I offer to pour the wine while he finishes at the grill. He holds my stare unabashedly over a glass of wine and my mind wanders with a fantasy of crawling across the dinner table, lowering myself onto his lap. Maybe a naughty nibble, a barely there brush of my lips, or a tantalizing tongue wiggle to the right area of his body and he'll hit that orgasm, thinking, *Wow, how'd she do that?*

"Rachel?"

Shit! I did it again. Letting my mind drift to a seductive play I wish I had the nerve to follow through with. "Sorry," I apologize without admission of what I wanted to do to him.

"How do you take your steak?" he asks, adding that he hoped I wasn't a vegetarian.

"Medium rare."

I maintain focus during dinner to avoid slipping back into my fantasy. It's like he sensed my nervousness. "I worried you might not show."

I admit I hesitated. "Just for a moment."

He sports that smile that for some reason relaxes me and excites me at the same time. Or maybe it was the wine. Whatever it was, I am enjoying his company and his food. I feel at ease with a man I barely knew. A man I want more as each minute passes. We chat about our likes and dislikes and laugh over the assumptions made from Sam's drunken behavior.

We keep the conversation simple, agreeing not to discuss work since we are on vacation. The more we talk, the more wine we drink. All of which makes me want to bring my earlier fantasy into reality. I release a sigh without thinking.

"Everything okay?" His genuine concern touches me deeply. Knowing he heard my sigh gives me the opportunity to make that first move.

"Not really." I pause and dig deep for courage. I take another sip of wine as he patiently waits for me to explain. "My mind travels sometimes," I admit.

"Where did you travel to, if I may ask?"

Oh, God. Do I confess? Share my fantasy. Be brave, I tell myself.

"I've been wondering how to make that first move since I arrived."

There. I said it. There's no turning back now. Not that I wanted to.

"You just did by telling me that."

He takes my hand, gently grazing his lips across it. The slight, subtle touch induces shivers I'd never experienced. One simple kiss confirms he'd show me an insane time in the bedroom. He stands, asking me to dance to the slow music playing softly around us. I melt in his arms as his mouth takes my earlobe between his lips and gently tugs. This gives me goose bumps, making me completely crazy for his lips against mine. He starts humming along to the music while he presses tender kisses along my neck. His mouth vibrates against my skin in a way that feels similar to a sex toy.

The varying pitch of his voice creates a range of sensations. Lower at first and then slower vibrations, followed with higher pitches and faster ones, suggestive of what he could do down below with that mouth. His kisses establish an *I want you now* connection and he takes the passion level up a notch, gently pulling back my head and to the side, exposing the extra-sensitive area from my ear to my shoulder. He works his way down the ridge, randomly alternating between small nibbles and gentle kisses, making my imagination run wild with hot and heavy possibilities.

Then he stops. I open my eyes. "Don't stop." His lips cover mine in a desperate, needy motion and then he takes my bottom lip between his and sucks on it gently before exploring my mouth, flicking his tongue along the roof of my mouth, throwing my senses for a loop. He breaks from our kiss, leaving me breathless.

"Are you sure you want this?"

I smile. The desire burning inside me wants to take him right here, right now.

"You said I made my move. That confirms I changed my mind."

He grins, asking if we could move this inside.

"Your mouth delivers such an incredible range of sensations. I'm curious to discover what else you can deliver." His lips brush mine softly, whispering what I want to hear. "I'll be more than happy to oblige your every want, your every desire." He takes my hand and leads the way, knowing this is about to be the best night of my life. A summer fling. Wild sex. No strings attached.

Chapter Six

I slip inside without making a sound, not wanting to wake Sam. I wasn't quite ready for his interrogation. I needed time to think about Lucas's invitation. But it could be dangerous to my heart. I already felt the trickling of emotions pulling at my heartstrings. Thankfully he had to go into the city today, so I could spend the time debating my pros and cons.

Why am I so analytical? Why can't I be more carefree like Sam? Talk it out in my head, Sam would say. I need to wake Sam.

As that thought enters my mind, I notice my beach list on the kitchen counter. *Really, Sam?* I laugh, noticing his handwritten addition of "Summer fling." Beside it—a check mark. Then I hear the approaching patter of footsteps.

"What happened to lover boy?"

I pour a cup and take a sip of the freshly brewed coffee, ready to be drilled.

"He had to go into the city." I turn to Sam. "Parasailing or jet skis?"

Like changing the subject would stop him. But I need both his advice and a fun day.

A day with Sam is well spent and parasailing was more thrilling than I'd remembered. "Why haven't we done that since college?"

Sam shrugs. "Busy lives. Work. Pandemic." My stomach growls and he adds, "Feeding you." He pats my stomach, adding he'll fire up the barbecue grill. I'll never turn down food and I offer to make the salads. Usually the only part of the meal he allows me to do. Pouring a glass of wine, Sam grabs a beer and the steaks and then escapes to the grill.

Sam offers to clean up while I get ready for my date. I decided to hold onto my one-night-virginity and accept Lucas's invitation. He said he hoped to be back by eight and told me to meet him in the hot tub, which made it easier to decide on an outfit. In a bikini and wrap, Sam kisses my cheek. Barely. "Don't want him to smell me on you. He's already questioned our relationship."

I laugh. "He knows you're gay."

Sam quickly asks if he has any friends who are. I shake my head. "You are hopeless."

He nods. "A hopeless horny romantic."

I agree, but I hold on to hope that he meets the one for him. The one who deserves him.

I head to Lucas's place. With the sun shining directly on the hot tub, I hold my hand over my eyes as I climb the steps. Then my heart sinks when I hear an unexpected female voice.

"Who the hell are you?"

A gorgeous naked blonde in the hot tub acts like she owns it. I answer her with the same question. Her reply stabs me in the heart. Flashbacks of Todd in bed with another woman who asked the same of me when I walked in on them.

"I'm Shelby. Lucas's fiancée."

I can't speak. My hands are trembling as I try to grip the rail to hold me up. I can't breathe. *Damn, I'm stupid*, I think as I turn and run down the stairs and up the beach. Once inside, I could hold the heartbreak no longer and collapse to the floor in a disheveled heap as my grief pours out in a flood of uncontrollable tears. My sudden presence alarms Sam.

"Rach? What the hell? Are you okay?"

Inhale. Exhale. I desperately try to even my breathing and answer him.

"Blonde. Naked. Fiancée."

Sam helps me to my feet, slowly walking me to the sofa. Kneeling in front of me, he takes my hands in his. My breathing eases but the tears don't.

"Rach?"

His gentle voice calms me, and he wipes my tears with his shirt. His loving nature warms my shattered heart. "I'm so stupid."

Squeezing my hands, he argues, "You're the smartest person I know."

I laugh, almost choking, and then decide to remain quiet to slow my heart rate. He always compliments me and means it. Why can't other men be more like Sam?

He checks my vitals; I roll my eyes at him. He ignores my gesture. Nurses must have patience, along with great empathy. We help people overcome anxiety—it's crucial in our profession.

"First, I'm getting you a glass of wine. Then, you tell me what the hell happened."

I close my eyes and focus on my breathing. I am no better than that woman I found with Todd.

I take a sip of the wine Sam brings, and then tell him. "Lying, cheating bastard. The respect I had for him just washed out to sea."

Sam sits beside me, comforting me in silence as we sip wine. I need time to absorb what just happened.

"I'm never dating again."

Before Sam starts in, I point my finger at him. "Don't try to convince me otherwise." He respects my wishes. For now.

And we sit, finishing our wine until our peace is abruptly ended by a knock at the door.

Immediately, I know who it is. "The nerve!"

Sam stood. "I'll take care of this."

I watch Sam close the door behind him. I can see them but can't make out what they're saying. Lucas brushes a hand through his hair. His focus turns from Sam to me through the glass and I look away. My heart is aching, not only for myself but for his fiancée. I've been there.

Voices simmer and the door opens, pulling my focus to Sam.

"You might want to come out here. It's not what you think."

I'm sure I know what I saw and what I heard. Sam pleads, "Give him a chance to explain." He walks past me, leaving the door open and Lucas standing there.

Slowly, I walk toward him, taking a deep breath. I'll accept his apology. Then I'll have closure. Not like I did with Todd. After two days he never apologized so I blocked him and never heard from him again. It was over. Still, closure is good.

Determined not to allow threatening tears to spill, I fixate on his perfection. He has muscles where it's attractive and a well-defined, chiseled jawline that starts my erotic engine, fueled by arousal. I truly didn't understand the power of arousal until last night. He knew how to build it. He knew how to maintain it. God, he's beautiful.

"Rachel, I'm sorry that this happened."

"This?" If he's edging toward an effective apology, he isn't hitting the mark. He shows no sign of regret or remorse. At least I only invested one night in him. That poor girl accepted his proposal to spend the rest of her life with him. I expected him to express some regret. I hope his apology to *her* went better, which I realized must not have because he was here.

"This—meaning last night with you and me, or this—meaning getting caught by your fiancée?"

He stops me. "She's *not* my fiancée."

Did he think I was *that* naïve? "I'm pretty sure I heard her correctly."

"I never proposed to Shelby." His voice is shaky and weak. I let him continue.

"I don't know how she found me here, but trust me she's gone." He sounded sincere, reminding me of the girl he told me he dated in high school. The one who cheated on him with his best friend. Lucas mentioned her last night, not in great detail, but I got the impression she did a number on him like Todd did on me.

"I hadn't heard from her in years until this year's tour," he says. I didn't remember him mention he was military.

"Tour of duty?"

He appears confused. I thought it a simple question.

"I'm not military, but my tours do hold tremendous duty to my fans."

"Fans?" Now I'm confused.

Lucas smiles. "You really don't know what I do for a living?"

I remind him we decided not to discuss work while on vacation. He nods, apparently remembering that part of our conversation, but still surprised.

"You've never heard of Lucas Locklin?"

I'm not sure whom I slept with now. My head is spinning. I slept with a man I barely knew and didn't think to ask for his last name. Though I hadn't offered mine either. Not that it mattered, but then I have to wonder who Lucas Locklin is.

"I guess last names weren't exchanged last night. I'm sorry, should the name mean something?"

Brushing aside a strand of hair that swept across my cheek, he half-smiles at the doubt my question implied, and he looks at me as his smile grows and his eyes light up as the setting sun shines against us. "I like it better that you don't know." His finger trails along the length of my neck, reminding me of the way his mouth moved against it last night. Remembering the most passionate night, I don't shy away my inner thoughts. I speak from my heart.

"Last night. I honestly haven't had a better time in my life. But now I'm worried I shouldn't have given in to one night with someone I don't know."

"Then let's not leave it at one night and I'll tell you whatever you want to know."

His offer is tempting. It is hard to fight the sensation his fingers are leaving on my neck.

"One quick question." He nods. His gaze, powerful and filled with affection, is arousing my need to kiss him, but I have to know. "Who is Lucas Locklin?"

His lips brush softly across mine as he whispers, "A musician, but with you, I'm just Lucas." He grazes my bottom lip gently with his teeth. Slowly, he pulls back and announces he's the man who wants to bring my every desire to life. That I already knew he could do. His kisses— so intimate. Yes indeed, great sex comes after, but it all begins with his kiss. And damn, this man can kiss.

Obviously, I made her feel good in the bedroom, remembering her words that it had been the best night of her life. What does Rachel desire? I ask myself, climbing the steps to my terrace. I offer to mix things up to deliver whatever she wants. To my surprise, her answer implies we don't have to go full-on *Fifty Shades*. "You have what I need."

Then she throws me for a loop. "What do *you* like?"

No woman had ever asked me what I wanted. If she could be brave, then so could I. "You can start with your mouth on my nipples." She reaches for the hem of my shirt, pulling it up and over my head. The silky texture of her tongue feels so sexy on the erogenous zone most women ignore. I often wonder why it's something only women should like.

She switches from one type of texture to another with her tongue, keeping all my senses on maximum alert. I knew my secret craving to have attention paid here would make me beg for more when she stops. Her hand grips the edge of my waistline.

"Can we move this inside?" I ask. We do.

She stops me at the edge of the bed, slightly releasing the pressure of my arousal, unzipping my pants, and slowly pushing them over my hips until they fall to the floor. Her hands follow the length of my legs, gripping the backsides until she lowers herself and she plants a light-as-a-feather kiss above my knee. From there she works her way up, increasing the pressure of her lips against my skin the farther she goes. Priming me for super hot sex.

Most women I'd been with typically didn't participate as equally in foreplay. I like this dominant side of Rachel and she prolongs the participation by starting over again down at my other knee, driving me crazy with anticipation. The sensitivity of her kisses lead a treasure trail right to where I'm dying for her to go. Her nibbling simply is hard enough that I can feel it, but gentle enough that I'm not jumping out of my skin. The pinpricks of slight pain she creates send jolts of electricity throughout my lower region.

Pushing me softly on the bed, she straddles me as I lie back, and presses her mouth firmly against my neck. Her tongue is flexed so it's pointy, probing behind my ear, working her way down using her tongue instead of her fingers and her lips instead of her hands. The massage instantly goes from relaxing to racy when she hits my nipples. The swivel of her tongue and a puff of air produce a thrilling hot-then-cold sensation. My body is so in tune to hers, giving our intimacy a surcharge.

In between licking and sucking, she grazes her teeth against my skin for a little added excitement, while she whispers demands and getting vocal about what she wants me to do to her. Repeating my name with each demand is such a turn-on, I whip her around until she's beneath me and I guarantee another night to remember.

Chapter Seven

Tapping my fingers on the table to the song playing, I hear Lucas come out onto the terrace with my morning coffee in hand. "You like my song?" he asks.

I look up in surprise. I'd forgotten he was a musician the moment his mouth took over with a guarantee of another night I'll never forget.

"This is you?"

He modestly nods and I answer, "Cool. I like it."

I think I've heard it before and confess I'm not good with names of songs or who sings them. "If I like it, I listen. If not, I move on."

He chuckles half-heartedly. "Then I take you like it since Spotify is still playing it."

I give him a thumbs-up and he kisses the tip of my nose. "Thanks for the raving review." I know he's joking, but still, I explain I'm more of a book and movie kind of gal. He smiles. God! That mouth reminds me of its talent. I blurt out my inner thoughts. For some reason, this man brings out my bravery.

"You are talented." I smile and add, "That mouth of yours brings sensations to my body I've never experienced before. And it's rather good for singing too." I wink. "But that's all you're getting." I remind him we agreed not to talk about work. He nods.

"I'm more flattered you like *me* and not *him*." Lucas points to the speaker playing his song.

He lowers his lips to mine in a soft kiss. "I guess we'll just have to talk about sex."

I admit I like a cooperative man, and he deepens the kiss, pulling me back inside.

One night led to one week and then closer to one month. We did enjoy each other and never discussed work again, no matter how many times Sam attempted. "Summer fling" was checked off the beach list, but I held on to my one-night-virginity. Lucas and I talked about what happens after our month, but we agreed our busy lives and schedules are too different. I tried not to think about it, knowing my heart would ache once it ended, but the memory of him would forever remain.

He'd been planning a special night for us when the call came, that Sam and I had to get back to work. "I'm sorry. I know you planned something special tomorrow night, but duty calls."

His eyes held sadness, but then he took me in his arms with one last trail of his kisses along my neck. My heart began to sink. I was going to miss him. I hope he will remember me as much as I'll remember him and our summer fling.

"I wish you didn't have to go, but I understand."

Sam loads the car and offers to drive. I don't argue. My mind is elsewhere. He attempts small talk but when I don't participate, he turns on the radio. Lucas's voice rolls out through the speakers. I look at Sam and he turns it off immediately. "Sorry, bad idea." He drives in silence after reminding me he's available to listen when I'm ready. I wasn't and leaned back, closing my eyes the rest of the way.

By the end of the first four shifts, exhaustion hits me hard. I start to pack up the supplies in the mobile unit Sam and I were called back to run, giving long-awaited vaccines. The curtain opens and Sam informs me we have one more patient. I hand him a package and he shakes his head. "This one is for you."

I open the curtain to find Lucas. I hadn't expected to ever see him again. He wanted to exchange numbers, but I told him it would only make it harder. It was best to leave *us* as a memory. His words reminded me how lost I felt without him.

"For a month, I was happy. For the past four days, I was miserable."

"But—"

He presses a finger gently on my lips. "I don't care what we agreed, I can't spend another day without you."

My heart races as he tells me about the call he received with sudden good news of an award. "You were the first person I wanted to share it with."

Confessing he can't picture himself going with anyone else. "You're the one, Rach." His hands rest on my hips, he pulls me closer, holding my stare. "I'll always be your first summer fling," he pleads. "Let me be your last."

I seal my lips over his in reply. Something great follows a kiss when it comes to us.

Angela Ford resides in Nova Scotia - Canada's Ocean Playground. Inspired by sunsets, the ocean, her family, and books! She is never without a book, whether she is reading or writing. Angela is a bestselling and award-winning author who has been in the top fifty, Readers' Choice Awards, and ScreenCraft. She has over 50 published works in paperback, ebook, audiobook, and foreign translation. An Award of Distinction sparked the idea for her first book 'Closure' that hit Bestselling Action & Adventure, Women's fiction. In between mysteries, Angela writes short contemporary romance. She loves to connect with her readers! www.angelafordauthor.com

Follow me on Facebook Twitter Goodreads Instagram

Most Recent Releases : The Healing Hearts Ranch Series (YA) & Love On Tour (Sweet Romance) Links can be found at my campsite angelafordromance.

Love On Tour is perma free (link at my campsite as well).

Spicy Beach Reads : Sunset Kisses (.99 Cents) & Seaside Seduction (links also at my campsite -angelafordromance)

Sea Change

by

Pam Binder

Chapter One

Under the protective glow of the new moon, a crow searched for Muirenn, the captured whale shapeshifter. Klem, Sage of the crow clan, had traveled along the coastline for weeks, and this remote location was his last hope of finding her. He circled the structure named the Whale Sanctuary, nestled against a grove of cedar, oak, and pine trees. He'd heard rumors of a shapeshifter having been captured and caged, but while battles raged across The Great Land there had been precious little time to investigate. While searching for Muirenn he'd discovered the grim rumors of captive shapeshifters were true.

He circled lower. Something would have to be done to free them all, but first he had an assignment to fulfill.

From Klem's view, the Whale Sanctuary resembled half of a wheel. The flat side faced the bay, while the rounded side abutted the forest. It was made up of five tanks of water separated by gates connected by passageways, with the largest tank facing the bay. Four water tanks housed killer whales and their young, who seemed content to swim around and around in a confined space. The one that contained only one whale caught the crow's attention.

Klem dipped his wing for a closer look, heading toward the tank that housed the lone killer whale. As an intuitive he could see the whale's aura, and the human image caught him by surprise. Not only was the whale a shapeshifter, a being with the ability to shift into human or animal image, but Klem recognized him from descriptions. How was that possible? Max'inux was supposed to be dead.

Klem watched Max'inux as he swam in his whale image through the water, acting as though the shapeshifter didn't care that he was in a cage. Klem knew differently. Nothing was ever as it seemed.

Chapter Two

Max'inux felt the stark, white walls of his tank close in around him. He'd thought after all this time in captivity he'd get used to swimming in a confined space rather than free to explore the vastness of the oceans. He made another turn around his tank, fighting the urge to listen for the caw of seagulls, the surge of waves against the shore, or the distant song of whales. Those sounds were part of his past. A past he could no longer claim.

When he first had been captured he had been too injured to escape. During his recovery the handlers, fearing he might die, wasted little time and drew his sperm, impregnating one of the female whales. Later, after he'd recovered, he'd learned the female whale had died in childbirth, giving him a son. He knew the child was not shapeshifter, but it didn't matter. The child was his. It had been a long time since Max'inux had cared about anyone or anything. Learning he had a son had changed that.

A short time ago another female whale was captured and days away from giving birth, he had made sure he was there to help. He didn't want another child growing up without a mother. Sometimes those invisible scars never healed. During the difficult labor, he'd learned the female whale was shapeshifter and her name was Muirenn.

He felt a stirring in the air, a prickling of the skin, and then a crow landed nearby. He knew the crow was a shapeshifter. Most whales were intuitives, both a gift as well as a curse. Max'inux hadn't seen a crow shapeshifter since... Darkness rolled over him, bringing back the memories that he wanted—no, needed—to forget. He ignored the crow and rolled in the water, maneuvering his massive whale body in a slow, deliberate turn.

"I know who you are." The crow had shifted into his human image and his cloak fluttered around him like wings. He had the look of a man who'd seen battles and come out the victor. "My name is Klem and I was sent to find Muirenn, but the council will be pleased you are alive. I can help you escape."

If Max'inux had wanted to escape, he would have. No, this was where he belonged. Correction—this was where he deserved to be. He flipped his tail in the air as though to turn and leave and then paused, remembering Muirenn, her child, and the other shapeshifter, Tatkret. He had his reasons for staying, but he couldn't make that decision for the others.

Out of respect, Max'inux began to shift. His body became more defined as legs formed and arms extended. He would remain in the water. Over seven feet tall and built for battle, his size alone instilled fear. But what made the blood of both shapeshifter and singlesight run cold was the tattoo on the left side of his face. It was the totem image of a killer whale posed to attack. His size, even in its human image, instilled fear.

Max'inux's instincts proved correct when Klem swallowed and stepped back. Max'inux treaded water, keeping his distance. "There are those here that have need of your help," Max'inux said. "But they need more than the cunning of your kind to pick a lock or steal a set of keys. They need the will to want to leave. Who amongst your kind can accomplish such a task?"

"Can you not conjure the will yourselves?" When silence reigned, Klem continued. "I know someone. Zimp of the red cloak."

Max'inux heard it then. In the performance pool on the side of the bay, a woman cried for help.

Chapter Three

Muirenn swam in her whale image until she was convinced the human-only handlers who worked at the Whale Sanctuary had left for the evening. It grew increasingly more dangerous to shift into her human image, but there was more risk if she didn't. If she didn't shift into her human image every few days, she would remain a beast forever. Forever longing to be human and forever denied the gift of shapeshifter. She'd chosen to swim in the performance pool rather than her own tank because the Sanctuary's handlers had neglected to draw the net-like dome over the top. As a result, there was more light from the new moon and stars. Without the dome, it would be an easy feat to leap over the seawall and into the bay. But leaving here was not an option.

She kept to the shadows in the pool while she willed the shift from whale to human to begin. Her body shrank. Her tail split to form legs and her flippers, arms. Her hair swept down her shoulders in dark waves. She twisted it into one long braid to keep it in place while she swam. At six foot five inches she was tall for a human-only, but average height for a female whale shapeshifter.

In her human image her senses were still heightened, but her reactions to her surroundings changed. The water was like warm silk as she swam with practiced ease through the moon-kissed water. As human she could block out the desperation she felt at being confined rather than free to explore the oceans of The Great Land. But shifting was dangerous. If she were discovered in her human image her cage would shrink not expand.

She fought against the waves of despair that threatened to engulf her. Muirenn's life had not turned out the way she'd imagined.

Her mother had groomed her to take over as the leader of their clan and The Few had been considering inviting her to sit on the Council. Even more extraordinary, her mother, as leader of the largest whale shapeshifter clan, had considered allowing her daughter to accept. Her mother's decision had been controversial. For thousands of years the whale clans had refused to get involved with the politics and battles of The Great Land.

"Help me," a woman pleaded. The cry rose above the lap of water against the sides of the tank.

Muirenn paused, treading water. Recognizing the voice, her pulse vibrated through her. The woman was a whale shapeshifter from the transient clan. Muirenn searched the shadows and found her huddled against the seawall. Tatkret was small for a shapeshifter whale and in her human image was only around five eight, made thin by her refusal to eat. She hugged her knees against her chest, slowly rocking back and forth. Muirenn scanned the area for anyone else, but the woman was alone.

Tatkret turned in Muirenn's direction. "I don't think I can do this on my own."

Muirenn's skin chilled at the tone in Tatkret's voice as she moved through the water toward the woman. What was she trying to say?

Each stroke Muirenn took was whisper soft as her mind raced. Tatkret had refused to eat and for weeks her handlers had been concerned that she'd given up the will to live. That could have been a large part, but another reason was that she was from the transient clan and they didn't eat fish. But Muirenn feared that Tatkret's refusal to eat hid a darker purpose. Was Tatkret trying to end her life? Muirenn shuddered. The mere thought of a whale committing such an act was unthinkable. When Muirenn reached the edge of the pool she glanced over her shoulder again, expecting alarm bells. None sounded.

She wondered why Tatkret had risked leaving her tank. Muirenn had overheard the doctors say that she had developed an infection and her organs were shutting down. Her doctors had advised the Sanctuary against having Tatkret performing until she'd recovered. In a rare moment of compassion, they'd agreed.

Muirenn pulled herself out of the water. "I will be happy to help you return to your own tank. You shouldn't be here."

The woman's smile was paper-thin as she tried to push to her feet. The effort cost her. "None of us belong here. Even the legendary warrior, Max'inux, chafes against his captivity."

"And yet he stays," Muirenn said.

"He has his reasons."

Muirenn took in a breath of calming sea air. Tatkret and Max'inux were from the same transient clan and maybe that was the reason Tatkret didn't blame him for what had happened. Muirenn knew he'd tried to convince Tatkret to eat fish like he'd learned to do, but she'd refused. And true, he'd helped her through the birth of her child, with a tenderness she hadn't expected in someone from his clan, but he had a dark side she couldn't reconcile.

"Whale shapeshifters take a vow not to kill humans," Muirenn blurted, fighting down her contempt. "And yet your legendary warrior murdered his handler."

"Max'inux may have had his reasons. You would do well to ask him."

Muirenn waved away Tatkret's comment. The last thing Muirenn wanted to do was get involved with a beast that was out of control. Muirenn took Tatkret's hand in hers. "You need to rest. I'll help you back to your tank."

"I will not go back."

The woman reached out and grasped Muirenn's arm with a strength that was surprising in someone who looked so frail. "I'm going home," she said.

The home Tatkret spoke of was Whale Island, a haven of beauty, safety, and peace. After two years in captivity, however, Muirenn was beginning to believe the Island was more a dream rather than reality. "You're too weak to make it that far. They'll find you and bring you back."

"There will be nothing of me to find."

Muirenn's eyes blurred, realizing Tatkret wouldn't survive the jump, and perhaps that had been her plan all along. "What you're asking me to do is against our beliefs. I can't..."

Tatkret lifted her chin. "It was wrong of me to ask for your help in this matter. I see that now. This is something I must do on my own."

"When you are stronger..."

The woman drew in a breath and hauled herself to a standing position. Muirenn rose with her. It was late October and the surf climbed the seawalls as though opening its arms. The sound of the surf thundered in Muirenn's ears and vibrated through her body. The call was so powerful she staggered and reached out to the seawall for support.

The woman's smile reminded Muirenn of warm sandy beaches. "You should come with me. Even if I don't make it, at least you will be free."

"I won't leave my daughter," Muirenn said evenly.

The woman's eyes unfocused as though she had already drifted into another realm, the second realm of their ancestors. When her vision cleared, her voice was so feather soft Muirenn had to lean in to hear her words. "Save her, then."

"It's not that simple. At least if we stay here we will survive."

The woman shook her head slowly. "Without risk, there is not life."

Muirenn couldn't breathe. Her mother had said something similar the day she'd been murdered by a human-only. A tear traced a path down her cheek, tasting of salt, as she searched for words that might change Tatkret's mind. She cleared her throat. "The fall will kill you."

"Only our bodies die."

A disturbance in the water drew Muirenn's attention. Max'inux had swum through the interconnecting passageways and was shifting from whale to human image. In one fluid motion he rose from the water and stood before her. Over seven feet tall, his dark skin glistened with water as he pushed the hair out of his face.

He glanced toward Muirenn as though there was something he'd wanted to say, words that were left unsaid between them.

She stepped toward him and nodded, grateful that he'd come. She might disagree with some of the decisions he'd made, but she never doubted his dedication to his clan and those in his care.

With a silent nod and a shadow of a smile, he turned toward Tatkret. "I had an interesting visitor. Krem, the crow shapeshifter, paid me a visit. He's left, but said he'd return with more shapeshifters to help us."

"Why would he bother?" Muirenn said.

"Krem said the council sent him to find you."

Muirenn clenched her hands at her side. She'd told no one about her mother's involvement with the shapeshifter council, and how Muirenn suspected her mother had been betrayed. But why after all this time had they sought to find her?

She forced her hands to relax. She couldn't worry about Krem or the Council. She had to help Tatkret. "Maybe Krem's appearance is a good sign," Muirenn offered.

Tatkret shook her head. "We are on our own."

"Please listen to Muirenn," Max'inux said. "She is wise. Wait until you are stronger. Until then, what can I do to help you?"

She laid her hand on his shoulder. "Forgive yourself."

Without warning, Tatkret leapt onto the ledge and dove over the side of the seawall. She arched her body into a graceful dive and shifted into her whale image. Both Muirenn and Max'inux reached out for her but they were too late. Tatkret was a blur of black and white as she disappeared into the surf.

Chapter Four

The morning was overcast as Sam Thorne entered the Whale Sanctuary's employee locker room. To a city dweller, the tile, metal, and chrome were a welcome relief. He'd spent the last ten years of his life hunting shapeshifter whales and building his reputation. If this latest assignment panned out, he'd be up for a promotion.

It also felt like a sauna. He didn't mind. It probably meant that those in charge of the Sanctuary were keeping the water in the animals' tanks uncomfortably warm in an effort to keep them docile. He chuckled under his breath. He'd known he was going to like this place the moment he'd applied for the whale handler's opening.

But even with his successes at hunting shapeshifters, he'd had to talk his ass off to convince his commander to send along a few extra men in case his theory proved correct. The guy was an idiot. The men he'd sent were camped in the woods beyond the Sanctuary, waiting for Sam's signal, and were already grumbling that this was a dead end.

Sam swore under his breath. He was surrounded by idiots.

He had traveled a long way with no more to go on than an article in a newspaper written by an animal rights activist. The incident was over three years old. Very few humans paid attention to these ramblings about animals involved in the death or injury of their handlers in zoos, game preserves, or aquariums. Big corporations involved made sure the incident was covered up and the story excused away. Maybe that was why it had taken so long to see the light of day.

But Sam paid attention. That was where he discovered his best leads. What had confirmed his suspicion was what he'd overheard when he'd applied for the job opening. A woman's body had washed ashore overnight, and this morning a female whale was reported missing from the Sanctuary. The owners hadn't seen any connection.

He smiled, congratulating his detective skill as he folded his belongings neatly and placed them in his assigned locker.

The article he'd read had involved the drowning death of a whale handler a few years ago. Sam had learned that it was more than a reported drowning. That was the cover story. His sources claimed that a killer whale by the name, Max'inux, had bashed his handler to death against the sides of the tank. Grisly stuff.

Naturally, not many people had applied for jobs in Whale Sanctuaries like this one after the story had broken. The message was clear. In captivity, killer whales were unpredictable and dangerous.

Sam bit back a smile. Underestimating the dangers of going up against a predator that could also be a shapeshifter had almost destroyed the human race. They constantly underestimated their foe. But this time, their naïveté had worked to his advantage. Humans always seemed to believe they controlled this planet. But they were only renting the space. He and others like him didn't like the concept and were working to change the balance of power. The first step was the extinction of shapeshifters.

Securing a job under the current circumstances had been even easier than he'd expected. They weren't being picky. All they wanted was someone who wasn't afraid of the water, naïve enough to believe that humans could tame a wild predator, and who looked good in a skintight wetsuit.

The interview process had been a joke. Especially, after he had removed his shirt. The woman hadn't tried to hide her desire. It was pathetic. Of the five who applied, she'd hired three: a woman with big boobs and a guy who looked like he had straw for brains. So much the better. Sam could do what needed to be done with no one the wiser. He had one task. Find the shapeshifter, if there were any, and kill them.

There were still those who searched for the shapeshifter in the old ways. Hunt them down and engage in a messy battle. Sam had made his reputation by thinking outside the box and searching in unexpected places. Sometimes the shapeshifter, while in their animal image, were captured and taken to game preserves, zoos, or aquariums. With the advent of cameras it was difficult for them to escape their prisons without being exposed for the plague they were.

But they couldn't escape their nature. He made it his job to investigate every occurrence of an animal behaving against the norm. Killing a human for sport or revenge was an indicator that something wasn't right. Even in captivity the shapeshifter reproduced and so their offspring had to be killed as well. All stain of the abomination had to be wiped out and all trace of their bloodlines destroyed. This was genocide on a global scale and he was the weapon, the tip of the spear that would bring it all about.

He slammed his locker door and headed for the Sanctuary's performance pool. It was time to confirm his suspicions that Max'inux was a shapeshifter, and then he'd investigate the other whales. He'd learned that with whale shapeshifters, if you found one, others were close behind.

Chapter Five

Muirenn couldn't shake the image of Tatkret shifting into a killer whale and disappearing into the surf. It was mid-afternoon and the Whale Sanctuary was on high alert. A woman's body, with no identification, had been discovered on the shoreline early this morning. No one made the connection with the mystery woman and Tatkret's disappearance, or even considered that when shapeshifters died they reverted to their human image.

Muirenn had shifted into her whale image immediately after Tatkret had jumped, seeking the connection with her daughter and the two other animal-only, female whales in her tank, while Max'inux had returned to his. On the other side of the tank, her daughter played with two female whales. Muirenn had christened her daughter *Anu*, in memory of her mother. Muirenn smiled to herself. In true whale spirit, Anu and the whales sang to each other and sprayed each other with water.

Normally, the calm demeanor of the whale image, together with the presence of the other whales, helped separate her from the turmoil going on around her. Not today. Tatkret's words, *"Without risk, there is not life,"* would not leave her thoughts. They echoed, growing in strength with each hour that passed.

It didn't help that Tatkret's name meant "moon." Her mother had held a deep devotion to the Great Mother Moon, and Muirenn wondered if her mother had tried to send her a message from the other realm through Tatkret. Before being captured, Muirenn, like many whale shapeshifters, was an intuitive, as were crow shapeshifters. But captivity had nearly crushed her ability.

She and her daughter were all members of one of the oldest sea clans in the world and could trace their ancestry back to a time when oceans covered the earth. They were the largest predators and were called by many names— blackfish, orcas, killer whales. They were also being hunted into extinction. As long as she and her daughter remained at the Sanctuary, Anu would be safe.

As though Anu sensed her mother thinking of her, she swam over to Muirenn and nudged her playfully. *"Mama, please tell me a story."* Although Anu was too young to shift into her human image, Muirenn could use the whale shapeshifter ability to communicate telepathically. Like any child, her daughter wiggled with excitement at the prospect of the stories.

Muirenn cherished these moments together, where she could share happier times with her daughter and the history of their people. Her mother had said that whale song had been developed to create their oral history. *"Which story do you want to hear, little one?"*

"Tell me about our island," came the fast response.

Muirenn nodded. It was one of her daughter's favorites. *"Whale Island is a magical place created long beyond any of our ancestors' memories. We are peaceful creatures and needed a safe place where we could walk on legs and dwell in our human image without fear of being drawn into the battles of The Great Land."*

Anu twisted around to stare at her tail and fanned it through the water. *"What does it feel like when you shift into your human image, Mama?"*

Muirenn was pleased with the question. Anu had asked many questions about Whale Island. What type of food did they eat? Did they wear clothes like a human-only and were their songs as beautiful as whales? Muirenn was pleased at her daughter's curiosity. She hoped the well-thought-out questions indicated that Anu's human image lay dormant, just waiting for the key to unlock the door.

Muirenn nodded toward her beloved child. *"A good question. In our whale image we feel everything in the water around us, from a change of temperature to the sound of an approaching school of fish. In our human image we can detect these things as well, but it is our reaction to them that is different. In our human image the beauty of a sunset, splashed with reds and golds, evokes joy and the feel of sand beneath our feet tickles and makes us laugh. But when it comes to the love we feel for our children, we are the same."*

The sound of a whistle vibrated through the water in Muirenn's tank. It was too early to perform. More likely it was one of the handlers exerting their control. It was time to pretend that she liked them, time to pretend that she was tame. She'd fought back when she was first captured and had received a scar over the left side of her face and another across her ribs. As a result she had been weakened and had almost lost Anu when she had gone into labor. After that she realized fighting back was futile.

When the whistle blew again, Muirenn eased away from her daughter. The last thing she had to remember was the most important. She must guard against shifting into her human image in public. If a human-only knew what she was, it would not only alert those who hunted her kind, but jeopardize her daughter's safety as well. It was not uncommon for human-only to massacre all animals in pursuit of the few who might be shapeshifter.

As she swam into the center of the tank, the new handler had come out to the landing deck. He was tall for a human-only. His hair was tied at the nape of his neck and he wore a bodysuit. He glanced in Muirenn's direction and then dove into the tank.

Muirenn waited. How easy it would be to drag him under the water. Everyone would believe she was being playful. After all, whales were friendly and easily controlled. They would never attack humans. If a human drowned, it must have been that the human had been careless. She shook the dark thoughts from her mind, wondering at their origins. In the wild she had never considered harming a human.

Killing a human only was forbidden. Throughout the whales' long history they'd been taught against committing such an act of violence. For thousands of years they'd kept this treaty. When humans violated its parameters, they'd still upheld the laws of the treaty, praying the violence would stop. But the violence was getting worse. When humans hunted for sport or stole their children, it grew harder to reconcile or control the killer whales who sought revenge. *"What choice do we have but to fight back,"* was a common response. The sea was seething with unrest. Soon it would boil over.

The human-only broke the surface a short distance away, treading water. "My name is Sam Thorne."

It wasn't unusual for handlers to speak to her or tell her their names. She supposed it made them feel like they were making a connection, or what they liked to call "bonding." She wondered what they would do if she shifted and spoke back? For starters it would be all over the news. She didn't have to worry about being dragged off to some medical facility for questions or worse. She wouldn't make it that far. The shapeshifter's enemies would have killed her long before then. Still, if it weren't for her daughter, it might have been worth the risk just to see the handler's expression.

"How are you doing this morning?" he said, easing closer.

Her thoughts churned out the answer to his question. *I'm in a cage, treated like a slave,* she wanted to shout. *How do you think I'm doing?* No wonder many of her kind had gone insane, harmed their handler, or like Tatkret, refused to eat.

His pasted-on smile never faltered. "I'm sorry about Tatkret."

He'd made the connection to the woman on the beach and the missing whale. How? She drew back. There was something about him...something about him she didn't trust.

The human-only talked to her about how he loved animals, wanted to make their lives easier, wanted to be friends. The standard speech all handlers peddled. Some handlers Muirenn felt really meant what they said, but in this case his words rang hollow and his eyes looked as cold as the dead fish she was fed each morning.

She didn't want to hear his ramblings. She turned to leave.

He raised his voice and a dark shadow crossed his features. A whisper of the man inside, perhaps? When it cleared he continued and the smile cocked into a leer. "I overheard the handlers say that they sold another whale. The calf named Anu. She's scheduled to leave in two weeks. She's your daughter, right? What do you plan to do about it? Let me take you in and I'll..."

A dorsal fin rose from the water. Max'inux had entered Muirenn's tank and begun a slow circle around the perimeter. Sam glanced at the killer whale as though mesmerized.

"Sam," a woman shouted. Athletically built, the woman paced the deck. "Max'inux is in the tank," she said, clearly panicked. "You know the new rules. Handlers aren't allowed in the water anymore. Get out of the water, Sam. Now."

He twisted around toward the woman. The friendliness in his voice sounded forced. "There's nothing to worry about. Muirenn and I are just getting to know each another."

As Sam turned, a jagged scar along the back of his neck became visible. The breath caught in Muirenn's throat. No wonder Sam had seemed familiar. She'd attacked him with a knife after he'd murdered her mother.

The woman handler continued to shout for Sam to get out of the water, but her words seemed far away. All Muirenn could hear were her mother's cries of pain as she lay dying.

Sam turned back toward her. "This is not over," he said to Muirenn before swimming away.

It took all the strength she possessed not to shift into her human image and tear him apart. *"You're right. This is not over."*

Chapter Six

In late afternoon, the October sun hovered over the performance pool, its light so dim it looked as though it were losing its grip on the day. The net-like dome arced over the area, which only added to the gloom. Lights were usually reserved for nighttime performances were turned on and heaters brought in to keep the people in the stands warm.

In her whale image, Muirenn hovered near the surface of the water. Soon after the encounter with Sam, she had been ushered into the performance pool, while Max'inux waited in the adjacent tank. She would do her tricks first to warm up the crowd, and then they'd bring Max'inux in for the big finale.

She began swimming in a tight circle, growing more and more uneasy. Her daughter had been sold. The words thundered in her ears. What was she going to do? She knew she should consult with Max'inux and tell him about Sam, or at least thank him for intervening. What was she waiting for? Was she afraid Max'inux would ask questions? She'd judged him for attacking a handler. No matter the reason, she'd done the same thing to a human.

Muirenn stayed close to the surface, awaiting the signal from her handler. She couldn't stop shaking. The Sanctuary had sold her daughter. How was that possible?

The first whistle blasted, shrill and impatient, alerting the crowd that their wait was almost over. More overhead lights were powered on and the glare struck the water like a flat-sided mallet. Music blared, harsh and loud, Muirenn's signal that the show was moments away.

Muirenn wanted nothing more than to retreat back to her tank and spend time with Anu, but the consequences were dire. The humans had learned a few tricks in dealing with whales. They'd learned that whales cared about each other and used this knowledge against them. If one whale got out of line or missed a cue while the crowd was watching, that night no one ate.

The whistle blew again. A long shrill sound, followed by two shorter bursts. It was the signal for her appearance. Muirenn glided to the surface. She didn't care if they fed her today. Maybe Tatkret was right. Starvation and then death was a form of escape. As soon as the sacrilegious thoughts sprang into her mind, she struck them down. Even if it weren't against their beliefs, if she were dead, who would protect Anu? Muirenn had to remain strong.

When Muirenn surfaced, the crowd roared. There was the stench of bodies. Fish rotted in tin pails, simmering in their own juices, the reward for a well-executed trick. It was an assault on the senses.

The crowd's expression reflected their impatience. The humans told themselves that they came to this exhibition because their children would enjoy the spectacle. Seeing whales up close would be a life-changing experience. They endured the screaming children and being splashed with water for one reason. They wanted to be here if Max'inux killed again.

The adults all looked alike to her. Forced smiles, waiting to be disappointed. It was the children she didn't mind. They were like the young whales of her clan. Curious, fearless, full of energy, and inspired by everything around them.

Another whistle. Three short notes. Time for the rollover trick. Muirenn complied and turned on her side and raised her flipper, then did a turn around the pool. Halfheartedly, the crowd clapped and cheered. But it was only a polite gesture. They wanted more drama, more sense of danger. Muirenn finished her lap and glided toward her handler.

The handler rubbed Muirenn on the nose. Muirenn cringed. She didn't like to be touched by humans. It had to be endured. It was what the crowd liked. It made them think that the beasts could be controlled, and that they liked being kept captive against their will, or at the very least, they didn't know any better. The crowd was also told that whales lived longer in captivity. Another lie.

The handler gave Muirenn one of the rotten fish from the tin pail. The stench made Muirenn's stomach clench, but she accepted it. She sensed the tension in her handler. The woman was trying to read the crowd. What would please them? How far could she push Muirenn?

Beyond the roar of the crowd and the crackle of lights her daughter sent her a message. *"Mama, Max'inux is under attack. They won't let me..."*

"Anu." Muirenn turned in the direction of her daughter's tank. *"What is wrong, little one?"*

The link broke as frantic whale sounds ate up the void, vibrating through the water. A few handlers rushed in the direction of the sound. Even if Muirenn had wanted to help, she was confined to the performance pool with all the exits to the other tanks locked.

Muirenn heard a splash on the far side of the pool, then screams. A child had fallen into the water. Muirenn noticed the hesitation on her handler's face. What must have been the child's parents rushed from the stands. Security guards fought to control the people as more handlers pressed around the edge of the pool. The child had already sunk beneath the water.

Muirenn could almost read their thoughts. Everyone was afraid of entering the water with a killer whale. The one person who might not be afraid was Sam Thorne, and he was nowhere in sight.

While the handlers debated the child would die, Muirenn dove beneath the surface. It didn't take long to spot the child. The little girl must have been rendered unconscious the moment she hit the water. Muirenn located the child at the bottom of the pool and nudged the girl with her nose, trying to maneuver the child onto her own back. The child was too small. There was only one option left. She had to shift into her human image.

Before she could rethink her decision she began the process from whale to human. When the child was safely in place on Muirenn's back, Muirenn shifted into whale image. The process had taken only seconds, but the child had been underwater a long time. Muirenn prayed to the Great Mother Moon the little girl would live.

With the child in place, she rose to the surface, but not before Muirenn caught a glimpse of a human-only staring back at her through the glass in the bottom of the pool. He pressed against the glass and grinned. She recognized him at once. Sam Thorne had witnessed her shift.

Chapter Seven

The moon had just appeared on the horizon, partially hidden behind the clouds as though fearful of what she'd seen. While Muirenn had rescued the human-only child, Max'inux had been attacked so badly he'd been unable to perform. At nightfall the atmosphere in the Whale Sanctuary mirrored her state of mind. Confusion and panic reigned. There had been a momentary celebration after she'd rescued the child from drowning. The child's parents had declared Muirenn a heroine for saving their daughter and had bought a toy orca whale.

It was a mystery as to how the child had slipped past her parents, opening the locked gate that separated the audience from the performance pool to end up in the water unnoticed until it was almost too late. The distraction had proved too convenient. While Muirenn was rescuing the child, killer whales had entered Max'inux's tank and attacked him. Killer whales never attacked each other in the wild, but it was not uncommon in captivity. Still, the coincidence bothered her.

Sam had witnessed her shift. He would know that she was shapeshifter. Would he also have recognized that she was the one who had attacked him?

She and Anu had survived these past two years by keeping to themselves and behaving like docile, tamed animals that knew their place. But a new paradigm was forming and as yet Muirenn didn't know what it meant or how it would end.

The whale shapeshifter clans had survived thousands of years by adhering to a strict set of rules. They kept to their own clans, neither intermarrying nor waging war against each other. They were neutral as well when it came to the politics of The Great Land and the five Great Powers: Stilth Alshore, Selan, Weilk, Dgosh, and Bredndern who had drawn the dragons, griffins, minators, and harpies into their battle and then targeted these creatures for extinction. But the different clans of killer whales were left alone to develop a matriarchal society and honor the Great Mother Moon, their creator and healer, unchallenged.

Her mother had wanted to change that paradigm. Was that the real reason she had been murdered? Sam and his men had known where to find her mother. Was there a shapeshifter informant? Could the killer whales change the balance of power?

As though the Great Mother had heard her daughter, clouds parted over the moon and she peered down on Muirenn, challenging her reluctance to help Max'inux. Muirenn was a healer, as her mother and grandmother had been before her. Hereditary healing was not a choice, like the type of fish you hunted for breakfast or the mate you chose in the evening. A healer was who you were.

Max'inux was not of their clan, she argued to the watchful moon and her warring thoughts. In the wild he would have been driven away by her people. These rules were not hers but had been the custom of both their clans for thousands of years. She was from the resident whale clan, while he belonged to the transient. The two clans did not declare war on each other, but neither did they coexist. They did not hunt together nor mate, nor join together against a common foe. Her clan would not blame her if she left him alone to bleed to death.

The moon glowed brighter, once more challenging her. It was the same pale, starflower blue moon that had both consoled her and stilled her revenge the night her mother had been murdered.

"I hear you, Great Mother," Muirenn said as she shifted from her whale image to human.

Chapter Eight

The Sanctuary was deserted with only the moon to guide her. It had risen in the sky and beamed down on Muirenn as though in approval. Those who owned the Whale Sanctuary seldom left lights or security cameras on during this time of night. It was not thrift that guided the practice, but caution. Nighttime was when they transported whales in and out of the facility, and the fewer witnesses who overheard the panicked cries of the whales, the better.

Muirenn shifted into her human image and slipped along the narrow walkway that joined her tank with the others. She'd overheard that they'd placed Max'inux in isolation for his own protection after the attack. If his injuries were as severe as she'd heard, why was he being left without supervision?

The walkway ran along the seawall and the air of the shoreline smelled of seaweed and wet sand. The perfumed scent flowed over her with every step she took. It would be so easy to climb over the wall and dive into the welcoming arms of the sea. Her heart raced as she paused and pressed her hand against the coarse wall of rock and mortar.

Max'inux's great bulk hugged the side of his tank. His breath was labored and blood stained the water. One of the Sanctuary's doctors had sutured his wounds, but Muirenn knew their efforts would fail. Max'inux's injuries ran deep; she could tell by the amount of blood in the water. The story was that he'd been attacked by the other whales, but the bruising wasn't consistent with what she'd seen in the past.

Muirenn knelt and put her hand on Max'inux's head. He flinched and pulled away. His eyes were glazed over in pain, and he looked as if he had retreated deep into his whale image. If she had any hope of saving him, she had to pull him back into his human image. But how could she reach him? If she were honest, she knew very little about him. She hadn't wanted to know. Even after he'd helped deliver Anu, she'd kept her distance once she'd learned he'd killed his handler. He was a wild beast, beyond redemption. And yet here she was, about to help him. She cast a glance toward the moon, but it had slipped behind the clouds once more.

She eased into the water so as not to startle him, sending her message telepathically. *"I'm a healer. Let me help you."*

He pulled farther out into the water, leaving a trail of blood in his wake. The moonlight turned the water a pale shade of liquid silver.

She followed, swimming slowly after him. *"I promise I won't hurt you."* She reached out to him again. *"Hold very still."* He shuddered under her touch and looked at her, and for a moment she held her breath. *"I can heal you, but only if you shift. I fear that the wounds are too deep."*

His whale image shimmered as his human image fought for control. *"Leave me before they return."*

"They can't hurt you anymore. The handlers have secured the whales in their tanks."

A wave passed over his features as his whale image took over.

"Shift," she ordered, fighting the rising panic. Extreme emotion or physical pain could prevent the whale shapeshifter from shifting. *"Shift,"* she repeated.

"You should let me go," he ground out.

"Would you abandon me?"

"How could I?"

"Neither could I abandon you."

With a shudder he shifted into his human image. She caught him before he slipped beneath the waves. "Stay conscious," she said as she swam with him over to the side of the tank.

"Can't...promise." His eyes fluttered shut and his body went limp in her arms. "No you don't," she said, pinching his shoulder.

"Hey," he said. "That hurt."

"Sorry. But if you lose consciousness I won't be able to lift you out of the water, and if I can't do that, I won't be able to heal you. You weigh a ton." She reached the side of the tank and leapt up, positioning her arms under his shoulders.

He grimaced as he pulled himself out of the water. Holding his side, he lay against the tile floor, taking deep breaths. "I need to tell you something."

"Whatever it is, it can wait. Save your strength."

He reached for her hand as it hovered over the sutured wound. "It's important. I murdered a human-only. I'm not asking forgiveness, but I want you to know why."

Muirenn slipped her hand out of his. She knew she'd judged him for his actions. In fact, she felt as though she'd spent her life in judgment. She'd judged her mother for wanting to change the course of how her clan interacted with the shapeshifter of The Great Land and herself for not being able to protect those she loved. "Not now."

"The handler was beating my son."

She paused, her hands trembling. That was not what she'd expected. She imagined how she would feel if someone harmed Anu. Great Mother Moon, she might have done the same thing.

"It's not an excuse, although I know it must sound that way. I'm not proud of what I did. We live our lives in peace and cooperation. I should have found another way."

"I fear times are changing for us all."

"I fear that as well." He grew silent, and then shook his head as though to banish his dark thoughts. "I don't weigh a ton, by the way, at least not when I'm human."

She grinned at his attempt at humor, examining his wound closer. "My apologies. What do you..." She gasped. "You were harpooned. Who did this?"

"Sam Thorne's men. I may have to kill again."

Chapter Nine

The moon had drifted low over the horizon, spreading its light over the lush forest framing the western side of the Sanctuary. A creature of both land and sea, Muirenn had drawn upon the healing properties of plant and tree aura. From the oceans she'd called upon the seaweeds and grasses that strengthened the blood. From the emerald green forests she'd summoned the cedar trees for their cleansing and protection, pine for its balance of pain, and oak for its strength and endurance.

Muirenn released them now, feeling wisps of the nature power remain as though it were their gift to her for resuming her calling. She expanded her lungs to drink in the gift, giving her thanks as she glanced over at Max'inux.

He leaned against the seawall, his eyes closed, but she knew that he wasn't asleep. It had taken longer than she'd expected to heal him. His wounds had been deep. Not only those caused by the harpoon, but bruises where it looked like he had been beaten with a flat surfaced board. If she hadn't healed him when she had, he would have died from his injuries. Sam Thorne had tried to make it look like the other whales had attacked him, and no one would have questioned the supposition.

A healer didn't just heal the outward wounds; they glimpsed of the person inside. She knew that he had been in captivity for a long time. Such creature's eyes were dulled into acceptance or reflected the glow of madness, and their spirit crushed. This had not happened to Max'inux. There was an intensity about him, a sense of purpose and inner strength. She wondered how it was possible for him to hold onto his core self after all he'd been through.

She knelt beside him and spread her hand over the bruise on his shoulder. "When you were attacked, why didn't you fight back?"

His eyes opened slowly as his muscles corded under her touch. "Thorne said he'd kill you and then find my son and turn him into shark chum."

Muirenn sank down and pressed her lips together at Sam's cruel words. "Do you know what happened to your son?"

His voice was a whisper. "Sold and hauled onto a ship. That's all I know. They drugged me the night they took him away."

She clenched her jaw to quiet the catch in her throat as she rested her head against his shoulder. Max'inux had been locked in his own version of hell. She threaded her arm through his. "I'm so sorry. Nothing is worse than the helplessness of not being able to protect your child."

He wiped a tear from her cheek with the pad of his thumb. "If Krem and the shapeshifter don't return in time, I'll find a way to get you and Anu to safety. I don't know what it is about you," he said with a smile. "Whenever I'm around you, I want to protect you, bare my soul, or ask forgiveness. Sometimes all three at once."

She leaned her face into his hand, feeling her heart swell. She had not expected to feel so much. "I'm a healer. We have that effect on people."

He shook his head. "I've been around healers before. That's not it."

She drank in the silence, trying to quiet her newfound surge of emotions. She took a ragged breath. "I should probably get back."

He reached out to her. "Why did you help me?"

She settled back against the wall. "I'm a healer and you were hurt."

His eyebrow rose. "I've been hurt before."

His words spoke the truth. But their tone did not accuse her of abandoning her calling; her conscience accomplished that task. She'd been locked in her own world, keeping everyone at bay and using her daughter as the excuse. She realized that she was the one who was afraid of losing herself if she made any real contact with the others here.

She took his hand in hers. "When you are a healer, you can't help but become connected and attached to those you heal. I was afraid to feel."

He squeezed her hand. "What changed?"

She shook her head and shrugged. "One thing. Many things. I don't know for sure myself."

His voice was a deep rumble as though made from the depths of the ocean. "You have the saddest eyes for someone so young. What heavy mantle do you carry?"

Her eyes brimmed and she blinked. "Max'inux. I'm in a cage. We both are."

He brushed hair off her forehead with a gentle touch. "The cage that threatens your soul is not this one, but the one of your own making."

She lifted her chin, clenching her jaw to keep it from trembling. "My mother trained me to be the leader of our clan. Instead, not only did I fail to protect her, but I was captured, and because Anu was born in captivity she may never experience freedom. I let everyone down, including myself."

He leaned his head against the wall, deep in thought. "We are not that dissimilar. You judge your actions before you were captured, and I afterward. It paralyzes us both." He pushed away from the wall. "A shapeshifter once told me this proverb. There are two wolves. One represents light and hope and the other darkness and despair. In a battle which wolf will prevail?"

She drew closer to him. "I know the answer. The wolf who will prevail is the one you feed."

He nodded with a smile.

Pulled by an invisible force as old as the seas themselves, she moved toward him, kissing him lightly. "You are not what I expected."

He framed her face with his hands. "And yet, you are exactly what I expected."

His words were a caress that gently opened her heart to possibilities. The confines of the Sanctuary wall fell away. There was only the pounding of the surf and the rustle of the trees. She leaned toward him, pressing her lips against his, feeling the textures of his mouth and the strength of his arms as he pulled her into an embrace.

Chapter Ten

It had been twenty-four hours since she'd spent time with Max'inux. They thought it best, as they knew they were being watched. He had told her as much as he knew about Krem. Would the shapeshifter return? When she'd first learned about him, she hadn't been sure, but now...

Muirenn had shifted into her whale image and hovered near the bottom of her tank. Clouds had snuffed out the stars and moon and plunged her tank into shades of gray. The only illumination came from the lights at the bottom and sides of her enclosure. Muirenn was restless and couldn't sleep. She couldn't stop worrying about Anu. For some reason they'd moved her daughter to the performance pool.

The two other female whales were in with Muirenn and they seemed just as restless. She knew they weren't shapeshifter, but even as singlesight they were intuitive and sensed that something was wrong. Two more men had been hired on and seemed to be working with Sam Thorne. Cruelty had awakened even the most docile of the whales and the unrest had spread.

The sounds of muffled conversation, now raised in frustration, flowed toward her from the direction of the performance pool. The two other female whales had heard the disturbance as well and moved in closer. Anu cried out. Muirenn felt her heart stop.

More voices carried through the water. Human-only voices.

"Anu was uncooperative so we had to tie her to the gurney," a male voice said.

"Get more rope," snapped the order. But this voice she recognized. It was Sam Thorne.

The female whale's song of concern echoed through the water. An innocent was in danger. Their echoes bounced against the walls, growing in intensity.

Anu's cries grew frantic. *"Mama, help me."*

Through Anu's description, Muirenn knew what was happening. Her daughter was being forced onto a canvas gurney, strapped down for transport and taken to an unknown location. This was exactly what had happened to Max'inux's son.

Muirenn imagined the human-only words the handlers spoke. They were meant to soothe, but would instill only more fear. How could they not? They were taking her away sooner than expected. Muirenn had thought she had more time.

Then the lights in her tank went out.

A weight pressed against Muirenn's heart as her mind raced. Why was this happening now, after all this time, and all that she and her daughter had endured together? How could they take her daughter from her? Because humans didn't value the connection animals had with their young, came the answer to her own question. That was obvious when they'd taken Max'inux's son. Still, it didn't make any sense. Next to Max'inux, her daughter was one of the Whale Sanctuary's biggest attractions.

Max'inux was on the other side of the Sanctuary. She reached out with her mind, but he didn't answer. Perhaps he was too far away. Did he know what was happening? If she shifted into her human image she and Max'inux could find weapons, but would the two of them be enough to fight Sam's men and free Anu? Muirenn remembered what Max'inux had said about the crow, Krem. Even if he returned, would he be bringing an army or just a few of his kind?

She couldn't wait.

Muirenn rose from the bottom of the tank toward the surface. The humans had planned well. Her daughter was a favored attraction. The locals wouldn't want Anu to leave. There would have been a public outcry and protests, which was all the more troubling. Why had they sold her daughter in the first place?

The reasons didn't matter. All that mattered was preventing her daughter from leaving on the transport. Muirenn knew where the women's lockers were located. It would be a simple task to change into one of the uniforms. She'd pose as a visiting veterinarian, and claim that the young whale was too sick to travel. She knew enough about the clan of men that if a whale died in transport, it would bring down the press. Next only to the loss of revenue, bad press was what the owners of Whale Sanctuary feared the most. That was plan A and for the plan to work she had to get past Sam without being recognized. If not, she'd have to come up with a plan B.

Even with the lights turned off, Muirenn knew the location of everything in the building. Like all whales, she had an uncanny sense of direction and awareness of her surroundings. She didn't need lights to guide her. She would rely on her instincts.

She neared the surface, sensing something was wrong. Everything was still draped in shades of gray. She'd thought the lack of star and moonlight was caused by the cloud cover, but as she approached the surface she realized the real cause.

A dark foreboding clutched at her heart. Someone had rolled the lid across her tank shut and locked it. There was only a space of only a few feet that separated the top of the lid from the surface of the water.

Muirenn began the process of shifting into her human image. In all the time since her arrival, the lid had never been closed. She pressed her hand against it. It was a patchwork of alternating glass and metal squares, each a foot in diameter. A simple bolt secured the lid over the tank. Muirenn worked her way toward the side where she remembered the bolt was located. All she had to do was...

A beam of light flashed through the glass square nearest the bolt and blinded her.

Sam knelt close to the glass and dangled a set of keys. His dark eyes were filled with hate and his face was a mask of insane delight as he stood and tossed the keys over the side of the seawall. She was locked in, with no way to reach Anu. His mouth opened and she knew he laughed, but the only sounds she heard were those of her daughter's cries for help.

Chapter Eleven

Muirenn could feel the presence of the other female whales just below her. The water vibrated with their contempt for Sam Thorne. In their own way, they were lending their support. They wanted her to know she wasn't alone.

"You're beautiful for a shapeshifter," Sam said, oblivious of the turmoil below him. "If there was more time I'd take you for a ride."

Muirenn treaded water, ignoring his crude remark. She suspected that he was behind expediting her daughter's transport in an attempt to expose Muirenn as shapeshifter. She no longer cared that he'd seen her shift. All that mattered was Anu.

"Release my daughter and I'll come with you."

His laughter was brittle. "I have no intention of taking you alive. I've come to kill you." He smashed the glass panel directly over Muirenn with a hammer. Shards of glass rained down, cutting her face. She steeled against the pain as he aimed his gun.

Muirenn sank lower in the water. If she shifted into her whale image, would she be strong enough to break through the lid? Or would he kill her before she had the chance?

Max'inux appeared out of nowhere. He grabbed Sam's gun with one hand and slammed his fist into Sam's jaw with the other. Sam staggered back, fighting to gain his balance as Max'inux yelled to Muirenn. "Shift. Break down the gate. It's our only..." Sam drew a gun from his boot and charged Max'inux.

Muirenn didn't waste time. She shifted into her whale image. She felt the power and strength of her animal image surge through her. She knew breaking down the gate so she could reach her daughter was their only chance, but would she be strong enough?

She swam around the tank with a speed born of a mother's desperation. Each turn she drew on more strength, more power, more speed. The gate that separated the tanks was reinforced steel. It was made to hold the whales in their tank, but it would not prevent her from reaching her daughter.

The barrier would be no match for a mother's love. She would not allow it. She slammed against the gate with the force of her strength. It held. Just then the other female whales appeared. They weren't shapeshifter, but they understood her need to rescue Anu and were willing to help.

No one would keep her from her daughter and now she had help. She didn't know if Max'inux had been able to disarm Sam, but she couldn't worry about that right now. She had to reach Anu before it was too late.

Her daughter might not know she was shapeshifter. She might believe the world was as small as her cage and that the life she'd known here was all she deserved, but Muirenn knew that there was more. They might both die in their attempt to gain their freedom, but it was worth the risk.

Muirenn and the two female whales took turns slamming against the gate and she could feel it weakening. It gave them the will to continue. Blood flowed in the water from the injuries she and the other whales endured to break through. It churned and foamed in the waves caused by their attack. Pain rose through Muirenn. Still she fought to free her child. No one would take Anu from her.

She slammed into the gate and this time it buckled. The men working to secure Anu noticed the breech and shouted in panic. Seizing on the chaos and still in her whale image, she leapt through the opening and sped toward her daughter. Fearing the mother, Sam's comrades abandoned the young whale and ran.

Out of the corner of her eye she saw Max'inux climbing the scaffold that held the ropes binding Anu to the transport gurney. He had a gash on his shoulder and blood ran from a bullet wound on his leg. Neither injury slowed him down as he cut the robes. The female whales had followed Muirenn through the opening and joined her in a tight, protective circle around her daughter. Anu struggled to free herself of her constraints, but she was having trouble.

As Muirenn shifted into her human image to help release the buckles, the fear in her child's eyes changed into recognition. For the span of time that it took to draw a breath, her child's eyes resembled a human's. A handler's shout brought the beast back in her child, but Muirenn had seen enough to hope. Her daughter was shapeshifter and for a split second had recognized her true nature.

Max'inux raced to lower the nets across the seawall. If anyone came into the pool she would kill them. Her child was her life. They had starved and beaten both Muirenn and the other whales in the Sanctuary and she had stayed back and watched, believing that would save her. If she didn't risk, she would survive, she had reasoned. Tatkret had taught her a valued lesson. Merely surviving was not living. It was a slow death.

"Hurry," Max'inux shouted. "We don't have much time. I've lowered the nets across the seawall. You and Anu will have to jump."

"I can't free Anu," Muirenn shouted. "The buckles are stuck."

Max'inux reached for a knife and dove into the water. Surfacing near Anu, he begun cutting through the straps. "As soon as she's freed I want you to jump over the seawall."

"Anu will never make it. She's too afraid."

"She'll follow your lead. They all will. They know you'll keep them safe."

Muirenn shook her head. "You and I are stronger than the handlers. We can force them to tell us where they took your son."

Max'inux released the strap and patted Anu as she swam over to Muirenn. He shook his head. "There are too many. I can sense Sam is calling on more reinforcements. Soon we will be surrounded. We can't wait. I know the rage you're feeling, and it will destroy you. Remember that you are a healer, not a killer." Max'inux kissed her lightly. "Take your daughter to safety. We will find a way to find my son."

A gunshot split the air. Sam stood near the scaffold. Blood covered his body. His right arm drooped loosely at his side while his left pointed a gun in Muirenn's direction. "Well, isn't this a pretty picture of domestic bliss."

Max'inux leaned toward Muirenn. "Shift. That's the only way you'll survive the jump into the bay. Wait for my signal." Treading water, he held up his hands as though in surrender and edged in front of Muirenn and Anu. "You want me. Let them go."

"Not a chance." Sam waved the gun. "Get out of the tank. Your kind is easier to kill in your human image."

"Now that's an interesting folktale," Max'inux said with a smile. "I wonder who started it?"

"Move faster or I'll start turning the water red."

"I could shift into whale..."

"No," Sam shouted. "Just hurry. I don't have all day."

Muirenn knew Max'inux was stalling for time. They had to hurry. She nodded toward Anu. *Little one, this might sound scary, but I know you can do it. We need to jump over the seawall.*

Anu turned her head to gaze at the wall. Her whale eyes widened. *What is beyond the seawall, Mama?*

Whale Island.

Muirenn swore she saw her child smile as she nodded.

As quietly as possible they both eased farther away from the scaffold. Max'inux was providing the distraction while she and her daughter built up enough speed to make the jump.

Max'inux had moved to within a few feet of Sam when he turned toward her and winked. In the next instant Max'inux had shifted into a killer whale. She hadn't known a shift that fast was possible. In a blur of black and white, Max'inux leapt out of the water toward Sam. Sam fired off a round of shots as Muirenn, Anu, and the female whales raced toward the seawall.

Chapter Twelve

Dawn was breaking through the clouds in shades of crimson and silver light. With Anu beside her, Muirenn felt the ocean envelop her in a welcome embrace. It felt like freedom and rebirth. It also felt lonely. As Max'inux had predicted, the two female whales had followed Muirenn and her daughter. They circled waiting for direction. Muirenn vowed to take good care of them. She glanced toward the seawall, searching for Max'inux.

Before she'd made the jump, she'd seen Max'inux pull Sam under the water, but she'd also seen human-only, with weapons drawn, surge into the Sanctuary.

To the less aware, the seas and the killer whales that inhabited their domain were all alike. Like the great oceans of the world, killer whales were part of dozens of unique cultures, guarding their secrets, maintaining their histories and traditions. Muirenn could feel her clan's history in these waters. Currents sang of both joys and tragedies. Waves roared the names of ancestors. Would they sing of the sacrifices of the killer whale Max'inux?

Overhead crows headed in the direction of the Whale Sanctuary. From this distance Muirenn couldn't tell if they were shapeshifter or animal-only. She prayed...

Anu nudged Muirenn, flipping her head in the direction of the shoreline. Large boats were warming up their engines as crews readied the vessels to cast off and begin the hunt. It wouldn't be long before the search for them began.

Muirenn nodded to her daughter, proud that her child had sensed the danger. With Anu and the other female whales close behind, they dived beneath the surface of the water that pulsed with life. Gone were the concrete boxes that had held them. Muirenn sensed her daughter's wonder as they sped through the open seas. The ocean was alive, vibrant with red coral reefs, schools of fish, and underwater caves to explore. The currents helped them outdistance their enemies and over each mile they covered, Muirenn repeated the same pledge.

"Max'inux. I will return for you."

Pam Binder is a USA and New York Times Bestselling author of over 10 novels, and four anthologies, a conference speaker and the president of the Pacific Northwest Writers Association. Pam loves Irish and Scottish myths and legends and writes historical and contemporary fiction, as well as middle grade fiction, fantasy and time travel novels. She believes that time is an illusion and love the only reality. Her newest 2020 summer releases are the 14th century Scottish Time Travel, *The*

Quest, and two anthologies *Beach Reads*, and *Summer Vibes*. Pam's contemporary romance, *Christmas Deadline, will be released in the Fall of 2020 in time for Christmas.* You can learn more about Pam Binder by visiting her website, http://pambinder.com, or following her on Facebook: https://www.facebook.com/Pam-Binder-820665554640308/ and Twitter https://twitter.com/PamBinder183.

Lakeside Love

by

Mandi McGuire

Chapter One

Sarah Oliver raced into her kitchen as the smoke alarm blared in her ears, blocking out every other sound with its whirling reminder that she was a terrible cook.

She quickly opened the kitchen drawer next to the stove, pulling out the oven mitts her mom had sent her from Florida last year for Christmas. She didn't know if the mitts were a joke, but the bakers' hat print was now worn from repeatedly pulling out charred remains from her latest attempt at feeding herself.

With her hands covered, she used the back of her wrist to push a strand of hair out of her eyes as she opened the oven door. Black smoke billowed out and swirled upward like a campfire just getting started in the open air, and puffs of smoke fought each other as they raced to the top of the heap before disappearing into the night sky.

"Sarah!" Her roommate, Leah, screamed as she opened the front door of their downtown Tacoma apartment. Rushing to grab the broom that was just inside the coat closet, she ran toward the smoke detector, waving the black-bristled ends back and forth in the air. "You've got to stop cooking," she yelled again just as the alarm stopped, allowing the much-needed reprieve so the neighbors would stop worrying that Sarah might burn down their building. Sadly, they'd received far too many warnings from the tenants' association.

Sarah held the cookie sheet with both mitts as she looked at her friend. "I wasn't even cooking. I was just heating fish sticks." Her gaze moved from the sheet to Leah, as she bit the side of her lip. Letting out a heavy sigh, she tossed the cookie sheet with the ruined dinner onto the stove top before turning off the oven.

"What happened?" Leah leaned the broom handle against the refrigerator door and sat her purse on the island.

"I'm sorry. I got distracted. I put these in," Sarah motioned to the fish sticks, "and then I turned on *Vanderpump*." Her favorite TV show had a way of sucking Sarah right into the drama of the bartenders and waitresses at the Hollywood hot spot.

She tossed the pot holders on the counter next to the stove and opened a window, letting the blistering summer heat override their cool apartment. She sat heavily on the barstool at the kitchen island, resting her chin in the palm of her hand. "I'm never going to learn to cook."

"Don't say that." Sarah watched as Leah moved the pot holders away from the still hot stove, resting her hip on the counter. "You need to stay in the room. You can't go to the bedroom if you're cooking. You never remember to set the timer."

Sarah had seen the look Leah gave her before, a look usually reserved for six-year-olds who had accidentally made a mess in the kitchen, not a twenty-six-year-old who was supposed to be a fully functioning adult. "I know." She let another heavy sigh escape. "I need to marry a chef. A cook, or a baker." A laugh escaped her lips as yet another ruined dinner tested her patience.

"Agreed." Leah left the kitchen, walking the ten steps in their apartment toward her bedroom. "It's a good thing you have other skills. How are the daisies coming?" She rested her hand on the doorframe as she looked at the easel in the corner of their apartment.

"Good." Sarah turned and looked at the canvas, half bare, directly between two windows. Her makeshift art studio had perfect lighting. "I think." She cocked her head, hands on her hips. "It's coming together."

She was working on a collection of oil paintings from pictures she had taken while out camping—white daisies with their faces to the sun and wild lupine, standing tall along the river bed.

"I love it," Leah added. "I think it's one of your best so far. Hey, since you're still hungry, why don't you come out with me tonight? Brian is taking me to see a new band. One of his friends is the drummer. He said a bunch of people will be there. It'll be fun." She turned and waited before going into her bedroom.

"I don't know," Sarah replied. "I was going to spend the night walking the aisles of the camping store. I need a new tent and some of those little battery-powered lights. Everyone uses them to light a path. I don't want to head into the river when I'm looking for a place to go to the bathroom in the middle of the woods."

"Oh, come on. Why are you spending a Friday night shopping? Live a little." Leah shimmied her shoulders, the bangles on her wrists making their own music. "Sandra cancelled on me and I don't have any other girlfriends going tonight. Please." Leah pressed her hands together in front of her chin as though she was saying a prayer.

"Okay, why not." Sarah raised her shoulders in acceptance as she sat at the island. "I haven't been dancing in ages." Her mood immediately lifted at the idea of an evening out, a few cocktails, and her hips getting lost in the music. "Where are we going? Do they have good food?" she yelled into the other room.

Leah poked her head out of her bedroom door. "Yeah, the band is playing at The Swiss. You love their chicken wings."

"That I do," Sarah said, more to herself than Leah, as she moved to clean up the kitchen. She turned on the oven fan, which would have been helpful ten minutes ago, swatted the air with a dishcloth, and scrubbed the remains off the cookie sheet, before heading to her own bedroom to get ready.

After getting dressed in a short, red, floral dress and brown ankle boots, Sarah met Leah at the front door. Sarah had kept her makeup simple, with only mascara and lip gloss.

"Is that a new dress?" Leah asked. "I love it when you don't wear jeans."

"Yep. I picked it up for Sandra's bridal shower, but thought I would try it out now." Sarah smiled. "You look great too."

"Thanks." Leah's voluptuous curves were highlighted in her low-cut tank top and mini-skirt, while her strawberry hair cascaded down her back in wavy curls.

A knock at the door interrupted them. Sarah gave Leah an exasperated look.

"You know it's her," Leah whispered, digging in her purse for her car keys.

"We can pretend we're not home," Sarah whispered back, stepping away from the door.

"Oh, come on, chicken. Let's make a run for it."

Giving Leah a smile and a nod, Sarah opened the door with a flourish. "Mrs. Hamming," her voice purred as she plastered a huge smile on her face. "It's so great to see you." Sarah walked right past the older woman and Mitsie, her yappy little dog that always tried to bite Sarah's ankles. Leah followed and pulled the door shut behind her as Mrs. Hamming stretched her neck to see inside the apartment.

"Is everything all right in there?" Mrs. Hamming asked, a worried look making the wrinkles around her eyes look like creases in her aged face. Her hair was in curlers, and she wore a pale pink bathrobe with florescent green slippers. Sarah admired her nosy neighbor's Friday night attire.

"Oh, yes," Leah said. "Everything's okay. We're headed out to dinner." Sarah saw Leah wink at the older woman as they walked down the hall.

"Oh, thank God." Mrs. Hamming's voice was loud enough for the entire floor to hear.

That stung. Sarah knew her cooking skills needed improvement, and that she was the butt of every cooking joke in her building. She played along, and it didn't *really* bother her, but she'd always wanted to learn to cook. Martha Stewart had been her idol growing up. Gardening and crafts were one thing, but put Sarah in the kitchen and everything went south. Real fast.

Someday she would learn to cook, but not today. She swung the outside doors open, putting on her sunglasses as the dry heat of summer hit her face. Her long hair pushed back with a light breeze and she forgot all about her failure in the kitchen. "Don't you just love summer?"

Mike Russell hated bars. He hated the noise and the crowds, the weak mixed drinks served at the bar, and he hated the bathrooms most of all. Disgusting. But, he loved music and he'd promised his buddy from work that he would go hear his new band. Pulling his Jeep Wrangler onto Jefferson Avenue, he looked for a parking spot while Pitbull, Mr. Worldwide, blared from his stereo. He winked to a group of ladies as they stopped to stare.

He knew he was good looking and he didn't mind the attention. There was never a shortage of girls who liked his air force style crew cut, five o'clock shadow, and outdoor, masculine vibe. The girls often thought he was military or a cowboy.

His dad was in the Air Force, but not him. He wasn't a cowboy either, by any means. He hadn't ridden a horse in ages, even though his grandpa owned a horse ranch in

Montana. But he liked to camp, get outdoors, and get his hands dirty.

Some nights, out dancing, he would play it up with the ladies depending on his mood, and go with whatever story turned the girl on. It was harmless because he never took anyone home. He liked to dance and have a few laughs with his buddies. A bar wasn't the place to find Mrs. Russell. He was ready to settle down, but he hadn't found the right girl. And if he was honest with himself, moving around a lot with his family had made him a little guarded when he met new people.

The Swiss sat right behind the University of Washington's Tacoma campus and was always packed with college students. It was the best place around to hear live music and from the sounds blaring out the door, and the long line waiting to get in, it was busy.

Mike parked and walked up the sidewalk to the bouncer, ignoring the line that snaked around the corner and down the block. "Hey, man. I'm on the list. Mike Russell." While he waited for the bouncer to find his name, he turned his head, looking down the row of ladies, wondering which one could keep up with him for the night. As usual, there were more girls than guys, young girls, probably too young for him.

He was turning twenty-seven on Sunday, with a full-blown family party at his parents' house on base. His sister and her kids would make him a cake, his mom would make spaghetti with her homemade meat sauce, and someone would pick up balloons. He and his dad would sit outside on the patio and have a cold beer—one of the benefits of a summer birthday. His family was awesome. He smiled as a feeling of security flooded him.

The bouncer unhooked the velvet rope, letting Mike walk through, and into the dark, smoky bar.

"Hey, Doug." Mike slapped his friends' shoulder. He'd found him standing at the edge of the large wooden bar, surrounded by people. Mike lifted two fingers at the bartender. "Two shots of tequila, please."

"Thanks for coming, man." Doug was dressed in black jeans and a Led Zeppelin T-shirt. He introduced Mike to his band mates and he shook hands all around.

"I wouldn't miss it, man," he told Doug. "What time do you go on?" Mike rested his elbow on the bar.

"Not until ten."

Mike picked up a shot glass that the bartender sat in front of them and held it up. "To good music and good friends. Kick ass tonight."

They each took their shot in one gulp and slammed it on the counter, as Mike shouted over the noise to the bartender for two more.

The woman sitting at the bar next to Mike leaned over, pushing her breasts up against his arm. "A tequila man. That's my kind of guy." She smiled at him.

"Oh, really." Mike turned from the guys and smiled at the pretty redhead. He immediately noticed her friend, sitting next to her at the bar eating a huge plate of chicken wings. Her brunette hair, the color of dark chocolate, hung in waves around her face and her eyes flashed with a sparkle of amber as she glanced his way.

"Do you ladies like tequila?" Mike tapped the bar and ordered two shots for the ladies. "How's it going?" He leaned over his arm, pressing toward the redhead, but his eyes stayed on her friend.

"Oh, we're great. I'm Leah." The redhead put out her hand like a debutante for him to kiss.

"Hello, Leah." He took her hand and kissed it. "I'm Mike. Are you girls ready for some fun tonight?"

"Ha!" Sarah covered her mouth to stop from spitting out her food. "You lay it on thick, don't ya, buddy?"

"I'm just here for a good time. Aren't you?" Mike watched as Leah's friend continued eating. She raised her eyebrows at him and offered him a mischievous smile.

"Oh, I'm sure you like to have a good time." She laughed.

"Hey, hey now." Mike moved between both girls and put his hands on each of their shoulders. "Which one of you has the best dance moves?"

The bartender brought their shots and Mike motioned for the girls to join him. He raised his glass. "To Leah, and..."

"I'm Sarah." Her voice sounded like a cascading waterfall, soft and gentle, but with a strength underneath it.

The three of them downed their drinks.

"Sarah is the best dancer. For sure." Leah motioned to Sarah and smiled. "And she's single."

"Oh, no." Sarah waved her hand. "You're too cool for me, dude."

Mike could tell she was trying to be light-hearted, but she meant it. She wasn't interested in him. That was all the more intriguing.

"Is that right?" Mike flashed his megawatt smile. "I'm not sure if that's a compliment." Sarah had sass. He liked that.

"Are you in the Air Force?" Leah placed her fingers on his forearm.

"Do you want me to be?" He smiled at Leah.

"Oh, brother. You've got to be kidding," Sarah interrupted, turning toward him. "Does that line really work? It's so cheesy."

Mike noticed her little nose wrinkled when she laughed and he had the overwhelming urge to kiss it.

Sarah put him at ease and he could tell she wasn't like every other girl. She was willing to put him in his place. He held his hand out to Sarah. "Would you like to dance?"

"I'm afraid not. Thanks." She winked at Leah and turned back to her wings. "Thanks for the drink."

"I'll dance," Leah said. "I have a boyfriend, but he doesn't dance." She grabbed Mike by the arm and dragged him onto the dance floor. Mike smiled as he looked back to the bar. Sarah watched them from across the room.

He danced with Leah, liking the way she moved and her friendly smile. "So," he said over the roar of the band. "Tell me about your friend."

Four hours later, Sarah stepped outside to get fresh air. The night had been fantastic, better than she could have imagined when Leah had asked her to skip her shopping trip. The music was upbeat and she had danced for hours.

Brian's drummer friend was Doug, Mike's friend, and the group had stuck together for the first half of the night before the band took the stage. Everyone danced and laughed. Sarah didn't love going out to bars. She didn't like getting hit on by guys too drunk to keep their hands to themselves, but she liked to be with a group of friends that she could hang with. She'd even spent a large part of the night dancing with Mike.

He was a great dancer. He was also tall, dark, and handsome, exactly the type of guy she was attracted to. He was cocky, but once the night got going, he'd been super fun. He got along with all the guys and danced with all the girls. Sarah couldn't stop watching him when he was dancing with the other girls. Her eyes were drawn to him as he moved to the music, a smile on his face. She could tell he was having a great time.

As she stepped outside onto the bar patio, she caught the end of, what looked like, a fight between a guy and his girlfriend. The girl, surrounded by a group of her friends, was yelling, tears streaming down her face. Mike stood right between the two, talking calmly to the guy, with his hand on his chest.

"Let her calm down," Mike said.

"She's drunk!" the burly man yelled. "That guy had his hands all over her!"

Mike slapped the guy's shoulder and turned him slightly. "Come on, buddy. Why don't you get some water?"

Sarah watched as Mike steered the guy back towards the entrance door. He caught sight of her and nodded before joining her.

"What was that?" Sarah moved toward the railing in the corner of the patio as Mike followed her. "Too much to drink?"

"Yeah, I think so." He moved close to Sarah, resting his elbows on the railing, his shoulder brushing hers. "They'll be fine in the morning. They're getting married tomorrow." He smiled.

"Oh! Really? Let's hope they sober up." She laughed. "That was nice of you to step in."

"Ah. They were almost done when I came out." He waved her off before staring out into the dark night as the music blared from inside the bar, getting louder each time the patio door opened. "What brings you out here? Just cooling off?"

"Yes. You?"

"Yeah, the same. I don't like bars. It's not my thing."

"Really? You could have surprised me. You were quite comfortable in there."

Mike shrugged. "Well, I can adjust to my surroundings, and Doug's a good guy. I'm here for him."

"I don't like bars either. I came for the chicken wings." Sarah rested against the railing.

They laughed easily together, settling into a silence as they both tilted their heads toward the night sky. She was comfortable next to him. He radiated confidence and strength. A calm, which she always struggled to find in the city, settled over her.

"Tomorrow I'm having a barbecue at my house." Mike interrupted her thoughts. "That's more my style."

Sarah could picture him standing around a barbecue grill, drinking a beer with his buddies, telling jokes. Her stomach flipped and she felt the heat on her cheeks that had nothing to do with dancing. She wanted to see him like that. Relaxed. In his element. She lowered her eyes before he saw her desire.

"What are you and Leah doing tomorrow?" He turned to look at her.

"Ah. Not much." Her heart raced. Had he read her mind?

"Why don't you two come over? It's the whole group here tonight so you'll know people, and a few of my neighbors. I'll have plenty of food and it's going to be really hot. You can swim."

Sarah's head snapped up. "You have a pool?"

"Oh, no. I live on a lake." He turned toward her, their hands only inches apart. "You can cool off. Swim. I have two paddleboards. Why don't you come?" He reached out and gently touched her hand, his fingers brushing hers for an instant, sending tingles up her arm.

"Yeah. Okay." Her words came out in shallow bursts as she fought for breath. "I'll ask Leah."

He smiled at her. A radiant smile with blue eyes that looked into her soul, reaching down and tugging at her insides. Sarah's world shifted, like the earth settling beneath her feet, forming a more solid foundation. Her eyes met his. "Yeah, I'll come."

Chapter Two

The next morning, Mike woke up early as the summer sun shone through the large picture window in his bedroom, casting rays of light across his bed. He moved to the window, still in his underwear, and stretched. The spot was his favorite in the whole house. He could see the entire south end of the lake from there, the view of the calm waters grounding him. The houses around the lake, tucked in between the hundred-year-old pine trees, were just waking up for the weekend.

With a fresh rush of emotion, he remembered the way Sarah moved on the dance floor. When she'd agreed to come to his lake party, a calm sensation had flowed over him. Safe. Secure. He was excited to get to know her and the smirk she gave him hadn't left his mind since last night.

He spent the morning cleaning up the yard. His house was on Lake Retreat, a small, private lake community a few hours outside of Seattle. The rustic cabin was old, built in 1933, but had been remodeled multiple times over the years, with modernizations on the inside. The most recent owner, his father's friend, had completed a major remodel last year when he was getting ready to list the cabin for sale.

When Mike had first seen the property, the lake captivated him. His dad had brought him along to a going-away party and somehow Mike had convinced their family friend to sell him the house on a private contract. Mike had moved in two months later and loved every minute of waking up in such a magnificent spot.

He had a private gate that led to the house and garage. The house had a full covered deck along the lake side of the house, and a concrete stamped patio beyond that. Mike cleaned up the deck area, setting out chairs, and watering the potted plants his mom had given him as a housewarming gift. He swept off the patio area and moved the barbecue grill away from the hot tub toward the middle of the patio next to the picnic table that had come with the house.

Then he moved on to the large, multi-level yard that flowed down to the lake and his own private dock. He gave the yard a fresh mow and used the weed-trimmer along the side of the yard, before pulling fold out lounge chairs from the deck shed and setting them up in a row, facing the lake. His row boat and paddleboards were already tied to the dock.

After taking a quick shower, he grabbed a beer and sat in a chair on the porch, his feet up on a little wooden table. He'd had a rushed work week and now it was time to relax. The summer sun was starting to cross his yard. It would be sweltering by noon, but the porch, with its ceiling fans, would keep people cool if they wanted it. He surveyed the manicured lawn and smiled taking in the smell of freshly cut grass.

His house was definitely built for parties. Fourth of July celebrations, birthdays, and summer nights in the Pacific

Northwest. When the sun came out, and the clouds lifted, the lake was a deep blue. He often had friends over, but when everyone left, he had the night sky to himself. The roots he had found for himself would last a lifetime.

Today would be a great day. Sun. Friends. And Sarah. He smiled thinking about her.

"I can't believe you said yes." Leah was sprawled out on the sofa in their living room, pillow under her head, and a large, fluffy blanket across her chest. Her legs were up, sideways, over the top of the couch. "I'm so proud of you." She smiled.

"Proud of me?" Sarah sat in the arm chair, across from the couch, a cup of hot coffee in her hands. "It's not like I don't date."

"Well, it has been a while." Leah nodded.

"I don't just jump from one guy to the next." Sarah pulled her legs up underneath her.

"I know, but I like to live vicariously through you." Leah sat up and picked up the cup of coffee Sarah had put on the coffee table for her. "Mike is *hoooot!*"

Sarah could feel the heat on her cheeks. "Yeah, he is." She smiled. "But I don't know. At the beginning of the night I thought he was a major jerk."

"But then you got to know him." Leah took a drink of her coffee before a sigh escaped her lips. "You make a great cup of coffee."

"Thanks." Sarah smiled. "I can't burn that."

"Back to Mike," Leah said. "He's nice and he's got a lake house."

Sarah sat quietly for a minute, before taking a drink of her coffee. She held the mug under her nose, breathing in the nutty scent. "There's something about him." She shook her head. "I can't put my finger on it, but, last night we had a moment together outside."

Leah leaned forward, her elbows resting on her knees, her coffee still in her hands.

"He came on so strong when we first met. Once he relaxed, let his guard down...I liked him."

"Yeah." Leah smiled. "Me too." She stood up, tossing the blanket on the couch behind her. "Why don't you get ready? I'll make breakfast."

"I was hoping you would say that." Sarah didn't trust herself anywhere near the kitchen after last night's disaster.

Half an hour later, Sarah had gotten ready for the lake party and cleaned the apartment. She was giddy as she hummed a song, walking into the kitchen. Leah had made scrambled eggs and bacon, along with toast covered with peanut butter, bananas and a drizzle of honey. "This looks amazing."

"Girl. You know how to scramble eggs." Leah gave Sarah a sideways look.

"Yours are always better." Sarah hopped up onto the barstool and dug into her food. "Thank you. I'm starved."

After finishing breakfast and cleaning up the kitchen while Leah got ready, Sarah grabbed her beach bag filled with sunscreen, a towel, her flip-flops, sunglasses, and the newest release from her favorite author. She was filled with excitement as they left the apartment, putting Mike's address into her smartphone.

It was close to a forty-five minute drive to Mike's house. Once Sarah turned onto Lake Retreat Drive, she knew they were close. She rolled her window down, breathing in the fresh air. "What a beautiful place."

Leah pointed to the gate on the right. "I think this is it." The black metal gate was unlocked and swung wide open. A large wooden sign over the garage read *Russell*.

Sarah turned into the driveway, heading down the long drive, and parked next to the house, just as Mike walked around the corner, a black lab at his side. He was in swim trunks and his chest was bare. Sarah's heart raced at the sight of him. She opened the car door and his dog jumped up with his front paws onto her lap, covering her with kisses.

Mike laughed. "I'm sorry. He's a lover. Butch. Come here." He pulled the dog off Sarah as she stepped out of the car.

"It's okay," Sarah said. "He's adorable." The dog sat right next to her, touching her leg, as she reached down and patted his head.

"What an amazing place." Leah stood up on the door frame, looking at Mike over the roof of Sarah's car. "It's perfect out here."

"Thank you." Mike's smile was huge. "Come on in." He waved to Leah, but held his hand out for Sarah.

As they walked down the path to the house, Sarah felt like she'd entered a resort in the woods. The property was truly breathtaking. His house had a large deck and massive lawn that all faced the clear blue lake. "Wow," Sarah said under her breath, as the sounds of kids splashing in the water pulled her attention.

"I know, right?" Mike asked. "I feel like that every day." He walked over to the grill, next to a table filled with all kinds of food, lifted the cover and started turning chicken drumsticks, as a sweet, smoky scent filled the air. "Make yourself comfortable. My house is your house." He pointed to chairs down by the water where a few people sat and others walked around the grounds and dock. "I have lounge chairs if you want to get some sun. Feel free to use the boats or play in the water. The bathroom is just inside the kitchen, first door on the right. Lunch will be ready soon."

"Thank you for the invite. We brought a cooler with drinks and watermelon." Sarah placed the big bowl full of cut-up fruit on the table.

"Great, thanks." He smiled at her.

"This looks like a feast," Sarah said. "Oh my goodness."

The picnic table was filled with all the traditional fixings for a barbecue as well as paper plates, plastic silverware, napkins, and condiments. Across the table were platters filled with hamburgers, pulled-pork barbecue sandwiches, ribs, and chicken. Barbecued prawns, baked beans, corn on the cob and grilled vegetable skewers were more than standard fare. There was also a green salad with pineapple, strawberries, and goat cheese.

"This is no ordinary barbecue," Leah said and whistled, looking up at Mike.

Just then, a dog raced through Mike's yard as an older lady, running along the far edge of the fence yelled, "Fraaaank. Frank. Come back here!"

The dog barked at his owner, as if to say "Come and get me," but kept on running.

Sarah noticed that Mike's attention quickly turned toward his neighbor as a small dog raced through his yard, along the water's edge. The dog ran onto the dock, before sprinting around Mike's yard, sniffing leftover plates along the way.

"Would you please take care of the chicken?" Mike handed Sarah the barbecue tongs as he kept his eyes on the dog, a smile on his lips.

"Of course. Is everything okay?"

Leah slid up next to Sarah and took the tool out of her hand.

"I think so. This happens a lot lately." Mike moved past Sarah, touching her hip as he walked by. "I'll be right back."

"I'll take care of this." Leah looked at the older woman along the fence. "You help Mike," she said to Sarah.

~

Mike reached for Sarah's hand as she ran to catch up to him. He held it for a moment before letting go. He regretted dropping it a minute too late. Her small hand had fit perfectly in his.

"Can I help?" Sarah looked up at him as they reached the main road at the end of the driveway where he met June, his next-door neighbor. His dog, Butch, was at their side.

"Is everything okay, June?" Mike asked. "Frank took off again?"

"Yes, he did." She rubbed her hands on her jeans. "I let him out to go to the bathroom and he bolted. I guess I left the gate open again."

Mike had loved his neighbors, Frank and June, from the first day he'd moved in. They'd been sitting on their dock as their granddaughter played in the shallow water when he'd walked out and stood on his dock, surveying his new view. They'd waved him over and had been the best neighbors ever since, always watching out for strangers on the drive, inviting him to parties, and helping him chainsaw when the winter wind had knocked a tree onto his fence. When Big Frank had died last year, Mike spent more time helping June with chores around her lake house.

"I've got Butch." Mike patted his black lab. "Why don't you go back inside? We'll go find Frank and bring him home. Maybe he just needed a good run."

"Thank you so much." June still had a worried look on her face as she walked back to her house.

As Mike turned to walk down the drive, Sarah fell in alongside of him, her steps matching his. "Frank?" she asked.

"Her dog." Mike smiled. "She named her cocker spaniel after her dead husband."

"Oh." Sarah laughed.

They walked in silence around the drive. Mike loved the quiet, even though they were just a few miles outside of the nearest town. He was at peace in the woods. He loved the way the breeze blew through the trees, cooling his skin in the summer heat.

"You have an amazing home," Sarah said. "Do your parents live around here?"

"No, my dad's in the Air Force. My parents live on base, but my house used to be owned by one of my dad's friends." Mike looked down a driveway as they walked passed, before continuing on. "A year ago, I came here for a party and fell in love with the place. I was lucky that he was willing to sell it to me. I moved around a lot as a kid, and I've never felt like I had a home base. When I came here, it felt like home."

"It's spectacular."

Mike's steps slowed as he reached out and touched Sarah's arm, pointing to three deer that stood in the road ahead of them.

"They're so beautiful," she whispered.

"Yeah. Isn't it cool? I see deer every day." They resumed walking as the deer moved along the path. "So, tell me about you."

"Well, I'm the youngest of three. An oops baby. My parents are older and they moved to Florida a few years ago. I have two brothers. I work for a vitamin company and... I love to go camping. That's me in a nutshell." She smiled up at him.

"Camping? I love camping," he added.

"I saw your trailer next to the garage, but with a place like this, do you go camping very often?"

"Yeah, I still do. My family goes camping at least once a year in eastern Washington and I have a few friends who go camping and we take the quads."

They had turned down a side road and he called out for the missing dog. "Frank!" He listened for a distant bark. "He has a girlfriend a few houses down. I'm not sure June knows, so let's not give away his secret." He smiled at Sarah. Butch ran ahead of them, meeting Frank as he came racing out of the next driveway, his tail wagging. "Here, Frank." Mike knelt and petted the little dog as he ran into his arms. "Good boy."

"Hi, Frank." Sarah reached down and patted the cocker spaniel. "You naughty boy."

"Let's get you home." Mike turned back toward his house as both dogs ran ahead of him, sniffing the ground and chasing a bunny into the bushes along the way.

"Sarah. I know we just met, but I really like you." He walked along the peaceful road. He didn't rush to get back to the party, but instead, enjoyed the opportunity to spend time alone with Sarah.

She looked over at him and laughed. "You're definitely not shy."

"No, I'm not." He laughed as he waved at a car that drove slowly along the lake road.

"I like you, too." She picked up a leaf from the side of the road. "I'd at least like to get to know you better."

"Ask me anything."

"You're close with your family?"

"Definitely. My parents are great and I have an older sister. She's married with two little kids. They live in Covington and I see them all the time." He looked over at Sarah. "My family gets along great. I don't have major family drama like I hear so many other people do."

"That's good. I have enough family drama for the both of us," Sarah said.

"So, there's a 'both of us'?" He winked at her. "It's because of my lake house, right?"

"Well, yeah. Of course. That is a perk." She smiled.

Sarah waited at the gate as Mike walked Frank back to his house. June answered the door right away.

"You found him." She bent down and buried her face in her little dog's ears. "Thank you so much. I was so worried."

As Mike and Sarah walked down his driveway, he waved to friends who had arrived while they were gone. He wanted to turn around and head the other direction, keeping Sarah to himself.

Heading to the picnic table, he chatted with Leah. She had taken care of the chicken and turned off the barbecue grill. "I'm sorry we were gone so long. Thank you for finishing the chicken."

"It was no problem. I helped myself to ribs," Leah added. "I was starving, and now I'm heading to one of those lounge chairs with a cocktail. Your friends are fun, too."

Sarah moved to the picnic table, looking over the spread.

"Sarah, are you hungry? Or what do you say we head out on the paddleboards?" Mike asked.

"Yeah, let's get out on the water. That sounds great. But first, did you cook all this food?" she asked, seemingly surprised.

"Yeah." He moved to stand next to her. "I found a few new recipes online and I'm always grilling meat. I like to cook."

A smile spread across her face. She looked from Mike to Leah, who gave her a wink before turning and walking down the lawn.

"You're a cook. That's perfect," Sarah purred.

Chapter Three

Sarah sat on her paddleboard, in the middle of the small lake. Mike's dog, Butch, lay on the front of her board, his customary place. After their first day at the lake, Mike had invited her to his birthday party at his parents' house the following day, and the last month had flown by as they'd dated. Sarah had jokingly called him a professional dater because he did it so well. He always picked her up, holding the car door open for her, when they'd dressed up for their dates. They went to upscale restaurants and ate delicious food. They went to museums and plays, movies and festivals, but they always ended up back at the lake.

It had become her favorite place, and just like Mike, she felt like she was escaping the real world every time she came out to his house. The stiffness left her shoulders the minute she pulled onto Lake Retreat Drive.

Today was their one-month dating anniversary and Mike offered to cook her dinner. She was giddy at the thought. The fact that he loved food was a huge perk and now she got to eat his cooking again. Life didn't get much better.

"What are you thinking about?" Mike asked. He sat on his paddleboard next to hers. They had been paddling around the lake for over an hour.

"This place." She soaked in the calm, carefree air of the lake. She watched as a few kids, on the far end of the lake, jumped on their water trampoline. She waved to Claudia, one of the neighbors she had met, and she watched as a grandpa fished with his grandson in a little rowboat.

"I really hope you feel comfortable here. I love it when you come out."

"I do. Thank you." Sarah looked over at him, now lying on his back on the paddleboard, soaking up the rays from the blistering summer sun. His hair was still wet from when they had swum a bit earlier and water glistened off his chest. Her heart raced as she looked at his body.

"You're okay with just hanging out? We can go into the city if you want to," he said, his eyes closed.

Sarah laughed. "No. Why would I want to go out? This is perfect." She lightly splashed him.

"Just making sure you're not bored."

"Bored? Not a chance. It's nice to relax for a change."

He opened his eyes and looked at her. "Yeah. I love it here. It's calm and peaceful. I could swim or paddleboard all day. Heck, I could do yard work or sit on the porch with a cold beer and never leave this place."

"Well, so far, I'm in heaven. It's such an escape for me. I love it. I would want to travel a bit or see my friends, but if I lived here, I bet I wouldn't leave if I didn't have to." She laughed.

"Are you hungry yet?" He sat up on the board, his feet hanging off one side in the water. "I didn't know it was going to be this hot. It was cloudy this morning so I made comfort food. I hope that's okay." He smiled at her and her stomach did a little flip.

"That's totally okay." She smiled. "It's nice to stay in for a change. We've mostly eaten out and we've been on the go a lot."

"What about another loop around the lake and then we can head in?" Mike stood on his board, paddle in hand.

"Yep. Sounds good." Butch woke up from his short nap and sat at attention on the front of Sarah's board as she started slowly paddling. She was in heaven. As they rounded a corner, into the cove on the south end of the lake, a flower she hadn't seen before caught her eye. She slowed and studied the color. It was the perfect violet needed for her painting.

After coming off the lake, together they pulled the paddleboards onto the dock and put the paddles away. Mike liked how Sarah always helped clean up any towels or food they had left out. She was considerate and helpful. He hadn't seen that in many other girls he'd dated.

As they entered the lake house, the smell of pasta and cheese filled the warm kitchen air.

"Oh, it smells delicious." Sarah put their empty beer bottles in the garbage and put the leftover snacks from earlier on the counter. "What is that?"

Mike used two oven mitts to pull a baking dish out of the oven warmer. Sarah closed the oven door for him as he set the dish on the stove top. They stood next to each other, shoulders touching, as they took in the warm, deliciousness that smelled like home. Comfort food had a way of making even the best day better.

"Homemade macaroni and cheese. It's a new recipe using half and half, whipping cream, parmesan, and blue cheese." Mike smiled as Sarah bit the side of her lip.

"Hmmm. That sounds amazing. You're my hero." She took another deep smell, closing her eyes before opening them and smiling up at him.

"I also have an iceberg wedge salad with blue cheese and homemade rolls."

"Now you're just flirting with me." Sarah grinned as she reached out and held his hand. "If you keep this up, you'll have a hard time getting rid of me. Did I tell you I can't cook?"

"I could teach you." He loved how her hand fit into his.

"No, seriously. I'm terrible." She took a step away from him, pulling him toward her as she leaned against the sink, his body facing hers.

"That sounds like a challenge. I'll have to give lessons." Mike held her gaze as he stepped toward her. "It would be long days, maybe even longer nights, if you didn't get the hang of it."

He wanted nothing more. When she was with him, he felt content. Happy. He was surprised at how much he wanted to spend time with her. To have her at his house, his sanctuary in the woods. He wrapped one arm around her waist. She smiled up at him, patiently waiting while he searched her face.

"Mike," she said softly.

"We could cook pasta." He lowered his mouth to hers, gently tasting her lips. "Pork chops are my specialty." He whispered into her ear.

She wrapped both arms around his neck and leaned into him, her breasts pressing against his chest, deepening his desire. Looking into her eyes, he saw his future. Their lips met, hunger and passion colliding.

Mike Russell and Sarah Oliver are neighbors on the lake in the Lake Retreat Series.

Not yet published are *Falling for Blake* and *Running from Beau*.

Mandi McGuire is a sweet contemporary romance author living in the Pacific Northwest. Most days you can find her sitting on her patio, reading her favorite authors, and drinking a chai tea. Hot or cold, both are delish! Mandi is polishing the first two books in her Lake Retreat series.

Visit Mandi online at: www.mandimcguire.com

Touched by Magic

by

Gerri Russell

Chapter One

"Hello, gorgeous."

Caitlin Baxter ignored the comment. Holding a glass of champagne, she continued to study the beautiful woven cloth on display before her at the African exhibit of the Seattle Art Museum.

"Why would a beautiful woman like you be here all alone?"

She was far from alone. Caitlin waited in the foyer with a hundred other people. As conversations swirled around her, she prayed the newest exhibit would open soon, at least before the gentleman who had been following her since she arrived wanted to further his one-sided monologue.

"I would be honored to be your escort through the exhibit. Might be dangerous to see an exhibit on witches and witchcraft all alone," the fifty-something balding man in a black tuxedo pursued.

Caitlin turned her back on him, hoping it would signal to him to leave her alone. She'd made her way toward the front of the room on purpose and she wasn't about to give up the chance to be one of the first people inside the exhibit. The exhibit wasn't open to the public yet. As a history professor at the University of Washington she'd used her department connections to secure one precious ticket to the donors and sponsors' showing of *The World Bewitch'd*, an exhibit on loan for the next month from

Cornell University. Caitlin had flown to New York to study the collection many times, but the latest piece to join the collection was why she was here. She'd been trying to purchase the artifact herself for the last five years, but it had sold for far more than her meager savings would allow.

The journal had gone to auction two months ago and had been purchased by a private collector for two million dollars. The collector had promptly lent the artifact to Cornell. No one but the collector, the curator of Cornell's collection, and the staff at SAM had had the privilege of seeing the piece, no matter how many phone calls Caitlin had made explaining her academic interest. She'd claimed her interest was to benefit her own studies into the period of history known as "The Burning Times." But her interest was personal.

Very personal.

"Come on, gorgeous. Won't you at least look at me?"

With a sigh she turned toward the man. "I'm perfectly capable of navigating this exhibit by myself. But thank you for your offer."

The man grinned. "Playing hard to get? I like that in a woman."

Caitlin set her champagne glass down on a tray beside the wall. If he pushed her much further, she would show him just how hard she could play, despite her hip-hugging red velvet gown and four-inch stiletto heels. No one messed with the female ancestor of Mariam Swinton Sinclair.

"There you are, darling." Another total stranger touched her arm, then leaned in to kiss her check. "I've been looking all over for you."

What was happening? She forced herself to focus on the total stranger beside her instead of the fifty-something man frowned.

"They are going to let us in early, before the doors open. I thought you might like a few moments of privacy with Mariam Swinton Sinclair's journal. This way." Her rescuer stood back, motioning for her to go in front of him, and Caitlin stepped toward the doors. Excitement wedded with unease as the stranger beside her placed a hand on the small of her back, guiding her into the exhibit. It wasn't as if she couldn't handle herself. And she was getting what she wanted—more, in fact, than she'd imagined she'd have tonight. *A few minutes alone with the artifact.*

Once the doors closed behind them, Caitlin turned to the man beside her. He was exceptionally good-looking, in his mid-thirties with an athlete's slim and supple strength. He revealed an easy, charismatic smile. "Who are you and what do you want?"

"You're welcome," he said with a laugh. "I was trying to rid you of your unwanted companion."

Caitlin frowned at the confidence reflected in his gray-blue eyes, the intensity of the confidence he exuded. Why wouldn't he be confident? The tuxedo he wore probably cost more than her entire wardrobe. "Thank you for that."

He held out his hand though his gaze was fixed intently on her face. "Logan Ross."

Caitlin took his hand into her own and tried to ignore the rippling sensation that moved up her arm. "Caitlin Baxter."

His smile broadened. "I know who you are. You've been calling the museum for the past month, begging to see the journal."

"I never begged," she said as she released his hand.

He raised a brow. "Would you like to see the journal?"

It was all she'd longed for over the past five years since it had resurfaced. Her heart was pounding so hard she doubted she could speak, so she nodded instead.

"This way." He led her through the maze of rooms. The first contained statues and paintings from the fifteenth century to the present featuring artistic imagery of witches. The next room examined themes such as gendered stereotypes, beliefs in night flying, demonic pacts, forced confessions, and the witch epidemic of centuries past. The third was a collection of torture devices used to extract confessions.

Caitlin walked quickly through and into the fourth room that housed rare and unique editions of manuscripts from the fifteenth and sixteenth centuries on witchcraft, demonology, and a treasure trove of testimonies and trial records, and—Caitlin's gaze went to the leather-bound journal encased in glass—her ancestor's journal.

The breath left Caitlin's lungs as she froze in the doorway. "Oh, my goodness." She had thought she'd been prepared for seeing the journal. She knew now she hadn't been. An overwhelming sensation of belonging came to her—as if everything in her life had led her to this moment.

The journal lay open to pages twelve and thirteen. The yellowed parchment was still in pristine condition, even though the ink had faded to a rusty brown. Making out the elegant script of the work, Caitlin read the events of the day described by her ancestor. She was reading about historical people, and yet, it felt as though she were right there with Mariam as that lady wrote her thoughts a few months after she and Cameron Sinclair were married.

September 26th, 1592

The witch hunts continue. King James is as determined as ever to rid the country of all those whom he sees as a threat to society. Today, Mistress Critchen and her three daughters were arrested and taken to await questioning by a new witchpricker who has taken over the role from my father. I had not thought it possible, but Alaric Wyth seems to be even more brutal to his victims through the use of his pricker's needle than my father had been. The only crime Mistress Critchen and her daughters are guilty of is not having a husband or a father to protect them.

Cameron and I are planning to intercede on their behalf. And if that fails, Cameron and his men will ambush the cart on its way to the tribunal chamber. His men can easily overpower the four guards that usually escort the cart the few miles from the gaol to where the trials are held.

Since they will not be safe anywhere in North Berwick ever again, Vivian and Quinn Douglas have agreed to take them into their home—the one place in Scotland that King James himself has granted immunity to those who are accused of witchcraft.

October 12th, 1592

Mariam Douglas has confirmed what I have suspected for the past few weeks. I am with child. Cameron and I are excited and scared to bring a new life into this upside-down world right now...

"Caitlin?"

"Is there any way I can touch the journal, turn the pages, and read everything she wrote?"

"Not today, but in the future, perhaps. Come, now. It's time we step back so others can enjoy the journal."

"But it's only been—" She turned to him to protest but realized the look on his face was one of puzzlement. Then she looked around her to see the entire chamber was filled with others who'd been waiting in the foyer with her only moments ago. "I thought you said we would have time alone with the journal."

"You did. You've been staring at the pages for the past ten minutes without saying a word."

"Ten minutes—no, it was only a matter of seconds."

He shook his head as he offered her his arm and led her away from the glass case. "You were definitely caught up in studying it."

How could time have passed so quickly? Still unsure of what had just happened, she allowed Logan to escort her out of the room and into the last chamber that featured the continuing cultural preoccupation with witchcraft and possession, particularly through fiction and cinema. They sat down on one of the benches toward the back of the room, but instead of watching *The Witches of Eastwick* on the screen, she turned to Logan. "You said I might be able to see the journal and read it in private. How soon can I do that?"

"You are certainly determined to see that journal."

"I've been trying to either buy or view the journal for the past five years."

"It's that important to you?"

She probably shouldn't let him know how desperate she was to see it, but she couldn't help herself. If her family legends were true, there were things in that journal she needed to know, needed to understand. "I would do anything to read it from beginning to end."

"Anything?"

Caitlin frowned, not liking the presumptuous look on his face. "Well, almost anything."

"Then I'll make you a deal. Spend one day with me—morning until night—showing me the sights and tastes of Seattle and I'll give you the same number of hours with your ancestor's journal."

Her eyes widened. She hadn't told him her connection with the artifact.

He chuckled at her response. "It wasn't hard to put two and two together. Not after the way you were mesmerized by the journal."

She frowned. "How can you make such an offer? The journal is on loan to the exhibit."

"I can make the offer because I own it. I bought it then lent it to Cornell for this exhibit. And, it is because of me that *The World Bewitch'd* came to Seattle at all."

Caitlin stood and threaded her way back through the chamber they had just vacated, making her way to her ancestor's journal. She peered past the shoulders of a man and a woman currently viewing the pages to read the placard: *On loan from the private collection of Logan Ross.*

Having the confirmation she needed, she returned to Logan.

As she approached, a slow, lazy smile swept across his face. He stood to greet her. His fingers lightly caressed her arm as he bent his head close to hers. "Do we have a deal?"

She stepped back, noting that his gaze glittered in the dim light as they met her own. "I shouldn't say yes. I know nothing about you."

"I'm an American citizen like you whose ancestors migrated from Scotland. I grew up in New York but moved to Seattle two months ago. I own my own business, and collect relics from the past."

Those were things he did, not truly anything about who he was, but she had to admit he didn't sound too dangerous. And he was in some small way connected with her past, now that he owned her ancestor's journal. Swallowing back her reservations, she nodded.

"Great. We'll start first thing tomorrow. Shall I pick you up at eight?"

She nodded. "Then the day after tomorrow, I will have my chance to view the journal."

"You're really that anxious to read through your ancestor's chronicle of the past? Some might call you obsessed."

"I don't expect you to understand."

"I understand," he said softly with a look of compassion in his eyes. "I can be fairly obsessive myself at times."

Caitlin retrieved her cell phone from the small shoulder bag she carried and shared her contact information with him. "Until tomorrow, then."

"Until tomorrow," he agreed.

Caitlin smiled all the way back to her car. In one more day, she would have access to the information that might help her not only come to know her ancestry more fully, but she would also—hopefully—understand the magical abilities she possessed.

Chapter Two

Caitlin waited outside her Capitol Hill condominium building in the early morning sunshine for Logan to arrive. This wasn't a date, and she didn't expect him to come up to get her. She would show him the sights and flavors of Seattle in order to get what she wanted.

Exactly at eight o'clock, Logan pulled up in a silver Mercedes-Benz convertible with the top down. Though Seattle never seemed to shake its rainy reputation no matter the season, summer in Seattle was glorious. She'd dressed simply in a pair of Bermuda shorts and a lacy light-blue top with blue strappy sandals that were made for walking. Around her neck she wore Mariam's shell necklace that had been passed down through the generations of her family. The bag she carried had a few other options in case their travels took them to fancier locations.

"Morning," he greeted as he stepped from the car and took her bag, placing it in the back seat before opening the car door for her. She hated to admit how handsome he looked in his cargo shorts, white linen shirt, and Birkenstocks. He might have only arrived in Seattle a short while ago, but he certainly knew how to dress like a Seattleite.

"Ready for your adventure?" she asked as she slipped into the passenger seat.

"I can't wait." The words were spoken with silken sensuality as he returned to the driver's seat. He turned the ignition and the car growled to life.

"What a lovely car." Caitlin drove a very practical Nissan Leaf. "What is the name of the company you own? I don't believe you ever told me."

"I'm the owner and CEO of Seattle BioGen," he said as he pulled into traffic. "Which way should I go?"

"Turn right and head down toward the water. We're going to Pike Place Market." She gazed at him in wonder. "You own a biotech company? Why didn't you say so last night?"

"Would you have given me a different answer to our deal if I had?"

"No." Nothing short of harming another or stealing would have stopped her from agreeing to his terms.

"Then it doesn't really matter."

She shifted in her seat. "It's a little intimidating."

He smiled. "No one's ever said I was intimidating before."

"I said your job was intimidating. Not you." She returned his easy smile.

"Great, then for today I am just Logan and you are just Caitlin. Okay?"

It was early enough in the morning that Logan slipped into a parking space right off Pike Street. He closed the top on the convertible then exited before coming around to open her door. "This isn't a date," she admonished as she got out. "You don't have to—" She broke off as she stood, moving almost into his arms since he hadn't backed away. He smelled fantastic. Like cedar and citrus.

He ignored her comment and offered her his arm. "Shall we? I'm all yours."

Caitlin had had boyfriends before, but nothing serious ever came out of those relationships. She'd always been too busy either studying for her degrees, or researching her ancestral past. But she had to admit she liked the feel of Logan's arm beneath her hand, and the feel of his warmth at her side. Wrapped in his fresh, clean scent and the salty smell of Puget Sound, she led him to Le Panier.

At the counter, she spotted George, her favorite French baker. "Two of my favorites to go, please, George."

He smiled as he nodded then lifted his brow as the older man's gaze lit on Logan. "Of course, *ma petite.* Anything for you and your friend." George filled her order and handed her the brown cardboard box with her favorite breakfast inside. "On the house today, *ma petite.*"

"Thank you, George," Caitlin said with a smile. She'd find some way to pay the man back in the future.

As if reading her thoughts, Logan asked for a business card and tucked it into his wallet, withdrawing one of his own and handing it to George. "I'll reach out in the future when we need a caterer for a corporate event."

They left the French baker behind with a huge grin on his face. "Now for coffee," Caitlin said as they headed for the first Starbucks Coffee Co., which had opened its doors over forty-five years ago. "Don't be intimidated by the line," she said as they neared and saw that the waiting line extended down the street, past the stop sign and around the corner, where they slipped into place. "The line moves fast. The baristas here are the best in the world."

"What's next?" he asked as they crept forward.

"We'll go enjoy our breakfast at the Olympic Sculpture Park and watch the ferries sail by."

"Perfect." He was stopped from saying more as they arrived at the counter to order. After he had his cold brew and she her iced green tea, they headed for the car and quickly traveled to park beneath the Paccar Pavilion. They walked along the waterfront until they came to a bench near Alexander Calder's abstract sculpture of "The Eagle."

The big orange structure didn't look anything like an eagle, but Caitlin could definitely see curving wings, an assertive stance, and a pointy beak. But that wasn't why she chose this spot. It was because of the view. "From here you can see Elliott Bay, the Olympic Mountains, and watch the ferries as they glide across the water on their way to Bainbridge Island."

"New York was beautiful in its own way, but Seattle has a natural beauty that is hard to beat."

"Agreed," she said with a sigh as she took a sip of her tea.

"What's in the box?" he asked, peering at the pastries she'd set between them.

She opened the box and held it up to him. "Twice-baked almond croissants that are as big as your face. They're my favorite."

He reached for one and took a bite. "Delicious. I can see why you like them. Sweet and crunchy."

"Was it the biotech firm that brought you out here?" Caitlin asked as she took a sip of tea.

"That and other things." His tone was reserved, but since this wasn't a date, she didn't take it personally.

She took another bite of her croissant and chewed it thoughtfully. It didn't sound like he wanted to talk about his work. That was fine by her. She'd get right to the heart of what she really wanted to know without the small talk. "Why did you purchase Mariam's journal? I've been studying the English and Scottish witchcraft trials for the past twelve years, and your name was never listed among those who were researching or even funding the research in that area of study."

"It's a recent interest." He set his croissant down on the napkin in his lap and looked at her. "Can we not talk about this today? I'll answer all your questions tomorrow. I know history is your passion, but can we focus on having fun today? I haven't had a day off since I moved here."

"Okay, since work talk is forbidden, then tell me something about yourself that's personal. If I'm going to spend the day with you, I should know something about you other than that you like your coffee straight up."

"I mix it up sometimes with a Frappuccino."

She snapped her fingers. "Nope. You're avoiding my questions. Something personal."

He was silent a moment. "I'm an only child?"

"That's a start."

"I read a lot."

"Books?" she asked excitedly.

"Reports. Mostly having to do with drug research and clinical trials. It's not that exciting, and that's about my work." His voice faded off as he frowned. "I never thought of myself as a boring person before, but now that I think about it, outside of work, I have no life."

"Do you have a skill? A hobby?" Caitlin prompted, not willing to give up just yet. There had to be something he might say that would help her plan the next several hours of their day. She had a few ideas, but nothing concrete.

"I can whistle." He demonstrated with a melodic release of air through his lips.

"You can whistle?" Caitlin forced herself not to smile. "You like black coffee, you're an only child, you read a lot, and you can whistle. I must say, Logan Ross, you are the most interesting man I have ever known."

"I can be interesting if you give me a chance." He reached for her hand and gently brought her fingers to his lips. His touch was warm and suddenly very intimate. She found herself staring at him, unable to look away from his gray-blue eyes as her heartbeat accelerated and her blood ran faster in her veins. He released her hand, and though no part of his body was touching her, she still felt his warmth.

He sat perfectly still beside her and she could see the pulse drumming at his temples. She tried to think of something to say that would bring an end to the sudden tension between them. "The Great Wheel," she forced out on a breath. "We should go to the Great Wheel along the waterfront." She stood, defying the fact that her knees were weak. She could feel the heat in her cheeks and wished desperately for a breeze to wash all signs of her sudden attraction away. This was not a date.

That charming smile reappeared. "Sounds like fun. Let's go." Logan finished off the rest of his croissant then picked up the empty Starbucks containers and the empty cardboard box, which he took to the nearby recycling bins. The cups went into the blue, the paper in the green. He might not be a Seattle native, but he was a pro recycler already in a town that valued earth's precious resources.

They walked the length of Seattle's historic waterfront before stopping at the Great Wheel to buy tickets. On a Saturday, the line already extended all the way down Pier 57. "Looks like we'll have to stand in line for a while."

Logan shook his head. "Come with me," he said, taking her hand in his. "There are some perks to being a CEO of a local company. And this is one of them." He pulled her out of line and went to the attendant at the rope gate. Logan exchanged a few words with the man and the rope suddenly dropped, allowing them to not only enter, but to head straight for the VIP cabin, number forty-two.

Caitlin slid across the supple leather seat as Logan slipped in beside her. Beneath them, the floor was made of glass, and as the gondola door slid closed and the Great Wheel set into motion, the cabin lifted to reveal the waters of Elliott Bay on one side and the Seattle skyline on the other.

"What did you say to that man?" Caitlin asked as she gripped the edge of her seat.

Logan smiled. "I bought out the entire wheel for the next twelve minutes."

"We're the only ones on the ride?" She couldn't keep the distress from her voice. "Everyone in line will hate us."

"The wheel hadn't officially opened for business for the day yet. We are technically taking it out for a safety check—at least that is what the gate attendant will tell everyone." His smile faded momentarily as he noted the death-grip she had on the seat. "Relax. Enjoy."

Caitlin forced herself to breathe. "Easy for you to say. You're obviously not afraid of heights."

He pried her hands from the seat and pulled her close, taking her hands into his own. "Why did you suggest this activity if you're afraid of heights?"

The heat of his body warmed her, and she had to admit to feeling slightly less distressed. "You wanted classic Seattle. This is as touristy as it gets." She swallowed.

"Can I do anything to help?"

"Distract me," she said, her throat tight.

"You asked for it." He chuckled, and for the next eleven minutes he whistled her Bobby McFerrin's famous tune, "Don't Worry, Be Happy." By the time the gondola door slid open once more, they were both whistling and laughing.

Over the next several hours, they had lunch at Ivar's on the waterfront and fended off aggressive gulls as the birds begged for a taste of their fish and chips. They took a ferry ride from Seattle to Bainbridge Island and back again, watching for orca whales that came to Puget Sound during the summer months. They walked for miles along Alki Beach and splashed their bare feet in the cold, salty water.

As they walked along the shoreline, they came across two little boys, perhaps five and six years of age, trying to fly a kite. The wind was lighter than normal, causing the cloth kite to lift but then to pitch into the sand a moment later.

"Want to help them?" Caitlin asked. At Logan's nod, she walked over to the two mothers who were sitting close by and asked for permission to help the youngsters. At their agreement, Caitlin returned to Logan. "Why don't you take one of the boys down the beach with the kite and help him catch the wind. I'll stay here with the other boy and help him put tension on the string."

"Sounds like you've done this before," he asked, with a lift to his brow.

"More like I've failed so many times that I learned a thing or two along the way," she said, laughing as they parted to talk with the boys. At their suggestions, the boys jumped up and down with delight.

Once Logan was away from her, Caitlin focused her energy on the kite in the distance. She searched deep inside herself, pulling forth a uniqueness she still did not understand and thought about the wind. Finally, she brought her hand to wrap around her shell necklace. It was the one thing she needed to make the wind do what she commanded. Gradually, the wind began to stir, picking up speed as the very essence inside her grew stronger. The kite lifted, caught the wind, then soared higher into the sky.

"Hold tight," Caitlin advised the young boy. "Tug against the wind while you release more line. Let the wind pull the kite higher." Once the kite caught the wind higher up, it sailed all of its own accord and Caitlin relaxed her mind. She looked around her, hoping no one noticed anything out of the ordinary just as Logan and the younger boy returned to them.

"Well done, boys," Logan said with a charming smile.

"Thank you!" The boys moved farther up the beach, squealing with delight at their accomplishment.

"Seems you made them very happy."

"It wasn't just me. You played an instrumental role." Caitlin smiled back. Then, determined to return to their own fun, she took off her shoes and ran into the surf and kicked salty water at him.

"Two can play that game." He took off his shoes then joined her in the surf, and soon they were both a little wet and laughing as they continued down the beach. Logan fell into step with her and their strides matched comfortably.

As the day progressed, Logan shared more about his life. He told her about his childhood in New York, his time at Cornell for his undergraduate degree then at Massachusetts Institute of Technology for his master's degree.

He talked about how his father had died in a car accident four years ago, and that his mother had been ill during his entire lifetime with an incurable disease, which was what had sparked his interest in biotechnology. The only strange part of the day had been while they'd been at Alki, a blood donation vehicle had appeared in the parking area. He'd encouraged her to join him in giving blood. She'd never done something like that on an almost-date before.

After donating blood, they had changed their clothing in the public restrooms nearby and then headed to Salty's restaurant on Harbor Avenue for dinner. They were seated outside on the deck, with Elliott Bay on full display before them. Outside, the weather was warm, but a breeze made the temperature tolerable.

When they'd finished dinner, and the sun was sinking lower in the sky, he turned to her. "This has been the perfect day. Better than I imagined. Thank you. But could I ask for one more indulgence?"

She met his gaze. "And what might that be?"

"Will you come with me to my favorite location and watch the sun set?" The words were spoken with such intensity they acted like a magnet, drawing her toward him.

She leaned closer and caught the faint scents of citrus and salt. It would be the perfect end to the day...a day that had started out feeling like a business deal, but with each passing hour had become more like a date. Watching the sun set together would definitely tip things into the "date" category.

A breeze stirred, touching her face and throat with its hot breath, pressing the cotton of her dress against her breasts. She swallowed to ease the tightness in her throat and gave him the only answer she was capable of at the moment. "Yes. Let's watch the sun set together."

Chapter Three

Logan held the car door open for Caitlin to exit. He'd started the day out with her, hoping that they would make it to this moment. But what had started out as cool and calculated had now become an honest desire for her to meet the woman she would ultimately help if she agreed to the proposal he would soon offer her.

"Where are we?" Caitlin asked. "This looks like someone's home."

"My mother lives here."

"You brought me to meet your mother?" Caitlin froze. "I thought we were going to watch the sun set."

"We are. My favorite place to do that is down on the dock. You can't beat the view." Logan took Caitlin's hand in his, pulling her along the pathway and into the house that featured dramatic glass walls as well as fabulous views of Seward Park, the Olympic Mountains, and the Seattle skyline. He opened the door and headed into the main open-concept living area, where his mother was just finishing up with Dr. Sabario.

The tall, gray-haired doctor wrapped his mother's arm with a compression dressing after her plasma infusion before he turned to greet them. "Hello, Logan. We're just finishing up your mother's treatment." His gaze shifted to Caitlin. "You must be—"

"Mother, this is Dr. Caitlin Baxter." Logan cut off Dr. Sabario, not wanting the doctor to give away too much information before Caitlin was ready to hear it. "We met yesterday at the Seattle Art Museum exhibit. I hope you don't mind that we came over to watch the sun set on the dock."

His mother's face held an almost normal pallor, making her appear much healthier than she had last night. "You know how much I love having guests."

"Caitlin, my mother, Josephine Ross, and her doctor Anthony Sabario, a blood disorder specialist from the Fred Hutchinson Cancer Research Center."

Dr. Sabario inclined his head in acknowledgment as he continued to place his equipment in his medical bag. "An honor to meet you."

"It's nice to meet you both," Caitlin said, hesitating. "We didn't mean to intrude."

Josephine Ross stood before Caitlin in her white Givenchy slacks and pink silk blouse. Her dark hair was coiled into a chignon, and her nails were perfectly manicured and painted in a popular shade of rose pink that matched her lipstick. No matter how sick his mother became, she always looked fashionable. "I'm so pleased to meet you, and call me JoJo. Everyone does." She stepped back and motioned to Caitlin to join her. "Would you like a quick tour of the house so you can still get down to the lake before the sun sets? Perhaps you'd like to choose a bottle of wine from the cellar?"

Caitlin visibly relaxed as a smile came to her lips. "I'd like that."

"You two have fun," Logan said. "I'll see Dr. Sabario out." As soon as Caitlin and his mother disappeared from view, Logan turned to the doctor. "How is she? When will we know if this particular plasma treatment worked?"

Dr. Sabario walked beside Logan as they headed for the door. "I'll return early tomorrow and take a blood sample. We won't know anything until then. But she tolerated this injection better than others in the past. You might have found the perfect donor for her."

"I hope so. We'll talk more tomorrow morning once you have the blood results." Logan saw the doctor to his car before he went downstairs to find his mother and Caitlin in the wine cellar. Caitlin had selected a French champagne for them to share. He picked up two champagne flutes from a nearby rack. "Nice choice. Champagne and sunsets are a perfect end to a perfect day."

"I'll leave you two to yourselves," his mother said. "Nice to meet you, Caitlin. You're welcome to visit anytime."

As his mother walked to the elevator he'd had installed last year, he took Caitlin's hand. "Come with me." He led her outside and down the terraced stairs to the shoreline of Lake Washington. At the end of the dock sat two teak Adirondack chairs. He sank into one and set the champagne flutes at his feet before reaching for the bottle she carried. He popped the cork and poured them each a glass of the bubbling liquid.

She slid into the chair beside him, staring out at the water. "It is beautiful here." Then, with a sigh she added,

"What's wrong with your mom? You said she was ill. It's not terminal, is it?"

He handed her a flute then held his glass up for a toast before answering. "My mother has a rare blood disease. Her blood doesn't clot normally."

She nodded. "That explains the injection she was getting when we walked in."

"She has plasma treatments every two weeks in order to restore and maintain normal fibrinogen levels."

"Is that why you wanted to give blood when you saw the blood donation site today?"

"Blood donation is a simple and safe way to make a huge difference in the life of another person." He turned back to the setting sun. The day was perfectly clear, giving them a spectacular view of the large, orange fireball in the distance that splashed the horizon with hot pink, red, and a hint of purple.

"Where shall I meet you tomorrow to study Mariam's journal?" Caitlin asked, breaking the silence that had fallen between them.

"We'd have to meet at the Seattle Art Museum. They have a conservation room we can use. And since tomorrow is Sunday, no one will be there to disturb us. Sound good?"

"I don't suppose you'd let me make a digital copy of the journal," she asked sheepishly.

"I couldn't allow that. The contents of the journal are private. I chose to display for the exhibit the two pages of

Mariam's journal that had the least amount of personal information on them."

Her brows knotted in thought as she drained her champagne. "I still don't understand why you would be so interested in Mariam's journal. I mean, two million dollars is a lot of money to sink into a hobby."

He refilled their glasses before answering. "The Sinclair and Ross families are connected through their mutual histories. Both Alexander Ross and Cameron Sinclair were members of King James VI of Scotland's private guards. In the seventeenth century, the two families were joined through the marriage of Lena Sinclair to Ian Ross."

Her eyes widened as she set her glass down beside her chair. "You're descended from *that* line of the Ross family?"

"Yes. Our family lines crossed some three hundred years ago."

The animation in her face faded. "That means we're...related."

He set his glass down and stood, pulling her up from her chair and into his arms. "Centuries have passed. There is nothing stopping us from pursuing any relationship we might want to explore."

She didn't back away from the desire he knew was reflected in his eyes. "And what kind of relationship do you want with me?"

The cooling night air rustled the flyaway strands of her red hair about her face as her hands slid upward and locked behind his neck. He heard the quickened pace of her breathing, felt each exhalation like a wisp of magic against his face.

Slowly he drew her head forward, and he felt the slight shifting of her body as she pressed up on her toes to meet him. His lips touched hers, feather soft at first, then more firmly. He slid his hands down her sides until they came to rest on her hips. He closed his eyes and drew in the scent of lemons, salt, and sunshine. The sweet taste of the champagne lingered on her tongue as he slipped between her parted lips to explore her more fully.

It felt so right, holding her in his arms like this. It was as if no one and nothing else existed. He focused on only this moment, letting all the things he knew she might not appreciate slide from his thoughts as he deepened the kiss.

A jolt of pure desire shot through Logan's body. His groin tightened, and he moaned against the deep-seated ache that burned through him. Not wanting to pull back, but knowing he should before things went too far, he lifted his lips from hers.

A soft breeze continued to tousle Caitlin's hair as she turned her head toward the horizon. The sun slowly sank into the horizon, reflecting its shimmering rays of red and orange across the still water.

They stayed like that, locked in each other's arms until the descending sun was tucked behind the Olympic Mountains and the sky faded into darkness. Finally, with no other lights around, the stars came out, glittering like tiny diamonds overhead.

"That was beautiful," Caitlin breathed into the night. "I can see why you like watching the sunset from here."

He pulled her closer and kissed her on the top of the head. "I've seen this sight a hundred times, but tonight, with you, it's like seeing it all over again."

She shivered. Once the sun disappeared, the temperature cooled quickly in the Pacific Northwest. "Come, let's go back inside and then I'll take you home. We have an early start again tomorrow."

Logan bent to retrieve the champagne bottle and their two glasses while Caitlin wrapped her arms around herself. "How soon can we get into the exhibit and retrieve the journal?"

"I'll pick you up at eight again. I've arranged for the guard to open the doors for us by eight-fifteen."

"Can't wait."

Neither could he.

Back inside, they headed up the open staircase. At the sound of their footsteps on the hardwood floor, his mother emerged from the living room. "Are you headed home so soon?"

"Yes, I'm afraid so." Caitlin shivered again. "It's getting cold outside, but thank you for the tour of your lovely home and for letting me enjoy that fantastic sunset with Logan."

JoJo slipped the pashmina scarf from around her own shoulders and placed it around Caitlin's. "Take this. It will help you stay warm on the drive home."

"I can't take this from you." The beautiful pink and gold cashmere scarf cloaked her in warmth even as she protested.

"I insist, dear."

Logan simply smiled at the two women. "I wouldn't argue with my mom. She always wins, no matter the argument. Just take it for now. You can return it to me tomorrow."

"All right," Caitlin finally agreed. "Thank you again."

"Come back soon," JoJo said as they parted.

Traffic from Mercer Island into Seattle was light, and the drive flew by. Before he knew it, he pulled up in front of Caitlin's condominium building and they said good-bye.

He saw her to the security door. Before she turned away, he gathered her against his chest and pressed his hand against her cheek, reveling in the silken texture of her skin as he lowered his lips to hers. He angled her head back so he could explore her mouth in deep intimate strokes. He took the kiss deeper then, tasting her, breathing her, forcing her lips further apart, wanting to take in her very essence. He heard her whimper, felt the vibration in her throat, and it inflamed him more.

Good God, he'd never felt anything like this before. The more he tasted her, the more he wanted. Finally, with an anguished groan he tore his lips from hers. He had to stop before he lost control. "You're so beautiful."

He heard her quick intake of breath, saw her green eyes widen as if he'd said something shocking. The sight of her that way, startled, aware, slightly embarrassed sent a twist of longing to his heart and a stab of regret to his soul. He'd started the day intending to use her for his own purposes. Now, he wanted nothing more than to keep her by his side.

Would such a thing be possible once she learned why he'd baited her with her ancestor's journal? He would know the answer to that question tomorrow, once he told her the truth. "I should let you get some sleep." He forced the words out.

She drew a breath and seemed to gather herself for a moment before she nodded and pulled her keycard from her purse.

"Until tomorrow," she said softly, slipping inside the door and letting it shut behind her.

Inside her apartment, Caitlin closed the door and leaned her hot cheek against the wood. Her heart was pounding so hard she could scarcely breathe. She wanted to go back downstairs and invite him up. But not on the first date. Never on the first date!

Oh God, it had been a date all along.

She pushed away from the door and headed for the shower. What she needed was a splash of cold water to knock some sense back into her brain and cool her overheated body.

As much as she hadn't wanted to admit it at first, she liked Logan Ross. She really liked him, and not just because he could give her access to her family's past. She liked him because he was funny. He was fun to be around. He'd actually whistled a tune to calm her fear of heights on the Ferris wheel. Every single one of the men she'd dated in the past would never have done that— humiliated himself merely to make her laugh.

She stripped off her clothes, leaving them in a pile on the floor as she headed to the bathroom. Logan was handsome, successful, confident, and fun. Caitlin shuddered as she stepped into the stream of icy water. It took only a second before she cranked the dial to warm the water.

Something must be wrong with him. Wasn't that always the case with her and men? She fell into the relationship headfirst only to find out later that they were either cheaters or liars, or both.

Maybe this time would be different, and Logan would be exactly the man who'd spent the day with her today. Caitlin tipped her head back and let the warm water wash across her body, willing the water to work its magic and help her to relax.

She doubted she'd be able to sleep at all tonight. Not only was she eager to see Logan again, she would finally get to read Mariam Swinton Sinclair's journal. There had to be something within the pages of that document to help her understand what made her different.

Her hand crept up to the necklace still at her throat. Touching it calmed her thoughts. Since the time she was a young child, she'd been able to manipulate the wind. She'd never revealed that fact to her parents, her friends, or anyone else—terrified what they might do to her if they found out.

There were no witch trials any longer, but that didn't mean she was safe if someone discovered her secret. And she'd watched too many spy movies to trust any medical or government authorities. Nope, she was on her own with this problem, just as she'd always been.

She shut off the shower and dried herself. She'd waited for this moment for so long. Even so, she didn't want to get her hopes up. Mariam might have left a clue in her journal for her descendants, something only they would understand. But she might not have either.

In a matter of hours, Caitlin would know for certain.

Chapter Four

Caitlin's heart raced as she sat before Mariam's journal in the conservation room at the Seattle Art Museum. She'd donned white cotton gloves and a mask, and using tweezers, she opened the nine inches wide and twelve inches high leather-bound book to the first yellowed page. Excitement built as her gaze traveled over the handwritten script.

Logan sat beside her, but he remained silent as she lost herself in history.

What seemed like minutes later, but in reality had been four hours, Caitlin carefully set it open to the display pages and refocused her gaze on the modern room in which she sat. She would give anything to read the journal again, and again.

"Well?" Logan asked.

Caitlin brought her gaze to his. "You've read the journal?"

He nodded. There was no fear or suspicion in his gaze, only interest.

"Then you know Mariam wrote a lot about what she and Cameron Sinclair did to save people from persecution."

"Yes, but Mariam also wrote about herself, about possessing a secret ability she revealed to only those closest to her."

Caitlin nodded hesitantly. "It's understandable that she kept her abilities a secret, especially during the sixteenth century. It didn't take much back then for someone to be arrested and tried for witchcraft. Of those who were arrested, they died either from the torture they endured, or eventually they simply confessed, despite their innocence, just to make the torture stop."

"It seems Mariam and Cameron saved as many as they could." Logan straightened in his chair as though suddenly uncomfortable.

They had been sitting still and not moving for four hours. Caitlin stood, stretching the tightened muscles of her neck and shoulders.

Logan stood as well. "What did you think about what she wrote about her friendship with Vivian Douglas, the healer?"

"I'm glad she had a friend." Caitlin knew how lonely her own life had been, always keeping people at a distance, fearing what they might discover about her. She had a few close friends at the university where she worked and two close friends from her college days, but she, like Mariam, kept mostly to herself.

"What about the part of the journal where Mariam wrote about helping Vivian with her patients, especially the part where Vivian used Mariam's blood to help that young woman who was hemorrhaging after the birth of her child. Mariam saved the young woman's life."

"I am amazed Vivian and even Mariam knew enough about how blood worked in the human body to even consider such a thing."

"Science was emerging in the sixteenth century." An odd thread of tension entered his voice. He drew a breath and looked down at a thick sheaf of papers on the table in front of him. They had been there beside the journal the entire time, but Caitlin had hardly noticed as all her attention had been on the journal. "Caitlin, I know about your special ability. You used it yesterday helping those boys to fly their kite."

Her heart skipped a beat and her muscles tensed as fear swept through her. He was avoiding looking at her but she could tell he wanted something in return for his silence. "What do you want?"

He slid the sheaf of papers toward her. "I want your help to save my mother."

"How can I possibly do that?"

His gaze fastened on hers. "Your blood is special, just as the blood of all your ancestors has been."

Caitlin couldn't breathe. She couldn't look away. "My blood?" Her eyes flared. "Yesterday?"

He nodded. "I set up the blood donation vehicle to arrive where it did so that I could collect a sample of your plasma. Dr. Sabario retrieved your blood, processed it in his lab, then administered it to my mother yesterday just before we arrived. Your blood has interesting healing properties. I don't really understand all the technical aspects of it, but let's just say your blood holds magic...just like you."

"You tricked me," she whispered. "You stole my blood, and now you want more?"

He flinched at her words. "Yes, I won't deny it. I did it deliberately and with considerable forethought."

A flare of anger pierced her shock. "The museum exhibit? You brought it here to snare me in your trap?"

"At first, yes, but once I got to know you, things changed. I never meant to hurt you, Caitlin. I'm prepared to offer you an impressive deal if you help me and my mother." He reached for her.

She took a hasty step back and glared at him defiantly. "I don't want to hear anything more. You got what you wanted. I got what I wanted. There's nothing more we need from each other."

"There's a lot more we need to discuss." Desperation tinged his voice as he flipped the sheaf of papers to reveal a contract. "Mariam's journal is yours and I will personally fund your historical research for the rest of your academic career if you agree to four more blood donations over the next month. That's what Dr. Sabario thinks is needed to build up the fibrinogen levels in my mother's blood."

She crossed her arms. "What then? You'll pass me along to the next person who needs medical assistance? Then the next person? It will go on forever, and I'll never be free. No. Even with the journal as payment, the price of revealing my magical roots is still too high."

"Dr. Sabario and I are the only two people who know your secret. The contract, which I drew up myself so no one else would be involved, has a gag order in it. We can never speak of the matter ever again or else Dr. Sabario must surrender his medical license and I will turn over all my shares in Seattle BioGen to you."

The pain of his betrayal twisted her stomach. One date with him and now her life was forever altered. She had no choice but to quit her job and move to another state where she could start all over again. She forced herself to stand tall. "You're not going to get what you want from me. Not today. Not ever."

She headed for the door without looking back. She flew down the stairs and since he'd driven her there this morning, she started running away from the museum and back to her condominium. She needed the exercise to focus her thoughts and keep the pain of his betrayal at bay.

She and Logan had shared one day of friendship and laughter. And what she'd hoped might be a beginning of sorts for them was now nothing but a bitter memory.

Chapter Five

After a week of staring at the pashmina scarf Logan's mother had let her borrow, Caitlin decided it was time to return it. Only then could she truly be free of all ties to Logan, despite how much she missed him. He'd betrayed her. What future did they have if everything they had experienced was built on deception? Even so, no matter how much she tried to forget him, he filled her thoughts.

It was ten in the morning. The day was already starting to warm as Caitlin drove to Mercer Island. She turned onto Forest Avenue then into JoJo Ross's driveway, surprised to find the security gates open. No other cars were in the driveway, so Caitlin parked and made her way to the front door. Along with the scarf, she'd brought Logan's mother a bouquet of irises and six of her favorite twice-baked almond croissants from Le Panier.

She knocked on the door and waited. She knocked again after a long while, and was about to leave the items on the front entry when she heard a soft *thump, thump, thump* shortly before the door cracked open.

"Caitlin?" JoJo opened the door farther, revealing a woman who looked nothing like the one she'd met only last week. Logan's mother was still dressed impeccably in blue cropped pants with a floral Carolina Herrera silk tunic top. The hair that had been so meticulously styled before hung in disarray about her shoulders. Her face was pale—almost gray—and the lines about her eyes were etched so deeply she appeared skeletal. And, the woman who had walked without assistance before now leaned heavily on a cane in her right hand.

"I'm so sorry to disturb you," Caitlin said, forcing a bright smile to her lips even as she felt a sudden ache in her heart. "I wanted to return your scarf."

JoJo stepped back. "Come in, dear. You just missed Logan. Will you stay and talk with me for a few minutes? I'm not feeling my best. Company might help."

Caitlin fought for calm, then stepped inside. JoJo shut the door behind her then hobbled slowly forward, leading to the living room where she sank into one of the chairs near the floor-to-ceiling windows. How could the woman have deteriorated so quickly in the past week? Caitlin cleared her throat against a sudden thickness.

"I don't know if Logan told you, but I've been sick for some time now. I thought maybe last week the doctor had finally found a cure." Her features filled with sorrow. "I was wrong."

"I'm sure the doctor will find a cure or at least a treatment that will help you very soon."

JoJo sighed, and her frail body shuddered. "I've learned over the years not to get my hopes up. But there is still one last thing in this life I want to do."

"What is that?"

"Hold my grandchild, a child who would most likely be free of the disease. Logan isn't a carrier."

A lump lodged in Caitlin's throat. She could put an end to this woman's suffering. All she had to do was agree to donate her blood. Suddenly, possessing Mariam's journal didn't matter. Helping another person, as Mariam and Vivian had done in the past, was what mattered most. Caitlin would give JoJo her blood not because of any agreement, but because she wanted to.

Caitlin glanced up to find Logan standing there, looking at her with uncertainty, saying nothing.

Tears welled in Caitlin's eyes and spilled onto her cheeks as she got up and moved to stand before him. He watched her with anxiety in his eyes, as if he were afraid to believe she was truly there. "Caitlin—" he breathed.

"If my life can help another, then that's what I want to do." She wiped the tears from her face with the back of her hand and swallowed painfully.

Logan reached out and took her hand, wrapping his fingers around hers then leaned forward and kissed the damp trail of tears on her cheeks. "You're a good person, Caitlin Baxter."

She pressed her lips together and offered him a fragile, trembling smile. "This is a big step for me. I'm afraid, but I also realize I can't withhold the gift my ancestors passed down to me if it will heal your mother in the long or short term. It's what I want to do."

"There's no need to be frightened. I'll be right beside you today, and if you'll let me, for the rest of your life." He grinned down at her with bright shining eyes. "And if you ever find yourself in need of distraction, I could always whistle for you."

Caitlin laughed and moved into his arms. "Now that's an offer I can't refuse."

Gerri Russell is the award-winning, bestselling author of historical and contemporary novels including the All the King's Men series and *Flirting with Felicity*. She is best known for her adventurous and emotionally intense novels set in twelfth through seventeenth-century Scotland. Before Gerri followed her passion for writing romance novels, she worked as a broadcast journalist, a newspaper reporter, a magazine columnist, a technical writer and editor, and an instructional designer. She lives in the Pacific Northwest with her husband and three mischievous black cats.

If you enjoyed reading about Caitlin and Logan, you can find more about their ancestors in the All the King's Men series.

Seven Nights with a Scot
Romancing the Laird
A Temptress in Tartan
A Laird and a Gentleman
Much Ado About a Scot

Or check out Gerri's other contemporary romances:
Flirting with Felicity
Along Came Mr. Right
Married at Midnight

You can find more books by Gerri as well as ways to keep in touch through social media on her website at www.Gerri Russell.net

A Note from Nick Morgan:

I was thrilled with the opportunity to collaborate with Danica on a project for such a good cause. The song and story came together perfectly making for an incredible marriage of two different mediums. It turned out better than I ever dreamed and I am glad to be a part of it. You can follow along with me on Instagram @steelandstrings for more music, events, and other shenanigans.

Youtube link: Short and Precious Time

Made in the USA
Columbia, SC
29 August 2020